NIGHT RAIDERS

Colin Stubbington

Night Raiders

Futura Publications Ltd

A Futura Book

First published in Great Britain by
Futura Publications Limited in 1980

Copyright © 1980 Colin Stubbington

ISBN 0 7088 1787 4

Typeset, printed and bound in Great Britain
by Hazell Watson & Viney Ltd
Aylesbury, Bucks

Futura Publications Limited
110 Warner Road
Camberwell, London SE5

To Ian and Ros Fraser, who knew the unfledged Seraphim . . .

AUTHOR'S NOTE

On December 18, 1917 – so Mr Raymond H. Fredette tells us in his book *The First Battle of Britain* – a raiding force of Gotha bombers, followed by a solitary Staaken Giant, set out for London. The night, apparently, was a nearly moonless one, and southern England lay covered under a light mantle of snow.

All I have done is to add a second Staaken to this raid, together with an equally fictitious 'D' Flight stationed on the 'Roman marsh'.

On these small pegs, and on a few – hopefully plausible – liberties taken with the geography of south-east Kent, the substitution of a later Training Manual for the Bristol Fighter, and the construction and organization of the products of Zeppelin-Werke, I have hung my story....

PROLOGUE

Age will come
By stealth, as an insidious patrol,
Until we are surrounded by our heirs,
All lusty, young, and greedy for account
Of battles long ago and heroes dead;
Till all our strength is gone and nought remains
But an old greyhead mumbling by the fire
A bedtime story for the innocent.

H. V. S. Page: *Prospectus.*

Midsummer, 19—.

Standing vertically on her port wing-tip, and revolving lazily around its axis, the Beagle-Pup, Juliet Echo, completed a tight clearing-turn and, steadying back on course, halted the compass needle's playful pursuit of its own tail. Free to look inboard once more, the girl piloting the little plane glanced across at her passenger, an elderly, alert-looking man with a neatly clipped moustache and hair that, although snowy, stood in a defiantly boyish and unruly shock. No wonder, she thought, that people found it difficult to believe her grandfather was a month or so the wrong side of eighty. His eyes, she noticed, were today quite different from their usually benign and placid selves. Now, they were never still, but constantly and methodically probing the creamy drifts of cloud three thousand feet above, tightening themselves into narrow slits whenever they focused — as time and again they inevitably did — on the broken and blinding dazzle round the high June sun. Almost without his being aware of it, atavistic and half-forgotten habits of self-preservation had reasserted themselves in the old man from the moment Juliet Echo had left the ground.

Looking sideways at his watchful face, the girl was startled by the sudden realization of what her grandfather was doing; understanding that what till now had been for her a slangy catch-phrase out of the past, a fragment of flying-lore picked up from books or airfield gossip, was to him something immeasurably more – a reality still retaining all its ancient, dangerous potency and near-scriptural force. Despite skies long innocent of prowling enemy, it was plain that to her grandfather 'Beware-the-Hun-in-the-Sun' was no mere form of words, but an authoritative text – to disobey which admitted neither appeal, nor forgiveness, nor second chance. . . .

For a few moments the girl surreptitiously studied the old man's face, seeing him from a new perspective and with a more acute perception. The aura of quiet distinction in which he moved had been won, not given. It was like the tie he was wearing – a reticent and unboastful statement of merit. Earlier, in the club-house, the girl had caught the knowledge-able eyeing her grandfather's tie with something like awe. Those few left who had the right to wear its sober, faded stripes were a diminishing, dying yet immortal breed. Already the things it represented were barely matter for the memories of living flesh and blood, but something almost lost; just one more study for the curious, the academic, the incurably romantic; as fabulous and insubstantial as those Fokkers for whom the old man was so intently quartering the sky.

As if guessing her thoughts, he turned towards her and winked.

'Come on, Liz! Get on with it!' He jerked a thumb up at the clouds. '. . . Before old Immelmann's ghost comes down and peppers our arses!'

'You're quite ready?' The girl grinned back at him.

'As ready as I'll ever be . . . !'

'Straps tight?'

Her grandfather pulled a wry face and tugged at his shoulder harness.

'I can't escape, if that's what you mean . . . !'

The girl laughed out loud, looked carefully round the horizon once more and then, her left hand lightly but firmly on

8

the stick, eased gently back on the throttle with her right.

They were big hands for a woman, her grandfather noted; capable, well-made, rather beautiful hands – his own endowment to the cool and competent creature who sat on his left. Funny.... If Liz's hands were beautiful, then so must his own be, he supposed. Strange: he'd never thought of them in that light before....

But then, he'd never before been flown by a woman.... And the fact that the woman in question was his own granddaughter he found exasperating and yet oddly piquant and stimulating. For, dear God! the child flew quite as well as any man in his experience – always excepting one, of course.... Always excepting that lost, drowned face out of the past....

Liz cut across his thoughts.

'Do you want me to talk you through the next bit, Gramps?' He growled and shook his head.

'Just cut the blasted natter and get on with it, girl....'

'Right....'

She eased the throttle back still farther, and the bawling clamour of the engine faded; the Pup felt lumpy and uneasy on the summer air. Suddenly, Liz pulled the stick hard back into her stomach and kicked on the rudder-bar. For a tense moment, Juliet Echo's nose seemed to lift as her feebly-turning airscrew clutched vainly at the sky. Then she fell away to port, plummeting downwards, spinning frantically widdershins, with the only sound the howl of air over her wings.

For a moment the old man was tempted to close his eyes as a clump of Kentish woodland screwed up to meet them. Instead, they reluctantly focused on a solitary farm gate at one end of the coppice, and his mind struggled to make itself quite sure just *which* was spinning – the aircraft, or the gate – or both....

Liz's voice came calmly to him from a great distance, like that of a priestess crooning some arcane yet healing ritual.

'Full opposite rudder.... Pa-a-use.... Ease the stick sl-o-wly forward.... Centre rudder.... E-e-ase gently back on the stick....'

As unexpectedly as the spin had begun, it was over. As the

9

Pup's nose rose above the horizon, Liz opened the throttle again, and the engine resumed its cheerful burble. The old man drew a deep breath — and the farm gate disappeared beneath the starboard wing. Her lumpy heaviness gone, Juliet Echo danced lightly on the air — as though she would never dream of tumbling precipitously through the twelve-hundred feet of air that the altimeter recorded.

'Again, Gramps?'

Her grandfather muttered an unparliamentary negative — then grinned at Liz like a naughty urchin. Whatever else a chap of his age might think of them, there was this at least in favour of modern womanhood: there were times when a man could now forget himself and say *exactly* what he felt like saying. . . .

Liz pretended to be shocked.

'Did you think I was trying to kill you?'

'If someone had done that with me in 1915,' the old man snorted, 'they'd have damned-well succeeded. . . . I wouldn't be here now. . . !'

'Which means that Daddy wouldn't have been born — and therefore I couldn't have been either. . . .'

'Exactly, my girl. . . .'

The old man fell silent. He was troubled yet again by an inward vision that had come to perplex him more and more as he grew older — a shadowy, haunting image of faceless and unborn generations, lying with their sires in France dead and unconsidered. How much genius, how much delight and plain, ordinary decency lay lost a few short miles across the Channel. . . . Was it *really* any wonder that the world seemed such a blasted blighted mess? Only chance randoms of that bright and innocent generation still showed themselves here and there, the unmistakable sprigs of a dying stock — like this lovely girl beside him whose own father, younger then than she was now, had gone down over Essen in a burning Wellington a quarter of a century ago.

A dull ache gnawed at the old man's heart. Even now he could scarcely think of his dead son without pain. Sometimes he wondered that he should find so much pleasure in

Liz's company – she was so very much her father's daughter that just to look at her was to be taken back in time.... Her smile was Larry's, and that disarming trick of looking at you gravely from beneath one raised eyebrow was his. Only her hands were different, the old man thought, looking at them again. Yes ... heredity's puckish entail had skipped a generation here: Larry's hands had been small, almost delicate. Desperately the old man struggled to rid his mind of the nightmare spectacle it still too often fashioned for itself: of Larry's hands clutched agonizedly around a dead and useless control-column – and burning ... burning. ...

He came back to the present as Juliet Echo rocked suddenly, her wings buffeted by a playful thermal of air lifting off the last scarp of the down – a grey-green slope against which the sea had once pounded before its sulky banishment behind Dengechurch Wall, fifteen miles away.

Below them now, lay the Marsh itself, stretching away into the distance like an emerald velvet counterpane, scored with a haphazard grid of dykes and ditches, bounded on its westward flank by the long, shingle arm of the Ness. Beyond this lay the sea, blue and mauve today in the clear, sparkling light; and further, half-hidden in heat-haze, the indistinct gash of the French coast.

Was this *really* the same Marsh he had briefly known fifty years ago, the old man wondered. He supposed so – though the passage of fifty years and a different angle of sight implied more significant changes than he cared to think about. *Then* it had been winter, bitter with ice and snow. Now it was midsummer, and he was here again, a survivor, unlikely and out of place.

Liz banked the Pup and turned to fly once more along that last ridge of downland, losing height, and – as the landscape below gained focus – gently weaving Juliet Echo's tail from side to side as though casting about for landmarks. Liz fumbled in the pocket of her blouse, bringing out a folded slip of paper which she held up mockingly for her grandfather's inspection.

'Having one of these takes all the fun out of low flying... !'

'What's that? Your permit from the CAA?'

'Yes.... Though I was sure we'd never get one – not with that Fleet Air Arm Station being so near over at Aischurch.'

Her grandfather grunted complacently. There were things the young couldn't do.... It was nice to be able to say casually: 'Oh, I got old Charlie Bramshott to square it for you....'

Liz whistled: there were times when she forgot some of the people that Gramps knew. To her the name Bramshott meant Air Chief Marshal Sir Charles Bramshott – and a lot more besides. Most certainly *not* someone she could 'phone off-handedly – as her grandfather apparently could – with an: 'I say, Charlie....'

Her grandfather laughed: 'It's all quite simple really, Liz.... Even Air Chief Marshals have to start off as pilot officers – sometimes very young and *silly* pilot-officers, who need their backsides kicking....'

'And he remembers you kindly for *that*? ...'

'He does.... Besides: he reckoned that getting that piece of paper of yours would give him a cast-iron excuse to go and drink the Navy out of gin....'

Liz looked at the permit for a moment with a new respect before tucking it back in her pocket: 'I'd say he must have succeeded....'

She dropped the nose of the Pup even further until the altimeter steadied at five hundred feet, and they were once more flying over the Marsh. Below and parallel to their course ran the overgrown and tangled trackbed of a long-abandoned branch line. The old man's complacency left him, and he found himself trembling expectantly – he'd got his bearings now, and knew exactly where they were....

The railway finished at the ruin of its terminus with only an ugly and inhospitable-looking inn for company. About a mile beyond this, half-hidden and enclosed by a windbreak of trees, stood the grey, crenellated tower of a church leaning above a cluster of low, red roofs. The Pup dropped a wing and banked above a meandering lane, now metalled and wider than the old man remembered it, though still moated on either side by a pair of deep and menacing ditches. Curving back on itself, the lane lifted over first one hump-backed bridge and then another. . . .

And then, there it was, the place he had come to see. . . . The place that in actuality or memory he had consciously avoided for fifty years – a huddle of buildings in the corner of a meadow flanked by two fill-dykes, and the tell-tale green scar showing where at sometime a third had been ploughed in. . . .

But what had this colourwashed, refurbished and generally tarted house to do with him, or his past, he thought, noting the swimming-pool in its walled garden, the brace of expensive cars in the paved and straightened drive, and the ornamental trees – weeping-willow and Japanese cherry – replacing the wind-bitten straggle of oak and thorn he so clearly remembered.

Ten to one, the house's owner – now sunbathing there beside the pool – had renamed it 'The Nook' or 'Smuggler's Den' – anything rather than the ugly and prosaic name by which a handful of airmen had once known it: 'Brick-Kiln Farm'.

But, Brick-Kiln Farm it had once been, the first and temporary home of 'D' Flight and, therefore, the birthplace of the proud squadron into which that flight had grown. And, whether its present owner knew or cared, it had been from his house and that meadow behind it, that this Squadron had incurred its earliest casualties one bitter night late in 1917 when 'D' Flight had flown its first sortie.

The old man tried to remember the faces of the four men who'd died that night. Three were beyond recall, vanished now, apart from their neatly inscribed names on the Roll of Honour: Thomas Albert Peters; Reginald Julian Denbigh Browne; Angus Mackail. . . .

The fourth name and face were different. . . . They survived – after a fashion – in those glossy, coffee-table books, so much to contemporary taste, slick accounts of the 'Aces' and their doings: their kills set out in league tables; their techniques and abilities all discussed and cleverly analysed.

13

It puzzled the old man that the fellows who wrote these books seemed to know so much more about the Flying Corps than *he* did – except that the war of which they wrote scarcely seemed to tally with anything he remembered at all. . . .

And Laurie Destrier?

The clever young men seemed to know a great deal more about Destrier than he ever had. . . . They gave detailed accounts of his thirty-eight accredited victories, and his possible fifteen more; they knew how and why he had won his several decorations; his favourite methods of attack, and the precise manner of his final defeat. . . . Most mentioned that a non-commissioned observer had survived this, though few mentioned the observer's name – and of these, two got it wrong. . . .

And how damned neat and tidy they all managed to make it look in print, the old man thought; so different from those last, cataclysmic moments of confusion, uncertainty and sheer screaming terror that he remembered. Had Destrier been dead, unconscious or simply beyond caring in that long, insane fall to the sea?

The Roll of Honour was equally reticent and enigmatic on this point. Captain Laurence Destrier, it read: Missing, believed Killed.

The old man sighed. By rights this should have been his own epitaph also. . . .

ONE

Already, the short December day was beginning to draw in. A last, fitful gleam of sun undershot the low cloud resting on the southernmost scarp of the downs with an ugly, pinkish glare before fading abruptly, leaving their snowy flanks stark and colourless.

A single railway track eased its way carefully round these last outposts of hill, rumbled over a rutted lane and then, coming to the Marsh, lifted itself onto a low embankment that marched straight as a Roman road across a waste of dykes and willow-flanked ditches. Comically self-important, an ancient engine, followed by a short train of even more ancient six-wheelers, puffed its way towards the distant coastline.

For all its pretence at urgency, the train moved slowly. It paused at half-a-dozen halts, each seemingly of greater remoteness and lesser importance than the last. No one boarded the train – though at two or three of the sleeper-platformed halts shawled and basket-laden women climbed down, each dressed in the mourning-black that by now seemed European womanhood's sole reward for patience and endurance in the face of forty months of war.

From his seat in a first-class compartment near the rear of the train the man watched them go. They left the low, snow-dusted platforms, striking off down paths that led apparently nowhere, till the dusk, rising out of the hollow marsh, swallowed them up as carelessly as the swamps of Somme and Passchendale had sucked down their menfolk. . . .

For a moment the man – a captain dressed in the double-breasted tunic of the Royal Flying Corps – was deluded into confusing this peaceable marsh with those others – those he and his generation had grown to know so well, bludgeoned by shrapnel and high-explosives and corrupted by lethal, lung-rotting gases. From nowhere came the stench, the indescribable reek of putrescence that reached for a man's nostrils even as he flew a mile high above the battlefield. It was only with an effort that the man succeeded in dragging his mind back to the present. The Roman marsh became itself again: the seventh continent, as its people sometimes boasted – a hundred square miles of brooding mystery and legend.

The train moved on, its self-importance lessening in face of the marsh's dubious twilight. At the last halt, a porter had laboriously climbed onto the roof of the carriage to slip a brace of pot-lamps into place. The feeble light they gave out barely reached the corners of the airman's compartment. Not that it mattered; there was not much farther to go now.... One more halt, two, and then, in a sort of no man's land, the terminus would be reached, a long mile short of the village it purported to serve, and another three from the coast.

Obscurely, the man felt sorry his journey was ending. Once, the leisurely fussiness of the little train would have aroused in him a half-irritated, half-humorous contempt. Now, its asthmatic inertia and clamorous rattle reminded him of an almost forgotten world – a world where journeys finished in the everyday decencies of work or pleasure, not – as now – in the likelihood of death or mutilation.

The man stood to lift his heavy new valise from the rack. As he did so, he caught his reflection mirrored in the sepia photograph of a pre-war holiday resort, with its beach and bandstand, its sun-bonneted and boatered crowds. As poor a looking-glass as this made, and as feeble the light in the compartment, he saw his own face all too clearly, its left side from jaw to eye a mask of barely-healed scar-tissue, twisting a once generous and sensitive mouth into a devil-mask parody of a smile. Involuntarily, the airman covered his face with his hands – hands that were themselves scarred, transparent, hideous....

Flight-Sergeant Hopkins – waiting at Marshingfold station

for 'D' Flight's new Commander and fully aware that the branch-line was scarcely famous for its punctuality – had decided that a warm fire and ale were preferable to a long and icy wait in an open car. After a minimum of skirmishing with the landlady of the Station Inn – and heedless of wartime licensing laws – he was now propped in the warmest corner of the snug, busy with his second pint of flat, wartime beer.

To do him justice, Hopkins fully expected to pay for insinuating himself with a well-spun yarn or two. A dozen years of soldiering had given him the old sweat's gift of the gab – the narrative style which, while neither precisely true or false, had become so embroidered and advantaged with each successive telling that it reached at last into the realms of lyric fantasy. This time, however, Hopkins was to be disappointed. The landlady, Mrs Swale, had no interest in his tales. Married to an old soldier herself – one with his own stock of romantic lies – she was not to be impressed.

No! What Mrs Swale most wished to know was *was it true*? Was *what* true?

That *he* was coming *here* – to Marshingfold. . . .

Who was *he*, for Gawd's sake?

Why, *him*, of course. . . . *Destrier*. . . . The VC.

Hopkins finished his beer and pushed the empty mug towards the landlady. Now that depended, he conceded. He might be. . . . And then again he might not. . . .

To the Flight-Sergeant's disgust, the old woman ignored his empty glass. Instead, she reached down under the counter and, after a moment or two of searching, emerged triumphantly with a crumpled newspaper, jabbing at a front-page article almost swamped beneath banner headlines. Hopkins had no need to read the half-dozen paragraphs thrust under his nose. He knew them by heart. . . .

The landlady shook her head admiringly. 'Now *that's* what I call a man. . . .'

Hopkins nodded in agreement and tapped his mug noisily with a thumbnail. Mrs Swale laid the newspaper on the counter and leaned forwards, peering shortsightedly at the newsprint.

Now, Hopkins realized sadly, nothing short of violence

would stop the old harridan from reading this six-month old story aloud. He was embarrassed – not for himself – but for Destrier. Mrs Swale cleared her throat and coughed to make sure of the Flight-Sergeant's fullest attention.

'It says here –' she paused portentously before continuing in a sing-song voice – 'it says here that "Lieutenant Destrier, a gallant and intrepid officer of the Royal Flying Corps, downed four enemy scouts in as many minutes, while engaged in strafing enemy trenches near what has become known as Nine-Tree Wood. Lieutenant Destrier was himself most severely wounded in this action, but succeeded in regaining his own lines, where his aircraft crashed in flames.

' "The rescue of this brave airman was hampered by vicious machine-gun fire from the Hun who, devoid alike of sportsmanship or decency, endeavoured to harass several stretcher parties intent on their errand of mercy.

' "Lieutenant Destrier, who already holds the Distinguished Service Order, Military Cross and Bar, and the Distinguished Conduct Medal, is reputed to have destroyed over thirty aircraft since the beginning of 1916." '

Mrs Swale put down the newspaper with such an air of reverence that Hopkins was reminded of someone finishing reading a lesson in church. The piety of the gesture disgusted him. For Christ's sake! What on earth did this old fool think was going on in France? A nice game of cricket, with the opposing fielders expected to clap the batsmen in after a successful knock?

If anyone deserved decorating it must have been those poor bloody stretcher-bearers. . . .

And of course Jerry had done his best to finish Laurie Destrier off – as he would have done in their place! Two days Destrier's squadron had spent plastering that little kink in the German line, just north of Nine-Tree Wood: two days in which the grey-clad masses had been decimated and demoralized – but never broken.

A professional to his finger-tips, Hopkins respected that. . . . But –

'Cowards!' the old woman spat like an angry cat, brandishing a bottle fiercely as if expecting a whole troop of Uhlans to come stamping and marauding into her trig bar. 'The papers are right – they've no guts when it comes to real fighting.... Not one of 'em! Oh, they're brave enough when it comes to dropping bombs on women and children – I'll give 'em that. Them Zeppelins of theirs – and the bombers.... What do they call 'em? Gothas? One dropped a bomb out on the march a mile from Dykebridge not a month back.'

Hopkins did his best to keep his expression grave.

'That must've put the breeze up you....'

'Not *me*!' the landlady retorted, at last filling his glass. 'No one can accuse us of not being in the front line hereabouts. We know what this war's all about in Marshingfold. Still –' she went on, taking Hopkins's money and moving towards the till, 'We'll do for 'em in the end, don't you fret. And that'll be the day.... We'll see how brave they are then. Put 'em all against the nearest wall and shoot 'em, I say....'

Hopkins drank his beer in silence. Civilian belligerence no longer dismayed him but bored him, leaving him obscurely aware that when peace came – if ever – it was likely to be a bitter one.

God alone knew how the returning PBI put up with such atavistic bloodlust, Hopkins thought. Unless a man had experienced the Front for himself, how could he possibly have any conception of what this war was all about? Even himself – apart from a short but terrifying spell in the air, his own war had been safe and comfortable enough: an occasional trip up the lines to help recover a crashed aircraft, the odd tip-and-run raid from Jerry – but these dangers were as nothing.... He stretched and clamped his hand round his glass.

His mind was scarred by certain memories, though. He wondered whether this old witch of a landlady could possibly imagine what a man's body looked like after it had fallen the best part of ten thousand feet....

Hopkins drank deeply and considered peace. It would be pleasant, he thought, to get back to real soldiering again – everything decently regimental, pay-night booze-ups, exercises comfortingly designed to fight the last war but three. . . .

Nowadays it took Hopkins something of an effort to remember the army that had been like that, the army that had disappeared in the autumn of 1914, three and a half years and a whole lifetime ago. . . . He grinned wryly as he recalled how they had all welcomed the declaration of war. Then, its coming had seemed like the arrival of a long-promised treat – a romp that would be over by Christmas, with England on the winning side, of course.

Instead, and with the war reaching towards a fourth Christmas, there was only bitter stalemate – a situation which, Hopkins considered, scarcely said much for the wit of man, or the so-called goodness of God. . . .

No, Hopkins decided, that particular God – the one his orphanage had taken such pains to make him aware of – had long been shown up as a fraud. All-loving and omnipresent? *He*'d been conspicuous only by his absence – AWOL – since this little barney had begun. If God still existed – and it was *only* 'if' – then it was in some safe, cushy base-area with a staff-officer's flash on His halo. . . . Hopkins detested staff-officers. Now if old Mrs Swale here had suggested putting *them* against the nearest wall, he could have agreed with a clear conscience. That made sense. . . .

Hopkins liked things that made sense – clear, logical, sequential sense – which, perhaps, was why he was so good with engines. Their precision represented for him an intricate yet definite and apparent purpose that seemed lacking in the rest of creation. Their ills and eccentricities, their quirks of behaviour and performance left him unsurprised and unruffled. The merest change of note in Clerget or Le Rhône shouted to him that a bearing lacked oil, or a valve was sticking, or a carburettor was doing something less than its duty.

By and large, engines served Hopkins for wife, family and friends. With his own kind, man or woman, Hopkins was less sure. While friendly and approachable enough, he was sparing of anything deeper than surface affection. That way a fellow avoided hurt; in this life people came and went far too rapidly for a man to be over-generous with liking. . . .

Since August, 1914, such an attitude had proved a blessing. War had made love a luxury. For one person only would Hopkins admit any deep attachment: the man for whom he was waiting – Laurie Destrier. . . .

For all the Flight-Sergeant now knew he might once have had brothers and sisters of his own – but, an orphanage brat, he had long since lost touch with them. Destrier was the nearest thing to a relation Hopkins had owned to since the two of them had been brought together nearly twenty years before. Then, Destrier had been a rather wary newcomer whom Hopkins, for no very good reason he could remember, had taken under his eleven-year-old wing. Whatever the reasons for their friendship, the two boys had become inseparable, brothers in everything but blood. In all this world, probably only Hopkins now knew that Captain Laurence Destrier, VC etcetera, etcetera, was the casual by-blow of a drunken matelot and a Pompey whore. . . .

The orphanage had been austere but not unkind, and the education it had provided had been first class. Syd Hopkins sometimes remembered to bless the name of the philanthropist who had endowed the orphanage with its splendid workshops – for it had been in these that his love-affair with metals and machinery had begun. Here his hands had first learned that hard steel could be persuaded, given the knowledge and tools, into something tractable and obedient. And here, the smell of hot oil had come to have for him the same significance that freshly-turned earth has for the farmer, or linseed-oil the painter.

It had been in the class-room and on the playing-field that Laurie had excelled. From somewhere – his boozy father or raffish mother? – Laurie had inherited brains. Syd had noted this, at first with boyish dismay, then pride – the kid was a bright one all right! Besides this, Laurie had possessed all and more of any normal boy's penchant for scrapes and trouble: he climbed trees like a squirrel and was the most murderous shot with a catapult that Syd had ever seen. . . .

Only one thing worried young Hopkins about his protegé – the youngster's tendency to dreaminess, his not infrequent withdrawals into a private world from which no amount of prodding could recall him until he himself chose.

Hopkins now guessed that Destrier's secret world had been one in which a man might fly as easily as a bird. In a world which had only just recently seen the deaths of Lilenthal and Pilcher, and the first, tentative experiments of the Wrights, Laurie Destrier, not yet thirteen, was absorbed by the same questions. . . .

When the lads had left the orphanage they had gone their separate ways – Hopkins to one of the newly founded motor-works, and Destrier to a City counting-house. They had kept in touch by letter. Neither had been happy and, by mutual consent, both had gravitated towards the army. Wise counsel kept them from the infantry. Instead, they became Sappers – Royal Engineers – members of that Corps famous for being Jacks-of-all-Trades and masters of most. Joining had meant a white lie or two about their ages, of course – but what were white lies to the army?

Hopkins had quickly learned to wear the Service like a glove. His officers thought well of him, and he was soon marked out for promotion – the ideal NCO in embryo – disciplined, smart and intelligent. Destrier, on the other hand, had been less than happy: for a long, long while he had been the squarest of pegs in the roundest of holes – dreamy, unkempt and perpetually in trouble for a whole series of minor military crimes.

It had been at Dorrington Heath near Farnborough that all this had changed. Before overseas postings had separated them, Hopkins and Destrier had been seconded to a detachment at the Balloon Factory experimenting with man-lifting kites. Destrier had come alive. For a while he had gained a brief notoriety when he had taken a hair-raising and involuntary ride on one of the kites when it had broken free from its tow-line. Somehow – by luck, or the first small glimmerings of his almost preternatural skill as a pilot – he had brought the silk-and-bamboo contraption safely back to earth, and had found his own, true self in the process. . . .

Now, a decade later, in the snug of the Station Inn, Hopkins leant over the counter and turned Mrs Swale's paper towards him. Even for the Flight-Sergeant who had known both the orphanage brat and the young soldier he had become, it was difficult to equate them with this man whose exploits, it now seemed, made him a name to be reckoned with in the same breath as Ball or Immelmann. . . .

Hopkins emerged from his thoughts to find Destrier standing beside him, the ruined side of his face looking all the more ravaged in the chiaroscuro of the inn's solitary lamp. The Flight-Sergeant came to attention and smiled uncertainly.

'Sorry, sir. I forgot the time. I got to daydreaming about the old days. . . .'

Destrier looked pointedly in the direction of Hopkins's glass.

'Is that what you call it, Flight? You'd have done better to get the tonneau-cover on the car. It's beginning to snow again. . . .'

These days Hopkins felt uncertain as to how exactly he should treat Destrier – or even how the other man wished to be treated. Mention of 'the old days' had drawn no answering flicker of response. Indeed, judging by his frown, Destrier appeared to have resented it. His reprimand concerning the uncovered car had been made in curt, neutral tones; the voice of any officer issuing a mild if unmistakable reprimand. Which was *exactly* as it should have been, the good NCO in Hopkins insisted: KR's were adamant concerning the proper distance to be observed between commissioned and non-commissioned ranks. And quite right, too. . . . That way everyone knew where they stood.

Without resentment, Hopkins accepted that the old easy quality of his friendship with Destrier was a thing of the past. To think otherwise was foolish. Destrier's rapid promotion and the conventions of the Service saw to that. It was sad – but inevitable. Hopkins knew himself to be quite guiltless of envy or jealousy. He also knew himself to have sense and manners enough not to trade on an old intimacy – for the memory of this to Destrier was, he saw, an obvious embarrassment.

And yet, as Hopkins was well aware, he had only been posted to Marshingfold because Destrier had specifically demanded him, and had, indeed, pulled strings and gone far out of his way to arrange the matter. Puzzling. . . . Very. But perhaps this hadn't altogether been done for old time's sake, Hopkins told himself. Perhaps Destrier had only requested him for coldly professional reasons, as a disciplined, reliable tool. Nothing more. . . .

No, Hopkins reminded himself, trying not to stare at Destrier's face, it wasn't easy to envy the man. Yet there were those who did, despite his record – or, maybe, even because of it; pretending to see in the man's natural reserve a stand-offish pride and the arrogance of a jumped-up ranker made swollen-headed by success. Well . . . if that had ever truly been the case – which Hopkins doubted – then Destrier had paid for it. Oh, yes, he'd paid. . . . Destrier's critics should try looking their victim straight in his ruined face. . . .

Struggling to keep pity out of his voice, Hopkins said, 'I reckon that journey of yours must've been a cold one, sir. . . . Could you use a finger or two of whisky before we go?'

Destrier shook his head – then changed his mind. 'I don't see why not. You can tell me about Brick-Kiln Farm.'

Hopkins pulled a wry face. 'It's a bloody shambles. . . .'

'Did you really expect otherwise?'

'No-o. . . .' The Flight-Sergeant sighed. 'Not really. . . . The powers-that-be have got themselves into a rare old panic with all this civvy wind-up over Jerry's bombing. Everyone's yelling for Home Defence Squadrons – so Home Defence Squadrons there must be, even if that only means half a flight of barely serviceable aircraft operating off a four-by-two cabbage-patch. . . . We've no proper establishment of officers or men. I've never seen such a bloody Fred Karno set-up in all my service!' Hopkins thumped angrily on the bar for Mrs Swale's attention.

When she came, the landlady made no attempt to hide her distaste for Destrier's ravaged face, and shook her head when Hopkins ordered whisky, insisting that with all these dreadful shortages she hadn't a drop in the place. Hopkins thrust her newspaper across the counter to her.

'I reckon four Albatri should rate a noggin from somewhere, wouldn't you?'

Mrs Swale shot Destrier a resentful glance – then disappeared into her private sitting-room behind the bar.

Destrier, when he spoke, was quietly angry. 'Was that necessary?'

Hopkins was unrepentant. 'You should have heard the old cow ten minutes ago. You could've had the top-brick of the chimney – *then*. Besides, you're going to need a gill inside you when you see Brick-Kiln Farm. I called it a bloody shambles – and that's just what it is. There's hardly leg-room enough for a bluebottle to get up flying speed – let alone a Bristol.'

Destrier merely shrugged at this information. 'Go on....'

Hopkins took a long pull at his half-empty glass.

'Whoever chose the place must've been blind-drunk at the time. One side of the field's all trees, and the other three end in ditches. Not your ordinary ditches, mind, but dykes – part of the marsh drainage system. We've been half-promised pioneers to fill the smallest of 'em in. I'll believe *that* when I see 'em, and not before. There seems to be an unaccountable shortage of manpower all of a sudden.... I can't think why....'

Both men were silent, thinking of the profligate carnage of the last four years. Yes ... there was a shortage of manpower.

Mrs Swale reappeared, hugging a bottle of whisky to her scraggy bosom. Sniffing, she poured Destrier an ungenerous measure. In Mrs Swale's opinion, heroes owed it to other people to be handsome and godlike.... This Destrier was neither. The landlady shuddered genteely as Destrier stretched out what looked like a bunch of withered talons to his glass. Wounds should be kept respectable and decent, not like these – a sickening affront to a woman in her own bar-parlour.

Destrier gulped down his whisky and the two men went out to the car. The snow shower had been brief, and a casual slap or two from Hopkins's gauntlets served to dust the seats of the open-tourer. Destrier heaved his valise into the back of the car, grimacing at the effort and stifling an involuntary gasp of pain. The big Sunbeam was started, and Hopkins, conscious of his dimmed lamps, set about the tricky job of driving back to Brick-Kiln Farm along the hazardous marsh lanes.

For a mile or so they drove in silence as the Flight-Sergeant negotiated the abrupt corners and breakneck bridges looming suddenly at them from out of the darkness. For much of the way their road was bordered on both sides by ditches whose cat-iced surfaces threw back to the masked headlamps a menacing glint of steely light. Twice the heavy tourer skidded into patches of swirling mist, causing Hopkins to curse and brake suddenly, until the car burst through the clinging vapour and out onto clear road again.

'Is it often like this?' Destrier wanted to know.

'Often enough,' Hopkins grunted. 'You've got to remember that most of the marsh is ten or twenty feet below sea-level, sir – and riddled with dykes and streams. . . .'

Yes, Destrier thought, it would be like this often enough. There would be times when the marsh simply disappeared, hiding itself beneath a shroud of fog: times when anyone caught above would have no option – if his fuel was low – but to cross his fingers, say his prayers and put his plane down regardless. No one was likely to survive the odds implicit in that sort of landing for very long. And certainly not *here*, in this crazy wilderness of dykes and ditches, where every pocket-handkerchief of a field seemed to end abruptly in a belt of wind-bitten trees, or a bottomless trough of black water. . . .

In imagination this flat, bitter countryside became all too easily confused with that near Nine-Tree Wood – his brief moments of delusion in the Marshingfold train had been no coincidence: a week of blanket-bombardment would make the picture complete. And how many crash-landings had he himself survived in such moonscapes? Was it four? Five? He forgot. . . . The details of each had been much the same – except for the last time, and those frantic, searing moments over Nine-Tree Wood.

It was by a conscious and deliberate act of will that Destrier now frequently chose to let imagination re-enact the nightmare of that wild and awesome fall to earth, his Pup a wheeling torch, striking the earth, turning over and over again like some monstrous Catherine wheel, before throwing him clear and exploding into fragments. Mercifully he now remembered little of what had followed: of the efforts of various stretcher parties to get him in; of being half-carried, half-dragged through knee-deep mud to a field hospital – a field hospital where, on first examination, he had been laid aside as dead. . . .

No: what little he knew of that was mostly hearsay. . . .

But what came next *was* branded into his memory: his first steps back into life; the torments as he'd regained lucidity. Destrier clenched his fists as he relived that agony – fists made from hands whose flesh was still too inelastic for him to close them without pain. . . .

Yes, Destrier promised himself: he would remember.

At first the crash had been something to shut out of his mind, something that, despite the evidence seared into his flesh, he must deny had ever happened. Then, memory had been an enemy waiting its moment to slip under his guard; an enemy whose delight it was to take him unawares with evil dreams and the remembered stench of his own burning flesh.

For a while Dolly had been able to keep memory from him – his own dear Dolly. There was neither waking terror, nor nightmare strong enough to resist her gentle exorcism. . . .

No. . . . Nothing. . . .

'What was that, sir?'

Destrier sensed rather than saw the blur of Hopkins's face momentarily turned towards him in the darkness. Christ! Had he been thinking aloud? That was beginning to be a habit he would have to watch. . . . He answered Hopkins with abrupt formality.

'Watch the road, Flight-Sergeant. . . .'

At last, the Sunbeam slowed and then juddered off the road onto what felt like a cart-track. Hopkins changed down and slowed even further to save the car-springs as the rutted

27

surface sent them lurching and bumping down an enclosing tunnel of hedge.

'Not far now. . . .'

Almost as Hopkins spoke, they came out of the tunnel and braked at a five-barred gate. A sentry's challenge rang through the darkness and was answered: the gate was opened, and the Sunbeam moved on again. Ahead of them, a huddle of buildings and trees was dimly silhouetted against the sky.

'This is it. . . .'

Hopkins drove slowly across a field whose poached and broken surface had been firmed by frost and a thin layer of clinker. Aircraft loomed up at them out of the night. Destrier was stung from his introspective apathy.

'God's teeth! BE12s? They promised me Bristols!'

'We've only the one Bristol as yet, sir.'

'Drive me round the field. . . .'

'Sir!'

Hopkins slowed the big tourer to walking pace, edging round the field on a tour of inspection. Dark as it was, Destrier was able to see that the Flight-Sergeant had spoken no more than the truth when he'd described Brick-Kiln Farm as a shambles – and a pocket-sized shambles at that. . . . Even in the thick country darkness, Destrier saw that the perimeters of the field were close and hazardous. One of the ditches mentioned by Hopkins turned out to be almost a small canal. Under the dim light of the tourer's lamps, its waters looked leaden and dangerous.

'Show me the aircraft. . . .'

Without a word Hopkins drove back to the opposite end of the field, stopping in front of one of the gawky BE12s. Both men climbed from the car and walked towards it.

Destrier laid his hand on the tautly-doped fabric of its wing and gestured towards the shadowy outline of its companion a few yards away.

'What sort of nick are they in?'

Hopkins shrugged in the darkness.

'They're a pretty job pair – even for BEs. We've done our

28

best with 'em. But they're not what *I'd* call right, even yet... !'

'And the Bristol?'

Hopkins sighed.

'One of the first batch. A training-school hack according to her log-book, poor old girl. Got more flying hours in than the Archangel Gabriel. . . .'

'Show me. . . .'

Hopkins led the way through the darkness, till the Bristol loomed up over them, blunt and purposeful.

'Mr Peters has had charge of her till now – though I told him you'd most likely want her. If she didn't break his neck for him, then it's only because she's a thorough lady. . . .'

'What's Mr Peters like?'

'Bloody awful. . . .'

The way Hopkins spoke, Destrier knew him to be summing Lieutenant Peters up as a pilot, as an officer and as a man. Destrier climbed up onto the Bristol's wing-root and stared down into the absolute blackness of the front cockpit.

'Has she – have any of them – got instrument lights?'

'Nothing that works, sir.'

'Why not, for Christ's sake?'

Hopkins knew that no excuse would satisfy Destrier.

'We've had no time,' he said flatly.

'Then you should have made time. . . .' The tone of Destrier's reply was equally flat; its apparently unaccusing accent was like a blow in the face.

'Everyone's been working round the clock,' Hopkins said after a pause. 'The lads have been out on their feet. *You* know how it is. . . .'

Destrier grunted, then swung himself awkwardly into the darkness of the Bristol's cockpit. In the darkness he felt the machine around him, vibrant and alive, her wires softly murmurous even in such small wind as was blowing. It was odd now to think that the Bristol had first reached the Front with a dubious and quite unfounded reputation for structural weakness. Details of this had filtered through to Destrier in hospital. Afraid to manoeuvre, the earliest Bristol pilots had paid for their hesitation and had been shot out of the sky. Time, fortunately, had disproved the original myth of frailty. The Bristol had proved herself a winner; a 'thorough lady' as Hopkins had just now put it – a virtue which, in the present circumstances, was perhaps just as well, considering his crippled hands. . . .

Hopkins, it seemed, had been thinking along similar lines.

'Have you had one of these up before, sir?'

'A couple of times. About an hour all told. . . .'

The Flight-Sergeant drew in his breath sharply. Destrier felt a flush of anger as he clambered from the cockpit. Damn Hopkins! Did the man think he needed a bloody nursemaid?

Pitched high with petulance, a voice challenged them out of the darkness.

'What the devil's going on out here?'

Recognizing the voice as being that of Lieutenant Peters, Hopkins answered, 'It's the Flight-Commander, sir. . . . Just taking a look-see.'

'Oh. . . .'

Peters sounded unwelcoming. The Bristol was by far the best of 'D' Flight's scratch collection of aircraft. With Destrier's coming, Peters knew he would now almost certainly be relegated to one of the less-than-glamorous BE12s – a notion which did not comport at all well with the lieutenant's idea of his own dignity.

Destrier moved stiffly forward in Peters's direction. Neither man attempted to shake hands and, when he spoke, Destrier's voice was icy.

'Have you been in command in my absence, Mr Peters?'

'More or less, sir . . . I –'

'It appears to have been a case of "less" rather than "more" to me, Mr Peters. I'll tell you, and I'll tell Flight-Sergeant Hopkins here, that what I have just seen is not bloody good enough! I want an improvement – and I want it *fast*. By the day before yesterday. . . .'

'Yes, sir. . . .' Peters swallowed in disgust. These bloody

upstarts from the ranks were all the same, given the chance. By God he'd –

·But Destrier gave him no chance to argue.

'Mr Peters,' he said, 'I'll give you just one hour to get some sort of instrument lighting fixed up in the serviceable aircraft. One hour. . . . If the Hun comes over tonight, then this Flight will be ready for him. That means we'll be wanting a flare-path, too. . . . You *can* arrange that, I suppose? And –' Destrier's voice accused both Hopkins and Peters equally – 'For Christ's sake try and make a better fist of things than the pair of you have managed so far. . . .'

Without waiting for a reply, Destrier turned away, making for the farmhouse tucked away among trees at the corner of the field. Bitter experience had taught Hopkins precisely what officers of Mr Peters's calibre could be predicted to do and say in such circumstances. Indeed, he would have been almost prepared to bet a month's pay on the lieutenant's exact choice of words. Nor was he disappointed. His voice taut with outraged dignity, Peters snapped, 'Well, Hopkins? You heard the Flight-Commander, didn't you? Get on with it, man!'

'Yes, sir . . . right away. . . .' Hopkins answered, stifling an urge to kick the lieutenant's backside. Instead, he sketched an ironic salute into the darkness and spat silently onto the turf, suddenly ashamed of himself as he did so.

That was the worst of Lieutenant Peters. You found yourself sinking to his level. . . .

TWO

Corporal Mendelssohn heard the big Maybach engines of the Staaken Giant running up with something of the same, tingling pleasure he had once felt in pre-war days when listening to the symphonies of Beethoven. Indeed, for Mendelssohn, it was impossible to think of the giant bomber at all except in terms of Beethoven, or – he unwillingly conceded – Wagner. To call R.45 merely BIG was to lose the value of the word. The aircraft was a phenomenon, a colossus. Standing on the tarmac, Mendelssohn stared up at R.45 with pride. Only German imagination, coupled with a superlative national ability for engineering and organization, could have conceived and produced such a monster.

From the far side of the airfield came a new tumult of sound as a second Staaken's engines were started, joining their clamour to those of R.45 in a deep and sonorous Woom-Woooom-WooooOOOOOM of bellowing accord.

No! Their music was nothing like that of Wagner at all, Mendelssohn decided. Of all composers, only Beethoven could possibly have created a sound so compactly rich, or so expressive of Titanic force. In answer to the Maybachs, Mendelssohn hummed a few bars from the *Eroica*, unconsciously bringing up his hands like those of an orchestral conductor as he did so.

A chuckle came from behind him and, turning, Mendelssohn sensed rather than saw Captain Count von Trier in the darkness. Mendelssohn clicked his heels and saluted smartly. In the gloom such ceremonial was hardly necessary. But, Mendelssohn knew, the Count would appreciate the gesture – not because he was a stickler for that sort of discipline but because a tongue-in-cheek observation of the proper conventions always amused him. It was all part of a rather arcane game. . . .

Senior officers found Count von Trier odd, not to say downright disconcerting. True that – outwardly at least – he appeared the very epitome of the pattern expected of the very best type of Prussian officer: correct, able and aristocratic. Yet there was something in his manner that made him not quite credible; something suggesting a performance, or worse – *much worse* – parody . . . masquerade . . . *mockery*. . . . This feeling was more than a suspicion to those who actually served under the Count. To the crew of R.45 their captain was a sardonic, dead-pan joker absorbed in some esoteric military comedy of his own invention.

As other-ranks will when liking an officer, von Trier's crew – ground and air alike – took a proprietorial interest in their leader's whims and fancies, humoured him, dubbed him 'The-Last-of-the-Junkers' and allowed themselves to be drawn into his charade, developing their own similar brand of po-faced irony.

Were other crews smart, efficient and soldierly? Then R.45's crew set themselves the task of being that much smarter – but, in a way, only just marginally short of dumb-insolence that suggested mockery of the war and the system they served.

Self-conscious young officers went a hundred metres out of their way to avoid being saluted by von Trier's men, whose wide-eyed punctilio came suspiciously near to insult. Senior officers felt their prestige and authority subtly undermined, but in such a way impossible to counter without appearing either pompous, or foolish – or both. . . .

Yet, at the same time – there was no denying the fact – von Trier's crew and aircraft were possibly the most efficient at Gontrode. The fifty men responsible for maintaining and flying the huge Staaken had developed an amazing unity of their own.

To the disgust of outsiders, it sometimes seemed that von Trier and his willing minions were not only hell-bent on fighting the war on their own, but that it was a quite different war to that being fought by the rest of Germany. . . .

And, indeed, perhaps they *were*, von Trier thought as he returned Mendelssohn's salute. In his own mind, the Count

33

was quite sure that Germany – whether she would admit it or not – had already lost the war. Soon the Americans would arrive in Europe to complete the Fatherland's humiliation and to pick up the pieces of a broken continent. And for the owners of that foolish continent, there would be neither victors, nor losers, but only survivors. . . .

He himself survived – though two younger brothers had been killed: one at Verdun; the other blown to fragments on the Somme. And, throughout his crew, the Count was aware of a score of similar cases. There was scarcely a man among the whole fifty who hadn't one familiar ghost to dog his footsteps – father, brother, son or cousin. Any system *proud* of demanding such service, such sacrifice, deserved only to be mocked. . . .

As the Maybachs coughed gruffly into silence, von Trier followed Mendelssohn towards R.45. Perhaps of all his men the Count was fondest of the little Jew. In civilian life he knew Mendelssohn to have been a violinist – a not very accomplished café musician. But von Trier was also aware of Mendelssohn's other ambition: his desire to follow in the footsteps of his illustrious namesake as a composer. Once, the Count had heard Mendelssohn whistling a strange, haunting little threnody. In answer to questioning, the corporal had admitted this to be part of a projected violin concerto – the main subject of its slow movement.

Von Trier hoped that Mendelssohn would survive to finish his composition, for in that whistled fragment of adagio had seemed so much that was an epitaph for all that had happened since 1914.

Reaching R.45, von Trier climbed up into the aircraft's cavernous and blue-lit cabin. Sergeant-Major Mann was giving everything a last check, a worried expression on his jowly, gloomy face.

Von Trier grinned.

'Everything as it should be, Sergeant-Major?'

Mann's face became – if possible – even gloomier. He sighed gustily.

'It *seems* that way, sir. . . .'

A worrier and a perfectionist, Mann was always disturbed when things went right. He sighed again.

'I've run the rule over as much as I can. The generator didn't seem to be quite itself – but we've ironed that out. Nothing very serious, so Müller reckoned.... A loose connection that he's seen to and retested....'

Von Trier looked up to see Corporal Müller eyeing the Sergeant-Major with satirical disrespect. Mann's pessimism was a family joke with R.45's crew – and an excellent omen. When things went really wrong, the Sergeant-Major became quite disconcertingly cheerful.

Slipping out of the cabin, von Trier climbed out onto the enormous lower wing, picking his way among the maze of struts and wires to the starboard engine-pod. Here, he found Mendelssohn already in place, stowing drums of Lewis ammunition into their racks. Von Trier tried to imagine what it must be like for the corporal and his port-side opposite number, Schmidt, to be out here in their exiguous cockpits between the Maybachs, cut off from the rest of the crew, lonely, exposed and vulnerable. Nor was this the most terrifying part of the gunner-mechanics' duty. In action, both Schmidt and Mendelssohn were expected to climb from their cockpits, out into the eighty-knot slipstream and up precarious ladders onto the Staaken's upper wing, where the bomber carried a second brace of Lewises.

Von Trier's bowels contracted as he contemplated such a climb, twelve-thousand or so feet above the ground, in icy darkness, with one's limbs impeded by bulky flying-gear and nearly rigid with cold. On daytime exercises, the Count had watched both Schmidt and Mendelssohn perform this feat with apparent unconcern. Schmidt, in particular, contrived to make the whole performance look as hair-raising as possible – a circus act to end all circus acts.

Even so, the rest of R.45's crew had more than enough reason to bless the skill and agility of their gunner-mechanics. On the bomber's very first raid over England they had between them accounted for a marauding fighter. Unsuspectingly it had dropped down over the huge and seemingly vulnerable wing of the Staaken, only to be caught in the murderous crossfire of the Lewises. It had fallen past the cabin windows, a fragmenting, blazing wreck, from which two frenzied shapes had hurled themselves rather than face death by fire.

Afterwards, von Trier had found it difficult to equate this brutal little victory as – in part at least – the handiwork of the gentle Mendelssohn. He had shrugged the feeling off. In three years of war, such massacre had become daily routine.

Climbing down from the engine nacelle, von Trier returned to the cabin. Lieutenant Horst and Sergeant Walter, his copilot, who had been seated at the bomber's controls during the engine-test, were now quietly busy in their places, the sergeant jotting figures onto a clip-board at the officer's dictation. Both seemed relaxed and satisfied. The Count eyed his pilots with amusement. They were an unlikely pair, he thought: the officer, large and fat, the sergeant, small and almost weedily spare; yet, together, they made a competent team.

Only Horst, as von Trier was aware, kept himself aloof from the rest of the crew's determined irony. A deeply serious man, such levity both shocked and disturbed him. Horst thought in large and important words – words like PATRIOTISM, HONOUR and DUTY. When Horst uttered the word FATHERLAND, his voice trembled and each syllable vibrated on the air. But von Trier knew him to be a good pilot – a trifle heavy-handed, maybe, but safe, reliable and with about as much imagination as a cow's backside.

Nor, in an emergency, would Walter be a bad substitute. By inclination a scout pilot, though he had previously flown two-seaters, the sergeant had schooled himself into a bomber pilot's disciplined and cool detachment. Von Trier gave his sergeant full marks for the strain involved in this. An ex-scout pilot himself, he knew what it cost a man to tie his impatience to R.45's lumbering stolidity.

Moving to the rear of the cabin, von Trier found the fuel-mechanic, Wendel, tapping the gauges beneath the petrol-tanks and looking to his pumps. In flight it was Wendel's duty to keep the bomber's engines equably supplied and the tanks balanced. He always did so with the apparent indifference of a man getting through some dully routine factory job. Von Trier half-suspected the mechanic to have more imagination than he ever showed – though just *why* he should think this the Count was unsure. To all outward appearances, Wendel was the completely phlegmatic, even bovine, Saxon. No disaster, or threat of disaster, seemed to move him. Even when on one occasion, a bursting anti-aircraft shell had sent red-hot shrapnel fragments whining through the cabin, drenching him with petrol from punctured tanks, Wendel had remained unflurried and apparently oblivious to danger. He had drained and shut-off the damaged tanks with unperturbed efficiency. A dumb-ox he might seem – but a hearteningly reliable one.

Von Trier ducked and slid out of the cabin into the tapering rear of the fuselage to inspect the Staaken's ventral defences. Here the original clumsy mounting had been replaced by a captured and adapted Scarff-ring, around which a brace of Lewises was free to travel. In action, the gunner swung above empty void, supported only by a webbing harness.

It was this gunner – Rossi – who was the only member of R.45's crew to give von Trier doubt. Perhaps it was something to do with the fellow's ebullient Italian ancestry, but, in practice, Rossi had proved to be either quite brilliantly outstanding or impossibly bad.

Now, seeing his commander beside him, Rossi grinned, then, kneeling astride the opening in the floor of the fuselage, pulled up the spade-grips of the Lewises and, swivelling them round on the Scarff-ring, went through the motions of firing.

'I shall be good, sir, tonight! Very good!'

Von Trier forced himself to sound severe.

'Just make sure that you are, Rossi. After all, we don't want you puncturing our own tail again, do we? The Sergeant-Major was most upset about it.'

Rossi's grin faded.

'He asked me whether I was trying to win a Victoria Cross. . . .'

'He wasn't the only one who got that idea....' The Count did his best to sound unamused.

The gunner busied himself with his Lewises.

'It won't happen again, sir,' he promised miserably.

'If it does, I'll arrange to get you transferred to the RFC.' Crouching, von Trier turned and made his way back for'ard into the bomber's cabin, where he found Mann waiting.

'Satisfied, Sergeant-Major?'

Mann's face fell into folds and creases of ineffable gloom, suggesting that were von Trier to give the order to start up, R.45 would immediately fall to pieces round them. By this, the Count knew that everything was just as it should be and that, short of last-minute hitches, the Giant was in superb working order.

'Right then....' von Trier instructed, 'providing the Flying Corps don't choose this evening to pay us a social call, our orders are to be ready for 21:00 hours. That means I want everyone rested and on the ball by 20:15. Is that clear?'

The men in the cabin nodded. Only Horst found it necessary to answer aloud, his voice deep-toned and determinedly martial; the voice of a man in whose ear clamoured the distant echo of trumpets, and the crash of arms....

The orderly whose job it had been to take Destrier to his room in Brick-Kiln Farm was soon left wishing that some other poor fool had been detailed for the job. Even before they had reached the top of the stairs, Air Mechanic Smith had been charged twice – once for his over-long and unkempt hair, then for the state of his boots. A third charge had followed when Destrier, running a gloved finger along the cracked window-sill, had inspected his finger-end in the candlelight and had found it black with dust.

Told off to report himself to Hopkins on all three counts, Smith felt very near to tears. As he put it to his friend, Dusty Miller, if that be-medalled Bastard upstairs could nail a fellow three times in two minutes by candlelight, then what hope could there be for anyone in the broad light of day?

Thus, it took 'D' Flight the minimum time to discover that in its Flight Commander it had found a tartar....

Destrier himself, left alone in the small, dirty, old-fashioned bedroom, looked about him without emotion. He had dismissed Smith, preferring to do his own unpacking. Despite his scarred and mangled hands, he accomplished this with the deft precision of a man most of whose military career had been served in the ranks, placing his few belongings in the small locker beside the grey-blanketed truckle bed, using that impersonal layout expected of a private soldier. Only one small object suggested individuality – a silver-framed photograph of a girl in nurse's uniform.

His unpacking finished, Destrier lay down on the bed, staring up at the cracked ceiling and willing his mind into some sort of composure. Christ! Just what sort of a set-up had he let himself in for? Three half-clapped aircraft of dubious provenance operating from a glorified paddock.

Destrier's eyes glowered at the feeble amateurishness of it all. Worse, Destrier found himself regretting the stubborn persistence, the obstinacy, which had betrayed him into arranging Hopkins's transfer. Already he knew that to have been a mistake, a foolish surrender to weakness and sentiment. Hopkins was a reminder of the past – a past which Destrier wished to forget utterly.

Yet, against his will, Destrier found his mind trespassing on forbidden ground. Thought of Hopkins brought to mind Dorrington Heath, Farnborough, and breathless, exciting days on Laffan's Plain. Lost days when the mingled scents of petrol, dope, castor-oil and bruised grass had contained no threat. Recalled even now, those scents were subtly different from the same ones today, magically restored to their lost and primal innocence, redolent not of fear or death, but of faith and aspiration. Yet, even in those days, there had been death and sadness, Destrier remembered. But those early, pre-war deaths had been different; a harsh, but acceptable, necessity; part-price for man's increasing mastery over the air.

His body drawn up and hunched on the bed like that of a

frightened child, Destrier turned towards the silver-mounted photograph. The girl in nurse's uniform smiled back at him. But her smile held no comfort for him now.... Only pain.

Alone at last in R.45's great cabin, von Trier sat himself at the navigator's table and methodically began checking maps and charts. It was from this table with its radio and morse-key that he would command the Staaken while, two miles high, she would bellow her way towards England. Only when the bomber was nearing her target would it be time for von Trier to make his way forward to the bomb-aimer's position in the nose.

It was this moment in each raid that he always detested. Despite Higher Command's pious claim that its bombers' targets were all strategic and military, the Count knew otherwise. With the bombsights available, such an assertion was all too manifestly untrue. In von Trier's experience, the target aimed for and the object hit were rarely if ever the same. Perhaps it was a mercy, he told himself, that in the nature of things he would never know where his bombs had landed....

With a sudden, sour taste in his mouth, von Trier fished in his pocket and took out a monocle, wiping it on a silk handkerchief before clamping the gold-rimmed circle in his eye. In his own way this was Claus von Trier's considered comment on all things Prussian.

Chilly and one-eyed....

No one – not even the kindly and perceptive Mendelssohn – knew just what sort of a man lay within Karl Wendel's impassive, ploughman's frame. Nor was anyone at Gontrode aware – apart from himself – of the secret battles against fear that the big man found it necessary to win before each flight. For Wendel knew himself to be that most outcast and despicable of humankind – an arrant coward. And he no longer had even one real friend to whom he might unburden his dreadful secret, since Jacobs, his only close companion, had been killed three weeks back, during one of the RFC's retaliatory raids on Gontrode. Besides, such terror and dreadful self-knowledge a man ought properly to keep to himself – a guilty secret that no one must ever be allowed to guess.

Up till now, Wendel knew he had been successful in this. So far as he knew, the rest of R.45's crew saw him as a mindless and emotionless cabbage, reliable and efficient, phlegmatic to the point of imbecility. Whereas other men might have felt slighted by such obvious disregard, to Wendel himself this seemed a small triumph, one indicating that his secret battles had not been in vain.

Now, a new fear was beginning to stalk him. How much longer could he keep up his charade? When – and where – would this crack? His main dread now was not of *being* afraid, but of giving way to fear. Already his appearance of calm indifference was becoming more and more difficult to maintain. In the hour or so before each mission, when apprehension and terror of the unknown were at their worst, his guts dissolved into water, and imagination showed him a hundred ways of meeting death, each more terrible than the last. . . .

Once into the aircraft, and off the ground, Wendel knew he would instantly become the man the rest of R.45's crew expected to see: one more addition to the bomber's manifold mechanical systems, detached from all but the purpose in hand – the precise balancing and distribution of the six-hundred odd gallons of fuel in the tanks above his head. Nor, till now, had Wendel experienced difficulty in giving this appearance of robot insensibility. In the air, he knew himself to be a man without choice, moving towards whatever fate might have in store for him, a dead man in all but name. . . .

No, it was on the ground and in the long-drawn hours prior to each raid that Wendel experienced his worst times. Then, prepared and briefed, with nothing to do except wait, fear claimed him. A machine he might be, but one with bladder and bowels to shame him. To cure this, Wendel had tried stuffing himself with a whole variety of panaceas and medicines. Now, even chloral failed to have much effect. Most of Wendel's last hours before each raid were spent alone in the chilly misery of the latrines.

And, tonight, the hobgoblin terrors stalking him were the worst yet. In imagination he had already been burned or mutilated, trapped in R.45's comet-falling wreck, or mashed to bloody pulp by a hail of Vickers bullets. But for some time now he had had a recurring vision in which none of these things happened. In this latest nightmare, the horror was new, different and dismayingly convincing. He stood alone in the Staaken's dimly-lit cabin, desperately juggling with pumps and gauges – and quite uninjured. The bomber thundered homewards – *or was it homewards?* – through the moonless blackness of the night. But, as he saw quite clearly, there was no one up front at the controls – at least, no one *alive*. Lieutenant Horst and Sergeant Walter sat in their places, and both were clearly dead, Horst, indeed, with the top of his skull blown off, and something horrible and grey showing where his helmet should have been. Lying near his pilots was the contorted body of R.45's captain, his face set in a manic parody of its familiar, sardonic self.

Try as he would, Wendel could not put this picture from his mind. His guts curdled and he retched dryly. Dear God above! Perhaps the coward's hell to which he was condemned would be no more than an extension of this world's torments, an eternity of icy, stinking latrines. . . .

Rolling off his bunk and dragging a greatcoat over his shoulders, Wendel staggered towards the door of his billet.

In the corner of a nearby barrack-hut, Otto Schmidt began clothing himself in the multitudinous layers of wool and leather made necessary by his exposed position out on R.45's port wing. When finished, he would no longer be recognizable as anything human, the clothing, goggles and helmet having transformed him into something grotesque and pupoid. Schmidt dressed slowly and with careful thoughtfulness, for the *exact* order in which he put on each article of dress had become part of an absurd and private ritual designed to propitiate those gods whose business it was to grant a fellow good luck.

Putting on the right-hand side of everything first was the key – sleeve, trouser-leg, sock, glove or boot. Schmidt was unsure how he had originally come to evolve this pattern, but he had, and – as things seemed to have worked out pretty well so far – Schmidt chose not to look into the matter too closely lest he break the spell. In Schmidt's considered opinion, half the trouble in this world was caused by people who had never learned to let well alone and who insisted on knowing the ins and outs of things far too deeply. And a fat lot of good it did 'em, Schmidt thought. It didn't make them any happier – at least, not so far as he could see. All people like that ever seemed to get for their pains was worry and trouble.

To Schmidt's simple mind, being a thoughtful man meant being an unhappy one, too.

No, he told himself, giving the Hebraic shrug of his shoulders he had learned from Mendelssohn, there wasn't much profit in that for a chap now, was there? Eat, drink and be merry – for tomorrow might come the Vickers bullet that knocked a hole in your head and put out the sun for ever.

And *then* where were you, eh?

Not that a Vickers bullet would ever get *him*! – of that he was sure. Schmidt knew himself to be one of those rare ones – an immortal. A thousand might fall at his left hand, and another thousand by his right – but *not* old Otto, as had been proved to him over and over again at Verdun. For all the shit and shell the Frogs had thrown at him, they might as well have saved themselves the trouble and gone home.

Schmidt stared down complacently at his still naked arms. There! Not so much as a scratch to show for three years of war. Nor would he ever have, not so long as he stuck to his proven rituals. With great care, Schmidt dived into a thick woollen vest – *right* sleeve first.

A few feet away, Solomon Mendelssohn looked up from his work and eyed his friend with amusement. Schmidt's brash self-confidence always amazed and delighted the little Jew.

43

Such certainty these days was rare and oddly reassuring; a reminder, perhaps, that mankind, though bloody, was not yet wholly bowed, and that plain and simple pleasure and an open enjoyment of living still had their proper place in the scheme of things. Something which Solomon was beginning to doubt....

For Mendelssohn shared none of Schmidt's blissful optimism. On the contrary, there were now few certainties in which he could find himself holding much belief. Even his religious faith, once strong and compelling, had become just one more war casualty: 'Died-of-Wounds' as Solomon told himself. God – if he had ever existed – had either deserted or was malingering in some safe back area....

Such cheap cynicism made Mendelssohn feel ashamed. Yet what alternatives were there for a man these days? Faith was a thing of the past. All that someone like himself had once felt free to believe in and take for granted – friendship, decency, honour and a happy, though formless, belief in the perfectibility of things – had long since been smothered in the mud of Flanders. What could any of these things possibly matter in a world given over to an orgy of lies and self-destruction? What could personal existence or survival count for when mankind was slaughtering itself in millions?

No.... If he was honest with himself, a man could no longer attach much importance to himself as an individual. The varying little lamps and lights that signalled and signified each man's existence were of small account. The blanket of war smothered them all. Only here or there, perhaps, a candle survived, its chance glow frail in the all-enveloping blackness. The effort to go on, to endure, to survive, was merely a gesture – a response as absurd and pathetic as that of a drowning man clutching at the proverbial straw.

Yet, despite thinking this way, Mendelssohn now spent most of his brief leisure working at the one thing which, these days, still retained something of its former value: his music.

It had been early in the year, at the time of Passover, that, unable to feel any of his old spiritual exaltation, he had first conceived his violin concerto. Now, sketchy though most of

44

it still was, the shape of the first two movements was clear. On the bunk beside Mendelssohn lay a sheaf of manuscript paper, black with corrections and second thoughts. Only one thing eluded him still – the subject of its final movement.

This he knew would have to be something extraordinary: a great, striding, triumphant melody, a reaffirmation of so much lost, thrown away or wantonly destroyed. Yet what shape this theme must take he had no idea. A dozen beginnings had come to him, only to be dismissed as unworthy or trite – Brahmsian pomposity, Wagnerian posturing. To descend to either, Mendelssohn knew, would be a betrayal of what his musician's instinct told him was a profound and original conception. He himself did not matter – but the truth of his work did. Humbly, and without conceit, Mendelssohn knew himself to be shaping a masterwork – a requiem for a whole European generation.

Nor could his last movement possibly be all rejoicing. At its end must come a coda, a ghostly echo of his threnodic slow movement, the solitary violin weeping above an echoing grumble of muffled drums and muted horns, fading gradually into silence.

Lachrimae. . . . Oh Lachrimae. . . .

With a sigh, Mendelssohn shuffled his manuscript pages together and stuffed them into a folder. It was high time he copied friend Otto and struggled into his flying gear. Mendelssohn always hated this business of turning himself into a brown caterpillar and usually chose to put it off until it could no longer be avoided. His flying-gear, though necessary, had come to symbolize for him the depersonalizing nature of war.

'Come on, Solly!'

Schmidt was impatient. His friend's reluctance to get ready for each flight always amused and exasperated him. He knew the reasons behind this reluctance and found them both funny and difficult to understand. A fine sort of fool a man'd look flying to England in his birthday-suit, wouldn't he? Supposing they were forced down. . . ? Schmidt conjured up a ribald picture of Mendelssohn's pink bum landing in a prickly British holly-bush.

The two young men finished changing in silence. In order to settle the folds of his bulky clothing about him, Schmidt began a curious little dance of his own invention, a clumsy, shuffling, knees-bend, stamp and hop which reminded Mendelssohn less of a grub or a caterpillar than of an old brown bear he had seen performing in the village square back home. There was something both endearing and comic in the sight.

But Schmidt slipped suddenly and the moment's humour was lost. He fell to the floor in a haphazard flurry of arms and legs. And, as he did so, his tumbling body reminded Mendelssohn of those others hurtling from the wreck of their blazing FE six weeks before....

As he fumbled in the dark of the Bristol's cockpit, barking his knuckles for the umpteenth time, Hopkins could not disguise the dismaying fact that he was about to make a bloody fool of himself. In order to stifle this unpleasant feeling, Hopkins growled at the young mechanic supposedly holding a torch steady enough for him to work by.

But firmly as he might try to push his intentioned folly out of mind, Hopkins failed. The notion he had conceived as his duty – his duty to an old and now tarnished friendship – would not now easily allow itself to be put from mind.

Almost desperately Hopkins cursed the mechanic again. The youth flinched, and his torch drew a wavering circle round the cockpit before coming to rest on the switch that Hopkins was screwing beneath the cockpit coaming. That's it! Hopkins jeered at himself; get at a youngster who couldn't answer back; pretend it was *his* fault that a man old enough to know better was about to make an unholy and irredeemable ass of himself. And all for reasons he could barely explain, reasons which, if put down on paper, would only look brainless and illogical.

The switch firmly in place, Hopkins tightened and taped its leads before testing his makeshift circuit. Immediately the instrument panel was lit by a dim green glow. Just what Destrier had ordered. Hopkins flicked the switch several times, the light faithfully responding on and off as he did so.

Yes, he told himself, it was all Destrier's fault.

But that wasn't really the crux of the matter at all, Hopkins derided himself, reaching down to make sure that the battery-leads were safely tucked out of harm's way. How long had he been in? A dozen years? Fifteen? And hadn't he learnt *anything* in that time? Not even that simple aphorism drummed into every rookie from the day he first joined. *Never volunteer for anything*. Never. Never. Never! And most especially not now. Not at this particular stage of this particular war. If there'd ever truly been a moment for committing the sort of daftness he was presently contemplating, then 1914 had been that time. But he *had* been daft then, too, hadn't he?

Hopkins fingered the emblem on his tunic, the faded braid with its embroidered 'O' and half-wing. Dyar! A man with his gift for mechanics volunteering to fly as an observer! People had been certified for less.

But then, Hopkins defended himself without much con-viction, the gesture had been right and proper, hadn't it? In time of war a soldier's rightful place was at the sharp end.... And the fact remained that he *had* volunteered, and that, scared stiff, frozen to the marrow and several times nearly killed, he had more than earned the right to wear that pretty scrap of ribbon on his chest.

Conscience would not allow Hopkins the luxury of dis-sembling – even to himself – the flood of relief he'd felt on being grounded early in 1915. A new CO, one who had known him in pre-war days, had arrived to take over the squadron. A cool realist, Major Driscoll had known Hopkins to be of more use to everyone alive and with a spanner in his hand than dying gallantly behind a chattering Lewis, and he had told Hopkins so, bluntly.

At this distance in time, all Hopkins could now hope was that he hadn't allowed himself to show his sense of reprieve too obviously. Oh, he'd protested, of course, but strictly for the look of the thing, hoping and praying all the while that Driscoll would remain adamant and not allow himself to be persuaded.

So now, the cool voice of reason queried, why this sudden suicidal urge on Hopkins's part to climb into a cockpit again and face those same terrors he had escaped so fortuitously? After all, the gunner whom Destrier would inherit from Peters was adequate, wasn't he? Adequate, young and almost pathetically eager at the prospect of finding himself teamed with someone of Destrier's reputation.

But young Russell didn't know Destrier as *he* knew him, Hopkins's conscience said. Nearly twenty years of friendship ought, surely, to count for something? But did it look as though memory of that friendship still meant anything to Destrier?

Hopkins shook his head angrily: that wasn't the point at issue, was it? It was what that friendship had once meant – and still did? – to himself alone.

For all this, he was now resigned to the certainty that he would be flying with Destrier tonight if the Huns came over. Just why this night of all nights seemed so important Hopkins couldn't explain to himself. It was a wholly irrational feeling that left him no room for manoeuvre or escape. Yes, he *would* fly tonight, and maybe once or twice more if need be. After that, the back seat of the Bristol was all Russell's – and he was welcome to it!

Hopkins glared at the young ack emma whose face was dimly visible in the muted glow of the torch.

'Is your mum much of a hand with a pair of knittin' needles, Russell?'

The boy nodded uncertainly.

'She never stops, Flight.... Sweaters, gloves, balaclavas. She's kitted me out a treat.'

'I'd say you and me were much of a size, wouldn't you, son?'

Russell nodded again.

Hopkins sighed resignedly.

'Good.... I want a word with you, my lad....'

Lieutenant Horst always did his best to avoid the company of his captain in the Mess. Von Trier's easy manners and confident air of self-possession always left him feeling gauche and discomposed. The son of a minor government official, Horst was well aware that he possessed none of his superior's enviable assurance and charm. It was only these gifts, Horst supposed, that enabled von Trier to get away with some of the things he said – things which should have sounded shocking and quite indefensible in the ears of any decent German officer, but which, coming from von Trier's lips, seemed only to cause general laughter.

Even as he slipped into the Mess, Horst heard the Count's clear and disdainful voice, pitched above the hubbub, embroidering some fancy for everyone's amusement.

'No-o!' he was saying, 'of course we shan't bomb the British War Office. Why harm our best friends? We shall simply land in the Mall, steal that ridiculous statue of Queen Victoria for His Majesty and then come straight home. Always providing, of course, that some fat London bobby doesn't tell us to "Move-along-there, please." '

'And what would you do if he did?' someone asked.

'Move along, of course. . . .' von Trier said, waving his cigar. 'As a good Prussian Officer what else could I possibly do but recognize the voice of authority – and obey!'

'Even British authority?' someone scoffed.

Von Trier's eyebrows shot up and his lips curled ironically. 'And why not?' he said coolly. 'It'll be good practice. . . .'

Ribald cheers greeted this remark. Horst turned away, unable to bear more. Count or no Count, von Trier shouldn't be allowed to get away with saying such things.

'Horst, my dear fellow –' he heard von Trier call across the room, '– I insist that you come over here and refute me! There should be no defeatism in a German Mess! Now come along, Richard. Do your stuff! The British blockade is a fantasy; the American threat is a myth; Germany's strength grows greater every day. And why shouldn't it? After all, isn't God a German like ourselves? A deity needing to be

49

propitiated with blood-sacrifices from time to time, in order that we may discover our true and irresistible German destiny?'

To Horst's simple mind, von Trier's statement seemed both reasonable and irreproachable. It was the *way* he said it that bothered the lieutenant: the bitter, inescapable ring of mockery.

'Well, Richard?' von Trier queried politely. 'Must I wait all night for an answer?'

Horst reluctantly cleared his throat.

'Sir, I don't think –'

'Ah –' Von Trier turned towards his brother officers '– Did you hear that? I have been most properly rebuked. Lieutenant Horst is an example to us all – on his own admission *he does not think*. Splendid! How much happier each and everyone of us would be if we could only echo that simple statement: "I am a German Officer – and I do not think." '

Von Trier stood, flicking the remnants of his cigar into a nearby ashtray.

'When we are over England tonight, gentlemen, bombing suburban streets in mistake for strategic targets, how convenient it will be to still our misgivings with that same absence of conscience, that same convenient denial of responsibility....

'Yes, Horst is right, of course. If a man dared to let himself think, then God alone knows what inadmissible conclusions he might come to, what dark sounds he might be forced to hear....'

'To hear?' he was asked.

Von Trier shrugged.

'The flutter of dark wings, perhaps. The wings of the Furies – or of chickens coming home to roost.'

Someone growled in protest, but von Trier silenced him with a look and left the room. Even as he passed the door, von Trier knew he had gone too far this time, even for him. The things he had just said back there in the Mess had been worse than a breach of discipline – much worse; they had been a breach of decent manners, an oafish trading on the amiable tolerance of his fellows.

Why was it these days that even the ordinary decency of his fellow men only served to set his teeth on edge and drive him to excess? Even poor Horst, suety-faced and unimaginative though he might be, wasn't at all a bad fellow, really. He was simple, kind, upright and honest by any reckoning. English, German, French, Belgian – the fields of Europe were by now choked with Horst's kind, the only reward they would ever get for their courage and unthinking patriotism.

And – honesty compelled him – von Trier knew it was *his* kind that had led them to this. The nickname his own crew had bestowed on him – 'The Last of the Junkers' – hurt. It came too damned near the truth. In his bitterest moments of self-denigration, the Count reminded himself of his English dictionary's definition of a Junker: 'A young German noble or squire; an overbearing, narrow-minded reactionary aristocrat.' Was *that* really himself? Perhaps. . . .

Von Trier paused in the ante-room outside the Mess; he found he was shivering and that one eyelid was fluttering uncontrollably. Perhaps, he accused himself, his outspoken concern with the follies of mankind was really no more than a sophisticated way of showing plain, simple funk. It was a salutary thought that he, Captain Count von Trier, was, for all his pretensions, no more fire-proof than the next man. . . .

Lieutenant Horst came out of the Mess. A look of apprehension crossed his pudgy features as he saw his superior. Von Trier felt ashamed. God help him! It was his job to pump confidence into the Horsts of this world, not to destroy what little they had. He moved towards Horst and saw the lieutenant flinch as he approached. Von Trier winked, then flung an arm round Horst's shoulders.

'Come along, Richard. Time to get ready, I think. We must have you in extra good form tonight.'

As they went upstairs together, amiably chatting, Richard Horst wondered just what devils drove von Trier. He could make you hate him and then, the next moment – just as he was

51

doing now – with a cheery word and an arm round your shoulder, make you willing to follow him *anywhere* . . . even down into hell itself should he suggest it. Sadly, Horst knew that *he* could never be that sort of officer. Such a gift was but one more inheritance that came with aristocratic birth. For half a millenium the von Triers had been born and bred to lead.

As Horst well knew, his own antics as an officer left men unimpressed; they neither loved nor feared him, but simply obeyed. As Horst was shamefully aware, R.45's crew had a nickname for himself as well as von Trier. But his was vulgar, plebeian: 'Horst der Vürst – Horst the Sausage.' He was too bitterly conscious of his failings as an officer to recognize in this name the beginnings of affection. To him it merely suggested disrespect, not to say downright contempt. Not even having the simplest gift of humour himself, it always worried Horst to find this disconcerting trait in others.

The world was far too serious for humour.

Sergeant Walter, R.45's second pilot, wondered whether he could possibly get another pair of trousers on over the two he was already wearing. Reluctantly he decided not. The electrical current heating the flying-suits of the Staaken's crew had an unpleasant habit of failing at critical times, and of all the discomforts that afflicted a man in this wicked world, Walter most detested cold. Before the war he hadn't minded it too much. But now, after a year in the trenches and then two more of open cockpits, being uncomfortably if not stiflingly warm was something that had come to obsess him. Never again, he vowed – always providing he survived the war – would he allow himself to be cold. Rather would he damn the expense, heap the coals up the chimney, pile his bed with blankets and, regardless of what she might look like, marry the fattest, warmest wench in Bremen. . . .

Come to that, Walter thought with an urchin grin, tucked up like that, he wasn't too sure he'd ever bother getting up again either – apart from visits to the can. Left to himself, he'd devote the rest of his life to copulation and pleasant postcoital sleep. Indeed, it was the thought of sleep rather than sex that really moved him. After three years of cat-naps and uncertain sleep, his body cried out and ached for rest. At twenty-four years of age he felt an old man. Worse, examining his face in a smeary mirror, he knew he was beginning to look it. Deep lines marked the side of his mouth and scored his forehead. Fear, indifferent food and this enervating weariness made him look older than his own father now comfortably profiteering in Bremen.

To date, Walter had been shot down three times. Flying for eighteen months in vulnerable and clumsy two-seaters, he had frequently experienced the helpless despair of knowing himself to be so much cold meat as a British scout had zoomed up into the blind spot beneath his tail. Once secure in that position, and given that his attacker could shoot with moderate accuracy or his gun didn't jam at a critical moment, there could only be one ending. Three times Walter had dragged the bloody rags of his observer from the crumpled ruins of Aviatic or Halberstadt. His rump still ached where a brace of Vickers bullets, slashing up through the fragile flooring of his plane, had lodged in his buttock.

As first his transfer to heavy bombers had seemed a move even more likely to get him killed than remaining in two-seaters. But, slowly, a new confidence had begun to grow in him. R.45 might present a target that no one, not even a blind man, could possibly miss, but flying alone, and at night, the Staaken provided her enemies with an exasperating and elusive quarry. Besides, even if an enemy *did* find her, R.45 was very far from being a sitting duck. Most of the other Staaken commanders had seen fit to strip their defensive armament down to the barest minimum – but not von Trier, who, by devious means, had even managed to equip R.45 as per manufacturer's specification – with the British Lewis.

Yes, Walter thought, thanks to the skipper, R.45 was able to ladle out at least as good as she got. The unwary FE they'd bagged on their first raid had proved that.

As he bundled his discarded trousers into a locker, Walter briefly allowed himself to contemplate a world after the war –

a world in which, please God, he still breathed and had his being. Winding a long woollen scarf round his neck, Walter assured himself again that his wants from that world would be few and carnal: food, beer, sleep and a plump, accommodating woman. Those and *warmth*, of course – never in that unattainable and far-off future would he allow himself to feel cold.

Not for so long as a single minute.

The fact that it was known to everyone at Gontrode that he had once managed to pepper R.45's tail was a continual source of embarrassment to Rossi. He knew himself to have inherited all the proverbial excitability of his father's race, and the fact that he himself was German by birth and education could never alter or eradicate that simple fact. The more he denied his roots and attempted to school himself to a proper appearance of German method and calm, the more the Italian in him fought and struggled for freedom. The greater his effort to appear more German than the Germans, the less credible his act seemed. His temperament was too definitely Mediterranean, too much a matter of squalls and sunshine. Among R.45's crew, he felt himself to be a man set apart by race and attitude – an outsider.

Nor had the behaviour of his father's people made his position in the squadron any easier. Despite her treaty obligations to the Central Powers, Italy had allied herself with the French and British. There were times, Rossi felt, when he was fighting a war all of his own. . . .

He had said as much to von Trier once, surprised at his own temerity. But the Count, despite his outward appearance of Teutonic hauteur, had proved very approachable. He had listened gravely to Rossi's stammerings and had then shaken his head. 'But my dear Rossi,' he'd explained in his precise voice, 'that is neither more nor less than what each and every one of us is doing. We are *all* fighting our own, pathetic, separate little wars, each one of us in his own, individual way.'

As he finished changing, the Italian considered this. Von Trier was right, of course. He usually was. He, more than anyone Rossi had ever met, seemed to have a clear understanding of what life and living were about. Too much so, perhaps, for his own good. However bitterly he might denigrate High Command for its prosecution of the war, to his own crew von Trier was the very fount of strength. If anyone could bring them all safely through the next few months, it would be von Trier. Rossi dreaded the terrifying prospect of being mustered with another crew.

Rossi crossed himself to ward off the thought of this dreadful possibility, then took from a locker those other guardians of his destiny — a rosary that had once belonged to his dead mother and an ugly little doll given him by a hero-worshipping sister. Both seemed fragile armour against anti-aircraft fire or marauding fighters. And yet — Rossi glanced down to where his flying-helmet lay on his bunk. A deeply scored mark down its right side showed where a bullet had come yearning for him out of the dark. A couple of centimetres the wrong way and....

Rossi tried to contemplate the world going on without him. He found it impossible. Without Giovanni Rossi, the world quite simply did not exist. How else could it, but by the grace and favour of his own continuance? Rossi crossed himself again. Thoughts like that were dangerous! A temptation to Death's dark angels! If a man allowed himself to think like that, then misfortune, surely, would find him out, making him prey for the random bullet, or the shell fired blindly at nothing-in-particular.... Rossi shivered as a cold apprehension about the coming raid took him in its grip.

Yes, von Trier was right. Each man could only fight his battles alone. But they were always battles with himself.

And each battle was worse than the last.

A timid knocking at the door roused Destrier from what had nearly become a merciful doze. The door opened to show the frightened face of Smith, his orderly. Behind him stood Hopkins. The Flight-Sergeant shoved the orderly unceremoniously to one side and came into the room.

'Eight o'clock, sir. Can we get you something to eat?'

Destrier shook his head. The thought of food these days nauseated him.

'No, Flight,' he said. 'I don't want anything.'

He sat up, conscious of his own remissness. How long had he been lying here like this in a limbo between sleep and waking? The room felt icy. . . .

As Destrier struggled to sit upright, Hopkins felt his stomach turn over. Up till now he had barely taken in the ruin that had been his friend's face. One side of this was puckered into a cicatrix of purple tissue round what must have been a bullet hole. A scar under the opposite side on Destrier's throat showed where the bullet had originally penetrated, punching upwards through mouth and cheek. Judging by Destrier's ungainly struggle to sit upright, Hopkins guessed at other wounds quite as hideous as those marring what had once been a personable face. And, judging by the spasm of pain twisting Destrier's mouth, such wounds could be scarcely healed.

Hopkins longed to throw a protective, affectionate arm round Destrier as he would have done when they were boys. Damn discipline! Damn KR's! Damn conventions! He and Laurie were still the same people, weren't they?

Yet, Hopkins thought sadly, it was difficult to see in this bitter, broken man the engaging, imaginative youth he had once been. What had formerly been a taut, reserved strength, now seemed a dangerous, explosive tension. Only in Destrier's eyes lurked something of the boy as Hopkins remembered him – and even these now expressed nothing so much as an infinite weariness; their old intelligent, interested gleam had become a dully defensive glare.

Hopkins turned on the lurking Smith and abruptly dismissed him.

'Here you, sonny – Hop it!'

The orderly vanished with relieved alacrity, and Hopkins closed the ill-fitting door. He turned to Destrier, said nothing for a second or two, then decided to chance his arm.

'Hell's teeth, Laurie – you've put the fear of Christ into that one!'

Ignoring the impertinent use of his Christian name, Destrier bared his teeth in the mockery of a smile.

'I'll be gentler with him tomorrow.'

'D'you still want him on the pegs?'

'No, providing he gets his bloody hair cut!'

Hopkins relaxed. This was more like the Destrier he knew. Not a man to take any untoward liberties with, but decent, fair....

Destrier painfully screwed his body round on the bed and put his feet to the floor.

'Was it your tom-fool idea to let me sleep?'

Hopkins nodded. 'You looked like you needed to.'

'Not one of your better notions if I might say so, Flight-Sergeant. This place, as you so nicely put it earlier, is a bloody shambles, and what does its OC do on arriving? He takes himself off to bed!'

'There wasn't much you could do. Not this evening.'

'I could've gone round and twisted a few tails. It's high time *someone* got a bloody grip on things.'

Hopkins looked hurt.

'We've only been here ten days ourselves. The lads have been at it all the time ... non-stop....'

'With you snapping at their heels, I suppose?'

'No!' Hopkins said firmly, 'I haven't needed to. Oh, we've been handed a pretty scratch lot – real odds and sods, mostly. But *willing* ... they've needed directing – not driving.'

'As you've tried telling Mr Peters?'

Hopkins looked up, startled.

'How in hell did *you* know that?'

'Because I've been an "other-rank" too, remember. I know the Mr Peterses of this world as well as you do.' Destrier grinned. 'Yes ... you'll have done your best if I know you, Syd. You're a good chap.'

Destrier was surprised to see the pleasure his unthinking

use of the other's Christian name had given. Christ! Was he getting maudlin as well as physically weak? Deliberately, he hardened his tone.

'But decisions as to whether I wake or sleep are *not* your responsibility, Flight-Sergeant! I should have been up and seeing to things for myself, not lying here. Do you understand that?'

Hopkins shuffled to attention.

'Yes, sir. . . .'

'It's our job to be ready for the Hun whenever the bastard chooses to come. That means by the day before yesterday – and not when we bloody-well happen to feel like it. Have those three machines been brought up to scratch?'

Hopkins looked pained.

'You know me, sir –'

'That's not what I asked.'

'All three aircraft are available for immediate use, sir!'

'Instrument lights?'

'Fixed –'

'Guns?'

'Checked and loaded 'em meself. Every round inspected . . . just ball . . . no Pomeroy or Buckingham to cut dazzle. . . .'

Destrier shook his head angrily.

'Scrub that! I want my belts made up ball, Pomeroy, Buckingham. Got that?'

'Hopkins sucked in his lips.

'That's not supposed to be very wise, is it, sir? At least, not at night?'

'I don't give a damn whether it's wise or not. If I hit something I want it to go off with a satisfying bang.'

'Including your own propeller?'

'That's my worry.'

Yee-es, and mine too, now, Hopkins secretly thought. He shrugged.

'D'you want the BE12s armed with incendiary, as well as the Brisfit?'

'That's a matter for Mr Peters and whoever the third pilot is –'

'Mr Browne....'

Destrier shrugged.

'I don't care who it is – just so long as he's ready and standing by an hour from now. So far as I'm concerned the Flight's operational as from now. Tell the Recording Officer to log that, and to inform whoever it is we're supposed to inform.'

'Yes, sir.' Hopkins opened his mouth to say something further, but changed his mind, saluted and left the room.

Despite his anger at having been left to sleep, Destrier made no attempt to get up from the bed. Weakness and inertia caused him to sink back again onto its comfortless springs. He turned to the photograph on the locker beside his pillow.

'You wouldn't approve of that, Dolly – you wouldn't approve of that at all, would you, old girl. Not Buckingham. But I want them to know what it feels like when the world blows up in their faces, too ... I want them to know what it feels like to burn....'

The sepia image to whom he spoke stared gravely back at him. Dolly had always possessed that look of cool serenity, moving through the world with a sort of sober, wondering gravity that had seemed to set her apart from other women. Her presence had always been unfussy, relaxing and comfortably reassuring. When her rare smile came, its recipient felt refreshed and reborn in its light; someone to whom a very special gift had been advowed.

Looking back on his time in hospital, Destrier could recall the exact moment when he had first become aware of Dolly. For two or three weeks, perhaps – or had it been three? – since he had first been wheeled into the ward, little more than a heap of suppurating, agonized tissues, Dolly must have been near him, busying herself with the unspeakable details of his nursing.

When at last her face had come swimming into one of his mercifully rare moments of consciousness, he had given himself up for dead. There was no such beauty in the living world that he remembered. Such a face as this could only belong in the hereafter. Awed, Destrier stared up at Dolly, her face haloed by its starched veil. A look of worry had come into her grey eyes, like cat's-paws of wind across quiet water; neat little teeth had come down to bite on a full lower lip. Then, prosaically, unromantically, this angel – this madonna – had asked him whether he needed a bed-pan. Trying to reply, Destrier had discovered the lower half of his face to be bound in a mummy-like swathe of bandage. This had frightened him, and he had vainly struggled to sit upright. Pain speared him from head to toe, and with a groan he had dropped back into unconsciousness.

But this time, in the dark places that filled his coma, he was not alone. In the boiling, tormented caverns of pain that reached down into his apparent stillness, a second figure walked beside him, held his hand, told him to be unafraid and drove away the hobgoblin chimera that filled his darkness. Twice, in this time, Laurie Destrier almost died. The second time he found himself standing beside a bottomless crevasse separating himself from the girl. In terror he looked down – and despair gripped him. He heard himself cry out. The girl stretched out her arms towards him, and he leapt, felt himself held – and, even in his delirium, knew that somehow he had leapt back into life.

In that moment, unconsciousness became a peaceful, healing sleep....

He had awoken from this on a bright April morning. Daffodils stood on the locker beside his bed, and he found himself worshipping them for their cocky, trumpetting arrogance. Through a window opposite he saw and heard a blackbird singing in a lilac bush, the sound falling across him in silvery cascades. The blackbird was plump and glossy; even the gold of the daffodils paled before the orient brightness of his beak. Yet, marvellous as these things seemed, Destrier was conscious, too, of loss, and resentful of his resurrection. Death had been bearable because of a girl's angel presence, and the prospect of life without her was desolate. Try as he would, Destrier could not believe such a creature to be incarnate, a being of sinew and blood like himself.

Hopelessness overwhelmed him – yet, even as it did so, he

remembered that the girl had once asked him whether he needed a bed-pan. Surely angels never asked a fellow questions like that? Once a man was through the Gates of Death, surely such mundane considerations became unnecessary? Destrier tried to laugh, but the sound – muffled by gauze and lint – came out as a choked gurgle. It was a small, quiet sound, but enough to bring the angel to his side.

'So, Mr Destrier, you've decided to stay alive after all, have you?'

She said it flatly, but her voice held a faintly perceptible timbre of relief.

'Yes. . . . I rather think I have.' Destrier managed to whisper. 'Thanks to . . . an angel.'

The girl laughed uncertainly.

'An angel? What's her name?'

'The same as yours. . . .'

'I'm Nurse Lyttleton. Dolly to you.'

Destrier noted with wonder that two large tears were brimming up in Nurse Lyttleton's eyes. Were *these* for him?

Dolly Lyttleton sniffed and then muttered something about daffodils always giving her hay fever. The sniff made Destrier's former angel approachable, human. Although still awed by her, he felt none of that gauche awkwardness he usually felt in the presence of beautiful women. Watching the girl stifle her tears, he realized with humility that they had indeed been shed for him. He struggled to see if arms and legs would obey him. It seemed they would – if pain was anything to go by. But, and he threshed wildly in the bed, was pain proof enough? Amputated limbs could ache quite as agonizingly as those still attached to the body. . . .

The girl leant forward, her gentle but firm hands pinning him to the bed.

'You mustn't do that. You must lie still. Absolutely still. It's the best way – the only way – to help yourself. You must have patience.'

In his weakened state there was nothing that Destrier could do but obey. Nurse Lyttleton smoothed his sheets, drawing them up under his chin, then tucking them firmly on either side of the bed to restrict his movement. To be made prisoner in this way, strait-jacketed by an ethereal slip of a girl, roused in Destrier a flush of petulant anger. At the same time, he felt relieved and freed of all responsibility. There was nothing for him to do now but allow himself to be treated as a child whom others must feed, wash, keep warm and see came to no harm.

Such an experience was quite novel to Destrier. His prostitute mother had never cossetted him, nor, during his brief illnesses at the orphanage, had Mrs Maubrym, the matron, ever treated him with more than a brusque if kindly detachment. To be mothered was something entirely new in Destrier's experience. The prospect left him half-resentful, half-delighted.

Nurse Lyttleton gave him a drink from a revolting little cup with a funny, awkward spout and then went away. Destrier felt suddenly bereft and alone. He whose life had been mainly solitary and self-contained was now brought face to face with his essential loneliness. Promotion had cut him off from the one real friend he'd ever made. He had killed his King's enemies – and each victory, achieved with what observers took for callous ease, had only served to make him more separate still, isolating him within a precious yet precarious privacy. Success had made him vulnerable, an object of curiosity; the inquisitive wished to know about his past, his antecedents. . . .

How intolerable, if, now, after almost twenty years, the unsavoury details of his background were to come to light!

There were events in his childhood that Destrier had confided in no one – even Hopkins. His transformation from harlot's guttersnipe to orphanage brat had been brought about in the best traditions of melodrama. A drunken matelot – one not dissimilar to his unknown father, perhaps – had, in a drunken rage, strangled the blowsy woman who had been the boy's mother. By chance, Destrier had seen this, and his had been the evidence that had put a hempen rope round Able-Seaman Waterlow's neck. Even now, Destrier could remember the poor devil standing in the dock, a puzzled, red-faced, roly-poly of a man, only half-comprehending as the foreman of the jury had pronounced that one dreaded and dreadful word: 'Guilty!'

With memories like that, a man tended to keep himself apart. Whatever his achievements, whatever his success or fame, the trauma remained. Indeed, the greater a man's fame, with all its attendant publicity, then the more likely was that past to come to light. Destrier dreaded that. There were those, he knew, who resented his rise from obscurity to something like a public idol. What pleasure the ancient scandal of his birth and upbringing would be to them. . . .

But even this dread lost its importance the first time Destrier was allowed to see his face in a mirror. Only after days of argument was he at last able to overcome his doctor's obvious reluctance. This doctor – a hard-bitten RAMC colonel – had put the matter off as long as possible, until one morning Destrier lost his temper. For all his abrupt manner, Colonel Mayo was a kindly man. He quickly weighed in the balance which was worse for his patient – knowledge of the truth or lying in bed fretting. Reaching his decision, Mayo shrugged and signalled for Dolly to fetch a looking-glass.

What Destrier saw almost broke him. He had never been vain about his looks. But the nightmarish run he saw in the little handmirror revolted him. With an involuntary blow of disgust, he knocked the mirror from Nurse Lyttleton's hand, smashing it to fragments on the ward floor. For the first time since he'd known her, Dolly Lyttleton ceased to be an angel for him. Instead, she became simply a beautiful girl – one who must have had to hide her revulsion every time she looked at him. . . .

For a week afterwards, Destrier refused even to speak to her. When she changed his dressings or straightened his bed, he simply ignored her. For her part, Dolly, if hurt, understood his reasons. Yet, she also knew that however much Destrier might choose to disregard her, he was in some peculiar and inexplicable way her own. At the beginning, she *had* felt pity for him – yes. But it was neither pity for his broken body, nor respect for the proud spirit locked within his burnt and bullet-riven flesh that moved her now. Without her willing it, Destrier had become the whole reason for her existence, and, scarred and broken though his body might be, the object of her frank and unashamed love.

But how was she to bring home to Destrier what she felt?

Too well she remembered his reaction to what the mirror had revealed. Now, she knew, he would never give the smallest sign of affection for her, but would take for granted that she, too, must share a similar disgust and revulsion.

No, if she wanted Destrier, Dolly knew she must make the running herself. She would have to fling herself at his head. The implications of this made her blush. Yet, despite this, she knew that in her heart of hearts she cared nothing for convention, nor orthodox morality, so long as she could make Destrier hers. The world could say and think what it liked.

Destrier's body set itself the task of healing quickly. It could never restore itself to muscled symmetry of face and body, but flesh and sinews began to knit themselves together as best they could. Colonel Mayo was surprised and delighted. Paradoxically, the extent of Destrier's wounds gave the doctor a sense of relief. Here was one body on whom medical skill would not be wasted. It would be a year at least, Mayo knew, before Destrier would be free of major pain or fully mobile. Aches and a degree of physical disability would be his for the rest of his life. There were still at least three chunks of metal in Destrier's body which Mayo had judged it prudent not to remove....

Early in May, the Colonel considered it was time for his patient to get up. Quickly though Destrier's body might be healing, it was obvious that his mind was not. There was a listlessness in his attitude, an apathy of mind and soul, that Mayo – who scorned the budding science of psychiatry – understood perfectly. Destrier's morale was round his ankles. Getting the man onto his feet again would be a start in taking care of that. After three months in bed, the effort of conquering bodily weakness would take his mind off other matters.

This diagnosis proved correct. Destrier's reaction on being allowed up had at first been amusement at his body's disobedience, followed by an irritated then angry determination to get the better of his mutinous limbs. He had snapped and snarled at would-be helpers. If he was to stand at all, then it would be alone. Above all, he would not be defeated by this treacherous, exasperating weakness of feet and legs. Their wilful determination to do anything but what his brain commanded *must stop*! Fellow-patients and nurses alike learnt to dread Destrier in the following month as, inch by inch, he fought his body into some semblance of obedience. Wasted muscles and sinews long-inured to idleness grudgingly remembered forgotten duties. Destrier's will fought a savage and bitter campaign against his rebellious body. Single-mindedly, he disregarded all else – including other peoples' feelings – till he knew his battle was being won.

By the end of the month, Destrier had fought his body into something like submission. Like a drill-sergeant with an unpromising platoon, he was beginning to recognize the first faint glimmerings of sense in the awkward squad at his command. Waking from his self-absorption, he was surprised by the hostility he had raised about him. Angrily, he blamed this onto his face. Who could blame the world if it found difficulty in looking at him without flinching? Yet – in that case – let the world look out for itself. He owed it *nothing*! The world had been none too gentle with him – why should he be gentle with it? His burned and ravaged face might be a cause for apology. But not by him.

Even Hopkins's visits (the Flight-Sergeant had been posted to Hendon) had been fraught with potential embarrassments. Neither man knew what to talk about. Both had been glad when visiting times were over.

It was in this time, too, that Destrier succeeded in stifling within himself that first, absurd flush of love he had felt for Dolly Lyttleton. Now, her calm placidity angered him. Nothing she could do for him was right and he set himself the none too difficult task of making this obvious to her, treating her kindness with so much contempt and disdain that one day she had finally slapped him.

Dolly's blow had not been a particularly hard one, But,

even so, delivered to the undamaged side of Destrier's face, it had proved too much for his unsure legs. He had staggered and fallen in a clumsy, self-pitying heap and, to his infinite shame, had begun to cry. Mayo, examining another patient at the far end of the ward, had seen Nurse Lyttleton's slap and what had led to it. Without ceremony, he abandoned his patient, dragged Destrier up from the floor, bundled him onto his bed, then drew the screens around it. For the next five minutes he verbally chastised the weeping man in language Destrier hadn't heard since his promotion from the barrack-room.

The Irishman's wrath cooled at last, and the usual tone of rough-and-ready compassion crept back into his voice.

'I can see it's doing neither you nor us much good keeping you here. You're to have a week, no, ten days, out of this place. Get yourself away somewhere! Go and have a look at that peculiar place outside we call the world. And, while you're there, just look around you. There's many a poor devil in worse shape than yourself, you'll find. Yes! And many a woman in black who'd get down on her knees and thank the Blessed Virgin for getting her man back – even if he did look like you.'

Destrier cringed back on his bed. No! he didn't want to go outside. He wanted to stay here, where it was safe. He heard himself begging and pleading with Mayo not to be sent on leave. But the big Irishman was adamant.

'So,' he scoffed, 'you've nowhere to go ... what are you – a child? Find somewhere.... There're hotels and places a-plenty. You'll be out of here by four o'clock. I'm away to sign a chitty to that effect this minute.'

Clamping an unhygienic pipe between his teeth, Mayo stumped off out of the ward. Desolately, Destrier began packing his few belongings. An orderly brought his kit from somewhere in the hospital; a nurse helped him dress. But another nurse – not Dolly. Dolly was nowhere to be seen.

The thought of leaving hospital without apologizing to her and saying goodbye filled him with shame. Brought to himself by Mayo's anger, Destrier cursed himself for a lout; an ungracious, ungrateful oaf who had thrown back into Dolly's loving face almost every small kindness she had shown him. . . .

The same orderly who'd brought him his kit carried Destrier's valise down the hospital steps. He himself tottered on a stick. The outside world seemed frighteningly vast, and its sunlight, dazzling. At the foot of the steps, a car was waiting – Mayo had seen to that. A door was held open for him by a driver whose face momentarily lost its urbane, disciplined expression at the sight of his passenger's features. For a moment Destrier was seized by a barely-resistible urge to bring his stick down across the man's shoulders – but the urge died as he realized the car had another passenger beside himself: Dolly Lyttleton.

The very unexpectedness of Dolly's presence completely took away what little remained of Destrier's self-composure. He settled himself into the corner opposite her and said nothing. He found that his hands were twitching uncontrollably. The effect upon his newly-healed skin felt horrible – it was as if insects were creeping over it.

As the car pulled away, Dolly looked at Destrier from the corner of her eye. Removed from the authority of her uniform, she found herself feeling unsure, and a little afraid of the man next to her. Suddenly, she felt shy; this man was no longer the familiar being she had come to know, but a stranger. But – stranger or not – he was still the man she wanted.

'Are you going anywhere in particular, Captain Destrier?'

Destrier looked confused and lost. He shrugged and then screwed up his face. For one dreadful moment she thought he was about to cry again.

'No-o. . . .' he said at last, 'I'm not going anywhere. . . .' He sounded ashamed, as if this small admission was some sort of guilty secret. 'C-Colonel Mayo suggested an hotel somewhere . . . I don't know. . . .'

'In London?'

'I suppose so. . . . Shows . . . theatres. All that sort of thing.'

'I prefer the country myself.'

'Do you?'

'It's much nicer.'

'I didn't know you were due for leave.'

Dolly laughed.

'Nor did I. Colonel Mayo seemed to think I needed it.'

'Oh. . . ?' Destrier's voice sounded flat, incurious.

Dolly had the sinking feeling she was about to make a fool of herself. Oh, well. Never mind. What she'd set out to do she'd best finish – whatever the cost in shame or humiliation.

'The Colonel seemed to think you'd been giving me a difficult time lately. . . .'

'I . . . I'm sorry. . . .'

Dolly stole another sideways look in Destrier's direction. Yes, he really *was* sorry, she could see that. He sat on the edge of his seat looking like an embarrassed little boy. She felt her confidence returning.

'So . . . when the Colonel suggested it was time I took some leave, I jumped at the chance.'

And who could blame her, Destrier thought. What the devil must it cost a girl to go on, month after month, patching up the remains of men such as himself? For the first time since his crash, such a notion came into his head entirely devoid of self-pity.

'Are you going home?' he asked.

Dolly shook her head.

'Not home, exactly. We've a cottage just outside Tolleswich.'

'We?' Destrier's heart sank.

The girl noted the pang of anxiety in his voice.

'Daddy and I. He's with the Grand Fleet now. My mother died just before the war.'

'So you're on your own now?'

'It'll be a relief!' Dolly bit her lip. Why, oh why, had she had to say anything so stupidly clumsy? Destrier looked chastened and muttered something about 'not being surprised'.

Dolly plucked up her courage and turned towards him.

'I didn't really mean that about wanting to be on my own.

Besides, it's not terribly good for me. I get very slap-dash and lazy.'

Her heart lifted to see the look of hope on his face. She ignored the fact that the glass partition separating them from the driver was not quite shut, took a deep breath and then, conscious of her rapidly dwindling courage, said in tones so matter of fact that she surprised herself, 'Why don't you come, too?'

For a moment she was afraid Destrier hadn't heard her. He sat quite still, his eyes half-closed, apparently intent on the driver's close-cropped hair and pimply neck. The blood drained out of his face, leaving it tired and strained. Then Dolly felt Destrier's hand reach tentatively for her own. She slipped her fingers into his and felt an infinitely gentle tremor of response – though still he wouldn't, or couldn't, look at her.

At Liverpool Street they dismissed both car and driver. Reaching the station's crowded concourse, Destrier was momentarily dismayed by its unaccustomed surge of humanity. Self-consciously, he put up a hand to hide his face – it was only with an effort that he told himself to stay calm and look the world coolly in the eye.

With an angel like Dolly on his arm, what reason had he to feel either apologetic or self-conscious.

He bought tickets to Tolleswich, and they found that they had only a few minutes in which to catch the train. They were forced to hurry down the platform (Damn his stick! Damn the porter with his valise!) and Destrier found himself panting and trembling at the exertion. But – to his infinite joy, and miracle of miracles in wartime – he and Dolly were lucky enough to find a first-class compartment to themselves.

A whistle blew. With a jerk and a grinding of wheels, the train got under way. The bleak wastes of the East End were left behind, and then they were beyond the suburbs and out into rural Essex. For the second time their hands reached for each other's. Neither spoke, and both felt afraid to break the silence, in which one trite or stupid remark might ruin everything. With his free hand Destrier lit a cigarette, its blue smoke dancing and uncoiling in the sunlight. Through the half-open window came pleasant country scents – woodsmoke, hay, a general green sappiness – all the more pleasant after the hospital odours both had become used to.

Though called an express, the train seemed in no particular hurry. It ambled and jogged its way sedately through the early evening sunlight, fleecing the fields with sudden drifts of steam touched with rose and gold by the lowering sun. To both Destrier and Dolly Lyttleton the war seemed suddenly very remote, a thing less of reality than rumour.

At last a landscape of black elms, blind hedges and secretive lanes opened out into marsh. The breeze coming in through the window now carried a tang of salt on its breath. The train rumbled over one muddy creek and then another, its wheels setting up a hollow drumming on the girdered bridges. And then they were slowing down, slowing, and at rest in Tolleswich. Doors slammed; a crowd of naval-ratings burdened by hammocks and kit-bags formed a scrum round the ticket-barrier – a cheerful, laughing scrum that smelled of soap, strong tobacco and beer. A petty-officer caught sight of Destrier, called the ruck of matelots to attention and saluted smartly.

'Need any help, Sir?'

Returning the salute, Destrier found himself wondering whether the burly man with the crossed killicks and good conduct badges had ever known poor Waterlow, the same sailor his childhood evidence had sent to the gallows. He was surprised how equably he could suddenly take this notion; up till now the sight of a naval uniform had always unnerved him. Now, it seemed, that grubby ghost of his past had at long last been laid to rest, had become something trivial and unimportant; an event in someone else's life.

Destrier thanked the petty-officer for his offer of help. A cheerful-looking sailor picked up his own and Dolly's cases and carried them to a waiting cab. Offered a shilling for beer, the man at first refused but then accepted with a grin and a wink on condition that 'the lady wouldn't take it amiss if it was used to drink her health'. Dolly blushed. As their cab moved off, some of the sailors raised a cheer. Destrier was unsure whether to feel embarrassed or elated. Dolly, it seemed, had no such doubts. Blush she might but her eyes danced with pleasure. The cheer had been meant as a kindly compliment to them both and she knew it.

They stopped off in the town in order to shop and, in spite of the shortages, stocked up with food as best they could. Dolly made her purchases with the same competence that seemed part of all her actions, and Destrier, who till then had always regarded shopping as a tedious necessity, found himself enjoying a pleasurable and entirely novel sense of domesticity. In a Dickensian wine-merchant's he managed to buy half-a-dozen of a claret he had heard spoken well of in the Mess. This, too, was a new experience for him. Never before in his life had he bought wine. As a ranker he'd drunk beer; as an officer, whisky.

When they had finished their shopping, their cab took them on through the town, past a few short streets of sleepy suburb into the country beyond. At a word from Dolly, the cabby – a bewhiskered, elderly man in a hard-topped bowler – called his horse to a halt, and they stopped outside the white gates of a cottage.

They got their belongings down from the cab and paid the man off. It took them several journeys from the gate to the front door before everything was safely inside and Destrier was free to examine his surroundings. He took to the cottage at once. Someone in the previous century – a romantic, perhaps, with a taste for gothic – had conceived the desire for a place in the country and this had been the result: a peculiar, red-bricked doll's-house with pointed windows and wide eaves overhanging the garden, on beams whose trusses were decorated with flamboyantly-carved bosses.

The interior of the cottage, too, was a similar essay in the imaginatively eccentric. The furniture was built in solid, dark, uncompromising lumps and the walls and floors displayed large areas of black, unpolished timber. Instinctively, Destrier knew that the house would be at its best after dark, lit by candles or oil-lamp. Inured to orphanage, barrack-room and the Spartan sameness of wartime messes, he found the unselfconscious individuality of the house strangely unreal and exciting – like a stage-set, waiting for some as yet unwritten play to begin.

Each of them set about separate tasks without any need for discussion. Dolly busied herself with laying out a cold supper and with airing the cottage after its long emptiness; to Destrier fell the business of lighting fires – for, as Dolly said, the cottage felt damp, and besides, June or not, the evening was surprisingly cool. Destrier slipped off his Sam Browne and tunic and went in search of kindling. He eventually found some in a small shed at the end of the garden. Someone – Dolly's father, perhaps – had been careful to leave a neat stack of logs and chopped wood. The kitchen-range – a monstrosity of black-leaded iron and gleaming brass – lit easily enough, but the fire in the L-shaped dining-cum-living room proved less amenable. Only at Destrier's third attempt did the flames begin to lick upwards into the black cavern of the chimney. Smoke billowed into the room; choking and coughing, Destrier retreated to the sanctuary of the open window.

Outside, the golden evening was fading into the cobalt and indigo of early night, though the long, midsummer afterglow would take its time yet before fading. Reluctantly, Destrier dragged himself from the window to attend to the task of lighting the lamps. He found them already filled and only needing the smallest adjustment before their wicks burst into aureoles of yellow light. Destrier gave the glass chimneys a quick polish before replacing them and setting the lamps strategically in kitchen and dining-room.

As with the shopping earlier, Destrier found this commonplace domesticity curiously stimulating. He had, of course, performed similar jobs as part of the daily routine in the orphanage, and as a private soldier. But then they had been activities to be got through as quickly as possible, without thought, and without enjoyment. Now, and for the first time in his life, he found such everyday simplicities oddly satisfying. Surely, he felt, these were the sort of things a man did about his own home? But then, Destrier was not certain. . . .

How could he be when he came to examine the matter? 'Home' was not really a word whose meaning he could properly understand at all except in an academic sense. 'Home' till now had always meant for him an impersonal dormitory or barrack-room. Perhaps, he suddenly realized, this house, and the short hour he'd already spent in it, were the nearest he'd come in his twenty-nine years to be sharing what most men took for granted.

The thought saddened him.

Supper was a peaceful, long-drawn meal. Both man and girl were hungry and ate with cheerful appetite. Wine and the intimacy of lamp-light loosened tongues that had somehow grown shy and stilted in the train. Quite naturally, Destrier found himself telling Dolly about his past; all of it, leaving nothing out – his mother's murder, Waterlow's execution, his years in the orphanage and army. It surprised him to be able to speak so easily – and with a certain wry humour – of things which, till this moment, had filled him with shame and self-contempt.

Dolly listened to Destrier's story as matter-of-factly as he told it. Unpleasant as some of it was, she showed neither squeamishness nor distaste. Nor, being a sensible girl, did she gush with a now pointless sympathy, realizing that only by telling her all this was Destrier able at last to come to terms with himself, and to accept that self just as she accepted it.

When he had finished, she accepted another glass of claret, and – to Destrier's slightly old-fashioned surprise – lit one of his cigarettes. As she smoked, she tried to tell him something of herself in return. She, too, had few relations. Her mother had died just before the war, and her only brother had been killed at Loos. Her father – a Paymaster-Commander – waited along with the rest of Beatty's fleet for the German Navy to come out of its bolt-hole.

They cleared the supper things into the kitchen, washed up, then returned to the big room. Destrier made himself comfortable in one of the massive winged chairs by the fire. To his delight, Dolly curled herself on the rug at his feet, her head against his legs, cradling the wine-glass in her hands and gazing into the hearth. Summer evening or not, the warmth and glow of the crackling logs was pleasantly comforting. The light from the leaping, drifting flames called up answering echoes in Dolly's hair and set a nimbus of amber light about her head. Almost without him realizing it, Destrier found himself stroking the smooth, cool tresses. His clumsy, crippled finger-ends plucked at the pins holding Dolly's hair in a chaste coil on the top of her head and, set free, the golden mane cascaded down and over her shoulders, like a stream of tawny flame. These hands had bathed in such flame before, he remembered. Yet, how different this second sensation of burning! It was restoration and renewal....

Dolly pressed herself back against Destrier's legs and turned her face up to his. In the changing glow of the fire, her eyes seemed huge, their irises fathomless.

'I love you.'

She spoke clearly, deliberately – yet Destrier failed to understand her. Till now, his experiences with women had been embarrassing and inconclusive, spectred always by his experience of sex as something bought and sold in dingy upstairs rooms – grubby transactions between such a creature as his mother had been and an endless procession of Able-Seamen Waterlows....

Dolly repeated her words. She saw their meaning at last get through to Destrier. He looked startled, she thought: frightened even. A third time she repeated the words, spacing them out, dropping them like stones into the silence of the room. Destrier sat quite still. In actuality, he was afraid to move, petrified – despite the girl's triple declaration – that he had misheard her. Why should this angel, this madonna, say such things to him? For a moment or two he thought she was teasing, playing some cruel practical joke on him to repay all his wretched ill-temper in hospital. But no, Dolly could never be capable of any such meanness of spirit, he knew that.

With the perception of love, the girl read each of these thoughts fleeting through Destrier's mind. They showed her an extra dimension to the man. Self-contained he might be – as self-contained and unbiddable as a cat – but his assurance was no more than skin deep. Where love and human affection were concerned, Laurie Destrier was as ignorant and ill-at-ease as a child. Now Dolly knew beyond all argument that whatever must happen – if, indeed, anything were to happen at all – was up to her, and her alone. Despite her declaration – or, maybe, even *because* of it – Destrier would do nothing. Not because he did not love, or was too selfish to give himself freely – but because he honestly believed that neither his love nor the gift of himself were worth any woman's possessing. To Dolly, such humility, in so proud a man, seemed strangely moving.

Yet Destrier, she knew, was like herself: someone who could love – and would love – once only. His affection, once given, would never be retracted or withdrawn. It would become part of himself, part of his deepest nature. Given time and peace, he would become – in degree, at least – herself, just as she would become him. They were both the sort of people to whom this final unselfishness of love was both joy and necessity.

Dolly raised herself onto her knees, then dragged herself upright, flattening her breasts against Destrier's body. She heard his sharply indrawn breath and almost laughed aloud as he at first pushed towards her, then pulled guiltily away.

'I'm going to bed now. . . .'

Destrier's eyes jerked towards her. Had she shocked him with her implicit suggestion? She didn't care. Perhaps it was quite true what her dead brother had once said, that all women were harlots under the skin. How scandalized she had been at the time. Yet now listen to her . . . I'm going to bed, indeed! The way she had said it had been more than an invitation. It had been a challenge. . . .

She stood and, carrying the smallest of the lamps in front of her, went up the stairs which led directly out of the room. A glance over her shoulder showed Destrier, apparently intent on the fire, in reality taking in her every movement.

As Dolly vanished from sight, Destrier struggled to his feet. Was he ill again, the way his flesh trembled and refused to obey him? His mind was a whirlpool welter of sense and half-

75

sense, utterly confused. Why did Dolly have to go off like that, leaving him? And what did she mean by saying she was going to bed? He hadn't the faintest notion of where he was expected to sleep. . . .

He supposed he'd better find out, and began to climb the stairs. The landing was a pool of black shadow, creased only by a single wedge of light coming from a barely open door. Without thinking, or without even remembering to knock, Destrier pushed this open and went into the room.

Dolly stood on the far side of the room, encompassed by the oil-lamp's hazy corona. But *was* this Dolly?

For the woman Destrier saw was quite different. Gone was the nurse. Gone, too, the angel or madonna he sometimes thought her. Here was the pagan goddess of man's first worshipping: a goddess who, unashamed, stood before him naked and deep-breasted, her arms outstretched as if in welcome. . . .

By a miracle — rough and clumsy and urgent though he was that first time — the thing came right. Beneath him on the big four-poster he heard Dolly's voice cry out in the immensity of void opening to accept him. His hands pressing into the glory of her breasts, Destrier at last flew as he had always instinctively known it was possible for a man to fly — beyond moon and planets, beyond time and place into the great orange eye of the sun. . . .

THREE

Dismissed by Destrier, Hopkins went down the worn, carpet-less stairs to the farm-parlour serving the officers of 'D' Flight both as Mess and makeshift office. Old calenders, steel engravings and agricultural almanacs covered the bulging, flaking walls. Above a lumpy, comfortless settle a moth-eaten stag's head leered cross-eyedly down.

Lit by a brace of pressure lamps, the room looked snug enough but, to Hopkins, felt damp and chilly. A small fire smouldered dully in a rusting grate and, from time to time, puffed acrid gusts of smoke into the room. Three officers were present – Peters, young Browne and a professorial-looking Artillery Lieutenant named Morton-Dunne, who was seated beside the room's one concession to modernity – a brace of telephones. Morton-Dunne, his neck swathed in scarves, was reading Plato in the original Greek – a habit that Hopkins felt vaguely unbecoming in an officer. Peters, as usual, was in-dulging in an angry, bitter monologue. He ignored Hopkins's entry, and it was some moments before the Flight-Sergeant could repeat Destrier's instructions concerning the Flight's immediate availability for operations.

In their different ways, each of the three officers showed surprise – young Browne with a joyful whoop, Morton-Dunne with the merest upward twitch of an eyebrow, and Peters with a further outburst of invective.

'So the bloody fool thinks we're ready, does he? I'll see about *that*!' Peters began to climb the stairs.

Morton-Dunne looked up from his book. 'Don't be an ass, Tom.'

Peters checked on the stairs, then climbed down again, his face scarlet with anger. He glared at Morton-Dunne as the gunner picked up one of his telephones and asked for a num-ber in London.

Foiled in his effort to rouse Morton-Dunne, Peters turned on Hopkins.

'I suppose we've *you* to thank for this, Flight-Sergeant!'

Hopkins stood his ground.

'Hardly, sir. The Flight-Commander. . . .'

This was Peters's cue.

'The Flight-Commander!' he sneered contemptuously. 'That damned, jumped-up glory boy!'

Morton-Dunne's head jerked up from his book a second time and he coughed warningly. But Peters was beyond stopping. Hopkins's mouth tightened in disgust. Just what sort of an officer did this blighter imagine himself to be, carrying on like this about his superior officer in front of an NCO? In ten years of soldiering, Hopkins had never heard anything like it. Oh, well, he consoled himself, Peters was always binding about something. It was probably his only defence against what must be an increasing and inescapable sense of inadequacy. The worse this got, the more Peters compensated for it by performing like this. As Hopkins was aware, most of the lieutenant's fellow officers had got his number by now. They contrived to treat him with a good-humoured, if sometimes weary, resignation. One or two, driven beyond patience, simply ignored the man altogether.

As the torrent of recrimination continued, Hopkins's features set themselves in a line that experience had taught him was just safely this side of dumb insolence. With the corners of his mouth tucked in, he stared over Peters's shoulders to where Browne – a mischievous-eyed monkey of a man – was winking and pulling faces behind his senior's back.

And there was *another* one who ought to know better, Hopkins thought, while finding it difficult not to laugh. He liked young Browne; the subaltern's high spirits and good humour were infections. The lad was a good pilot, too.

Peters on the other hand was quite dreadful and impossibly clumsy. How he had managed to survive the war so far was a topic of perpetual interest to officers and ground-crews alike. In their ribald opinion, Peters would be more at home behind the controls of a tram-car than those of an aeroplane.

Nor was his prowess as a gunner noticeably any better. Yet, despite these apparently fatal handicaps, Peters had somehow contrived to survive a spell in France. Presumably it had been in a quiet sector. And yet, to hear him talk, Hopkins thought with amusement, the Red Baron must surely count himself lucky to be in one piece. How galling it must be for Peters to find himself under the command of a natural like Destrier. Particularly so when, for no very good reason, Peters had confidently put it about that he expected 'D' Flight to be his.

Hopkins strongly suspected that Peters lived in something of a fantasy world these days, a world in which everyone and everything conspired to rob him of what he considered his proper due. It was understandable in a way, Hopkins supposed; anything must be better than living with Peters's unenviable burden of inferiority, failure and fear. Despite his bluster, the man must surely have some awareness of his patent absurdity and the miracle of his continuing survival. Better men and pilots had only lasted days, or even hours, in France before death had found them. Even Peters must be able to work out that he couldn't go on cheating the odds for ever.

But *nothing*, it seemed, would stop the fool's empty ranting, or his sense of affront that Destrier had taken the Flight's solitary Bristol as his own.

All three of the room's remaining occupants could have told Peters that this was the kindest thing that Destrier could have done for him. Each had watched with awe Peters's split-arse take-offs and sketchy landings in the Bristol, waiting for what so often seemed the inevitable crash. Stable and comparatively forgiving towards the ham-handed, the BE12 was an infinitely safer mount for Peters than the spirited Bristol – especially by night. Yet Peters refused to see things in this way. Still he railed on, his voice a monotonous whine of self-justification and complaint, moving from one imagined slight to the next with bewildering and sometimes incoherent haste.

Behind his back, Browne was by now openly mocking, and conducting an invisible band. Morton-Dunne ignored him completely, making it obvious he preferred the *Republic* of Plato to that of Peters.

'And *now* it's bloody snowing again, if you please!' Peters concluded, as if announcing the last trump. He glared at Hopkins accusingly as if suspicious that by some neglect of duty, the weather was somehow the Flight-Sergeant's fault.

Hopkins, long inured to the ways of officers – particularly those like Peters – took this calmly. The one thing he certainly wasn't going to do was allow himself to be goaded into losing his temper by this little squit. The tapes on his arm had taken too much earning for *that*. All the same –

Hopkins felt a sense of reprieve as young Browne saved the situation, moving round Peters to shake an admonishing finger and make a joke of things.

'*Snowing*, Flight? Now that's really very naughty of you. Most remiss. And there was me believing what my nurse told me – that a Flight-Sergeant could arrange *anything*!'

Hopkins grinned down at him.

'I'm afraid your nurse didn't tell it you quite right, sir. After December the tenth, it's Santa Claus as arranges the weather, not me. A matter of seniority. . . .'

Browne's answer came in a comic wail as he gestured towards the blacked-out window.

'But they're BEs out there, Flight – not bally sledges with pretty bells on. . . . I'm not going to get myself up in a red suit and false beard for anyone – even Fritzy. Besides, we haven't got any reindeer. . . .'

Peters turned away. It was plain he found such simple humour childish and annoying. Poor bastard! Hopkins found himself thinking with an unexpected start of compassion. It couldn't be much fun flying with Peters's dark familiars for company.

But now Browne was eagerly talking again, gesticulating extravagantly and fantasticating on the subject of reindeer.

'I suppose we might *just* work the oracle with a flock of marsh sheep. . . . What do you reckon, Prof?' He nudged the book out of Morton-Dunne's hands and onto the floor.

Unperturbed or offended, the quiet man picked up his book

while pretending to give the matter his serious consideration.

'It might just work,' he conceded judiciously, 'providing we rope 'em all together with little bits of string and tie bunches of twigs on their heads to look like horns. . . .'

Browne was wide-eyed with astonishment at the other's cleverness.

'Genius!' he breathed. 'Sheer, unadulterated bloomin' genius. . . . Yes! That's exactly what he must do. . . . *Immediately*!'

He swung round on Hopkins, making his voice a passable imitation of Peters's nagging word of command.

'See to it this instant, Flight-Sergeant! See to it! See to it!'

'Right away, sir!' Hopkins said, grinning and saluting. But, as he turned to leave the dreary little room, he heard Peters take up the bellyaching thread of his commination again.

The *absurdity* of being made to stand-to on a night like this. . . . An almost *moonless* night. . . . *Anyone* who knew *anything* at all about night operations – which that fool upstairs obviously *didn't* – must also know that the Huns *never* came in absolute darkness. *That they hadn't the guts. . . .*

Ah, well, Hopkins thought, closing the door behind him, so far as Peters was concerned the blame for the general bloodiness of things must lie *somewhere. . . .* In the weather, in the aircraft, in the ground-crews – anywhere, it seemed, but in his own unhappy and frightened self. . . .

Yet, once clear of the farmhouse, in the starless, snow-feathered night, Hopkins privately acknowledged that Peters might well have a point when he declared a raid unlikely. Brother Fritz *did* like a nice bright moon to show him home to bed – not through lack of courage, as the Flight-Jeremiah sneered, but as a matter of plain, common prudence. And to-night's moon – assuming it showed its face at all – would be the merest sliver of light.

As he trudged across the make-shift airfield, Hopkins found himself enjoying the sugary crunch of snow beneath his boots. This enjoyment gave him a sense of guilt. God help the lads in the trenches on a night like this. Nor were the frost and snow making life a picnic for his own chaps either. These, billetted under canvas, were even more drearily accommodated than their officers. Their tents were old and far from waterproof. Perhaps it was just as well everyone was being worked too hard to take in the misery of their surroundings.

Still, it was *his* job – and Destrier's – to do something about things. He'd have a quiet word or two tomorrow. Unless Laurie had altered, there would soon be a few smart changes around the place. And high bloody time, too, Hopkins thought. In the past ten days, Peters had been far too full of his own woes to spare any thought for other people's. Not, Hopkins thought with satisfaction, that any of his blokes had really griped as yet. Odds and sods they might be, but so far they had got stuck into things with a heartening, good-humoured will. What a blessing that had proved in the last ten days. The Flight was in a mess now, but without this cheerful spirit, things would have been a damned sight worse.

Suddenly, Hopkins began to feel cautiously optimistic.

The tall, angular figure of an NCO – Sergeant Mackail – loomed out of the darkness and fell into step beside him.

'Anything up, Flight?'

'The OC wants a change of fireworks in the Bristol.'

'Does he now.' The sergeant's voice showed neither surprise nor annoyance.

'He does. And another thing. . . . The aircraft – we'd better give their engines a swing while we're at it. Get 'em warm – and keep 'em that way.'

Mackail gave a grunt of satisfaction.

'Ah! Sounds to me as though someone's blown the whistle for kick-off.'

'That's right.'

'Good. Not before time, either, if you ask me. Things always get better once the game's actually started. Better than hanging about. . . .'

'I've just been thinking along much the same lines. Have you got enough blokes, Mac?'

'Enough for now. A dozen, mebbe. Potter, Wilkins, Davies –' Mackail ticked the names off. 'I can always rout out a few more.'

'Save 'em for later. Just give me the first three.'

'Ye'll re-arm the guns yourself, Flight?'

'Not half. . . .' Hopkins laughed. 'We've got the first eleven playing tonight.'

'Ye'll know best, Flight.'

An edge came into Hopkins's voice.

'Yes, I do, Mac – at least, so far as that's concerned. It's no bloody fun sitting up aloft with a jammed Lewis, I can tell you. We all know Jerry's not so black as he's painted. But there's not much future trusting his good nature that far.'

'No-o . . . I reckon not.'

The two men reached the line of waiting aircraft. Since Destrier had inspected them, all three had been swathed in tarpaulins to keep out the snow. Hopkins and Mackail fussed about the Bristol like a pair of grooms round a favourite but wayward and uncertain mare.

Mackail sucked his teeth loudly.

'I'd say the old girl's as good as we can make her, Flight.'

Hopkins agreed, doubtfully.

'Aye, Mac. She'll have to do.'

The Scot grunted and gave the Bristol a slap on her flank for luck.

'Just between our two selves, I don't reckon we've done so badly, what with one thing and another – if you know what I mean.'

Hopkins knew exactly what Mackail meant. All things considered, they'd done marvels, really. But the pessimist within him caused him to shake his head at such a notion. The proof of the pudding was in the eating, and now wasn't a fit time for self-congratulation – not when there was still plenty of work to be done. Hopkins squared his shoulders against the night's searching cold, and his quick brain began shaping orders as he turned towards Mackail.

'Right!' he began. 'Potter, Wilkins and Davies you said, Mac –'

It was high time to be getting a move on.

Hopkins was not the only pessimist at work that evening. Far away in Gontrode, Sergeant-Major Mann, warned that, bar some drastic worsening of the weather, the projected raid was now definitely on, prowled restlessly about R.45's dimly lit cabin. Beneath him, he could hear the various thumps and gratings that told him the Staaken was in the process of being bombed-up. In a few moments, Mann knew that he would have to leave the warmth of the cabin to make sure this was being carried out precisely to instructions. It was not that he really expected otherwise, or that he mistrusted the sergeant in charge of the arming party. It was just that conscience insisted that he made sure for himself that every last detail was as it should be.

Like Hopkins, the German NCO felt an avuncular concern for his men – and with more reason, perhaps: his ground-crew, unlike Hopkins's, was no scratch collection hastily drummed-up from transit camps but a team handpicked for ability. Even so, Mann knew that carelessness or over-familiarity could mar the work of even the best aircraftsman. Besides, no one could possibly argue that the Staakens were easy aircraft to keep properly serviced. Mann puffed out his cheeks and blew a gusty sigh from between tight lips. Whenever he dared to think of the multiplicity of parts going into each of the huge bombers, his head whirled. It only needed a failure or flaw in just *one* of them, down to the smallest screw almost, to bring disaster.

Again Mann blew out his cheeks and sighed. Squadron wits maintained that the Sergeant-Major reminded them of nothing so much as a worried old ewe. It was an unkind image – though apt. There was little in Mann's outward appearance to suggest the 'regimental'. True, he wore the almost obligatory moustache, properly waxed and upturned in homage to the Kaiser – but the effect was unconvincing. The fierce whiskers did not suit him; they looked patently false – like pantomime moustachios haphazardly stuck on the face of a favourite uncle. And indeed, among themselves – though not, of course, to his face – that is precisely what R.45's crew called their Sergeant-Major: 'Nunky'. Mann might seem a figure of fun, but amidst the chaos of war he was a comfortable rock to lean on when things went wrong.

Mann gave the cabin a final, all-embracing glance, and then, with surprising agility for so ponderous a man, slipped down through the access hatch onto the icy tarmac beneath. Here, as he'd known perfectly well it would be, the work was proceeding smoothly. The bombing-detail went about its duties with quiet competence. The Sergeant-Major was well pleased with what he saw and gave the detail a nod of approval. It gratified him even more when he noted that every single man was too absorbed by the job in hand even to have noticed the gesture.

His inspection finished, Mann gave R.45's elephantine flank an affectionate good-luck pat, much as Mackail had done with the Bristol. So far as he could tell, everything was just as it should be. And yet.... And yet, deep down inside himself, this good, stolid, not over-imaginative soldier experienced a sudden and disturbing twitch of misgiving. In a way that was impossible for him to explain, the sensation was subtly different from the anxieties he'd felt before any of the Giant's previous raids. Upset by this vague yet insidious disquiet, the Sergeant-Major cursed himself for a silly old woman, then stamped off in search of beer. Thirst played havoc with a fellow's sense of perspective....

Aided by his soldier-servant, Claus von Trier struggled into his flying leathers. For some reason he could not explain, he found himself thinking about his father. All in all, von Trier now realized, the two of them had been a pretty sore trial to each other, light years apart in attitude and sympathy.

As a family, the von Triers, whatever else their possessions, had rarely been noted for their intellectual capacity and for their part always mistrusted those so burdened. Intellect was all very well in the middle-classes and in Jews, but then – God be thanked! – no von Trier could possibly be expected to mingle with these. Besides, it had long been recognized in the family that brains were an almost insurmountable handicap to a successful military career. Nor were they any more seemly in a landed gentleman.

The old Count, Claus's father, had therefore been extremely put out to discover that his eldest son, by some inexplicable and underhanded trick of heredity, showed early signs of a prodigious and critical intelligence – something that hadn't happened in the family since the middle of the eighteenth century. Then, an eccentric ancestor, instead of keeping a string of horses or mistresses like any sensible fellow, had kept open-house to a motley succession of indigent poets and musicians, including one of the lesser Bachs, who had wasted his patron's time and money by scribbling a whole series of tinkling nothings which he had had the damned impertinence to call 'The Trier Sonatas'.

It shook the old Count even more when he learnt that his heir – now aged about twelve – could play most of these boring and trivial jangles. Count Heinrich had nothing against music as such – not so long as it came in the form of a rousing military march – the noisier and brassier the better. But to discover his son playing old Wolfgang Emmanuel Bach's wishy-washy nonsenses with evident and enraptured enjoyment was too much! The old man was shaken to his foundations. . . . *Du lieber Gott!* If the child were allowed to get away with that sort of thing, then he'd most likely end up as a lisping, spineless catamite. . . .

Count Heinrich, therefore, had seen it as neither more nor less than his plain fatherly duty to take a riding-switch to young Claus's behind: his corrupting tutor was dismissed without a reference, and a week later the boy himself was packed off to a military academy where discipline and a spartan regimen could be relied upon to lick him into line in the shortest possible time.

The school had certainly tried its best. To all outward appearances it gave back to Count Heinrich a son he could be proud of in his own simple fashion. But what the school had not been able to crush in young Claus were the youth's critical faculties. Indeed, by providing so many unintentional and rewarding targets for satire within its own fortress-like walls,

86

the school had unwittingly sharpened these.

As was inevitable after such a schooling, Claus went on to further military studies rather than to university. Rather to his surprise, he found that the mainstream of family tradition ran in his blood more strongly than he had ever guessed or supposed: slightly to his shame, he discovered an enjoyment in soldiering. Not all of it, of course. Mess-life, he found, on being commissioned into the cavalry, could be quite shatteringly stuffy and pompous, and the politer arts of social intercourse expected of a young officer left him yawning and bored.

But there *were* compensations, he discovered. Freed from the tyranny of his father's basilisk eye, young Claus was at last able to indulge his undernourished intellect. There had been women, too, of course – women far removed in class and kind from the sort of society brood-mare whom an officer was eventually expected to marry.

And, finally, there had been flying.

Perhaps it had been the distant rumour of his son's increasing interest in this hare-brained and totally heretical novelty that had at last proved too much for Count Heinrich's heart. Early in 1910, the old man died, leaving Claus a title, a large income, estates – and an overwhelming and delicious sense of liberty. The German government, less hide-bound, perhaps, than its British counterpart – or old Heinrich von Trier, for that matter – laid out a comparatively generous amount of money on the growing science of aviation. With his social connections, Claus had not found it difficult to enrol himself into the growing cadre of those to whom flying was both faith and religion. Besides its other attractions, it offered a welcome relief from the inanities of routine peacetime soldiering, and – von Trier that he was, scion of a long line of hard-riding country gentlemen – any activity which held out the prospect of a broken neck possessed an attraction that was not to be despised.

Indeed, von Trier very nearly had broken his neck – not once, but several times. To his chagrin, he found himself to be, at best, an indifferent pilot. Even with the sense of balance

87

and good hands inherited from his forebears, something vital had been left out of his make-up. Perhaps it had only been an eighteen-month return to regimental duties just prior to the war that had saved Claus from himself. Even so, he had found his return ineffably boring, and, with the outbreak of hostilities and the war hardening into entrenched stalemate, he had contrived to get himself returned to flying.

Here, at last, he had begun to gain a true understanding of his inadequacies as a pilot. It was not so much that something had been left out, but that something too much had been put in. He was really *two* von Triers: the outward one ironic and apparently cocksure; the inner, secret one diffident and uncertain. Once in the air, these two selves fought for supremacy. Between them, they managed to make his flying a lethal combination of foolhardy bravado and almost pathological care. Briefly, von Trier had flown with Boelke and Immelmann. He'd had his successes, certainly – a brace of innocent BE2s and a Morane – but in gaining these victories he'd crashed and smashed at least five of Anthony Fokker's famous if not over-handy monoplanes. To everyone's relief – his own secretly included – he was transferred at last to a squadron of two-seater Rolands, where, from the vantage of the rear cockpit, he could command without actually flying.

In retrospect, he had come to acknowledge this move – though a bitter one at the time – as having been beneficial to everyone, except the enemies who'd come under his guns. For von Trier had proved himself a virtuoso with the Parabellum mounted on the Roland. Here, too, he reflected, heredity had played its part: long generations of von Triers had shot everything that crawled, ran or flew in their gloomy Silesian woods. . . .

From Rolands, and then other two-seaters, von Trier had graduated to the command of R.45.

He settled himself into his leathers much as Schmidt had done, with a bear-like hop and shuffle. A fastidious man, he resented his plebeian, molly-grub appearance. How ironic that he, the one von Trier who in twenty generations had ever seriously doubted the military ethic, should himself be marked out to cut a figure that might have been designed to show that ethic at its most obscene.

Still, he told his reflection, what possible right had he to complain? The trouble with satirists, such as himself, was their disproportionate surprise and shock when the joke rebounded on themselves.

And, after all, for all his aristocratic pretensions, his half-digested philosophy and intellectual arrogance, what did he – Captain Count von Trier, with an assortment of pretty medals given him by a grateful country – really amount to these days? An airborne garage-hand who dropped kilos of high-explosive down onto women and children in the hopeful pretence that by some miracle he might just chance to hit something of strategic importance to Kaiser and Fatherland....

Even granted the limited perspective of the last forty months, von Trier's lucid intelligence could already sense the unmitigated disaster this war would one day seem, whoever won it. Who, in 1914, could have guessed that so many evils lay waiting their chance under the decent veil of European civilization? For perhaps the hundredth time in the last few months, von Trier wished he was a poet able to give his thoughts tangible and adequate shape.

For a while, as a youth, he had secretly considered that to be a true poet was the most important thing in this world. Like many another young man he had scribbled his verses and imagined himself another Schiller or Heine. Nowadays, he remembered how his naïve lines had, at first, always seemed so splendid and miraculous. But, then, he recalled sadly, how quickly had this brief glory faded. His verses had seemed to lose their lustre, like pebbles taken from the sea....

Gruber, Lieutenant Horst's servant, having folded his master's best uniform neatly onto its hanger and tidied it away into a wardrobe, saluted with excessive zeal and left the room in a thunderous crashing of boots. There was really no need for such a display of bull, but Gruber – slyly aware that Horst swelled visibly when on the receiving end of correct military compliments – deliberately went out of his way to be as regimental as possible. He had long since discovered that this paid. The implied respect and flattery put Horst into a malleable and complacent frame of mind which – as the orderly was well aware – could be exploited to his own advantage.

For Gruber despised Horst as a fool and systematically robbed the lieutenant of money, cigarettes or anything else that happened to take his fancy. Here Gruber had made the cardinal error of mistaking guilelessness for downright stupidity. But, fortunately for him, this was a mistake which, in the present circumstances, would never come home to roost.

Once Gruber had left the room, Horst moved across the floor to examine himself in the mirror, much as von Trier had done – but far less hypercritically. Unlike his commander, Horst saw in his reflection no sermon on the follies of war – nor was his mental equipment such as to trouble him with philosophical conundra impossible to answer.

No, what troubled Horst as he stared at his face in the glass was just why that impertinent lout Schmidt had seen fit to dub him 'The Sausage'! The name galled Horst. Not only did it offend his sense of military propriety, but it also sapped his none too certain self-confidence. Was that *really* how others saw him?

Horst gazed at his reflection with what he honestly imagined was an objective eye and saw no reason for Schmidt's misplaced humour. It seemed to Horst that what the mirror showed him was a decent, solid, flesh-and-bone sort of a man – not handsome, exactly – but, all in all, a fair advertisement for German values. Trying to improve his appearance, he twisted his heavy features into a ferocious and properly officer-like scowl of disdain and admired the result. Yes, that was better. He must cultivate such a look until it became second nature.

But Horst – who was basically a kind and harmless sort of fellow – found the strain of glaring too much for him. The moment he turned away from the mirror, his scowl slipped and his jowly face fell back into its normal, blood-hound folds.

Horst took a tin of heavy grease from a locker and began to lard the contents onto his face. Whenever possible he liked to fly with R.45's windshield open, at least for take-off and landing. At the aircraft's eighty knots, the slipstream hit a man's face like a wall of solid ice – especially in weather like this. When he had sufficiently greased his face, Horst picked up goggles, gauntlets and flying-helmet and glanced at his watch. Was it really that late? It was time he reported to von Trier....

But before he left the room, Horst set a little trap. He carefully counted the pile of small change left on his locker and the number of cigarettes in the case that looked like silver but wasn't. For some time Horst had been aware that Gruber was quite unscrupulously treating his officer's money and possessions as his own. And tonight Horst had made up his mind that this would stop. Over the last fortnight he had made a note of Gruber's exactions. Tomorrow he would charge the wretched fellow with being a thief and would lay the matter in front of the CO.

Being a kindly man, the thought of Gruber's pending disgrace gave Horst neither pleasure nor triumph. His batman had played his little game – and now he must pay for it.

Mendelssohn sipped a cup of rather horrid ersatz coffee, smoked a cigarette he didn't particularly want and listened while Schmidt laid down the law on the subject of women. On this topic, Schmidt considered himself an expert. To Mendelssohn, who was as shy and diffident with women as his friend was not, Schmidt's amorous adventures seemed as wide-ranging and cheerfully scandalous as his taste in girls was catholic. For, judging by what he said – with much laughter, innuendo and rib-nudging – blonde or brunette, tall or short, buxom or slim, they were all grist to his mill; charming, changeable, tantalizing creatures, without whose fascinating entanglements life would be intolerably grey and boring....

Not for the first time it occurred to Mendelssohn that he,

too, might well have devoted more time than he had to unravelling the deliciously intriguing enigma that was Woman.

The trouble with Art, he told himself sadly, was that it left too little time for life. . . .

Or was it just that the artist's life was simply a *different* kind of life? Perhaps. And yet, to Mendelssohn, more used to thinking in the refinements of musical notation than mere words, both questions seemed extravagant and rhetorical and suspiciously like an excuse for something. The plain fact that girls scared him? 'Of course, Beethoven liked women, but never married,' he said, half to himself.

'Very wise of him, I'd say,' Schmidt was opining. 'Better a complacent mistress than a wife any time. . . . Besides,' he went on, 'let's be fair. Just look at the thing from a woman's point of view. There must be artists, I suppose. . . . But, in God's name, what sensible woman would ever go and marry one? Just suppose you were a good little housewife; fancy having a fellow like Beethoven around the place, getting under your feet all day long – Ugh! It'd be enough to drive anyone crazy. Thumpitty-thumpitty-thumpitty-thump on that dreadful piano of his all day and every day, hour after hour. No-o, if I was a woman, I'd settle for the butcher, the baker, the candlestick-maker – someone who went out to work all day long and came back home in the evening with randy intentions.'

'But Beethoven was a great man, Otto,' protested Mendelssohn.

'I'm not saying he wasn't. But, great man or not, he had some pretty distressing habits, didn't he? I remember reading something about him once. . . . A great lady came to see him – a princess or a grand-duchess, something like that – and found him working on, what would it be – the *Kreutzer Sonata*, perhaps? Splendid! But what do you think was under the piano?'

Mendelssohn shook his head.

'You don't know? Well, I'll tell you. A damned great china utensil full of pee. . . . *Brim-full!*

'You could hardly have blamed *madame* if she simply

clapped her fingers to her aristocratic nose and simply bolted.'

'But did she?'

'Bolt? No; not the way my book had it,' Schmidt admitted. 'She stayed – and that old bear, Ludwig von B., put himself out to be charming – and the lady was duly charmed.... But can't you just imagine the unholy stink of that room? Pheeeeeeeeew!'

Mendelssohn stayed silent for a moment or two, digesting these facts – if facts they were; it didn't really matter. It was typical of the extrovert Schmidt to be able to knock the windy stuffing out of an intellectual dilemma with a few well-chosen and coarsely-apt phrases.

Yet, *had* he though...? The twin images – the *Kreutzer Sonata* and the chamber-pot full of urine – caught Mendelssohn's imagination. The one, one of the highest expressions of Man's musical thought; the other, the uncouth waste of a physiological function: both, in the end, the production – the *work*, if one chose to say it – of the same man.

Perhaps that, in a nutshell, was the answer to both questions. The artist was a creature of bodily as well as spiritual needs – the vocation was not a monastic one. Mendelssohn made up his mind. On his next leave he would try to forget his shyness and diffidence in an attempt to pick up a little of Otto's earthy wisdom.

Perhaps Schmidt guessed his friend's thoughts. He grinned like a monkey and slapped Mendelssohn on the shoulder.

'That's more like it, Maestro! Nothing ventured, nothing gained!'

Sitting some distance apart from Schmidt and Mendelssohn was the solitary figure of Wendel. Now, with only a short time before he must drag his protesting body upright and out across the concrete apron to the waiting R.45, was his worst time of all. This was when the fear inside him became a trapped and tormented animal frantically clawing and struggling to escape from the cage of his body. But to look at Wendel, no one would ever have sensed this; his colour and breathing appeared normal and there was no tell-tale fidgeting of hands or fingers.

Stealing the odd glance at Wendel from time to time, both Schmidt and Mendelssohn found themselves envying the fuel-mechanic's stolid indifference. What, they both thought, must it be like to be one of the Wendels of this world, without apprehension or imagination, a complete pudding?

Schmidt ironically concluded that to feel like Wendel must be like feeling nothing at all – no sense, therefore no feeling, *Q.E.D.* . . . Mendelssohn took a more kindly but no less erroneous view of their comrade. The big man's look of dumb composure set Mendelssohn's quick and questioning brain in hot pursuit of one of its usual hares. Was it better to be bright or stupid? To feel nothing at all – or everything too much? Either way, Mendelssohn concluded, there was something rather splendid about Wendel's monumental calm: the big man looked elemental, a force of nature. . . . Just how the devil did he manage it?

Lying full-length on his bunk, Rossi was surprised to find himself utterly at peace with the world. Never before had he experienced such a total and profound quietude of spirit. It was as if, in some mysterious way, he had moved outside his body altogether and was now poised above himself, looking down at the figure on his bunk with resigned pity. Not a *self-pity*, as he'd always understood it, but a quite impersonal compassion, an extraordinary, all-knowing sadness. . . .

It was some moments before the gunner understood the reason for this sadness. When at last he did so, it was without terror or fear, but only a serene indifference.

He, Giovanni Rossi, was going to die.

His two selves, the one disembodied, the other, flesh, fused together again and, coming to himself, the gunner rolled over and swung his legs to the floor. He took a writing-pad from the locker by his bed, and – after rummaging in his pockets – found a stub of pencil. Rossi sucked at this for a moment or two, then began to write. His letter was a simple one, misspelt and sketchily punctuated, a letter full of the sort of things most people find impossible to say until it is too late; a letter full of love and gratitude, begging his parents and sisters not to grieve for him; a final confession of his shortcomings as son and brother. . . .

When he had finished writing, Rossi read the whole thing through quickly and folded it into an envelope. He took a rosary from his pocket and pondered briefly whether or not to put this in with his letter. But no, on deeper consideration he knew the rosary must stay with him, come what may. He slipped it back into his pocket, stuck down the flap of the envelope and then printed his father's name and address on it as clearly as he could. When this was done, he bent down and placed the letter in his locker on top of his neatly folded kit, so that whoever might be responsible for clearing up his belongings would understand the letter's significance. On second thoughts, Rossi reached down into his locker and pulled out a paper package. This contained some exceedingly improper photographs, and the gunner tossed the bundle into a convenient waste-bin. It seemed as good an act of contrition as any.

This done, Rossi lay down on his bunk again and lit a cigarette. He decided that if he was going to get killed there was little further point in worrying and not the slightest reason in letting himself be uncomfortable while he waited. . . .

Hopkins and Mackail sat facing each other across a broad table set in the warmest corner of a room in one of the farm's outbuildings. On arrival at Brick-Kiln Farm the pair of them had quickly marked this down to serve themselves as billet and office and had already in their brief occupation made it a haven of comfort and warmth compared to the bleak little parlour used by their officers.

A few days had served to give the room an orderly, lived-in look: a good fire blazed in the grate and a pair of hurricane lamps threw a cosy glow across the ammunition-box table, neatly covered with a blanket, serving in lieu of a cloth. A

95

kettle sang to itself on an improvised hob – then began to whistle. Mackail wrapped a cloth round the kettle's shiny handle and poured the boiling water into a brown tea-pot warming in the grate.

After letting this stand for a while, Mackail filled two enamel mugs that were waiting on the table. Hopkins looked at the tea and grimaced his approval: as a military man, Mac certainly possessed the one cardinal virtue – he could brew tea. The liquid in the mugs was a solid mahogany colour, good hearty stuff a man could hurt himself stirring. If there was one soldierly crime above all others in Hopkins's book, it was the mashing of wishy-washy tea. He grunted in commendation, 'That looks something like. . . .'

Mackail looked at his handiwork, critically.

'It's a bit on the weak side, mebbe?'

Hopkins laughed.

'Gawd, Mac! If this stuff'd come any thicker, it'd be in lumps!'

'Aye. . . . Perhaps it'll stand just a wee bit of dilution. . . .'

Sergeant Mackail reached under the table and produced a medicine bottle, glowing a rich amber in the firelight. He uncorked the bottle and sniffed disapprovingly at its contents.

'Mind, this is no the real stuff at all to my way of thinking. But we'll just have to make do. . . .'

Hopkins knew that by 'the real stuff', Mackail meant whisky. Speaking for himself, the one whiff of aroma that had reached him across the table was good enough for him. You could smell Service rum a mile off; and issue rum was as near to being the 'real' thing as any other liquid likely to pass down a man's throat in this world – or even in the next, come to that. . . . Hopkins winked at Mackail and sighed resignedly.

'Just as you say, Mac. We'll have to make do. . . .'

The Scot allowed himself the merest flicker of amusement. He was a man who took care to sum people up slowly. But already instinct told him that in Hopkins he had found someone with whom he could work. In a way, his offering of the rum had been a test – and Hopkins had passed; he had been discreet enough not to ask any damnfool questions concerning its origins. Though normally a frugal man, Mackail slopped the rum into the steaming mugs with a generous hand. It amused Hopkins to watch him, understanding perfectly the reasoning behind the other's canniness. In the Service it always paid a man to know exactly where he stood and to establish to the last thou' just how far a superior's tolerances might safely be tried. In his own time, too, Hopkins had made explorations similar to the one now being made on him. He relaxed his face into a grin of complicity and flipped a packet of Goldflake across the table.

'Gasper, Mac?'

Mackail paused for half a moment before picking out a cigarette and tamping the loose-ends of tobacco against his thumb-nail.

'I'm a pipe-man, myself, Flight – as you've mebbe noticed. But, just this once. . . .'

Hopkins twisted a piece of paper into a spill and poked it into the fire, and the two men lit their cigarettes with an air of ceremony. Both men knew this small act was, of itself, significant: it signalled an alliance which, if not friendship as yet, was certainly an understanding. They raised their mugs to their lips and drank deeply, the supercharged warmth seeming to explode underneath their ribs.

'Ker-r-rist!' Hopkins murmured reverently, wiping his mouth with the back of his hand.

The two of them grinned at each other like naughty school-boys and drank again. Mackail decided that this was as good a time as any to air the doubt that was on his mind. He gave Hopkins a straight look and said, without preamble, 'The new OC?'

As he'd expected, a blankness seemed to come over Hopkins's face; the eyes, so friendly a moment ago, were now hostile.

'The new OC. . . .' Mackail repeated.

To the sergeant's relief, Hopkins relaxed.

'You've seen him yourself, Mac. . . .'

'Aye, I have . . . poor laddie. . . .'

The two of them considered Destrier in silence, until Hopkins came to a decision. He could trust Mac. The sergeant was no gossiping blabbermouth, but a pro like himself: one properly worried and concerned by 'D' Flight's deficiencies – just as any good NCO should be. And a certain Flight-Sergeant not so far from here was going to need all the muckers he could find before things were even half-straightened. Some of the officers looked useful – young Browney and that Greek-reading Gunner for a start. But Peters? That one spelt trouble.... Hopkins had served long enough to know the dangers of a stupid officer in certain situations; in his book, Mr-bloody-Peters was a considerable pain in the arse....

'He is that....' Mackail agreed.

Hopkins started.

'Gawd! Was I thinkin' out loud?'

'Ye were, Flight – a little, anyway. Enough for me to guess who you're on about. You're right. He'll be nae use to the Captain....'

'And what *you* want to know is whether Destrier'll be any use to us?'

Mackail drew thoughtfully on his cigarette.

'Look, Flight. I've served with him before – just over a year back at Etiennebois. He's changed.'

Hopkins snorted.

'Christ, Mac! Haven't we all in the last couple of years?'

'But not like he has – and I'm not just talking about his face, either. It's something that goes deeper than that. Much deeper. It's as if the man's hurt right down inside himself. It's made a killer of him....'

Hopkins looked at Mackail uneasily.

'How in hell've you got him taped so quickly? I didn't know you'd even spoken to him yet.'

'I haven't – apart from a salute and a "Good-evening, sir."'

'So ... how do you know?'

It was Mackail's turn to look uneasy.

'I just do – that's all....'

'Good old Highland second-sight?'

'Something like that....' Mackail pushed back his chair.

'Look, Flight, if what I hear's true, you and Destrier have known each other a long time. If I'm talking out of turn I'll shut up —'

Hopkins tossed his cigarette packet across the table again.

'I only wish you were, Mac — but you're not. Yes, I've known Destrier on and off for the best part of twenty years. But it's almost as if the bloke I knew isn't at home any more.... Oh, he's changed all right. This war's turned personal for him....'

'How come?'

'The same reason we're all sitting here on our arses in the middle of this cabbage-patch. The night bombers....'

'Yon's a bluidy dirty way to fight a war!'

'Is it? Jerry bombs — and we blockade. So where's the odds? Either way it's the innocent who get hurt.'

Mackail was silent for a moment or two before replying.

'None that he'd have been able to see — once....' He shook his head sadly. 'Do you think there's anything left of the fellow we remember him as, Flight?'

Hopkins shrugged and jerked a thumb in the direction of a heap of flying-kit — leather coat, fur boots and borrowed sweaters — lying piled on his bunk.

'Gawd knows .... That's what I'm going to have to find out for myself, Mac....'

The Scot stood, tossing his cigarette end into the grate.

'Then I'd rather you than me, laddie....'

FOUR

Destrier lay on his back watching the dismal play of the solitary candle on the walls of his room. Above him, the mildewed and sagging plaster of the ceiling was divided by half-a-dozen worm-eaten beams. From a crack behind one of these emerged a crumpled Peacock butterfly, still dizzy with midwinter sleep yet attracted by the room's meagre warmth. The little creature slowly opened and closed its wings, exposing then hiding the brilliant roundels on their rich sienna ground. Then, as if astonished by its own temerity and uncertain as to whether or not its wings would support it, the butterfly drifted down from the beam and began fluttering round the room in a series of erratic circles, its movements echoed on the candle-struck walls of the room by a grotesquely dancing shadow.

His own existence had been like that, Destrier thought, a tremulous and dreamy launching of self into an unknown element. Until he had met Dolly Lyttleton, his real life had been within himself, an interior monologue. He had lived and had his being as though from within a goldfish bowl, permitted to look out from his own world towards another, able to see, but not to touch. . . .

Even his flying – of itself, superficially, a purely physical act – had been part of an exploration of an inner mystique, marked 'Private and Personal'. Nor had he ever told anyone – not Dolly, not Hopkins – of the one particular image that in one particular moment of time had set him apart by giving him this compulsion towards the air.

It had been late summer, he remembered, when he was sent the orphanage, a very lost and unhappy small boy. Before Hopkins had befriended him, he had been left to his own devices a great deal and had spent most of his evenings walking alone in the orphanage grounds. And then, one sunlit evening, he had seen the swallows.

There had been two birds – the mother and a single, almost fully-grown youngster. They had been flying separately – and only rarely were both ever present in the same part of the field for more than a few seconds. Each was busy about its own affairs, apparently self-absorbed and quite oblivious to the other. And yet, at the same time, it had been as though both were in some mysterious way conjoined by invisible wires, related like two quite different but intertwining strands of melody. The youngster flew around the perimeter of the field, the archetypal sprog practising circuits – straight and level flight, followed by banks and turns, with the occasional self-indulgence of flying straight at a tree trunk for the pure pleasure of avoiding it by a last-moment sideslip. The mother was hawking for insects, bare inches above the ground, for, brilliant though the evening was, the atmosphere was thunderous and heavy.

At the particular corner of the field in which she was now flying, the ground appeared quite flat – but the sun was now so low that it undershot the close, rabbit-nibbled turf, throwing the meadow into a relief map of lights and darks, creating with shadow an intricate delta of valleys that in the normal light of day were so shallow as to be imperceptible. It was among and along these tortuous passages that the hen-swallow flew, jinking violently at high speed with pure joy at the unfettered glory of her movement. Perhaps it had been her exaltation that had so worked on his imagination, Destrier conjectured; in the flight of both swallows had been pattern and purpose – yet also, passion and delight. . . .

Several times repeated, there had been one crowning piece of flying by the swallows that had enchanted him, a manoeuvre so exquisite in its dangerous precision that even at this distance in time he remembered having shouted aloud at the wonder and mastery of it. Nearly grown as the youngster was, from time to time his mother apparently still found some choice insect for him. At a signal Destrier hadn't been able to understand – some instinctive telepathy, perhaps – the two birds had flown straight at each other from opposite ends of the field, closing at astonishing speed.

A few feet from collision, both had climbed almost vertically until, at stalling-point, within a whisker of touching, and over almost too quickly even for a boy's keen eyes, the mother had fed the youngster on the wing. Then, sometimes turning in mirror-formation and sometimes fanning away from each other in opposite directions, the birds had dropped and broken off contact in what Destrier had long since learned to call stall-turns, resuming their haphazard quartering of the field.

Remembering the swallows, it seemed to Destrier that the moment – the one, imperative moment for which his life seemed purposed – must surely come soon. Ever since he could recollect, the knowledge of that moment – that all-important and coming instant in time – had smouldered somewhere in the recesses of his brain. In that moment would be consummation, and the making clear of the for-why and for-what he had had his being at all. Several times in his lifetime, Destrier had thought that this moment had come and was NOW.

The first time had been when, as a small boy, he had given the evidence that had put a rope round the neck of his mother's murderer. But no, he had afterwards come to see that it was not for this that he had been waiting. The hawking swallows had been a harbinger of something – and for a brief hour or so after his involuntary, half-minute flight on that break-away kite at Farnborough, he had deluded himself into believing that this, in its turn, had been his promised rendezvous with fate. But again, no – it had been a rendezvous of sorts, certainly, but *not* the one for which he had been conceived, for which he'd been carried in a whore's womb before kicking his way bawling and yelling into the light of a dirty back bedroom in Fratton.

Now, he could see quite clearly that there had been several such instants in time, each one important, each significant, every last one containing within itself fragments of a continuously unfolding truth – a truth that would one day be wholly revealed to him. His first solo pre-war had been one such moment, his bloody flight over Nine-Tree Wood another. The moments were getting ominously closer together, he noted. His first entry into the sanctuary of Dolly Lyttleton's body; their brief courtship and marriage – all were parts of a rapidly telescoping pattern, as was that moment when ... when. ... But Destrier's mind refused even to acknowledge that lost instant in time when his whole world had been brought tumbling into ruin about him.

Moving closer and closer to the burning candle, the Peacock struggled frantically against the irresistible compulsion drawing it inwards to destruction. On the bedroom walls, the butterfly's shadow leapt and swayed in a cruel parody of its feebly beating wings. Suddenly, the candle-flame leapt and the creature's wings took fire. In that instant, the thread of compulsion broke and the butterfly at last succeeded in breaking free from the candlelight's pull. But it was now too late. The fragile wings scorched, then powdered to nothing, and the thing that only a few moments before had been so beautiful, so exquisite, now lay blackened and still on the bare boards of the floor.

His leave up, Destrier returned to London with Dolly. They separated at Liverpool Street, each of them making their own way back to the hospital, so as to avoid embarrassing comment.

Colonel Mayo, at least, was not so easily taken in.

'We-ell, boyo,' he said the next morning when examining Destrier's healing body, 'someone's been changing your dressings very professionally!'

'The local doctor.'

'Ah ... yes.... Of course.... Now I wonder what the fellow's name might be?'

'I ... er ... forget....'

Mayo rolled his eyes up to heaven.

'Glory be to God! The poor man's been treating you for ten days and you haven't even the grace to remember his name! Let's see now. It wouldn't perhaps have been Smith, would it?'

Destrier blushed. 'It might have been....'

Mayo roared with laughter. 'A likely bloody story, my lad!' He thumped Destrier on his uninjured shoulder. 'Well, *whatever* you've been up to, it seems to me you spent your leave in the best possible way.'

'I spent it quietly.'

'But not so quietly that you didn't succeed in putting the roses back into Nurse Lyttleton's cheeks. . . .'

'I don't know what you mean. . . .'

'Pull the other one, boy – it's got bells on. Besides, aren't you forgettin' something? The prescription was mine in the first place.'

'What was that, Doctor?'

Mayo had the grace to look embarrassed.

'Well, I – er. . . . Let's just say that the two of you weren't getting much forrader in here. . . . You both needed someone to give you a push –'

'Is that why you sent me on leave?'

The bantering note left Colonel Mayo's voice.

'There's a damned sight more to medicine than a few assorted potions and a sharp knife, Laurie. Besides –' he reached out and touched Destrier's scarred face, 'without a little help from someone, would you ever have let yourself believe that a girl as pretty as Dolly Lyttleton could ever be in love with you?'

'I don't know. . . .'

'Well, I do. And the answer's no, you wouldn't have. . . . For which little piece of extra-mural treatment the fee will be one bottle of John Jameson, to be delivered to my office on the day of your discharge.'

'I might even run to two. . . .'

'One'll do. And damned cheap at the price, if you ask me.'

'I'll have an illuminated citation made out and sent to the GMC.'

'You *dare*! Which reminds me. . . . Was there any mail for you this morning?'

'Only a bill from my tailor.'

'That's odd. Damned odd. . . .'

'Why?'

Mayo's eyebrows lifted in astonishment.

'Sweet Jesus! D'you mean to sit there and say no one's told you yet?'

'Told me what?'

Mayo's eyebrows threatened to vanish into his hair.

'Just this –' he said, pulling a crumpled newspaper from the pocket of his white coat. With a forefinger well-burnt from tamping down the tobacco in his dreadful pipe, he pointed to a closely-printed column, framed in a circle of red ink.

'Here! You'd better read this.... The whole hospital's buzzing with it. You must be the only one that doesn't know about it....'

Destrier found it difficult at first to make much sense out of the cold print. In clipped, official prose whose tone was borrowed from the London *Gazette*, which the newspaper freely quoted, the column spoke of events and persons both familiar yet outside and remote from his experience. Someone, it seemed – someone, by an odd coincidence with the same name as himself – had, in February, been attacked by four Albatros Scouts while he was engaged in a ground attack on a section of the enemy's line near Nine-Tree Wood. This other Destrier, it appeared, had succeeded in summarily despatching all four of his attackers before crashing himself, and was now reported to be recovering from serious wounds at a hospital in southern England.

His Majesty had been graciously pleased to accept the recommendation that the said officer, Captain Laurence Destrier, DSO, MC and Bar, DCM, of the Royal Flying Corps, should be awarded the Victoria Cross.

There was more – much more – but Destrier had read enough. He flung the newspaper down and lay back on his bed. His head buzzed, and the ravaged muscles in his chest and shoulder screamed. It dawned on him slowly, that he, *he* and no other was the Captain Destrier referred to. He felt himself go cold, and his disgust became spiced with anger. The whole bloody business was a mistake. No! It was worse than a mistake. It was a put-up job. He had allowed himself to be bushwhacked like any green novice, he had escaped more by luck than judgement – and now, the great and stupid 'They' who ordained such things wanted to pin a bloody VC on him.... Oh, Jesus! The crass stupidity of it all....

But, no.... Perhaps he'd been nearer the mark just now when he'd thought of the matter as a put-up job. There was method in the madness. The fact that the award should have been made at all, after this lapse of time, was a gesture designed to stimulate the morale of a populace growing ever more weary and depressed by news of the war. The country needed a paper hero – and he had been chosen. He felt like being sick.

Mayo was looking at him strangely.

'You don't look very pleased by it....'

'Should I be?'

'Why not?'

Destrier snatched up the paper and waved it under the doctor's nose.

'Because the whole thing was a bloody useless, senseless cock-up from beginning to end – that's why!'

'There's no need to shout, old boy....'

'Isn't there? I feel like bloody well screaming!'

Mayo retrieved his newspaper.

'Forget it.... You survived –'

'By luck, not judgement.'

'The modesty of the man!'

Destrier flung a pillow at Mayo's head. Suddenly the dam broke and his anger spilled out in a bitter denunciation of the war – a war which had been nothing but a series of bunglings and mismanagements from beginning to end. His voice reverted abruptly to the modulations and language of the barrack-room. Freed from inhibition, Destrier told the world what he thought about the war, and the be-knighted and beribboned buffoons running it.

He came out of his mist of anger at last to find Mayo gazing at him with friendly and quizzical concern.

'You must think I've gone mad.'

'On the contrary, my boy,' Mayo grinned, 'I was just congratulating myself on how remarkably sane you are.'

'Sane? Despite an outburst like that?'

'No-o.... Because you can *still* make an outburst like that.'

'It's your job to patch people like me up – and send us back....'

Mayo's grin faded.

'Yes... That's my job – may God forgive me. I save a man's arm or leg from amputation and know that if this war goes on for long enough, then I've probably signed his death-warrant....'

'And mine? Have you signed *my* death-warrant, Colonel?'

Mayo shook his head.

'No.... You're one brand I have plucked from the burning. You're out of this war for good now. And, whatever you might choose to think at the moment, you've not come out of it so badly for all your hard knocks. Scarred you may be – but, again, not so badly as appearances might suggest. You've a woman who loves you – and you've still got the sensibilities of a decent human-being. I could almost call you lucky.'

But, Destrier thought, nearly six months later, lying on a bed of grey army blankets in a half-ruined farmhouse, how much of that still held true? How much of that 'decent human-being' still remained? His sensibility was destroyed. Now, he was like a gutted and burned-out building: only the exterior shell remained, empty and dead; a habitation for ghosts, existing solely now in the echoes from a vanished past.

In the enclosed world of the hospital, it was difficult for Destrier and Dolly Lyttleton to keep their new-found happiness private. In public, each of them treated the other with an apparent indifference that both found disturbing and frightening. Doubts stirred.... Was the other *really* as neutral as appearances suggested? Into both of their minds sprang the fear that their shared, ten-day idyll had been nothing more than a dream.

It was Mayo who with characteristic good sense saved the situation. The announcement of Destrier's VC brought a stream of visitors to the hospital, both official and unofficial and all nearly equally unwelcome. These, Mayo declared, were of no benefit to his other patients, and it would be as well if Destrier were to be banished to a single room, both for his own good and that of everyone else. Gratefully accepting his cue, Destrier put up a show of reluctance before acceding to the change.

With the return of even this very limited privacy the sense of unease between man and woman faded. They picked up their relationship where the end of their leave had left it, occasionally escaping again, whenever Destrier's treatment allowed, for weekends in Tolleswich.

It had been on their third such visit, late in August, and safe in the bed that had sheltered their first loving, that Dolly told Destrier what she had suspected for some time – that she was carrying his child. The couple had moved together and had made love tenderly yet with a new and fresh intensity, made blessed by fulfilment. Then, when their flesh had grown quiet at last, they talked of marriage.

Destrier's proposal was the simplest.

'When?' he asked.

'Do you mean marriage?'

'What else?'

Dolly laughed.

'Soon, I think. Doc Mayo's been eyeing my waistline avidly for the last fortnight.'

'What's that Irish sawbones know about having babies?'

'Enough to drop a heavy hint or two.'

'I can imagine.' His fingers, cupped on her breast, tightened their pressure. 'Soon, you said? Good. It can't be too soon for me. So far as I'm concerned you're married to me already, Mrs Destrier.'

Dolly giggled and ran her finger up the shattered line of his jaw.

'Don't you believe it'll come true?'

'I don't know. . . . The thought that something good might happen to me always leaves me afraid.'

'Afraid? *You?*'

'Why not? It's not easy for someone like me to believe

that things will last. Not good things, anyway. I'm usually right.'

Dolly put her arms round him and pulled him close to her. Strange; she had never thought of Destrier before in this light, or as being a man with any particular uncertainty of mind and spirit. She scolded herself for lack of perception – that Destrier should be like this ought to come as a surprise to no one, least of all herself. With his background and experience, it was hardly surprising if he was mistrustful and emotionally unsure. Well, it was up to her to change that.

She pressed her body urgently against his.

'This will last – I promise you! Just as long as you ever want it to last!'

They were married quietly in a London Register Office a fortnight later, early on the September morning when, an hour or so later, Destrier was due at the Palace for his Investiture. Afterwards, he remembered little of either ceremony – both had seemed equally detached and remote from anything to do with himself. To his infinite relief, Dolly reassured him that at neither had he made an undue ass of himself. Indeed, the only thing he remembered with any clarity about that autumn day was his relief when he and Dolly at last arrived in Tolleswich.

Yes, it had been good to be home. . . . Home. . . . The candle guttered, its light blurred, and Destrier rolled over on the bed, burying his face in the sour-smelling pillow. The silly, pretentious, over-ornate cottage at Toleswich had been the one place in all this world he'd ever been able to sanctify with that one small word. . . . Until that night nearly three weeks later. . . .

His quarrel with Dolly had been a silly, stupid one. Jealousy was roused in him when she mentioned the name of an old friend – an officer in the Guards. But this first estrangement left them silent and unspeaking. Dolly went to bed early, while Destrier moodily chose to go for a long walk.

The day had been one of low cloud and drenching autumnal rain, he remembered, though in the evening the rain stopped and the clouds partially cleared. A mile or so of walking was enough to convince him of his own stupidity. Whatever Dolly's Guardsman might have once meant to her, that was something in the past – Dolly's past – and therefore nothing about which he had the least right upsetting himself over. Besides, a sudden fragment of memory sprang into mind, making him guiltily aware of the full depths of his own pettiness. From scraps of a past conversation he recalled that Dolly had spoken of her Guards officer before, and that the poor devil was long since dead – killed on the Somme.

Contrite and furious with himself, he turned back the way that he had come, but after a hundred yards left the lane to take a short-cut home across the fields. As he limped along their headlands, the rain-sodden tangle of grasses and briar dragged at his legs, soaking his trousers and quickly tiring him. The night was very dark, and only occasionally was he able to catch a glimpse of the moon through the broken overcast above him. Two or three times he lost his way, and it was nearly an hour before he reached a wooden barn which he knew to lie only a small field away from the cottage. Exhausted, he paused and leant his head against its tarred planking. It was only then, with these ancient timbers acting as a sounding-board, that for the first time he heard the menacing growl and moan of aero-engines.

During his three weeks of marriage, Destrier had allowed himself to forget the war. Its immediacies and dangers had faded into something remote and of small concern to him. He had managed to bundle the war from his mind in a way that only a few short weeks before would have seemed quite impossible. Even when walking down by the harbour with Dolly, watching the purposeful comings and goings of the destroyers about their business as an adjunct to the Harwich Patrol, he had been able to forget that German submarines were even now reaching the climax of their threat. Even the occasional echoes of gunfire, rolling and throbbing inland from the hazy sea, had failed to penetrate the comfortable serenity of his new-found repose. With Dolly by his side, sleeping and waking, he had been able to forget his ravaged face and bullet-torn body – for all that both still had the power to wake him sometimes, gritting his teeth and sweating with pain. At first he had felt guilty in concluding this separate peace – but the balmy September weather, with its own inward-looking and self-absorbed quality, had conspired with him to stifle doubt.

Now, the war was about to force itself on him again.

Perhaps it was due to the low cloud, that by some freak of acoustics, Destrier failed to detect the approach of the German bomber until it was almost over the centre of Tolleswich. Indeed, it was only when the Staaken burst down through the cloud that the immense diapason of her engines – a sound that could normally be heard for twenty miles – came to his ears as he leant against the barn.

Destrier panicked. Something inside him screamed that it was imperative he should get back to Dolly at once. He stumbled across the soaking lattermath of the small field and, when he came to the back gate of the cottage, began fumbling at its seldom-used and rusting latch. As he heaved and sweated at this, he felt the scar-tissue on his hands give way like damp paper and then the warmth of his own blood trickling and oozing over his fingers.

New sounds came to his ears beside those of the pulsing Maybachs. Down in the harbour it seemed that every gun the Navy could muster was barking, snapping or growling its defiance. Then, though the bomber still sounded some way off, over the flaring, searchlight-glowing centre of the town, there began a long moaning sigh which, heightening in pitch as it came closer, shrivelled his soul into the nerve-ends of his being. It was a sound he knew too well. . . .

Oh, Jesus Christ! A bomb!

Blindly, he renewed his struggle with the gate, wrestling and heaving at its reluctant frame. But the jobbing-carpenter who had built it had done his job well, and the gate remained immovable. In the darkness, Destrier began to sob and swear as he threshed about him, punching and kicking at that damnable bolt until at last it came free and the gate opened. Destrier flung himself into the garden and was promptly tripped by a tendril of honeysuckle that, wrapping itself round his ankle, brought him crashing down onto the garden path.

It was probably this tendril that saved his life, for even as Destrier felt himself falling, the shriek of the falling bomb rose to an intolerable crescendo – a crescendo that ceased abruptly as the bomb struck the ridge of the cottage roof. There was a momentary illusion of stillness as the bomb bored its way through to the cellar before exploding.... Then, the whole house appeared to lift itself – still intact – twenty or so feet above the ground, its windows lit from within by a ghastly parody of festive light.

And then the cottage simply fell to pieces – bricks, slates, glass, rafters and splinters of lath rained out of the sky. Hot fragments of bomb-casing whickered through the air and sizzled in the drenched grass. The blast-wave swept over Destrier's tumbled body and a shard of broken chimney-pot speared him in the buttock.

When the fire brigade arrived, together with a party of blue-jackets, they found Destrier scrabbling through the debris of the cottage with frenzied, broken hands. It took three of the sailors to hold him, while the fourth, a petty-officer with rough but kindly hands, jammed a syringeful of morphine into him.

Or, thought Destrier, rolling over and staring into the blue heart of the candle's guttering flame, perhaps it was all a dream that he had loved and had been loved in return. The girl in the photograph beside his bed seemed so very unlike Dolly as he remembered her. Had that trim, remote girl really been his wife? Only his gnawing, intolerable sense of pain and loss survived to tell him that she had.

Destrier remembered as little of Dolly's funeral as he remembered of their Register Office marriage. Afterwards, he and Dolly's father, a tall, silent man with eyes like hers, had got very drunk together in a quiet hotel down by the harbour, watched over by an elderly waiter with flat feet and a gentle smile. They had said little. To neither man had there been much that seemed worth saying. Both had seen their share of violent death – Dolly's had been quite pointless, an obscene joke thought up by a perverted and pitiless providence.

Later, Destrier returned to hospital. Somehow, news of Dolly's death had reached Mayo; he was unable to look Destrier in the eye and appeared ten years older. When Destrier first requested – and then demanded – to be passed fit for active service, the Irishman shook his head but then, seeing the other's determination, shrugged as if the matter was no longer of any importance.

'I'll see what I can do.'

It took Mayo the best part of eleven weeks. Only Destrier's bitter and sometimes insolent resolution had got him through the various medical boards arranged for him. Well-meaning and kindly attempts by senior officers to keep him permanently grounded were greeted with contempt and, sometimes, blazing anger. Perhaps only the short inch of magenta ribbon saved him from court martial. But at last the wheels for his return to duty were reluctantly set in motion. Early in December Mayo called him into his office and showed him the papers that, in the usual stilted jargon of the Service, gave instructions that Captain Destrier was to be sent on a fortnight's leave prior to posting as the commander of 'D' Flight, detached for Home Defence duties near Marshingfold in Kent.

'And that's the best I can swing for you, Laurie,' Mayo said flatly. 'They won't send you back to France – not at any price. But at least this way you'll be able to have a crack at the Hun bombers – if that's what you want.'

'That's what I want. . . .'

Mayo said nothing. There was no point at all in arguing with Destrier; no purpose in telling him to leave retribution to God – the man before him was not that same one who, a few months earlier, had fulminated against the stupidity of war. Whatever battles Destrier was now seeking would be personal ones. As he rose and made to leave Mayo's office, the doctor asked, 'This leave of yours. . . . Where will you go?'

The other shrugged.

'London, I suppose – now. . . .'

'Yes. . . . That's maybe the best thing. . . . I'll see you before you go?'

'Perhaps.'

But to Mayo's secret relief, Destrier slipped away from the hospital the next morning without a goodbye. Instead, the doctor found a bottle of John Jameson waiting for him on his desk, together with a note whose one word read simply, Thanks. . . .

Destrier's packing had not taken him long – most of his belongings had been blown to smithereens in the Tolleswich cottage. But the journey up to London was strange. For a brief moment he experienced a treacherous surge of the old exhilaration he had grown used to feeling when going on leave – when leave had meant Dolly and the cottage. But instantly reality came crowding back in. The train wheels began to build up a mocking clamour that shaped itself into three short, bitter words inside the head, the rail-joints thudding home their meaning with changing and tormenting emphasis, 'Dolly-is-dead. Dolly-is-dead. Dolly-is-dead. Dolly-is-dead. . . .'

Once into London, Destrier booked into a quiet hotel near Victoria. He spent a dreary succession of mornings moving between his tailor, the War Office and the Air Board – this last now coming to the end of its days at the Hotel Cecil in the Strand. Here, everything seemed to him in an incredible state of muddle and confusion, uncertain of its present status, or likely future – and conscious of bitter political storms blowing beyond its walls. The information Destrier gleaned about his new command was meagre. 'D' Flight, yes – but of what squadron? None seemed certain, or able to tell him. His visits to the Air Board brought him little in the way of tangible reward. After much skirmishing with a succession of clerks, he was able to arrange for Hopkins's immediate transfer to Marshingfold. Secondly, he heard it whispered, on good authority, that 'D' Flight would probably be equipped with Bristols.

Bristols! It was this information that brought out into the open a doubt that had been lurking in Destrier's mind ever since he'd demanded to be considered fit for active service again. Supposing, when it came to it, he was not able to nerve himself into a cockpit again? An answer to that question was imperative. And even having got himself into a cockpit, would he still be able to perform those simple mechanical actions necessary to get an aircraft off the ground? Or would he find his body terror-frozen into a petrified catalepsy? Such things had happened to others, he knew – men who, like himself, had beaten the odds, whose bodies had mutinied when put to the hazard again. Well, if that happened to *him*, Destrier told himself grimly, his body would not be the winner by it. Among his few belongings, there remained his service revolver. If necessary, there was always that way home. His will must be stronger than himself. Yet, even at the mere thought of flying again, his limbs trembled uncontrollably, and his stomach heaved.

It was quite by chance that Destrier, prowling aimlessly and unhappily around London, ran into an old acquaintance at the Piccadilly Hotel. A voice hailed him from across the crowded bar and a few moments later, after its owner had battled through the crush, he found himself being clapped on the shoulder by a lean major with an Australian accent.

'By all the wonders – Laurie Destrier! I was only talking about you earlier in the evening. Someone said you were in hospital still – down in Surrey....'

'I ... escaped....'

'Yeah, I can see that. You remember me, don't you? Spring? Pat Spring?'

Pat Spring. Yes, of course Destrier remembered him. The Australian was a clumsy if effective pilot. Destrier had briefly flown with him in the same flight of a DH2 squadron late in 1915. Spring ran an interested finger along the coloured ribbons on Destrier's chest.

'What's all this mularky, then? Flag Day? I heard rumours you'd been busy collectin'.'

Destrier evaded a recital of his doings by ordering drinks.

'Yes, I've been busy,' he said. 'What about you?'

Major Spring pulled a wry face and splashed a few token drops of water into his whisky.

'I'm instructing, so Gawd help me.'

'Where?'

'Cranwell.... Turning pilots into officers, and officers into pilots. All failures buried free of charge. Union Jack and Last Post provided....'

'Do you get many fatalities?'

'Only on Camels. There's just precisely two sorts of Camel pilot – the quick and the dead.'

'Aren't they any good?'

The Australian was quick to defend the formidable little fighter.

'No good? The Camel's the bloody tops, chum. It's just that the jokers we get flying 'em aren't always as hot as they might be – and the Camel won't stomach a fool.'

'And the Bristol?' Destrier tentatively asked.

'Now *she's* quite different. The Bristol's a lady....'

'I want to fly one.'

The Australian shrugged.

'I daresay I could swing that for you – unofficially, anyway. Take a run down to Cranwell with me in the morning.'

Driving to Lincolnshire the next day, Destrier bluntly explained his inner fears to Spring. The Australian's answer was simple.

'Pack it in then, sport.... Fly a desk for a change.'

'I can't....'

'You've had your whack.'

'Not quite. Besides.... The war. It's become personal.'

'And you want me to help you break your neck?'

'If you want to put it that way.'

'Just so long as you don't break mine at the same time.'

For a while they drove in silence, then Spring said, 'I tell you what. When we get to Cranwell, I'll take you up in an Avro and let you get the feel of things for a bit.'

'Back to circuits and bumps?'

'That's it. Then, if you're not positively hopeless, I'll see about lettin' you loose with one of our handsome Bristols. Is that fair?'

'Fair enough....'

On reaching Cranwell, Spring hadn't given Destrier time to think. Within half an hour of arriving, they were walking across the grass to a waiting Avro. Destrier's stomach heaved as he forced himself awkwardly over the cockpit coaming and began strapping himself in. Again, Spring allowed no time for apprehension or second thoughts. Even while Destrier was clumsily struggling with the last of his harness pins, the Australian sent the little trainer rocking and bumping across the grass. Fifty feet off the ground, he raised both hands above his head to show they were clear of the controls. Destrier grabbed at the stick and the Avro side-slipped drunkenly towards the ground, recovering bare inches from the grass. Destrier made a tolerable circuit of the field before coming in to land. Spring swore foully into the Gosport-tube and took the plane back under his own control. The Avro climbed steeply to seventeen hundred feet until she stalled and fell away in a spin. Spring raised his hands again. A little belatedly, Destrier pulled the Avro out of this, with a muddy field leaping up to meet them.

Again Spring swore. 'For Jesus Christ's sake –'

Then followed a half-hour during which the Australian put the trainer through every nerve-tingling manoeuvre he could think of, lifting his hands from the controls at critical moments and leaving Destrier to get out of the resultant tangle as best he could.

Despite the coldness of the afternoon, Destrier found himself wringing with sweat when they landed. Spring grunted in somewhat grudging approval.

'We-ell. . . . At least you didn't actually break anything. . . .'

Destrier managed a thin smile. 'Not quite. . . .'

'You forgot *two* things. . . . An Avro isn't a *bloody* Pup, and *these* –' Spring reached out and took Destrier's hands in his own, '– these aren't exactly what they were when you drew them from store. Most of their strength's gone – which doesn't matter too much. But more to the point, their sensitivity's gone too. . . .'

Destrier nodded. He'd worked out both points for himself. Even allowing for the docile clumsiness of a school hack, he had soon realized that his hands now only possessed a tithe of their former precision. Still, his most urgent problem had been sorted out. . . . His body had obeyed his will.

The next morning found Destrier and Spring aloft in the Avro again. Once more the Australian put his pupil through a searching catechism and later in the morning allowed him to solo, just like any other aspiring novice, taking-off, circuiting and finally landing with an orthodox precision that brought an ironic smile to Spring's face. He was less amused by what happened next, for without allowing the trainer to come to rest, Destrier blipped open the engine again and quickly lifted off the grass again in a steep climb. After gaining a few hundred feet in height, he proceeded to put the Avro and himself through a catechism of his own, concluding by landing off a loop.

When Spring reached the trainer, he eyed Destrier grimly. 'Just try those sort of larks in a Bristol, old son, and you really will be joining the rest of the lads up in Boot Hill yonder.' He jerked a thumb in the direction of the neighbouring cemetery. 'Whatever else you feel like doing today, for Christ's sake don't try tricks like that with a Bristol – otherwise it really will be the jolly old "Dead-March-in-Saul" and arms-reversed routine for you. That's a promise.'

Destrier nodded and climbed down stiffly from the Avro. No, he told himself, he'd try nothing funny with the Bristol. In his heart of hearts, he knew he had overreached himself even in the tolerant Avro. The abilities of the little trainer had been a known and familiar quantity – but, nonetheless, he had strained even her docile and forbearing nature to its very limits. There had been once or twice up there when he had been convinced he had lost her. . . .

By contrast, his afternoon flight in a Bristol was almost an anti-climax. Clambering reluctantly into the rear cockpit, Spring carefully pointed out the sketchy nature of the observer's dual-control: the short hand-grips sleeved onto the rudder-cables, the detachable control-column that operated the elevators but not the ailerons. The Australian pulled the stick from its socket and balanced it thoughtfully in his hand.

'More of a comfort to nervous observers than anything else,' he said. 'When all else fails, the bloke back here could at least while away his last few moments bashing his pilot's brains in with it, I suppose.... So nothing daft below three thousand, eh, Laurie?'

Destrier grunted affirmatively and signalled to a waiting mechanic to swing the propeller. Within the next few minutes he became convinced that the Bristol was a winner, a thorough-bred with virtues as ruggedly handsome as her looks. At a safe height, he put the Bristol through her paces, finding that though the fighter seemed a trifle heavy on his aching, tiring hands, she answered with all the nimble ability of a single-seater.

'Well?' Spring asked him, when they were down again.

'She'll do....'

'Too bloody right she will, mate.... The question is, will you?'

Destrier jerked a thumb upwards at the sky.

'Could you have done better?'

'No-o.... But that's not what I meant – and you know it.'

'Mind your own bloody business, Pat!'

'OK. If you want to break your flaming neck that's up to you, I suppose.' He slapped the coaming of the observer's cockpit. 'Just remember, you'll have some other poor joker to answer for as well, will you?'

Destrier appeared not to have heard him. He reached up and touched the Vickers mounted in the engine-faring.

'Why the hell couldn't they have fitted a pair of these while they were at it?'

Destrier left Cranwell that evening and arrived back in Town to find there had been a lull in the bombing. London hadn't been raided since the sixth of December, when sixteen Gothas, changing their tactics, had plastered the City with incendiaries. The casualties had been comparatively low, but the destruction heavy. A morbid and self-tormenting curiosity led Destrier to investigate one of the outlying areas of destruc-tion. He was struck anew by the air of unreality in what he saw. A half-flattened and burned-out terrace looked less like an ordinary street in which people had lived real lives than a half-completed stage-set, wanting only actors and a moving-picture camera.

The appearance of an RFC officer in this woebegone little street was enough to excite anger in one of its former occupants, an old woman hopelessly trying to retrieve some of her charred and pathetic belongings from the ruined shell of her house. Instinctively, Destrier stepped forward to help her, only to find himself being berated in a shrill cockney voice. Chance showed the woman only the undamaged side of Destrier's face – and she bitterly berated him for being a bloody coward. She shook her fist at him and then, reaching down into a burst cushion, produced a white feather which she thrust into his gloved hand.

'There, mate,' the crone shrilled at him, 'that's what them bloody wings of yourn seem to be made of!'

Destrier fled.

And, in a sense, he was still running when, early the next afternoon, he arrived at Charing Cross and took the train for the Marsh.

FIVE

Huddled in his tiny cockpit between R.45's starboard engines, Mendelssohn was always both elated and terrified by the moment of take-off. Looking at the huge machine on the ground, it always seemed impossible that such a ponderous bulk of wood and metal could be persuaded to heave itself off the ground and then fly just like any other aircraft. The prelude to each flight – the starting and running-up of the thunderous Maybachs – always induced in him an excitement that was almost sexual in its intensity.

The feeling generally vanished the moment R.45's sixteen wheels began rolling across the concrete apron in front of the hangars. Then Mendelssohn felt his body turn to a watery, cowardly jelly: an excruciating terror unnerved him, and very often he went through the whole business of take-off with his eyes tightly shut and his gauntleted fists flung protectively across his face.

This time, however, Mendelssohn's elation did not vanish as the Giant trundled across the tarmac and turned her reptilian nose into the wind. On the contrary, it increased. The bawling menace of the Maybachs sounded like some splendid symphony and he found himself wide-mouthed with excitement as R.45's speed increased and she threw herself down a narrowing avenue cut from the darkness by twin searchlights meeting in a dazzling apex at the end of the runway. Mendelssohn could imagine Horst and Walter, crouched over the throttles, striving to judge that moment when the battle with gravity was won and Horst could ease back on the control-column and allow the Staaken to lift herself into the air.

Mendelssohn watched the apex of light leaping towards him. The wheels of the Giant hummed and moaned on the concrete, were briefly silent as the plane bumped off the ground, moaned again – and then ceased their keening for good as R.45 left the runway altogether and began climbing away into the darkness. Mendelssohn roused himself to stand and look backwards into the night. Already the searchlights were a diminishing V in the blackness below; then, abruptly, they were switched off. There was no point in providing an unnecessarily easy target for any prowling British bombers bent on retaliatory action.

As he looked aft, Mendelssohn felt himself pounded and pummelled by the slipstream. He knew himself to be a fool for standing like this. The night's coldness would find him out soon enough without him presenting his body as a hostage to the buffeting wind. There would be time enough for that later, once they were over England and a likely target for British fighters. Then it would be a case of 'Up-the-ladder-and-to-hell-with-the-cold!' Not that there would be much likelihood of any fighter finding them tonight, Mendelssohn told himself; the moon would be the palest of slivers. If any fighter did manage to find the Giant at all, it would only be by chance. With her bellowing great engines, R.45 neatly reversed the old nursery dictum: she was heard, but not seen.

Mendelssohn huddled deep down into the spartan comfort of his cockpit – a cockpit filled equally with howling winds, body-jarring projections and the stench of petrol. Yet, despite these and the numbing chill already beginning to insinuate itself into his sinews he felt almost content. The theme of his slow movement began to throb in his mind – that solitary fiddle lamenting above muted horns. If only he could begin to get an idea for the main subject of his elusive third movement.

In the shaded blue glow of the Staaken's cabin, von Trier looked round him with a very similar contentment. Horst's take-off had been a beauty. R.45's commander had been pleased to note the second pilot's quick glance of approval at the 'Sausage' as they had lifted off. The dull and stodgy Horst, it seemed, was gaining in confidence and technique.

But, in these first few minutes after take-off, a small hitch occurred which took the fine edge off von Trier's satisfaction when it was discovered that the Bosch generator, supplying power both for the radio and heating their flying-suits, was not working. Von Trier remembered the electrician Müller's supercilious grin at Sergeant-Major Mann's old-maidish concern about the generator. Von Trier grimly promised himself that should this hitch turn out to have been caused by Corporal Müller's carelessness, then the fellow would be smirking on the other side of his face in the morning.

Not that von Trier was at all put out by the prospect of navigating without the cross-bearings supplied by the radio. Indeed, the necessity for operating with complete radio-silence pleased rather than appalled him. It was his opinion that several of the British victories over Zeppelins had been caused by over-anxious airship captains relying far too much on their radios and being detected as a result. But the loss of the generator for heating purposes was far more worrying. The Staaken had fuel for something like eight hours' flying, though – with luck – they would not be in the air for more than five. But five hours' flying – particularly on a night like this – was a long, long time. They would be damn near frozen solid by the time they got back.

To take his mind off this problem, von Trier examined the maps set out on the navigation table in front of him. The first part of R.45's mission was straightforward enough: military installations to the south-east of London – the Naval Dockyard and Arsenal at Woolwich. It was in the second part of his instructions that von Trier detected a note of optimistic fantasy. Woolwich bombed, R.45 was to fly south across the huddle of suburbs and market-towns adjacent to this corner of London, in an attempt to bomb a night-fighter station which – so Intelligence claimed – the British were setting up four miles or so south of Bromley in Kent. Von Trier grinned. Even supposing Intelligence *had* got its facts right for once – and he seriously doubted it – he wondered whether anyone had seriously considered the odds against a solitary bomber being able to pin-point such an uncertain location. It was the sort of daft notion that could only have been thought up by some Intelligence Officer anxious to justify a miserable existence. Some Intelligence Officer who had seldom, if ever, flown – and most certainly never by night. Perhaps, von Trier told himself acidly, he was expected to touch-down somewhere near Bromley and ask the way. . . .

He found himself idly wondering just what Horst's reaction would be if ordered to do just that. A look of hurt worry and then his level best to carry out instructions, von Trier suspected. Poor Horst! The lieutenant's addiction to the letter of any command, however absurd, both amused and exasperated his superior. Such stupidity amounted almost to a national trait. Given a few thousand Horsts to command, body and soul, and an unscrupulous man might conquer the world – or destroy it.

At that precise moment, Horst was feeling very pleased with himself. He hadn't needed Walter's sidelong glance to tell him his take-off had been a beauty. From now on, he promised himself, such copybook perfection would be his norm. Now, in accordance with instructions given him by von Trier just prior to take-off, Horst laid R.45 on a course that would bring a landfall over the North Foreland something under a hundred miles away. From here, they would fly up the Thames Estuary before bombing Woolwich and turning southwards to their secondary objective, finally veering southeast to fly out over the English Channel again, somewhere near Dover and its grandiose white cliffs. The idea of flying, inviolate, over these symbolic embodiments of British power amused Horst. Despite the cold, he made no attempt to huddle down in his seat but instead sat rigidly to attention with his back ramrod straight and his chin thrust aggressively forward. How proud his father would be if he could see him now! The spearhead of German might and purpose: the personification of the Fatherland's will to conquer and endure.

Seated next to Horst, Walter was quite unconcerned with himself as a symbol of German anything. Already he was beginning to feel cold. Bloody cold. . . . As the chill began to search and seep into the recesses of his being, Walter's thoughts turned once more to his dream woman – the fattest, warmest wench in Bremen. He allowed himself the luxury of imagining what it would be like to burrow into her flanks and tuck his head between her breasts, while her flesh – as warm as toast and soft as any eiderdown – enveloped him with a heady scent of acquiescent femininity.

For a small moment, Walter's dream became so real for him that it temporarily banished the present. But, after a few wholly blissful seconds, actuality proved too strong and the image faded. Walter sighed. There were those, he knew, who would envy him his place here in R.45's cabin.... Well, anyone who wanted his job was welcome to apply. If anyone really wanted to be frozen, bored stiff and scared, all at the same time, he would arrange the swap tomorrow.

For a second time Walter tried to persuade his thoughts down more pleasant paths. But by now his groin seemed filled with ice. The harder he tried to recapture his earlier and amiably salacious fantasies, the more elusive they seemed. Resentfully, he damned them and stared out of the ice-smeared windshield into the blackness of the night.

Crouched over his open hatch in the tail, Rossi was even colder – much, much colder – than Walter. Here, the slip-stream tore into R.45's belly, rushing round and round inside like a biting, demented cat. Rossi huddled deep into his cocoon of sweaters and flying-leathers but did not shiver. He was now too cold for that.

In the small, ice-bound centre of his consciousness he was wretchedly aware of having made a stupid exhibition of himself yet again. Climbing on board the Staaken, he had slipped and fallen, banging his nose and cheek against the hatch-coaming. He had sworn obscenely in two languages – and everyone had laughed. Now, he realized, the fall had been more serious than he had at first thought in his anxiety to minimize the incident. His nose was by now so badly bruised and swollen that it felt as if it covered the whole of his face. The feral blast from the open gun-bay clouted him about his pounding head; despite his goggles, his eyes were constantly astream with tears. Too late he cursed his own clumsiness. Why, oh why could he never learn to do things with even a semblance of German efficiency and thoroughness? No wonder he was a laughing-stock. He tried and tried, yet somehow things invariably managed to go wrong for him. It was a wonder, he told himself bitterly, that von Trier had not had him returned to unit as being unsuitable for flying service. Perhaps he would now, after this latest fiasco.

Out on the port wing of the Staaken, Otto Schmidt cheerfully cussed the cold and prepared to put up with it. Like his friend Mendelssohn, Schmidt was huddled down into the illusory shelter of his cockpit between the tandem 280hp engines. These compensated for their ear-shattering clamour by providing their attendant mechanic with a certain amount of warmth – but not much. And even this little was all too quickly snatched away and dispersed by the tearing slipstream.

Not that Schmidt let this worry him too much. Indeed, he rather enjoyed his exposed position, cut off from the rest of the Giant's company. There was something in this isolation that appealed to his youthful sense of singularity and grandeur. There were times, too, when it amused him to stand in his cockpit and engage in an exhibition of shadow-boxing with the blustering wind. But not now. With at least four more hours of flying in front of him, even Schmidt's somewhat adolescent high spirits were partially subdued. Above all, he knew he must preserve every last degree of body heat for as long as he could. A fine fool he'd look if he had to climb that blasted ladder up to the top-plane only to find he was too frozen to move – particularly if there was some bloody-minded Camel pilot screaming down on them with a pair of nicely warmed-up Vickers guns and a happy smile on his face. The Tommies were decent enough fellows on the whole. But, good God, only a complete fool would try their good nature *that* far. . . .

Thinking of smiles, Schmidt grinned at the thought of Rossi's, which would be distinctly west-of-centre for a day or two. Lord! the poor old hokey-pokey man had caught himself a frightful crack on that hatch-coaming. And the *language* he'd used! Schmidt decided that when they eventually got down, he wasn't going to bed until he'd got a word for word translation.

It simply never occurred to him that Rossi's injury might be the undoing of them all. . . .

Back in the cabin, his shoulders drawn as a series of blue planes in the dim light, Wendel, now the complete master of himself since R.45 had left the ground, watched over the pumps and gauges in his care. As he had known they would, his fears had dropped away from him in that same moment he'd felt the bomber lift herself into the sky. Now, although Wendel himself was quite unaware of it, there was something admirable and almost daunting in the stern line of his neck and shoulders as he wrestled with the refractory pumps equalizing the six hundred gallons of petrol swashing above his head.

These pumps were a constant source of amazement and blasphemous worry to R.45's ground crew. Among these it was slanderously rumoured that the design department of Zeppelin Werke had been given carte-blanche to come up with an idea as eccentrically perverse and impracticable as possible. Consequently the bomber's pumps were Wendel's anxious concern in the air and Sergeant-Major Mann's despair on the ground. Each time R.45 flew, her pumps needed reservicing – and, in the air, there was always the fear that one or more would cease to function altogether – as had already happened for a few heart-stopping moments on an early training flight.

But now, as Wendel knew, his battles with these particular monstrosities were almost over. At the cost of much paper-work and heated argument, von Trier had at last succeeded in his insistence that R.45 be refitted with pumps of a more orthodox and better-proven type. Tomorrow, Mann's fitters would rip these present horrors out, replacing them with pumps which would no longer necessitate their guardian-angel spending each flight in hours of endless gauge-tapping and agitated tinkering.

For the moment, therefore, Wendel felt almost content.

Von Trier sat at his navigation table moodily prodding a slip of paper with a pair of dividers; Horst and Walter sat at their controls – the one, stiff-backed and straight; the other, slumped well down into his seat. All was well.

Yet was it? Into Wendel's mind there came once more the latest image of his nightmare terrors. As vividly as though it had already happened, he saw this calm and orderly cabin turned into a chaotic, blood-spattered shambles, and his three companions lying dead or dying about him. . . .

Wendel's stomach heaved. He turned back to his gauges for reassurance. . . .

Savouring the rich taste of rum on his palate, Sergeant Mackail left Hopkins in their joint cuddy and strolled out into the night across the thin, crisp layer of snow in the direction of the Bristol and the two BE12s. In the thick marsh darkness, he sensed rather than saw the handful of mechanics huddled in the lee of the Bristol's fuselage. As he neared the aircraft, he clapped his hands loudly and called, 'Right now, lads! Let's be having 'em warmed up!'

'Bollocks!' a cold and mutinous voice answered him out of the darkness – a voice which Mackail pretended not to recognize. He grinned to himself, though his reply rang sharply on the brittle air.

'That was an order, laddie – not an enquiry as to what you use for brains.'

A stifled laugh came from the little group as it obediently broke up. 'Old Mac's got your number all right, mate!' he heard someone mutter to the culprit.

Reaching the Bristol's wing-root, the sergeant swung himself up into the cockpit. He was well familiar with the F2B and had no need of Hopkins's lights to tell him where everything lay. Almost automatically, he began the routine for starting the Falcon engine. As he did so, he heard someone curse and slip in the darkness, his studded boots evidently skidding on the frozen turf. The Bristol shuddered as a heavy body fell against her airscrew, every wire in her thrumming sympathetically as the shock was communicated through wings and fuselage.

Mackail half-rose from his seat, peering vainly forward along the length of the engine-nacelle. Although the faller would scarcely need to be told to be more careful in future, Mackail was unable to restrain himself from yelling angrily into the darkness and hopefully in the direction of the offender, 'For Christ's sake watch your bluidy step! Yon thing might be going round next time!'

A shaken and contrite voice – the same voice that earlier had insolently answered 'bollocks' to his order – replied more soberly now.

'Sorry, Sar'nt.... It's this bloody snow –'

'Never mind the fornicating snow!' Mackail snarled. 'Just watch where you put your bluidy feet, Potter!'

'Yes, Sar'nt....'

Mackail lowered himself down into the cockpit. The pleasant taste of rum in his mouth had been replaced by something sourer, and he was surprised to find himself trembling. A careful man himself, the sergeant considered that of all the accidents likely to befall an air-mechanic, walking into a propeller was the stupidest. Twice he'd been present when this had happened. The first time, drenched in blood, he had helped to tourniquet the victim's shattered arm. The second occasion had been equally messy – though this time there had been no need for any first-aid.

Mackail steadied his breath and began the starting-drill again, with Potter's cowed voice answering antiphonally.

'Switches off.... Suck in.... Switches on.... Contact....'

The big Falcon clattered uneasily into life, spluttered briefly and then – as Mackail opened the throttle – forgot its coldness and let its full, peremptory organ-note boom splendidly into the night. The RAF 4a's of the two BE12s added their harmonies. Mackail settled himself deeper into his seat, carefully listening to the Falcon and trying to separate each individual engine sound. He pursed his lips and nodded in a dourly satisfied way. No.... Not so bad at all, he told himself. He and Hopkins had made a fair fist of things....

He throttled the Falcon back and then killed it, hearing its hot metal pinking and pinging in the freezing air. The growl of the factory engines ceased, too, and, climbing stiffly from the Bristol's cockpit, Mackail made his way across to the nearer of the BE12s.

A small figure appeared beside him in the darkness: young Browne.

'You needn't check mine, Sergeant Mackail. I've done that myself. . . .'

Darkness or no darkness, Mackail saluted.

'Yessir! But no bones broken if I run the rule over her, too. For my own peace of mind, you'll understand.'

Browne laughed. 'I understand. Thanks. . . .'

'Thank you, too, sir.'

Browne sounded puzzled. 'Thanks for what, Mac?'

That, Mackail considered, was difficult to say. Just something to do with the way young Browne treated everyone as a human-being, regardless of rank, the sergeant supposed.

Not like *some* officers.

And certainly *not* like that bastard Peters.

Browne sauntered back towards the farmhouse, his hands thrust deep into his pockets against the cold. Try as he would, he still found it difficult to give orders to experienced NCOs like Mackail and Hopkins without self-consciousness – though he knew this was the sort of thing his expensive public-school education was supposed to have fitted him for. On the face of things, the system seemed to work – but was that enough?

It was all, he decided, rather like county cricket, where the pros – for all their long experience and fame sometimes – changed in different dressing-rooms and called any amateur 'sir', no matter how much of a useless liability he might be, loyally covering up the deficiencies, cricketing and otherwise, of their so-called betters.

Why! Browne remembered, such chaps had even called *him* 'sir' in those halcyon few weeks back in the now almost forgotten summer of 1914. Ah! That was a time, he thought, looking back with almost painful nostalgia. But, Lord, what a rotten season he'd looked like having at the beginning. It hadn't been till the last week of May that he'd been able to find any sort of decent form at all. Then his luck had changed; his eye had found itself well and truly in, firstly against Winchester, then Wellington – and, best of all, against Eton at Lords.

Here, his good fortune had been almost unbelievable – embarrassing even. He'd been dropped twice off his first two balls, once by mid-off and then by mid-on, and both catches had been as easy as pie; absolute sitters. After that, it seemed as if he couldn't make a mistake if he tried. A hundred and eighty-two had been his final tally. The next day an invitation had arrived from the County, inviting him to play against Kent and Yorkshire in the hols. . . .

Nothing he'd done since, in the war, had filled him with quite such feelings of apprehension and downright terror. Luckily he had managed to persuade the Pater to keep away from the first match and let him travel to Canterbury alone. How little of that journey he could now remember, travelling firstly to London and then down into Kent. And himself? He must have looked pretty odd, too, Browne thought; a shy sixteen-year-old, looking at least two years younger, carrying a cricket bag nearly as big as himself.

In London, he had bought the *Times* and the *Daily News*. The cricket correspondent of the former wrote that Browne was the youngest player ever to appear for the County – and, although kindly, didn't seem to rate his chances very highly. The writer had then gone on to question the wisdom of blooding a schoolboy against Kent, of all counties – then, probably, the most exciting as well as one of the strongest sides in the championship. In his heart of hearts, young Browne agreed with the *Times*. There were moments on his train journey when he had come very near pure panic. . . .

The next morning, Kent won the toss and batted first. The long day in the field that followed this, steadied as well as wearied him. Frank Woolley had been at his very best, tearing and worrying at the County's limited bowling resources with languid and imperious ease. When Woolley had been dismissed at last – and how happily Browne remembered taking the catch that had got rid of him! – K. L. Hutchings completed the day's disasters. When Kent declared at close of play, the score had been the sort to remain imprinted on memory for ever: 444–4.

The County had been nowhere near so successful. Within half an hour of the next day's start, Browne – at number six – found himself walking to the wicket. It must have been a loathsome journey, he supposed. Thank God he could no longer remember it. Perhaps (shameful thought!) they'd even had to carry him to the wicket.

Woolley was again performing – this time as a bowler; left-hander to left-hander. Browne took guard, while the field was brought closer; a silly-point and a pair of short-legs, almost within the proverbial pocket-picking distance. Neither had been necessary.

Browne could still picture Woolley as, tall and lissom, he'd stepped up to bowl. The ball had been beautifully flighted just outside his off-stump and had hung for a tantalizing moment before pitching and breaking back sharply on him, forcing a hurried, ungraceful lunge to counter the spin. There was the faintest of tickles on the shoulder of his bat up near the splice. From behind the wicket, Hubble let out a triumphant yell and hurled the ball skywards.

On his seemingly endless trek back towards the doubtful sanctuary of the pavilion, Browne kept his eyes averted from the scoreboard's merciless and uncompromising truth: 28–5. Last Man, 0.

After lunch, the County's five remaining wickets rallied bravely, if briefly – thanks mainly to Perkins, the grizzled and elderly all-rounder who had begun his long and undistinguished career back in the days of Dr Grace and Arthur Shrewsbury. But, despite Perkins – and on the best of wickets – the County allowed itself to be bundled out for a miserable hundred and thirty. It was too humiliating. Kent, of course, would insist on the follow on. . . .

In the brief interval between the innings, Browne chanced

to run into Woolley. In his shyness, the youngster tried to brush by as quickly as possible – the ease with which the great player had beaten him had left him feeling a complete fool. But Woolley, though fully aware of the boy's embarrassment, was too kindly to let Browne wallow in his misery. He restrained the youngster by placing a hand on his shoulder, relieved him of his bat – and then and there, in the passage, demonstrated the stroke that Browne should have played.

It had been done quite unpatronizingly and with great good manners, Browne remembered. And he – *the great Frank Woolley* – had even called him *Mr Browne*!

The classically handsome face had broken into a friendly grin of complicity as Woolley had handed him back his bat. 'I don't somehow think we'll be seeing the back of you quite so easily this time, sir. . . .' he'd said.

Browne had felt his confidence return.

'No! I should jolly well think you won't, Woolley!' he had said firmly. The memory of his words and tone now had the power to make Browne blush and long to kick himself. Oh, Lord! Frank Woolley hadn't patronized *him*; but he – like a little stinker – had dared to put on side and patronize Woolley.

The County's second innings began on much the same low note as their first. Only Perkins, promoted in the order to give at least some semblance of backbone, seemed likely to make any sort of headway against the Kent attack. Again Woolley was bowling – this time in double-harness with Charlie Blythe, the best slow left-hander in the world, some said – better even than Wilf Rhodes.

This time – thanks to Perkins – the County's score was at least in the fifties before Browne arrived at the wicket for the second time. As in his first knock, he was faced by Woolley – a Woolley, who had already taken three wickets for fifteen and who looked as though he could go on bowling for the rest of the afternoon.

This time, Browne took guard in something approaching a composed frame of mind. The lovely St Lawrence ground was packed, and the thought came to him that now might be the time to give the beribboned and boatered crowd something to talk about. Again the short legs were brought in close. Well, Browne told himself, that was their funeral. Suddenly, he felt very calm.

Woolley came up to the wicket, with that same easy stride and action. The ball, when it arrived, was identical to the one that had proved Browne's undoing in the first innings – but this time he made no mistake. As it broke back on him, he got his right leg well across the wicket and clipped the ball away on the on-side past mid-wicket. Perkins called, and they ran an easy couple. Off the last ball of the over, Browne took a single and found himself face to face with Blythe.

Like most great slow-bowlers, Blythe was also something of an artist, amateur musician as well as cricketer. A love of melody and cadence seemed to be built into his bowling. Browne played out a maiden over. Every ball had *seemed* the same, yet each had dropped off, or held its flight, to pitch inches either way of the ones that had gone before. Once Browne had been almost committed to a full-blooded drive before realizing that the ball would simply not be there as his bat swung through. Somehow he managed to chop down onto the ball and smother it. Blythe grinned, and old Perkins wandered down the wicket to mutter a few words of advice to his young partner. Impatiently, Browne waved him away.

Perkins then played out a maiden to Woolley, batting like a stiff and old-fashioned book. Browne felt a pang of contempt for the old pro – and then swung wildly at the first ball of Blythe's new over, watching it evade – but only just – the clutching fingers of long-on, before bouncing and going over the boundary.

Perkins shrugged resignedly – and Blythe grinned again. By the time he'd finished playing out the rest of the over, Browne was happy to stroll up the wicket and seek his fellow-batsman's previously scorned advice.

Perkins kept it simple and to the point.

'Look here, sir,' he said, 'we can't win this game – and these fellows can. Today, too, if we don't keep our heads. But if the two of us was to stay here together the whole afternoon, I reckon we could rob the buggers yet. . . .'

'How, Perkins?' Browne remembered asking foolishly.

Perkins didn't bother framing his reply into words. Instead, he jerked his head upwards, drawing the youngster's attention to the sky on one side of the ground. For the first time since he had come in, Browne noticed the darkening sky and the line of angry thunderheads that was beginning to loom ominously over Canterbury. He became aware, too, how heavy the atmosphere was becoming; stifling almost, and so still as to wrap the pavilion flags in drooping folds about their masts.

'We'll have that lot round our ears by close of play, I reckon,' Perkins said, with a countryman's certainty about such things. 'No play termorrer, neither, not if I know anything about it. The ground'll look like a boating-lake by six o'clock. So . . . it's all rather up to you'n me, sir. . . . Alfie Patch and Major Mauleverer used up their share o' luck in the first innings. . . .'

Browne remembered nodding as he'd begun to understand the knowledge and reasoning behind the old pro's words. By Jove, yes. It was jolly-well up to them all right. . . .

'I'll do my best, Perkins.'

'No one can ask you to do more, sir.'

As he went back to his crease, Browne noticed one or two of the Kent fielders beginning to give the thundery sky dubious looks. Yet none of them seemed seriously perturbed; so far as Kent were concerned, this game would be well and truly over by the time the rains came.

And then he and Perkins were up to their necks once more in the battle with the two left-handers. Perkins was jerky, stiff and defiant, scoring – when he scored at all – with awkward little prods and deflections behind the wicket. Browne was a shade more ambitious, yet between them the two batsmen allowed the fielders to creep in closer and closer. For all his inexperience, Browne realized it was up to him to crack the threat which these presented.

The opportunity came in the next over. For the first time, Woolley overpitched and, jumping into the ball, Browne unceremoniously punched it to the boundary. Woolley's next ball was on a length, but – taking his life in his hands – the youngster treated it as a long hop, moving quickly back onto his stumps and carting it round, just backwards of square. The two short-legs retreated. For the first time, Browne was pleased to note an anxious air in the Kent side at the end of the over. The light, though still good, had a livid, almost artificial look.

The tea-interval came and went, almost unnoticed. Afterwards, he vaguely remembered spending it at a pavilion window, watching that sky grow ever more ominous, willing it to rain....

From the first ball after tea, Perkins sneaked a single. Much as Woolley had done earlier, Blythe now overpitched, and Browne, leaping down the wicket, drove the ball straight over the bowler's head and into the pavilion. It was a splendid, defiant blow: the St Lawrence crowd gave vent to a sigh of frustration and then burst into a round of generous applause. This youngster was a confounded nuisance – but, Lord! he had pluck, and it was good to watch him. The next ball, Browne tried the same ploy he had successfully used against Woolley. But this time he was lucky to get a thickish top edge to the ball which, skidding over the solitary slip, went for an inelegant boundary. Somewhat shaken by the narrowness of his escape, Browne played out the rest of the over like a good little book.

By half past five, he and Perkins had put on sixty together. Browne's score now stood at forty, but what really mattered was that he and Perkins were both still at the wicket. There was now only just under an hour to play. Fifty-eight minutes – or however many of those minutes the gathering storm might choose to leave them.

The Kent side was in conference now. Fielder, the fast bowler, was brought on to replace Woolley. In the thick air – now almost palpably solid – the ball, still red and shiny, thanks to the lush outfield, swung and dipped in the air like a hawking swallow. With his third ball, Fielder got his success, slanting it late into Perkins who, jabbing down awkwardly, could only help it onto his stumps. Perkins's shoulders slumped with shame and tired disappointment. As he turned to go back to the pavilion, he called over his shoulder, 'I reckon it's all up to you now, Mr Browne.'

Major Mauleverer, the next man in, looked worried. An attacking player on his day, holding-actions of this sort were not his idea of cricket at all. Without moving his feet, he swung wildly at his first ball and was easily caught in the covers.

In two balls, the County had slumped from 120–4 to 120–6. Alfie Patch, the number eight, nearly completed the disaster. He, too, waved a wild bat at his first ball – a late inswinger – and was almost bowled. To Hubble's intense disgust, the ball sneaked through and raced to the boundary for four byes. The last ball of Fielder's over was a yorker which missed the stumps by the proverbial whisker. As the fielders crossed, Patch stood at the other end of the wicket, his face wearing a bucolic, gap-toothed grin. Browne longed to walk the twenty-two yards and shake some sense into him.

But there was much more immediate business at hand. Blythe was on his mettle now, bowling with a certainty of control and variation that called for every last ounce of Browne's skill and concentration. Once he was dragged forward, so that his heel momentarily popped out of his ground. There was a yell of triumph as Hubble broke the wicket.

'Not out!' said the umpire.

Off Blythe's last ball, Browne managed to steal a single. Now he was faced with Fielder for the first time and knew that somehow – anyhow – he must quickly try to establish an ascendancy over the fast bowler. But the first ball of the over was nearly his undoing. It left him late, and he felt the tingle as it flicked off the edge of his bat and into the slips. There was a groan from the crowd as that safest of fielders – Woolley – proved that even he was fallible. Wringing his fingers and calling a rueful apology, the left-hander tossed the ball back to the bowler.

Fielder's next ball was short – not by much, a foot and a

137

half at the most. It climbed waspishly up at Browne's throat. His left foot instinctively slid back across his stumps and he hooked savagely. The crowd's applause broke over him like a wave. There was a brief search behind a line of waggonettes, and then the ball – now scarred from contact with something immovably solid – was thrown back onto the field by a man in a fawn bowler hat. Fielder's next ball seemed quite ordinary and, getting inside its line, Browne glanced it easily to the boundary. Once again the applause broke over him.

Heavens! Had he really scored fifty?

Browne acknowledged the cheers. It was pleasant to have got his half century – very pleasant – but there was still plenty to be done yet. For a start, he must get a single at the end of this over – *anything* to keep Alfie Patch away from Blythe.

But the Kent players were wise to this and denied him his run. Fielder's last ball, touched just a little too hard, was allowed to run over the boundary unchased. The batsmen had to walk back to their own ends – and Patch was faced with Blythe. Two balls were enough. . . . The first was swatted at blindly; the second left Patch sprawling halfway down the wicket, while Hubble stood victoriously over the stumps from which he had removed a single bail. 139–7.

The light was truly awful now, a vivid, electric brilliance, sandwiched beneath a canopy of almost solid blackness. Everything seemed drawn in harsh, precise lines. The air had become so damp it was difficult to breathe, and Browne was suddenly aware that his head ached intolerably. Oh, Lord! This game was so near to being saved – and yet. . . .

Wakefield, the next man in, had no defence at all to offer Blythe. He walked in front of his stumps, and the ball struck him on the pad. The umpire's finger went up almost before the bowler appealed. 139–8.

Bullstrode, the number ten, arrived at the wicket, bemused by advice and clearly in a state of nerves. He fumbled clumsily with his gloves and managed to drop his bat while taking guard. Two more wickets to fall and three balls left to the over, Browne thought despairingly. He stared up at the sky, willing the storm to break NOW, to strike him dead with its first lightning stroke, if need be – *anything*, just so long as the County didn't lose this game. Not now. . . .

As Bullstrode finished taking his guard, Browne gestured with his bat, telling the older man to just concentrate on keeping the ball out of his wicket. And, somehow, Bullstrode survived. The smile was gone from Blythe's gentle face now. He, too, looked tense and strained, and Browne remembered that the left-hander was rumoured to be subject to nervous disorders.

But this thought was quickly put from mind. Blythe's over was completed, and now Browne must face Fielder again. The fast bowler's face was as majestically thunderous as the sky. Browne slammed his first ball wide of cover, ran a couple – and then had to send the panicking Bullstrode back from what would have been a suicidal third. Ass! The second ball followed the first but, harder hit, reached the boundary. The next two he could only jab down on and trust to luck – a pair of beauties! The fifth he punched to the famous tree just inside the boundary, and, off the last, he got his precious single.

But where – *oh, where!* – was that bloody rain?

Then Blythe was at him again, the graceful, wheeling action fraught with menace and hostility, the ball shaping its delicate, dangerous curves in the humid air. Five balls were played, and again Browne managed to snatch a single off the sixth.

Fielder was replaced by Woolley – but a different Woolley from the kindly, avuncular pro who had spared the time to give him advice in the pavilion. Now, Woolley's face was set and resolute, being even more certain than Perkins that there would be little chance of play tomorrow. There were just two wickets to be got before that storm broke overhead – and the sooner these were done with the better. With his arm brushing high past his left ear, Woolley strove to put everything he knew into his first ball.

Perhaps it was his very determination that did it – but the ball was a shocker – a rank long-hop outside the leg-stump. Browne dropped on his left knee and thrashed the ball to the square-leg boundary. As he did so, the first lightning flash flickered across the ground, followed by a drum-roll of thunder.

But still no rain. . . .

Woolley's second ball was better – but Browne, realizing how precious seconds were being won every time the ball went to the boundary, leapt out and, risking the deep field, sent the ball one bounce into the crowd. There were more cheers from the ring – but the applause had a strained, feverish sound to it now. Advice – not all of it polite – was being freely offered to the Kent side.

Woolley's third ball coincided with the second lightning flash – and was a beauty. It whipped back across the youngster and, beating his forward lunge, took the leg-stump. . . .

Only as Browne began walking back to the pavilion did he notice the umpire's outstretched arm signalling a No-ball. But Bullstrode, that dithering ass, was wandering around outside his crease like a lost sheep. Someone shied the ball at his wicket with swift and underhand accuracy. The bails flew –

'How's thaa-aaa-aaaat?'

'Out!'

159–9.

And *still* no rain. . . .

Four balls left to the over, and the Kentishmen like cats round a mousehole to prevent a single. But all the same Browne got it off the last ball – an impertinent, cheekily mocking dab, down through the slips, which brought him back to face Blythe again.

But even as Browne rechecked his guard, he at last felt the icy ring of rain-drops, big as half-crowns, striking through his sweat-soaked shirt. For a moment, the umpires glared impotently upwards at the purple-blackness of the sky before gesturing towards the pavilion. No one needed telling twice, and – *sauve qui peut* – the players reached the boundary in a mad, undignified scramble. Fast as they ran, they were soaked before they got there. In ten minutes, the field became a lake whose slaty surface was pitted and pock-marked by the drilling rain.

In the pavilion, Browne's shoulders were pummelled black and blue. A great many kind and generous things were said to him – but best of all had been Frank Woolley's wink and confidential grin.

'I said we wouldn't have you quite so easily this time, Mr Browne. . . .'

And now the glory of that moment was lost, far, far away in a golden and totally irrecoverable past, Browne thought sadly as he reached the farmhouse door. The brilliant, ebullient Hutchings was dead; so, too, was Blythe, that most intuitive and artistic of slow left-handers.

Yes, Browne reminded himself, guiltily; and what about Perkins? That same, slow, ageing, disregarded pro whose calm and experienced sanity had really saved that game at Canterbury?

Dead, too. . . .

He had dyed his hair and moustache black, and had then declared himself to be at least fifteen years younger than his true age to some casual or uncaring recruiting sergeant. . . .

Well, he'd paid the price for that piece of romantic, absurd and middle-aged gallantry, drowned in a shell-hole near Passchendaele.

Pushing his way into the farmhouse, Browne wished that his straying thoughts had kept well away from cricket. The gap between that former, half-remembered yet halcyon existence and his present one seemed unbridgeable. There would be cricket again some day, he supposed. But that the game could ever be its old summery, splendid self seemed unlikely. How could it, when – after this war – there would be so many faces missing?

His own among them, maybe. . . .

Alone in his room, along the corridor at the back of the farmhouse, Lieutenant Peters sat alone with his terrors and an increasing awareness of his failure to be the man he wished himself to be. His thoughts were unpleasant ones. They concerned his last leave and the grubby encounter he'd had with a prostitute in a room off Soho that had ended in his utter rout and humiliation.

For, during that leave – the first he had not spent at home with his parents – Peters had been determined to lose his embarrassing and unwanted virginity. Like many another man before and since, he had unwisely talked much bigger than experience warranted. Driven as much by a sense that his ignorance might one day be found out as by any real urgency of lust, Peters had made up his mind to buy that elusive intimacy he felt so necessary to knowing himself a man.

For the first few days of his leave, though, Peters had not been able to screw his courage to the pitch that would let him accost a tart. Nor, perhaps significantly, did one accost him. He had spent the daylight hours mooning about the West End, looking at the girls: some, young and pretty; others, old and faded, brought back onto the streets by a long and demanding war. Few had aroused his enthusiasm.

His leave had been all but over when Peters had been brought face to face with at least the nastier realities of sex. Chance led him into the company of some old acquaintances from France. They hadn't been particularly pleased to see him but, being decent fellows, had been prepared to tolerate him. Their one idea, it seemed, was to get as tight as possible in the shortest time.

High among Peters's many other inadequacies was his total lack of a head for drink. Within three-quarters of an hour, therefore, Peters was decidedly drunk. The talk – mainly flying-shop at first – had turned risqué and had then focused itself on the swapping of sexual encounters, real or imaginary. Perhaps only Peters of the dozen or so young men present was naïve enough to be quite unaware of the fictional nature of many – if not most – of these anecdotes. Even as he himself boasted of several wholly apocryphal exploits, it struck him how much more worldly-wise his brother-officers seemed to himself. In his over-anxiety to prove himself a man among men, he unwisely uttered the boast that 'wine and company were all very well, but what he personally needed most at this moment was a damned good blow-through. . . .'

A rather shocked silence greeted this remark.

'Then why the bloody hell don't you damned-well shove off and find one?' enquired a red-haired man who'd never had much time for Peters in the past and who, for the last half-hour, had found himself liking him even less.

'Yes!' someone echoed – himself only too glad of any opportunity for getting shot of Peters. 'That's a jolly good idea. What d'you say, you fellows? Let's club together and send our intrepid birdman here off with the wherewithal to get his leg over –'

'And a bloody good dose of the clap, too – given luck,' a third added quietly – but not so quietly that Peters failed to hear him.

There had followed a humiliating few minutes in which the party had taken the advice of the second speaker and had filled Peters's cap with small change before bundling him unceremoniously out of the bar and into the street.

Somewhat uncertainly – a bottle of claret was more than enough for him – Peters got his bearings and made his way across the Charing Cross Road, through Greek Street and thence into Soho Square. For some reason, the streets were almost empty of their usual lilies, and Peters was forced to pursue his search further afield, wandering up and down Dean Street, then through little Hollen Street before he found what he was looking for.

Or, rather, before Gladys Biggs found him.

A great many years before, Gladys might just – by the very charitable – have been called pretty. Now, in 1917, and an ocean of gin and numberless clients the worse for wear, she looked exactly what she was – a raddled and hideous old bag. But, Peters couldn't see this in the blacked-out street. True, he heard her voice – ugly, cockney and hoarse – but, Hell! a fellow didn't go to bed with a woman for her voice, did he?

'Lookin' for someone to ease your mind, soldier?' Gladys said.

Peters tried to say that he was, in suitably man-of-the-world tones, but to his horror his voice emerged as a stuttering gulp. But Gladys, after a lifetime spent ministering to the needs of randy young men, took command of the situation.

'In the doorway of that shop over there or at my place? My place is extra.'

'Your place,' Peters said, in a voice as hoarse as Gladys's own.

The woman led the way through a maze of rank, cat-smelling alleys to a block of dark tenements. A spiral staircase went up the side of this, and Peters followed Gladys up the ringing iron stairs and along a passageway to a hutch of a room, smelling only marginally sweeter than the alleys.

This, Gladys knew, was the tricky moment: the moment when she must light the gas-mantle and her client got a long, hard look at her. She struck a match and half-shaded it with her fingers, fending off the evil moment as long as possible. Then, swiftly, she turned on the gas, put the match to the mantle – and with her free hand made a grab between Peters's thighs. From long experience, Gladys knew that a fellow wasn't likely to try dashing away leaving *that* clutched in her fist.

Peters gasped, shocked equally by his first sight of Gladys and the steely grip of her hand in his thigh. Christ! But, the wine taunted him, the old bitch was still a woman, wasn't she? And, as such, equipped to provide him what he'd come for?

'How much?' he muttered round a tongue that seemed too big for his mouth.

Gladys named her price – doubling it, seeing she'd got an officer, literally, in the palm of her hand. Blimey! She'd reckoned her days for officers were long over.... Before the Boer War, let alone this one....

'We'll forget the extra for coming back 'ere,' Gladys added generously, 'but let's see the colour of your money before we gets down to it.'

Peters slapped down a ten-shilling note and a handful of loose change onto the old tea-chest serving Gladys for a bed-side cabinet. She eyed the money greedily. Gawd! There was as much there as she sometimes made in a week.... Gladys put her free arm round Peters and pulled him towards her, half-choking him with the reek of cheap scent on her unwashed body. The bed-springs creaked resignedly as Peters was half-dragged, half-shoved down onto the unmade bed. Gladys's mouth closed wetly over his own, and her fumblings became urgent.

What happened to Peters in the next twenty minutes was humiliating in the extreme. Despite Gladys's professional skills, such as they were – or maybe even because of them – the sleeping and virginal worm between the airman's thighs remained mutinously dormant. The bottle of claret, Gladys's total lack of allure ... and, yes ... something that he had since come to recognize as being even more despicable and profoundly shameful had kept his courting-tackle defensively flaccid.

At first, Gladys had pretended a patience she was far from feeling, cooing in what were meant to sound like encouraging tones and caressing his still flesh. Gradually as success eluded her efforts, she became, by turns, first mocking, then angry, then downright scornful, jeering at Peters's inability to become tumescent.

At last she sat up and dug Peters painfully in the groin.

'Public School, aincher?' she sneered. 'You shouldn't have picked yourself a woman, sonny. I know your sort. What you need is a nice little boy scout with a pretty pink arse. . . .'

Peters hit her then, and she became afraid. In nearly forty years on the game, she'd met all sorts and had had some pretty nasty frights in her time. One way and another, she supposed, she'd been beaten up on an average of at least twice a year. And, come to think of it, she didn't go much on the look in this fellow's eyes, either. . . . He'd been drinking, yes: and his eyes were pink like a ferret's. . . . But there was something of that same mad, dangerous meanness you saw in a ferret's eye, too. . . . Officer or not, this nasty little toad grovelling around in her bed frightened her. She opened her mouth as Peters raised his hand to hit her again.

'Piss off, yer nasty little bugger-boy! For Christ's sake, get outer here and take yer bleedin' money wiv yer!'

With a sudden, savage shove, Gladys rolled Peters off the bed and onto the floor, jumping after him and pushing him towards the door. She grabbed at the money lying beside the bed and hurled it at him. A flying penny nicked his cheek, and a half-crown opened a cut over his eye. With a final screech and a heave, Gladys bundled Peters out of the room, slammed the door shut on him and slammed home the bolt.

Peters found himself standing in the draughty passage, his trousers and underpants round his ankles, watched by a gawping private of the Hampshires and his tittering doxy. Ignoring these, he pulled his disarranged clothing together and buttoned himself up, an inglorious and contemptible figure, and slunk off pursued by Gladys's traumatic accusation.

Now, alone in his room at Brick-Kiln Farm, it seemed to Peters that in the woman's taunt lay the clue to an odious and unthinkable discovery about his own true self.... He remembered his almost jealous affection for certain boys at school – pretty fellows, always rather younger than himself.... Jones or Wilmslow.... Or Prendergast, who had always flounced around like a little tart....

Yes – and worse than this remembrance – was the shock his body had given him this morning. While doing his rounds with Hopkins, Peters's eye had been caught by a young aircraftsman bent across a work bench, his breeches pulled tightly across his buttocks. Unconsciously – at first, anyway – the sight had stirred something in Peters. Then the boy had stood, wiping a blond lock of hair from one eye. Peters felt the treacherous worm in his thighs thicken and erect itself, responding to some instinct that Gladys's caresses had failed to rouse. Peters had gasped and faltered.

'You feelin' all right, sir?' Hopkins had asked.

'Of course I am, you bloody fool!' the lieutenant had managed to snarl before putting the aircraftsman on a charge for some purely imaginary misdemeanour.

Was it imagination, or had he really caught in Flight-Sergeant Hopkins's eye much the same expression of recognition and accusation that he'd seen in Gladys's?

The legend of Destrier's short flight on that break-away kite had persisted and stayed with him in the service. As such stories will, it had become exaggerated in the telling, a flight of fancy, a myth. Nor had it done Destrier any harm. On the contrary, it had set him apart, making him someone to be watched with interest. By the time war came, Destrier had stripes on his arm and his name had been put forward for flying training by a CO who recognized in him someone with an instinctive flair for aviation. But, at first, Destrier had had to content himself with flying as an observer. In December, 1914, he had bagged an enemy plane with six remarkable and lucky shots from a Lee-Enfield, was awarded the DCM and posted home to Upavon in Wiltshire for that long-promised flying-training.

As had been predicted, Destrier proved himself to be a natural. In his hands, even the clumsy Farman – the immortal Rumpety – had been made to dance like a ballerina. When he had returned to France, late in 1915, he had been sent to a scout squadron – and had been commissioned. The DH2 with which his squadron had been equipped had pleased and suited Destrier, but his first two months at the Front had been quiet ones. It hadn't been till the Christmas Eve that he'd at last made his first definite kill – a Rumpler brought down with a quarter-drum of Lewis.

Once he'd made this start, his score began to mount rapidly.

SIX

With little or nothing to do now R.45 was ponderously churning her way towards the Kent coast, Walter allowed himself to remember again what it felt like to be shot down. Three times it had happened to him – and three times Fortune had smiled in his direction and he had survived.

On each of these three occasions, though, his observer had been killed. And, although each of these observers had been officers and therefore, in Walter's book, no great loss to anyone, the cumulative effect on his own nerves had brought him dangerously near to breaking point.

Against his will, Walter recalled the first time he had stared the Dark Angel squarely between the eyes and had survived to tremble at the memory of the experience.

Speaking no ill of the dead was all very well, Walter told himself, but the creator of that proverb had quite obviously never met Lieutenant Pohle. And Pohle had been a first-class, twenty-two-carat shit – a stiff-necked, supercilious snob who, from the rear-cockpit of a Rumpler, had made it very plain that he regarded his pilot as a not very bright member of the servant class; a mindless chauffeur, fit only to fly according to the lordly bidding of his master, and someone to be kept properly in his place at all times.

Walter had hated and feared Pohle. With painful clarity he remembered the last morning the lieutenant had walked this earth: vainglorious, arrogant, stupid and totally oblivious of danger. Theirs had been the third of a trio of observation planes sent out to recce and photograph an irritating little bulge in the British lines. Their expected escort had failed to materialize, and within a few minutes of realizing this to be the case, they had become the sole representative of the trio when its other two members had turned back with engine-trouble – or, to Walter's mind, plain cold feet. Not that he blamed them. If Lieutenant Pohle had had any sort of sense in that close-cropped bullet head of his, then they would have done likewise. But no, Pohle had chosen to press on to their objective alone, in solitary and vulnerable splendour.

When they had arrived on target, it had looked – for a short while at least – as though they might get away with their presumption. The sky appeared to be empty of British aircraft, and Pohle had shot-off a whole boxful of plates over that annoying little salient, while Walter, mouthing a ceaseless flow of obscenities to mask his fear, had kept the leeriest of weather-eyes open for the enemy as they'd stooged sedately up and down the line of trenches five thousand feet below.

The end, when it came, had been sudden, murderous – and totally unexpected. Walter had just begun to congratulate himself on their miraculous fortune when a ridiculous popping noise had begun from beneath the Rumpler's lower wing. The noise had been repeated and the two-seater had immediately fallen away, out of control. Walter had heard someone screaming distantly – himself! He'd wrestled with the controls. The Rumpler had answered him momentarily before falling away again. For a second time, Walter succeeded in righting her. The two-seater flew straight and level for a few moments – and then plunged down in a lunatic dive that tallied with nothing in his experience. The stick went limp and useless in his hands: a fountain of oil spewed back from the engine, smearing his goggles and clogging his nostrils. The engine clattered like a lawn-mower, and the airscrew ceased to turn.

Suddenly, and for no apparent reason, the Rumpler eased out of its dive. As it did so, Walter glimpsed a small angular shape whipping into the attack over his right shoulder. Christ! A DH2! It dived away, behind and beneath the Rumpler, as if coming in for a third attack. Walter heard himself pleading and sobbing frantically that this wasn't fair! that he'd had enough! that he was finished! Evidently the British pilot must have felt the same: that third attack never materialized. . . .

Gliding, falling, recovering and then falling again, the two-seater plummeted down towards the German lines. Luckily for Walter, it had hit the ground in one of its more controlled periods; and, paradoxically, by this time, he had ceased to be afraid. Detached and apart from himself, his interest was purely academic as he watched the jumbled earth rush up to smash him. Quite relaxed now, he sat back in his seat and waited for the inevitable. The Rumpler's wheels struck the sand-bagged parapet of a trench half-a-metre from its top. The two-seater's forward momentum stopped immediately and she stood vertically on her nose for a long moment before completing her somersault. The noise must have been incredible – but, so far as Walter was afterwards concerned, the crash had been as silent as a film. As he sat in his cockpit – still quite detached and unmoved – he had watched the Rumpler breaking into pieces around him, and even now he could recollect quite clearly and rationally the order in which everything had fallen off or been smashed.

The troops who had rescued him had been surprised to find him alive at all, let alone in one piece and without so much as a scratch. Pohle had not been so lucky. His body had been catapulted from the cartwheeling wreck and had fetched up some fifty or so metres away, sprawled across a thicket of barbed-wire like a discarded rag doll. Not that this mattered. Crash or no crash, Pohle would have still been dead – at least four of the DH2 pilot's bullets had ripped through the Lieutenant's body from rectum to skull. Either way, Walter thought, you could say that Pohle had got it through the brain....

To his rescuers' surprise, Walter had been calm and rational and able to view his observer's body with cool dispassion. Indeed, in their eyes, he seemed to regard the whole episode as something of a joke.... Only later – and in privacy – had the reaction set in....

Though he would never know it, Walter had been Destrier's tenth and final victim in a DH2.

'Out!'
   'Wha-at?'

'I said, "Out", O Recording Angel – and "Out" I meant. . . .'

For once Morton-Dunne forgot his habitual pose of classical gravity and allowed himself the luxury of an exceedingly rude monosyllable.

Browne put his hands over his ears, crossed his eyes and contrived to look shocked.

'Shhhhh! Not in front of the children. I know they didn't even try to teach you any decent manners at Wellington, but I've always thought of your parents as a most respectable couple – even if they did let you become a gunner. So just try to be a credit to them will you – and remember that the umpire's word is final!'

Morton-Dunne sighed and handed over the chipped ruler that served Browne and himself as a bat in their impromptu games of waste-paper basket cricket. He knew that doing so would mean the next quarter of an hour at least foraging in the darkest and unlikeliest corners of the room, searching for the india-rubber they used as a ball.

Browne took his stance in front of the waste-paper basket with all the formality of a batsman opening a test innings. He scratched an imaginary guard on the worn carpet, stared round the room as though inspecting Morton-Dunne's field-setting and then pointed his ruler at the flocculating stag's head over the settle.

'I say, old chap, your cover-point's an unpleasant looking bugger.'

'Shh! Not so loud. He's on the committee of the MCC.'

'Ah! that explains it.'

'Play!' Morton-Dunne flipped the rubber towards the waste-paper basket. The rubber's squared edges made its break quite unpredictable, yet with his quick footwork and keen cricketer's senses, Browne contrived to hit the rubber – and to keep on hitting it – with a precision that filled Morton-Dunne (no mean club player himself) with a despairing envy.

Failing to budge Browne from his place at the wicket, Morton-Dunne began pitching the rubber in faster and faster. His final shy dropped outside the line of Browne's legs causing it to duck and turn at a right-angle across Browne's body. Instinctively, Browne invented the shot to play it. He sank on his haunches and, cutting square, smashed the rubber deep into the smouldering fire-place.

'Lord!' Browne muttered, awed by his own virtuosity, 'I'll never play a shot like that again, I bet you.'

An inexplicable tingle of foreboding went down Morton-Dunne's spine.

'Don't be an ass, Reggie.'

Even as he spoke, the telephone began to ring.

Sitting alone in the cuddy that he shared with Mackail, Hopkins was completing some returns in his round orphanage hand. Like any sensible man, he detested unnecessary paperwork, though like any experienced soldier, he knew that, come-hell-or-high-water, both War Office and Air Board considered the correct filling-in of routine forms to be infinitely more important than the mere winning or losing of battles. At this very moment, the length and breadth of supposedly civilized Europe, men like himself – French, German, Austrian, Italian and Belgian Hopkinses – were all sitting in similarly make-shift offices, all busily indenting in triplicate for this or invoicing that, counter-signing memoranda, forwarding the appropriate carbon copies to the proper quarters, filing others, emending, reporting, requesting, advising. . . . Christ! What a way to fight a war. Perhaps the whole bloody business would only come to an end when it choked on a vile conglomerate of muck and cheap, buff paper – like some monstrous latrine.

Hopkins threw down his pen and poured himself another mug of dark brown tea. He stood and, stripping off his tunic, eyed young Russell's head of shapeless and oily woollens with distaste. Now, he told himself, it was high time he began thinking about climbing into that lot. . . .

He reached for the packet of Gold Flake – and then changed his mind. No – to smoke one more cigarette would simply be a putting-off of the inevitable. Better by far to be open with himself and to admit quite freely that what he had set himself to do this evening scared him sideways. Yes – he must confess his fear, his complete funk, and then get changed. Half-amused at himself, half in earnest, Hopkins scowled into a small square of mirror propped up over the fire-place.

'Hopkins,' he told his speckled reflection, 'you're a windy bastard....'

He thumbed his nose at himself, then turned away to begin changing. As he cocooned himself warmly in Russell's sweaters – too warmly in the room's well-heated atmosphere – Hopkins allowed his mind to ponder the question of just why it was he detested flying so much. It seemed odd, he knew – and yet, as he was aware, he was by no means unique among air-mechanics in this: Mackail had admitted much the same sentiment. It was a curious phenomenon that so many men whose lives revolved around aircraft and engines (and who, on the ground, treated both with the devoted and solicitous care of a mother for her children) should be loth to put their trust in either engine or aircraft when themselves asked to fly. Hopkins chuckled to himself; if you asked *him*, the answer to that was simple: both mechanics and fitters knew far too much to be at all easy in their minds once free of the ground. For someone like himself, with his clever hands idle and denied active purpose, what else was there to do when flying but to sit with ears strained for a false engine-note, or with finger-ends twitching, wondering whether a quarter-turn more or less on screw, nut or turn-buckle might not have been made with advantage? – and reminding himself all the while what a bloody long way down the ground was....

And yet, Hopkins thought, recalling his brief spell as an observer, a man would have to be pretty mean of soul if, when flying, he couldn't rise above his fears to a sense of glory. And there was something else, too, a curious paradox that puzzled him deeply. Never once – except returning in a shot-up aircraft – had he landed without experiencing a strange and sad sense of loss, of disappointment and anti-climax. There were more senses than one in which a man came down to earth when his aircraft's wheels touched the ground....

This last thought brought his mind back to the man up-stairs: Destrier. Surely, Laurie had *always* known such things, understanding them in some instinctive, intuitive way before he'd even flown, perhaps? But then, Hopkins thought, remembering distant days with Destrier, Laurie had never really given away more than a fraction of what was going on within him. And, although the two of them had perhaps known and understood each other as far as any two people with quite different personalities could, Hopkins had always been aware of, and had respected, those facets and places in the other marked 'Private – Keep Out.' From quite early on in their friendship, Hopkins had learnt to recognize the ex-istence of this reserve in the other: what Laurie Destrier saw fit to tell, he would tell – eventually, and in his own good time; that – and nothing more.

Hopkins considered the recent past, with its gradual sever-ing of the links that had shaped their friendship. Inevitable, really, he supposed. Even in the small world of the RFC, their postings had separated them. At first they had both written, but then their letters, in the usual way of things had grown less and less frequent, and had then ceased altogether. Once, Hopkins remembered receiving a torn and dog-eared letter that had apparently been chasing him round France for months. At the time, he had stuffed the envelope into a pocket with oily hands that he hadn't found time to wash for several days, and had turned back to the bench over which – so it felt – he had been bent for an eternity.... Later, he had read Destrier's letter without much interest. So.... Laurie had been commissioned, had he? The best of blooming luck. ...

Was it jealousy or just plain weariness that had made him react that way, he now wondered? Hopkins wished he could be certain; for unless a man was honest with himself, he could be honest with no one. Eventually he had managed to contrive some sort of a reply to Destrier – a stilted and rather pom-pously formal note that had begun 'Dear Mr Destrier' and had ended 'Yours, Respectfully, Sydney J. Hopkins, Sgt.' The Lord alone knew what Destrier had made of this at the time (though Hopkins now had a pretty good idea!). Anyway, their letters had once more ceased.

After this, he had only heard of Destrier by hearsay. A good officer, by most accounts; not a chap to take liberties with, but one quite lacking in side, and very decent – providing you weren't flying an aircraft with black crosses on it.

Their paths had crossed only once, a few weeks before Destrier's savage encounter over Nine-Tree Wood, when Hopkins and a couple of mechanics had been detailed to take a spare engine on a lorry up to a neighbouring squadron near Petit Mariecourt. Hopkins had been quite unaware that this was the squadron with which Destrier had at the time been serving and he had been taken completely off guard when someone had peremptorily tugged at his sleeve while he was supervising the off-loading of the engine. Angry at being accosted in this way, he had turned indignantly, only saluting at the last moment when he saw the offender was an officer – and, managing to imply that, officer or no officer, he thought him damned rude. Quite unabashed, the other had stared at him quizzically.

'Well . . . I can see you're a Flight-Sergeant now, but in my book you're still an awful bloody snob, "Yours respectfully" or not, Sydney J. Hopkins. . . .'

Hopkins had felt the blood rising into his cheeks and had been aware of a sudden feeling of shame.

'Was it *that* bad?'

The other looked surprised.

'Wasn't that how it was meant to be?'

'Of course it wasn't.'

'Well, from my end it was like getting a painful – and very deliberate – kick in the arse.'

'I'm sorry.'

Destrier had grinned suddenly, the smile masking just how thin and drawn his face had become.

'You always were an independent cuss. . . .'

Hopkins had found himself grinning back.

'That's bloody good, coming from you . . . sir!'

They had both laughed at this, suddenly and happily at ease with each other. They had chatted for a while as the two airmen finished their unloading and afterwards Destrier had climbed onto the running-board of the lorry and squeezed into the cab beside Hopkins, driving back with them as far as the village before taking his leave.

'So long, Syd. . . .'

Hopkins had leaned out of the cab to take the other's hand and say with a sudden impulse of emotion, 'Good luck and, for Gawd's sake look after yourself, will you, Lol!'

Destrier had gestured rudely and kicked at the lorry's rear tyre.

'Go on! Bugger off, you old sod!'

Two weeks later, Hopkins had been posted to Hendon. Here, he first heard the rumour that Destrier had been shot down and, later, when this was confirmed, had managed to discover his whereabouts in a hospital on the outskirts of London. He had paid Destrier one or two embarrassed visits. They had found little to say to each other, and Hopkins had been shocked and dismayed at the extent of his friend's disfigurement. It had moved him to see how one dark and attractive nurse obviously failed to share his distress. To Hopkins it seemed quite obvious that the girl was in love with Destrier, and that Destrier, whether he knew it or not, was in love with her. Later, he congratulated himself on his perception when he heard of Destrier's marriage – but, even in the same breath, so it now seemed, he had heard of the girl's senseless death.

Meeting Destrier again this afternoon, Hopkins had been shocked by the change in him. It had been nothing to do with his scarred face this time; it had been his eyes. They had been blank, empty, fathomless – the eyes of a man looking inwards on himself, contemplating an inner scarring worse than that borne by his body.

Hopkins finished his tea and sighed. At that moment, the door of the cuddy was flung open and Lieutenant Browne burst in, beside himself with excitement.

'The Hun's on his way!' he yelled. 'Morton-Dunne's just had it on the phone.'

'Where?' Hopkins demanded, grabbing up gauntlets and helmet.

'Somewhere over Northfleet, so far as we could gather,' Browne went on breathlessly. 'That's all we could get. The phone went dead before we could find out how many Huns there are supposed to be – or even where we're to patrol.'

'Did you try the other phone?'

'That was dead, too.'

'Bugger!' Hopkins moved over to the window and thrust its makeshift curtain aside. He flung the window up violently.

'Mac!' Hopkins bellowed into the darkness. A torch was flashed towards him and an answering yell told him that Mackail had understood. Hopkins turned to Browne.

'I'll go upstairs and see to the Flight-Commander. And you'd better be thinking of getting yourself kitted up, hadn't you, sir?'

Browne's grin and bubbling reaction were those of the schoolboy he might just still have been had the war not come.

'Lord, yes, Flight! I should say so. . . . How ripping! You can bet your sweet life on it!' he shouted and skidded out of the room as unceremoniously as he had entered.

'Gone to get his ruddy pads on, I shouldn't wonder,' Hopkins said to himself, but only half-mockingly. For, come to that, his own first reaction to this news of the enemy had been every bit as absurd as Browne's. Self-consciously, Hopkins picked up the gauntlets and helmet he had dropped in his rush to open the window. The way he had just thoughtlessly snatched them up in the first place must have looked pretty foolish. Such symptoms of nerves and excitement were all very well – laudable even – in a youngster like Browne. But in a man of his age and experience they were ridiculous. It was his job to give an appearance of steadiness and disciplined calm – even if he felt neither.

Hopkins sat down and unlaced and removed his boots. He reached over to his bed for the heavy, thigh-length socks that Russell had lent him. He wrinkled his nose with distaste at these. Pheeew! Evidently young Russell wasn't as meticulous in his laundry habits as his mother had been in her knitting. Still, beggars couldn't be choosers, and – clean or otherwise – the socks were at least comfortingly thick and warm. Hopkins pulled a pair of them up over his breeches and covered them with a second pair. Around their tops, Russell had sewn an unmatching pair of girl's garters, both inscribed in marking-ink, 'To Bobby' – one from 'Lily', the other from 'Kate'. Hopkins grinned. Ah-ha.... Trophies of the chase, apparently. There was evidently rather more to young Russell than at first met the eye....

Hopkins's grin faded as he remembered Browne's message about the broken telephone lines. He swore softly. The bloke who had chosen the route for these ought to be strung up on a length of his own wire. A mile from Brick-Kiln Farm the telephone lines had been carelessly strung across the only good road leading out of the army camp on the Ness. Twice already in 'D' Flight's short stay on the marsh, the lines had been brought down by ASC lorries moving along the road in darkness. Now, with no proper idea where to look – nor even what to look for – 'D' Flight's first patrol looked like being a proper Fred Karno affair. A monumental cock-up....

Mackail stuck his head in through the still open window.

'I take it we're under starter's orders, Flight?'

'We are.'

'Then I'll away and see to the flare-path.'

Hopkins reached for the heavy, fleece-lined fug-boots lying beneath his bed.

'Good old Mac....' he said; then, without thinking, he added the words which at the time sounded so innocent and which were to haunt him the rest of his lifetime, 'You know, Angus, come what may, I reckon you're the one bloke round here who can be counted on to keep his head....'

Despite the cold, von Trier had moved into R.45's nose, where, in the exposed for'ard cockpit, the icy slipstream boomed and bombinated against his helmeted head. As his night-vision improved with each passing moment, he became aware of northern Kent unrolling beneath him as something sensed as much as seen, an ill-defined and barely tangible facsimile of the maps left behind in the cabin, drawn with just sufficient and recognizable certainty for him to allow himself a small glow of self-satisfaction for his faultless dead reckoning. Regardless of the lack of moonlight, the light layer of snow which covered the landscape beneath appeared to glow with a grey and sombre luminescence.

Between its frame of the Kent and Essex shores, the Thames Estuary – an area of unrelieved blackness – lay like a half-open fan with its handle pointing towards London. Now, von Trier knew, that even were he the world's worst navigator, he could scarcely fail to find his target. They had raised Margate and left that town behind some twenty minutes earlier, and were now flying over the flat levels of the Isle of Sheppey where, from Sheerness or nearby, several batteries of guns were beginning to send up a storm of angry and remarkably inaccurate fire. With detached and academic interest, von Trier watched the shell-bursts splashing briefly against the pitch blackness of the sky and tried to gauge their distance. Two miles away – three, even – he guessed, before bowing into the direct blast of the slipstream again, peering down to where, slightly to port, the mouth of the river Medway – a sable gash joining the main estuary – gave him his next landmark.

Von Trier did a few rapid calculations. Only another thirty miles remained before R.45's main objective would be reached. At something just under eighty miles an hour that meant twenty to twenty-five minutes.

To von Trier's logical mind there was only one possible worry now – that a fighter, or fighters, would home onto them by the simple expedient of working out that a bomber's simplest and most obvious route into London was to follow that tell-tale ribbon of blackness beneath. Not that this worried him unduly. It would be a very exceptional – and lucky – pilot who, providing he had the necessary height and night-vision, caught a glimpse of R.45's ponderous bulk moving above the only marginally lighter terrain beneath – a shadow passing across a shadow ... and even then, von Trier felt, there was little to be feared from any fighter encountered singly, even supposing that an attacker managed to hold on to his tenuous contact. Should he do so, the advantage of fire-power would lie with the bomber. Other Staaken commanders had chosen to strip their aircraft of guns in a bid to save precious weight, but to the Count this had seemed an illogical, if not downright dangerous, policy, and he had made it his business to see that R.45 carried her designed complement of guns. Further, he had taken care to select his gunners person-nally, had trained them to concert pitch and was confident of their ability to deal with any fighter unlucky enough to find itself caught in the web of their crossfire. When attacked, R.45 was an exceedingly dangerous animal, well prepared and able to defend herself – as witness that wretched FE2b on their first mission. . . .

Damn! von Trier thought, why had he had to remember that? The two figures who had tumbled from their burning machine might have been any airmen, English or German; his own crew. . . . Walter, Schmidt, Mendelssohn, Rossi, Wen-del, Horst. . . .

Himself. . . .

Behind von Trier, in the Staaken's cabin – and quite un-troubled by any thoughts similar to his Commander's – Horst sat up very stiff and correct at the bomber's controls. The posture was an uncomfortable one which made his bottom ache, but Horst affected not to notice this, proudly conscious not only of being over enemy territory but of drawing nearer each minute to the very heartland of that enemy. Horst set his face in what he hopefully imagined was a sternly martial ex-pression, and wished again that his father – that despised small-town official – could see him now. . . .

Poor Horst. His attempt to look the epitome of soldierly belligerence was a failure. Seated next to him, glancing across at his superior, Walter idly wondered whether the poor old Sausage's look and manner were due to acute piles. . . . If so, Walter sympathized.

At the rear of the cabin – and solid as a rock now that the

time of danger had actually arrived – Wendel was concerned only with his pumps. As the gauges fluctuated and told their varying tales, his hands went down to the pump-wheels and with a few turns, on or off, equalized the tanks and, with them, R.45's trim. On von Trier's instructions, Wendel emptied the outer tanks first. Empty tanks – or rather, tanks full of petrol vapour – were infinitely more volatile and liable to explode when pierced by a bullet than full ones. Wendel put the thought of exploding petrol tanks carefully out of mind, returned his attention to his gauges and then moved his hand along the bank of wheels. Already no. 5 pump was up to its usual tricks and requiring twice the attention of its neighbours. Resolutely, Wendel kept his mind from wondering whether no. 5 pump had got an air-lock in its system – an air-lock which would finally come to roost in the carburettors of one of the thunderously cacophonous Maybachs. . . .

To Mendelssohn, gritting his teeth and beginning the long climb from the comparative security of his cockpit to his icy perch on R.45's upper wing, there was nothing at all cacophonous in this thunder of engines beating about his ears. On the contrary, the Maybachs' impassioned throb and roar, their harmonic surge of controlled violence, reminded him more than ever of a symphony by Beethoven. As he climbed, he began to analyse the instrumentation and form of this roar, his quick musician's ear sorting out the separate parts from the whole, so that with his knowledge of the internal workings of the Maybachs he was able to know just what notes each racing, pulsing, busy part played in the sum total of sound. It was in this moment that, at last, the small beginnings of his own third movement began to stir and shape themselves in his head: a solid thunder of brass and drums, a sort of clamorous groundswell, not dissimilar to that now bellowing beneath his booted heels. The rest of the movement was not yet clear in his head, except that Mendelssohn knew that what must follow demanded a shift in key – a daring shift into the hackneyed and unfashionable key of C Major. Somehow he must make the strings flow in unison out of the swelling brass and then, over all, would rise the voice of his solo violin, in half-sad, half-triumphant affirmation – like a huge *Te Deum*. . . .

Mendelssohn pushed his body through the lubber's-hole of R.45's top-plane and strapped himself into the safety-harness beside his Lewis gun. His limbs felt like soggy sponge in the icy argument of the wind as he groped for the drums which held the weapon's ammunition. He found them in place and then felt for the Lewis's spade-grip with his gauntleted hands, flexing the gun on its mounting to make sure it had not iced up. The Lewis answered him with fluid smoothness. Good! He released the safety-catch and fired a short warming-burst into the night, the spade-grip jarring on his wrists and the muzzle-flash dulling his hard-earned night-vision. Mendelssohn thumbed the safety-catch back into place and, ducking his head, hunched himself into a ball against the battering slipstream. From now on, his only part was to watch and wait. . . . Somewhere deep down in the innermost recesses of his brain, the majestic theme for his last movement began to bubble and ferment, fed on the yeasty tumult of the engines below him.

Out on the port-wing, in the corresponding perch to Mendelssohn's, Otto Schmidt felt infinitely less happy. In his climb up the ladder to the top-plane, a moment of carelessness had nearly flung Schmidt into the void below. He had slipped off the ladder and, for a moment, had been left swinging by one hand as the prop-stream, blasting against his body, had tried to stretch him out horizontally like some bizarre pennant on a flag-pole. In his terrified struggle not to lose his grip on the ladder, Schmidt had lost a boot and a gauntlet. These – as he had all but done – hurtled away into the darkness below, narrowly missing the wooden propeller of the rear Maybach.

Now, seated on the top-wing, with his Lewis untested, Schmidt was endeavouring as best he could to shelter both hand and foot from the searching cold. Already both extremities were shouting with an agony of chill far worse than that felt by the rest of his body. Worse, the agony was spreading upwards from his exposed limbs to affect the rest of his body like an icy gangrene. Schmidt gritted his teeth and, closing his

eyes in an effort to quell his rising panic, cursed himself for
the cocksure exhibitionism with which he had always treated
that hazardous climb up the ladder. Tonight – unseen – such
flamboyance had been as ill-considered and unnecessary as it
had also been foolhardy. Now, maybe, there would be a price
to pay for his stupidity. There remained the best part of an
hour still for him to endure, exposed above the wing, before
R.45 was back over the sea and he was free to climb down
again. A lot could happen in an hour. And, when the time
came, would his stiffening body still be able to force its way
down to safety? It had better be. There'd been a fellow in
R.126 who for some reason had found himself unable to make
it. . . .

And, bleakly, Schmidt was only too aware of what had happened to *him*.

Frostbite. . . .

Death. . . .

At Brick-Kiln Farm, Sergeant Mackail had taken charge of
the ground-crews and was busy organizing a flare-path across
the clinkered field. What little wind there was now blew from
that end of the field bordered by the deepest and widest
of the three ditches – a fact allowing only the shortest possible take-off run. In these conditions, the three aircraft –
particularly the two-seater Bristol – would have precariously
little leg-room to get themselves into the air.

Men disappeared into the darkness carrying sawn-off
petrol-drums filled with petrol-soaked cotton-waste. Each
man had been issued with a box of matches, and each – at a
signal (in this case, three longs blasts on his whistle, or a single
red Very light) – would light a match, toss it into his petrol-
drum and leap clear. The result would be a flare-path twenty
yards wide down which the aircraft would run before becoming airborne. On the low bank of the dyke, Mackail had placed
a trio of red storm-lanterns to mark the limits of the runway.
Looking towards these, their dim glow smeared by pale intimations of mist, Mackail thought the margin of error they

allowed was frighteningly small. If anyone made a cock-up of his take-off tonight or his engine failed to give full-revs at a critical moment, it would mean a chilly ducking at best. . . .

Mackail shrugged such possibilities out of mind. It was no good thinking that way . . . things were out of his hands now, and in those of providence. Between them, he and Hopkins – theirs hands sometimes frozen beyond pain as they had worked – had done their level best with the engines of the three serviceable aircraft. In record time they had stripped and refurbished these, pampered and tested them. Now, the rest was up to chance, and to the trio of very different pilots who would soon be climbing up into the cockpits of the three aircraft. Destrier and Browne could be relied on, Mackail knew – but that supercilious twat Peters? Never mind *him*, Mackail reassured himself callously. If Mr-bloody-Peters managed to break his neck, he'd be no great loss to anyone – himself included.

Over by the sagging Bessonau, Mackail heard the roar of the BE12's Factory engines being started. Despite earlier warmings, they seemed to be taking their time getting into stride, and he listened anxiously to their dubious and uncertain clatterings. Above this racket of warming engines, Mackail heard someone's voice raised in angry warning at the clumsiness of some offending aircraftsman as half a dozen mechanics began moving one of the BEs out to the beginning of the flight-path. Evidently the warning came too late and someone yelped with pain as 1700 pounds of aircraft were trundled over his foot.

Clumsy bastard, Mackail thought dispassionately.

Still, despite this mishap and, odds and sods though the majority of the men might be, Mackail was agreeably surprised by everyone's performance so far. At Hopkins's insistence, and despite the interference of Peters, Mackail had found time to practise the present procedure since 'D' Flight had first mustered at Brick-Kiln Farm. As he was well aware, this practising had done nothing to increase his popularity with men already sorely overworked and lacking even the simplest amenities of decent living. He hadn't cared – and now the way everything was going proved his perseverance to have been worthwhile. Despite his rehearsals, Mackail had more than half-expected the real thing to be a hickaboo; instead, there was a heartening lack of confusion and fuss. Mackail crossed his fingers – and allowed himself just the smallest glow of self-satisfaction. Mind! he told himself, the voice of native pessimism reasserting itself, there was still plenty of time even now for something to go wrong.

Mackail turned as he heard the scrunch of footsteps on the frosty cinders behind him. The tall figure of Morton-Dunne materialized at his shoulder, and Mackail was thankful that things were going so well. There was an indefinable something about the Gunner-Lieutenant that made a man want his approval – just as there was an all-too-definable something about that bastard Peters that made a bloke not give a toss either way.

'Everything under control, Sergeant?'

'What else, sir?'

Morton-Dunne gave a dry chuckle.

'That sounds dangerously like hubris to me, Mackail. . . .'

'What's yon when it's at home, sir?'

'The pride that goeth before a fall – so the old Greeks used to say.'

The pessimist in Mackail approved the idea.

'Verra sensible of them, I'd say, sir. I was just thinkin' along much the same lines m'sel. Funny how some puir bastard always seems to get it in the neck just when things look fine.'

Morton-Dunne turned his head sharply.

'That's not a piece of your Highland granny's sixth-sense, I hope, Sergeant?'

'No, sir,' Mackail laughed. 'More like her grandson's long experience of Sod's Law – if ye'll pardon the expression. "If things can possibly go wrong – then they will."'

It was Morton-Dunne's turn to laugh.

'Then you have no dark presentiments about impending fate, Sergeant?'

'No, sir – only about what Flight Hopkins'll have to say if

he finds me standin' round gossiping like an old fishwife.'

'Point taken, Mackail. I'll leave you to get on with it.'

Mackail watched Morton-Dunne's shadowy figure disappear towards the aircraft. It struck him that what had just passed between himself and Morton-Dunne had been a pretty odd sort of conversation for men supposedly preparing for war. Yet, all the same, he *was* conscious of a vague unease within himself, a small sense of impending danger.

Blast Morton-Dunne! Things *were* going too well. Mackail felt he would be grateful for some small, not-too-serious hitch to occur. And, at that moment, as if in answer to his wish, one of the flare-path detail, straying too near the edge of the field, lost his footing and, with a crackle of breaking ice and a splash, fell into the ditch, from which he was hauled amidst a general confusion of shouts and unsympathetic laughter.

Mackail grinned, his small moment of apprehension over. So that's what his presentiment had amounted to, had it? Well ... it would be something to chuckle over later with Hopkins....

Until he had become conscious of the sounds of increasing activity beneath his window, announcing the warning of a German raid, Destrier had pushed into the back of his mind the predicament he had faced a couple of weeks ago at Cranwell. Then, to his disgust, he had found it necessary for him to endure allowing himself to be dressed for flying like a child. Spring, the Australian, had done the job for him, and Destrier had forced himself to pass the whole thing off as a joke.

But it was a joke he did not like. In reality, he had found his weak helplessness a matter for distaste and embarrassment. Dressing himself in ordinary uniform he could just about manage — providing he took his time. But clambering into heavy flying-leathers was beyond him. At Cranwell, Destrier had attempted to try on one of the newly-designed Sidcot suits. But this, too, had proved impossible. On leave, therefore, he had bought a new leather flying-coat to replace the one cut piece by piece from his body after his crash in the

Pup. This, together with fug-boots, gauntlets, helmet and the flying-man's traditional assortment of woollens would have to suffice.

But, without Spring, the effort of struggling into these had proved beyond him. Half-dressed and exhausted, Destrier sat on the bed, his shoulders and neck showing as purple layers of knotted flesh and sinew where they were not covered by his vest or remaining dressings. For once he was lost as to his next move. Did he just remain here like this, sitting passively, or did he shout for assistance? Both alternatives were equally humiliating.

Destrier heard footsteps hurrying on the stairs and then Hopkins came into the room. If Destrier was surprised to see him in flying-leathers, he showed no sign of it but turned to pick up a heavy guernsey lying beside him on the bed.

As the candlelight mooned almost affectionately over Destrier's back, Hopkins caught his breath. Christ! He'd known Laurie had caught a packet ... but this? Despite his long friendship for the other, Hopkins could not altogether stifle a momentary feeling of revulsion. Perhaps Destrier guessed this; his twisted mouth flexed angrily and his eyes shone with a sudden hurt.

'If you're coming in, then come in! And, for Christ's sake, shut that bloody door!'

'Sir!' Hopkins obeyed, his feelings suppressed, his manner neutral and correct. The closed door seemed to seal both men within the bubble of a remembered intimacy that both had so nearly forgotten. Perhaps it was the candlelight that made for this, with its memory of orphanage bedtimes in the chilly dormitory they had once shared with a dozen others and – Why, Hopkins asked himself, should he suddenly remember it now? – that oleograph that had hung in the Superintendent's office: an uncompromisingly merciless crucifixion scene by Grunewald.

Perhaps Destrier's memory was working back along similar lines too. The hot, hurt look faded from his eyes, and when he spoke his voice was that of the friend Hopkins remembered.

'Brother Boche made a good job of me, eh, Syd?'

'He could've done worse.'

'Maybe better for me if he had.'

'Balls.'

Destrier's lop-sided mouth folded itself into a grin.

'Looks like you'll have to dress me.'

'It wouldn't be the first time, would it? Remember when you got your collar-bone broken that time, playing rugger against a crowd of thugs from some posh public school?'

'King's Witheringham? I remember. I seem to recall getting a cushy week in the san' out of that – before Matron pushed me back with the rest of you peasantry. Lord! What was her name now?'

'Mrs Maubrym.'

'So it was. I haven't thought of her in years.'

'Nor me.'

Both were silent as they contemplated their past. For the first time in his thirty years, Hopkins was filled with a sudden, panicky awareness of the fleeting nature of time and his own utter helplessness in the face of it. Destrier guessed his friend's thought, catching it on the wing.

'It's not all been waste, Syd.'

'Hasn't it?'

Destrier shook his head firmly.

Hopkins picked up the other's tunic, with its short length of magenta ribbon.

'Funny. . . . You always said you'd get one of these.'

'A lot of kids say that.'

'Not many get the chance.'

Destrier's mouth quirked bitterly.

'No? I should have said far too many have had the chance in the last four bloody years. The Somme – and this last show – Passchendale. . . . And all for – what?'

'Don't ask me, Laurie.'

'And don't ask me, either. Don't ask anyone. Don't ask God – He isn't telling. Don't ask the devil – he might tell you too much!' Destrier's voice thinned to a bitter wire of sound. 'All I know is that we've got to win now. We must! The bloody

Hun has got to be beaten. If the last four years have taught me anything, they've taught me that.'

Hopkins's eyes stole to the photograph of the girl in the silver frame. Yes, if someone like that had been his, he too might feel the need to settle accounts. But then, in his experience, vengeance was never more than momentarily sweet. Besides – a new and terrible notion suddenly shaped itself in Hopkins's head – just supposing this war *wasn't*, after all, the 'War-to-end-Wars' that someone had christened it? What then? To what further dark places of the soul would the next war take everyone? And the one after that?

Destrier's voice cut across his thoughts, impatient now, its friendliness gone.

'This isn't the time to get broody, Flight-Sergeant. You'll find another couple of sweaters in the drawer there, and a scarf in my valise.'

Obediently Hopkins found the sweaters and began helping Destrier into them. It took longer and was more difficult than he expected, for Destrier's movements, even the smallest, were painful and restricted. Once, when Destrier's head was deep in the folds of the guernsey and he was struggling to raise his arms, Hopkins heard him cry out, his voice muffled by the wool. And, as his hands worked, smoothing the heavy woollens into place, Hopkins felt the body beneath his finger-tips tremble and flinch like a nervous horse. But it was physical pain, not nerves, that made Destrier clench his teeth and go pale under the wind-burn that even his long months in hospital had been unable to erase. With his sensitive, craftsman's fingers, Hopkins intuitively understood the stresses and tensions in Destrier's body – just as he would those of a maltreated and damaged engine. This grinding lancination, coupled with an almost unspeakable weariness of mind and spirit, transmitted itself up through Hopkins's fingers and arms, and thence to his brain, so that for a brief, empathetic moment, he not only knew just how Destrier felt – he *became* Destrier.

As his fingers buttoned the other man's tunic, the feeling faded. Christ alone knew what held his friend together at all,

Hopkins thought. What more reserves of courage or will remained for him to call upon?

Well as he had known Destrier for twenty years, this man in front of him was a stranger. For the first time in their long acquaintanceship, Hopkins felt afraid of the other, repelled and daunted by his aura of cold and implacable obduracy. Compared with this, the hot anger that had won for Destrier the right to wear that coveted slip of ribbon on his chest was as nothing. Many men – knaves and cowards among them – might rise to that sort of courage, the courage of the blind moment, with rage dancing like a bright curtain behind the eyes. But this inexorable, self-driving fortitude was something far deeper and quite different in kind. Only will now served to keep this man upright on his legs at all. Only will would send him limping from this dingy room and set him once more in the cockpit of a fighting aircraft. Only will would send him rocketing into the secret dark like an avenging angel when to all appearances he should be in a hospital bed – or in his grave.

As Hopkins tightened the buckle of Destrier's flying-coat, the memories of two-thirds of a lifetime flashed through his mind in as many moments as it took to flick the end of the belt through its restraining buckle. Once again Hopkins felt a rising sense of panic. Was this really all that a man's life amounted to in the end? This seemingly endless vista of experience and achievement, as something to be recalled in the blinking of an eye, a momentary play of shadows – and no more?

Hopkins ran his fingers along Destrier's belt, making sure that the thick leather of the coat had not been rucked into clumsy and uncomfortable folds. Satisfied, he bunched his fingers into a soft fist and tapped the younger man lightly on the jaw.

'You'll do, I reckon.'

For the first time since Hopkins had been in the room, Destrier appeared to notice his flying-leathers.

'There's no call for you to start playing heroes.'

'I'm not. This is purely selfish. Just think how things could look to my grandchildren. "What did you do in the Great War, grandpa?" I wound up the elastic on Captain Destrier's Brisfit, made sure his wings were properly tied on and that his propeller went round – "And then?" Oh, then I waved him goodbye and toddled safely off to the Rose and Crown.'

'You're a good sort, Syd.'

'Arse-'oles – sir.'

Hopkins bent down and picked up a tin from Destrier's valise, removed the lid and wrinkled up his nose with disgust as he did so.

'Whale-fat? Christ! Jerry'll give up and fall out of the sky when he smells you coming!'

Destrier's mood changed abruptly.

'Good! I hope the bastard burns all the way down!'

He clawed into the whale-fat, clumsily plastering it onto his face, wincing as his insensitive finger-ends bit into the scar-tissue on his cheeks.

Hopkins shut his mouth. He'd been a fool to have made his last remark – a fool, too, not to have seen that there was more than just will keeping Destrier going. There was hate, also.

As though finally shattering the small illusion of intimacy that had sprung up between them in the past few minutes, Destrier reached down into his valise and picked up a bundle of soft leather. He unrolled it to reveal something that was half-helmet, half-mask.

'I got this made up for me in town.'

Hopkins nodded; he'd seen such things before. They were eminently practical for someone flying in an open cockpit. Yet, as Destrier slipped the soft leather over his head, pulled its draw-strings taut about his throat and lifted the collar of his coat to cover the gap, Destrier's changed appearance filled Hopkins with dismay. The front of the mask left only two round holes for Destrier's eyes and another – smaller – for him to breathe through. And, somehow, the total effect was peculiarly unpleasant – far worse than the facial scarring it hid. Uncovered, Destrier's face was still recognizably human. Hidden, all humanity was banished, leaving only the threatening, predatory glitter of his eyes. The will and the hate in the man Hopkins had already recognized. Was there also something worse than either, he wondered grimly. Madness?

'Well? What do you think?'

Hopkins tried to keep disquiet out of his voice.

'You don't look a bad imitation of old Nick himself from where I'm standing.'

'Good.'

Destrier pulled a pair of goggles on over his mask and then struggled into his flying helmet. With the putting on of each of these new disguises he became ever less human: a creature of darkness, inimical and dangerous. Hopkins suppressed a shudder and, to hide his unease, picked up Destrier's new flying-gauntlets, pretending to test the suppleness of the leather.

'A good dose of neat's-foot oil wouldn't do these any harm.'

'Tomorrow.'

'I'll see to it myself.' Hopkins opened the bedroom door and held it wide for Destrier to go through. 'Mind the stairs, sir. They're none too clever.'

The muffled figure nodded its zombie head.

'It'd never do for me to go breaking my neck when I've an appointment with Fritz, would it?'

But instead of going through the door Destrier paused at the threshold before turning and going back into the room, crossing to the bedside cabinet and taking from it the silver-mounted photograph. He paused, looking down at this for a long moment before tucking the picture into the depths of his flying-coat.

Hopkins found himself wondering just what the original of that photograph – the grave-faced girl he had once met at the hospital – would make of Destrier now. Then, despite his wounds, his weakness, his disfigurement, she had been able to love him. But now? This second flawing was something more terrible, and infinitely worse. It was a wounding of the very soul.

Looking down at the greenly luminous hands of his watch, von Trier saw that his ETA over Woolwich had proved accurate to the minute. The black snake of the river had completed its work of unconscious betrayal and, although searchlights quartered the sky – at his last count he'd reckoned there must be something like forty – none had come near to finding R.45. Westwards, an increasing number of gun flashes spoke of the mounting anger of London's defences. But the big bomber flew on, undiscovered and without hindrance. Beneath her, the white blankness of open country had long since given way to a patterning of grey and black smudges – suburb, and then town. Von Trier stationed himself at the Goerz bomb-sight, wedging himself firmly against the sides of the for'ard cockpit and peering down through the sighting-lens at the landscape below. Even thus magnified, what he saw was confusing and inconclusive. Where in hell was his damned target supposed to be? Was *that* a dockyard or wasn't it? Were those buildings sliding into sight (assuming they *were* buildings!) part of the arsenal complex or merely unimportant warehouses? They might be anything. Von Trier slammed his booted foot hard – once, then twice, against the cockpit's after-bulkhead. In answer to this signal, Horst eased R.45's nose round gently to starboard. Ah! That was better. Von Trier thought he could now recognize in the uncertain shapes below some similarity to those he'd studied in a group of reconnaissance photographs taken earlier in the year by daylight-raiding Gothas. True, this similarity was minimal – but it would have to serve. Von Trier pulled a short lever and sent his first stick of bombs spinning down from R.45's great belly. Then, after counting off a five-second interval, he sent a second stick down in pursuit.

On neither occasion was he able to see the fall of his bombs. He stood up and leant over the cockpit-coaming, staring down into the blackness, counting the seconds it would take his bombs to reach the ground. Eventually, two straggling clusters of flashes sprang momentarily to life on the ground – well wide, so far as he could tell from his point of aim. He swore and, ducking down, crouched over his bomb-sight again, kicking impatiently at the bulkhead as a signal to Horst to bring R.45 round for a second run over her target.

Even as the bomber began her turn, a sudden stutter of machine-gun fire, crackling through the roar of the Maybachs, made von Trier jerk his head up out of the cockpit. He grabbed wildly for the Lewis mounted in the Staaken's nose – and missed. Even as his hands scrabbled vainly for the Lewis's elusive spade-grip, a vague shape dropped down on R.45 from out of the darkness, spitting out a little line of glowing lights which, moving slowly (oh, so very slowly at first....), accelerated as they came towards him. Von Trier stared at this bracelet of tracer, unable to move, though each and every one of those innocuous-looking little lights seemed aimed at the plumb centre of his forehead, speeding closer and closer, before appearing to swerve away at the very last moment and whickering harmlessly off into the darkness.

Above his head, Mendelssohn and Schmidt became busy. But too late.... Despite their vigilance, neither gunner had had the least inkling of their attacker's presence until his tracer had come reaching for them out of the night. As with von Trier, it had seemed to both men that each and every round that their enemy had fired had been aimed at him personally, each bullet a little, glowing eye that could see and hunt down its prey even in a darkness such as this. Frightened and angry, both gunners had let fly in retaliation and, inevitably, missed, shooting wildly at the place their assailant had come from rather than along his probable path. Schmidt rattled off a whole drum before realizing the futility of his action. Now, with a hand that was already frost-bitten, he struggled in vain to change the empty pan.

In the British fighter, the pilot damned his stupid over-eagerness and climbed to the attack again. He had guessed at R.45's presence by the flowering glow of her bombs on the ground. He had been high at the time and had dived his SE5 down to where he had thought the bomber most likely to be. His guess had proved almost too accurate and he had all but crashed into R.45, only seeing her elephantine bulk when it was almost too late. He had fired and taken evasive action at the same time. For one horrific moment he had been quite sure his SE could not possibly avoid collision with the German aircraft. And then, his body icy with sweat inside his Sidcot, he was clear, having shot right over the bomber, now left a clear half-mile behind.

The flash of his guns had killed his night-vision. By the time he had banked the SE round to return to the attack, the night sky appeared completely empty. But this pilot was no fool. If, on a night like this it was possible for a bomber to see the ground, then, he reasoned, it should be equally possible, now that he knew what he was looking for, to see the enemy silhouetted between himself and the ground. The SE5's pilot, therefore, climbed, standing his fighter on her tail, so that her air-screw seemed to be chewing a vertical tunnel for itself up through the darkness.

The Wolseley Viper engine screamed its protest at such maltreatment. The thinning oil, failing to find its way through a clogged channel, boiled and, becoming impregnated with tiny grey fragments of metal as the bearings at each crank-end overheated, blued and then disintegrated. At 13,000 feet the engine seized into a solid mass. The SE5 stalled and fell away into a spin, recovering clumsily as her cursing pilot damned his luck. For, even as his engine failed, he had caught a glimpse of R.45's tell-tale exhausts sneaking away southwards.

Despite his dead engine, the SE's pilot brought the fighter's nose round in pursuit. He had a two or three thousand foot advantage in height over the bomber and he reckoned that, even in a glide, the speed of his dive might just bring him into range of the bomber long enough for one good burst with his Vickers. He eased the stick forward and, nursing his height, brought the long nose round onto a course which, with luck, would intercept that of the bomber.

The distance began to close and, for a few glorious moments as the glimmer of R.45's exhausts grew brighter, the SE pilot was convinced he would just make it. But, by now, his height advantage was almost lost and, as his glide flattened, he felt the fighter grow sluggish under his hands and very near stalling-point again. Angrily, the SE pilot emptied his guns at R.45 from a quite impossible range, firing first the Vickers and then the Lewis as the bomber seemed to lift effortlessly above him.

The fighter staggered, and the pilot pushed his stick forward, taking one last, resentful look after those vanishing exhausts. But his look was a brief one. It was now far more important to find somewhere to land.

As the SE5 dropped, the steep hummock of Shooter's Hill loomed dangerously out of the darkness; banking round the shoulder of this, the pilot dropped his aircraft among the trees of Oxtree Wood. Uninjured – though sadly out of temper – the pilot removed helmet and goggles and, releasing himself from his safety harness, set about clambering down from the oak in which his now battered scout was crazily perched. Clumsy in his heavy Sidcot, he lost his grip on the frost-slick bark of the tree and fell the last fifteen feet to the ground. He fell awkwardly, half-stunning himself against the rough bole of the oak, smashing his front teeth and biting agonizingly on his tongue. As his mouth filled with blood, he stood muzzily and began cursing anew, his voice distorted by his damaged mouth. The caped figure of a Special Constable, brought by the noise of the crash, moved cautiously through the wood and came close up behind the pilot, listening. The Special didn't much like what he heard. To him, the language used by the pilot seemed strange, guttural and unintelligible – and undeniably foreign. The Special was tired and middle-aged, and had recently lost his youngest son at Passchendale. He reached under his cape, brought out his truncheon and swung it fiercely in the darkness.

'That's for my Jimmy, you bloody Hun!' he swore as the luckless pilot collapsed.

There had been times in the past when von Trier had found it necessary to restrain himself from actually shaking the stolid and phlegmatic Horst. But in those first few moments after the SE5's abortive but frightening attack, R.45's Commander had found himself blessing the man. Horst's evasive action had been exemplary. Further, on his own initiative – something rare with Horst – he had brought the bomber round onto the course that Intelligence at Gontrode had estimated should lead R.45 very close to her secondary target – that airfield somewhere south of Bromley, less than fifteen minutes' flying-time away. For once, therefore, von Trier was able to think of his pilot without the least temptation to be satirical. Horst had done well. It would be a pleasure to tell him so.

High in his eyrie above the starboard wing, Mendelssohn was glad he had missed R.45's attacker and had thus been spared a possible repetition of that earlier raid when he had watched those two figures hurl themselves from their burning FE. Mendelssohn supposed he should feel guilty about being glad to have missed the enemy fighter – an emotion surely at odds with his proper duty as a good and patriotic German. Maybe; but the private man in Mendelssohn – as ever – found it difficult to reconcile himself to the martial ruthlessness of current opinion. After all, that fellow in the British scout was some mother's son, just as he was himself. Mendelssohn found himself marvelling at the absurdity of a group of otherwise civilized and intelligent creatures who, meeting the best part of three kilometres high, in a wholly unnatural and alien element, expended nerves and energy in trying to destroy each other. It was as silly as it was sublime.

Below Mendelssohn, the charcoal smudging that was London's suburbs began giving place to open country – rolling, hilly country, so far as he could see, and not dissimilar, perhaps, to that which had inspired his idol among contemporary musicians, Edward Elgar. On one memorable occasion in Berlin, Mendelssohn had played in an orchestra conducted by the great Englishman. And Elgar, too, as Mendelssohn remembered, had written a violin concerto, and was – like himself – largely self-taught. Perhaps after the war, his own work might become something to be spoken of in the same breath as the Englishman's. Perhaps even – Mendelssohn toyed pleasantly with the notion – he and Elgar might meet one day and exchange ideas, with himself no longer an obscure fiddler from the back desk of the second violins, but accepted in his own right as a composer.

In R.45's cabin, Richard Horst was complacently satisfied by his own part in the recent proceedings. 'We must have you in extra good form tonight,' von Trier had said to him earlier; and, to someone of Horst's inflexible thought processes, this simple wish, coming from his Commander, carried little less force than a direct order. Consequently, Horst was in *excellent* form. Rarely, if ever, had he previously experienced such a mysterious sense of one-ness with his machine as he did now. R.45 felt like an extension of himself, a tool which, like his own flesh and sinew, was expressive of obedience and strong Germanic purpose. . . .

In the seat beside Horst's, Sergeant Walter's flesh and sinew felt neither obedience nor Germanic purpose – only an icy mutiny. The chill had become a numbing, grinding nag, eating up from Walter's legs and into his groin and belly. Why hadn't that horse-faced old fool Mann checked Müller's work more carefully? Everyone knew that the electrician was a conceited, careless bastard. . . . Despairingly, Walter huddled down into his seat. A fat lot of use he'd ever be to the warmest wench in Bremen at this rate.

At the rear of the cabin, Wendel – that same Wendel who, between operations, lived in a nightmare limbo of fear at the prospect of the next one, had barely shown any sign at all of noticing the SE5's attack. Just one of the scout's bullets had made its mark on R.45. It had ripped through the bomber's plywood fuselage a few centimetres to the left of Wendel's head before tearing its way out again through the floor. Wendel had noted its passage with detached interest. He was far more acutely aware of his gauges. Pump no. 5 was demanding more and more of his attention. It was still doing its duty – just – but by now was requiring more nursing than the rest of its partners.

Out on the port wing, poor Schmidt was scarcely capable of conscious or coherent thought. He had failed to replace his Lewis's empty ammunition tray with a full one – and by now was past caring. Nor did it seem to matter much any longer when he realized that getting down the ladder to the sanctuary of his cockpit between the Maybachs was quite beyond him. Despite the cold, a new and delicious lassitude was beginning to insinuate itself through his body – a feeling that very soon he would fall gently and pleasantly to sleep. That he was unlikely ever to wake from this sleep troubled Schmidt not at all. He was done with caring.

In his wind-torn tunnel beneath R.45, Rossi felt for the rosary and its companion doll in the breast of his flying-suit. Despite the piety of his mother, and that of his sister Bianca who was bent on becoming a nun, Rossi was uncertain – despite that bullet-crease in his helmet – whether he believed in any sort of God at all, let alone a personal one. Yet the rosary – and, perhaps, even more the doll – brought him a vague sense of comfort, representing the familiar and certain rock that was his home, with its cheerful babble of Italian noise, its rich, garlicky cooking smells, and the open and unguarded affection of his family.

Rossi pulled himself back from visualizing his home too clearly. His only fixed points of reference now were the spade-grips of the Lewises in his gauntleted hands, the ceaseless, throbbing moan of R.45's engines – these, and the cold: the lambasting, everlasting, wearying cold.

Even as von Trier had pulled R.45's bomb release, a mechanic had swung the propeller of Destrier's Bristol, and Mackail – whistle in mouth – had sounded off the three blasts signalling the aircraftsmen lining the runways to light their flares. Suddenly the night bloomed as the twin rows of petrol-filled canisters ignited with a whoooo-ooOOMP into pillars of dancing flame. Despite its earlier warmings, the Bristol's Falcon seemed reluctant to come to life. The mechanic swinging at its propeller thrust and heaved, while Destrier fumed impatiently in his cockpit. Behind him, huddled down onto his small and comfortless seat, Hopkins cursed the folly that had made him volunteer for this. Young Russell was more than welcome to his flying-pay. After tonight, the little bugger could earn it. . . .

Fifty yards away, and now thoroughly warmed, the RAF engines of the two BE12s purred like self-satisfied cats. In contrast, the big Falcon remained perversely silent. Destrier struggled upright in his cockpit and waved to Peters to take precedence on the runway. Mechanics pulled the chocks away from the BE's wheels and swung the aircraft's tail round as it began to roll slowly forwards over the snowy clinker.

Tense and sick in his cockpit, his stomach gusting with apprehension and his throat dry, Peters hated Destrier. Why should that damned upstart ranker have all the luck? Why did it have to be Destrier's engine that refused to start and not his own? The bile rose in Peters's throat; he choked and swallowed hard to prevent himself from being sick. Nearly nine feet of cowling and a pair of chimney-like exhausts hazarded his forward view, so that he found it difficult to spot the line of dimly glowing lanterns marking the end of the runway. When he placed these at last, his apprehensions increased. The lamps looked terrifyingly near, and the foreshortened perspectives of the lines of leaping, flickering petrol flares seemed to bring the low bank at the end of the field almost into touching distance.

As Peters opened his throttle for full revs, he heard his voice shrieking curses at the nameless fools who had selected such a site for an airfield. He waved a reluctant hand to the mechanics lying across the BE's tail. As these leapt clear, the BE rolled forwards, increasing speed until the blazing petrol-drums seemed to blur into a continuous line. Soon – far, far too soon – Peters dragged back on the stick. . . .

To the men on the ground beneath him – used as they had become in the last ten days to the chancy nature of Peters's take-offs – it seemed he had finally done for himself this time. For what seemed an eternity, the flame-splashed bulk of the BE hung above their heads until its frenziedly screaming engine dragged it up into the night. Sergeant Mackail put his hands on his hips and swore, his face strained and white even in the ruddy glow of the petrol flares. It had not been Peters's danger that had sickened him, but the scream of that tormented engine. Its racketing, its howl of what, in a human body, would have been anguish, roused answering echoes in Mackail's every nerve-end.

'Great God Almighty!' someone muttered.

Mackail turned on him savagely.

'Just you get on with your work, laddie, and leave Him to His!'

The offender melted into the darkness.

In the second BE12, young Browne, too, felt apprehensive. In his case, this was not fear exactly; nor – in a curious way – was his apprehension entirely unpleasant. It was, he decided, a very similar sensation to that he always felt when about to begin batting in a big game – half a happy anticipation of success, half a shocking dread of making an ass of himself. Peters's take-off had been a little like watching the chap batting with him getting out first ball to a dreadful cross-batted swipe. As Browne knew all too well, such daftness could be infectious.

He put his hand up to his forehead and jiggled his goggles more comfortably into position. When he had done this to his satisfaction, he waved to his attendant mechanics and saw them pull the chocks from beneath the wheels. Browne opened the throttle wide and signalled to the men holding down the BE's tail to stand clear. As the aircraft leapt forward, he peered round that damnably long cowling towards the rapidly approaching lanterns guarding the end of the field. He was determined not to make the same so-nearly fatal error as his senior, and held the BE down as long as possible. By the time he eased back on the stick he had almost left it too late. The BE lifted with sluggish reluctance, its wheels skimming through the fuzz of frozen vegetation topping the low bank of the dyke. His starboard wheel clipped the central storm-lantern fair and square and sent it skittering into the black waters of the ditch.

For a second time the watchers on the ground gritted their teeth anticipating disaster. But Browne's BE climbed away into the darkness, its engine-note becoming a slowly fading drone.

Mackail hadn't watched Browne's take-off. He had been far too preoccupied in deciding just why Destrier's Bristol had failed to start despite its earlier responsiveness. Oiled plugs, probably, he thought. Christ! That would have to happen now of all times. Mackail moved across beneath the Bristol's engine-cowling, uncomfortably aware of Destrier's still figure in the cockpit above him – so still, yet so palpably accusing. Mackail shoved the sweating mechanic away from the propeller.

'Here! You give me yon, mannie – before you rupture yoursel'!'

Mackail scrabbled his boots in the clinker for a foothold and gripped the wooden airscrew.

'Switches off. . . . Petrol on. . . . Suck in. . . .'

The petrol-pump sighed.

'Switches on! Contact!'

Mackail tightened his grip on the propeller and swung. To Hopkins, by now half-leaning out of the rear cockpit in his anxiety and staring past Destrier's head along the angular cowling of the Bristol's nose, what followed was something that became scarred on his mind's eye for ever, and yet an event which he could never afterwards sort into coherent sequence or shape.

As Mackail heaved down on the propeller, the Falcon coughed, choked, and then sang out strongly with its rich, familiar growl. A swirling flood of blue smoke bursting from its exhausts confirmed Hopkins's own guess that oiled plugs were the reason for the Falcon's unexpected fit of temperament. It was through the drift of this oily cloud that Hopkins saw Mackail hesitate, then apparently slip and fall forwards into the shimmering disc of the airscrew. Even as he fell, Mackail tried desperately to slew his body sideways. He was almost clear of the propeller's arc when one brass-bound tip caught him squarely across the neck, all but severing his head. A hail of something red and sticky flew back in the slipstream like warm rain, smearing Hopkins's goggles. And, as the Bristol surged forward, the other propeller blade lifted Mackail's inert body and flung it contemptuously aside. Without even appearing to hesitate or even to have noticed the incident, Destrier opened the throttle to its limits and aimed the Bristol down the avenue of now dying flares. Long before they had reached the end of the runway, the fighter was in the air and climbing smoothly away.

Hopkins leant over the side and vomited.

Morton-Dunne was the first to reach Mackail. The Scot's body lay like that of a broken puppet, outrageous in indignity. Blood – a brilliant vermilion on the frozen snow that had most likely been the cause of Mackail's fatal hesitation – had been blown back by the Bristol's slipstream into an aimless delta of streams and rivulets. Faced with this tragedy, Morton-Dunne became a different man to the one who usually seemed so determinedly lethargic. He tore off his greatcoat and flung it across Mackail's body, hiding that dreadful wound gaping in his neck. Nor, as Morton-Dunne was aware, would it do morale any good to leave the Sergeant's body lying for long like that in the snow. A stretcher was needed – and urgently. He turned and yelled for someone among the gathering circle of mechanics to go and rip a door from its hinges. For a moment, no one obeyed, until a repetition of this order sent two men scurrying off into the darkness. . . .

Out over the sea, a few miles to the east, Hopkins was crouched miserably in his cockpit. Behind closed eyes, he felt like a man drowning beneath surging waves of nausea as, over and over again, his mind pictured for itself those nightmare moments before take-off. Oh, Christ Almighty – Oh, Jesus Christ Almighty, for Mackail of all men to go and get himself killed in that bloody silly way. . . . Surely the poor sod must have had time to see what was coming? Time enough to have ducked and leapt aside instead of hesitating for that single, fatal moment? Poor reliable old Mac. . . . He had pushed that useless oaf of a mechanic aside and had become the victim of his own haste, his own avoidable and unlikely carelessness.

But, within Hopkins, there was a second, more sceptical self whose voice would not be silenced, a voice which whispered, insinuated, argued that there was another and different explanation, a voice which insisted that the real blame lay elsewhere – with the man in front of him: with Destrier. . . .

But that was absurd. In what possible way could Destrier be held responsible? He hadn't seen Mackail slip, and if he had there was nothing he could possibly have done to prevent the accident.

But the inadmissible thought persisted in shaping itself in Hopkins's head that Destrier had seen Mackail *only too clearly*: had seen him as something standing between himself and his enemy; had seen him hesitate and slip, and had uncaringly – angrily even – opened the throttle and gunned the Bristol forward regardless, sweeping Mackail aside. . . .

There were other questions demanding answers, too. . . . Just how much had Destrier's obvious and barely contained impatience contributed to Mackail's totally uncharacteristic carelessness? And just precisely *when* had Destrier opened the throttle? In the moment *before* Mackail was struck down? Or a fraction later?

Just before nausea defeated Hopkins for a second time, one last question forced itself on his attention. He was now blaming Destrier for what had happened – but was this man with him in the aircraft really Destrier at all?

No, Hopkins decided as he heaved his body upright to the cockpit coaming again, Laurie Destrier was dead, as dead and done for as Angus Mackail now lying bloodily on the snowy ground far away behind them at Brick-Kiln Farm.

SEVEN

As R.45 flew deeper into Kent and Mendelssohn became colder, he found his thought processes beginning to accelerate and work with a startling clarity and concentration. It was as if, by some freakish chance of his metabolism, the cold was serving to clear his mind of extraneous clutter and forcing him deeper and deeper within himself towards that still, creative centre which, if anything, was the nearest he could claim to being a soul. In imagination, he was by now a whole world away from R.45 in place and time. He stood alone, dressed incredibly in tails and starched shirt on a rostrum above an orchestra of waiting yet barely seen musicians. Below Mendelssohn stood a violinist, his fiddle tucked ready under his chin and with his bow poised waiting above its strings. The violinist's face was quite clear. It looked up into Mendelssohn's own, obediently anticipating the first sweep of his baton. Without surprise, Mendelssohn saw that the violinist was himself. He had become two persons – virtuoso and conductor. His twin selves nodded at each other. And the Mendelssohn on the rostrum, with a compelling flick of his baton, called the orchestra to attention.

A muffled roll of drums began the concerto, and then the violinist – his alter ego – rippled his bow across the strings in a rising arpeggio of harsh sound. An oboe sighed in reply, 'Alas! Alas!' The orchestra muttered briefly and the strings took up the solo violinist's first exclamation. The oboe sighed a second time before the bassoons cut across its sorrowful yearning with a bawdily raucous chuckle. Trombones bellowed out angrily, while the rest of the orchestra snarled, shrilled or thundered its dissent. Only the solitary fiddle ignored the general uproar, lifting its voice high above the tumult in a taut ecstasy of self-communion.

Mendelssohn snuggled down behind his Lewis, forgetful of

the cold. This world within his head was the real world – a prelude to what that other prosaic one might be some day. A concert hall somewhere; himself on the rostrum, and his own concerto launched into its bitter and blistering first movement.

Fifty feet away in the for'ard cockpit, von Trier's mind was concerned with less aesthetic notions. He knew that at this moment, his target – always assuming it truly existed at all outside the fertile imagination of Intelligence – should by now be somewhere near. Back home at Gontrode, von Trier had been shown a British Ordnance survey map with the putative new fighter station confidently inked in at – Now what in creation had been the name of that insignificant hamlet? Cudham Hall? Biggin Hill? Von Trier couldn't remember.

But now, surprisingly well-defined as the snowy landscape was beneath the bomber, the Count could find little similarity between what he saw on that remembered map. How very plausible that idiot Intelligence Officer had made the whole idea sound earlier in the day!

But there – von Trier grinned – that was Intelligence all over. He should have told the fool exactly what to do with his blasted map. Like all professional soldiers he had had his bellyful of Intelligence's 'dead-certs' in the past; of worthless objectives to be attacked and taken, careless of cost, of genuine opportunities wantonly disregarded.

But for once, had von Trier known it, German Air Intelligence was correct. A few miles from where R.45 flew, a Home Defence Squadron really did exist – or a Flight, rather; one as exiguous in men and machinery as that other at Brick-Kiln Farm. For the past eleven nights, this Biggin Hill Flight had had a frustrating time. So far, its fighters had not intercepted a single enemy bomber. Nor would they do so tonight, for all three of the embryo 141 Squadron's BE12s were all well away, patrolling over London.

On the ground, the remainder of this Flight could clearly hear the booming beat of R.45's Maybachs as she approached. To the men listening, it seemed that not one bomber but a whole squadron of Gothas must be coming their way. Air-craftless pilots stamped frustratedly up and down in the snow and cursed their luck. It was all so bloody unfair! In vain they searched the darkness above for the tell-tale blue-green flare of exhausts that would show the approach of a returning BE12. But nothing. . . . The sound of aero-engines rose to a boastful crescendo of sound that was centred some way to the south-west of the village and then began to fade.

In a voice whose chagrin perfectly matched the mood of every man around him, a fox-hunting officer shouted, 'Gone-away!' He got his laugh, though it sounded edged and false.

Away to the south-west, von Trier knew none of this. By chance he had flown fractionally too far to the south and had arrived over the deep rift valley below Biggin Hill. Here, assuming the barely existent hamlet of Fickleshole to be his target, he had loosed his remaining bombs. These missed their target by all of a long mile. Apart from killing a luckless sheep and terrifying the wits out of a prowling poacher, they did no damage.

R.45 flew on.

Once more von Trier ducked back into R.45's blue-lit cabin. In some ways he was sorry to leave his exposed and solitary position in the bomber's nose. Like most airmen of his time he mistrusted enclosed cabins. They robbed a man of much of his ability to see about him while snaring him into a false and quite unfounded sense of security. But now, over open country once more, von Trier experienced the tiniest sense of relaxation. The worst was behind them now. As he emerged into the cabin, von Trier reached up and gave Horst's ramrod back a reassuring pat. It amused him to notice how that same back became even more proud in its bearing at his touch. Good, simple, reliable Richard! It must be pleasant to be like that – a dog, to wag one's tail at the smallest sign of authority's approval. When authority's hand reached down to pat *him*, he generally felt like biting it. But who was the happier – himself or Horst?

Von Trier shook his head and looked towards his second pilot. Walter, glancing over his shoulder, caught his superior's eye. The two men grinned at each other, both understanding that what they were really smiling at was Horst. Such a sharing of humour at a brother-officer's expense was shockingly bad, really. But – looking at Horst again, von Trier was irresistibly reminded, and not for the first time – of a good but rather stupid English gun-dog he had once owned. How that dog had loved him! And, because it had loved him, how it had tried. . . . With something of a pang, von Trier suddenly realized that he could no longer recall the dog's name. Were love and loyalty always rewarded in that way?

At the rear of the cabin, Wendel still juggled with the problems of balancing R.45's fuel. The faulty pump was now doing barely any work at all. But it would last – or he would make it last – for just so long as it was needed. Now, in the middle of a raid, Wendel's mind was completely blank, apart from its concern with the equation of fuel used and fuel remaining, all to be finely balanced in the tanks above him. There was no room in him now for fear. Even his treacherous bowels felt taut and assured. Like a boxer facing a cunning but often-beaten opponent, Wendel balanced himself in front of his gauges, answering their fluctuating needles with the touch of a pump almost before the gauges had had sufficient time to register any perceptible change. Up here, nine thousand feet above hostile territory, Wendel – daytime coward, prey to a whole host of fears and terrors – was totally master of himself.

Rossi, beneath the Staaken's fuselage, felt a similar relief to the rest of R.45's crew at leaving London safely behind. But the vortices of the slipstream, howling into his tunnel, soon chilled this small sense of safety. His bruised nose ached, and the buffeting wind, raging round his aching head, inimically seemed to be trying to suck him out of R.45's fuselage into the night.

His spirit, haunted by the recollection of his earlier forebodings, became as icy as the wind. Deep down inside himself, he knew the worst was yet to be. . . .

Without thinking what he was doing, Rossi crossed himself and muttered an act of contrition into the scarf which he had pulled up to protect his throbbing face. Almost at once, so it seemed, his spirit lightened. He experienced again that same calm acceptance of fate he had felt earlier at Gontrode. Somewhere out there, waiting in the darkness, was a bullet with his name, rank and number neatly inscribed round its rim. Soon that bullet would slide easily into a breech; the breech would close, a trigger would be depressed. . . . *Arriverderci*, Rossi. . . . Goodnight, sweet world. . . .

Still shaking from his near-stall and a take-off that even by his own standards had been monumentally clumsy, Peters flew his BE12 south-east for a few minutes before gaining his bearings over Dengechurch and then turning back inland again to fly due north. In the last few minutes before take-off, standing in that chilly and uncomfortable farmhouse parlour, Destrier had given brief but precise instructions as to 'D' Flight's tactics. The three aircraft, taking off a minute or so apart, were to fly in a triangular box that would take them firstly to Whitstable, then south-east to Deal, then, finally, roughly south-west and so back to Marshingfold and Brick-Kiln Farm again. This box was to be maintained for as long as fuel lasted and was only to be broken out of, or entered, in the event of an enemy bomber being sighted – its presence most likely betrayed by gunfire from below. The heights of the three aircraft were to be staggered a thousand feet apart, with the Bristol providing top-cover at eight thousand feet. Because of the varying speeds and rates of climb of the three aircraft, each was to pursue its own patrol without regard for the position of the others. This way, as with a shot-gun, there would be a greater 'spread' of shot and a marginally more optimistic chance of intercepting the enemy.

Soon, however, flying the lowest of the three aircraft, Peters lost all sense of direction and balance. With the night as seemingly impenetrable as a blindfold tied over his eyes, he chose to ignore or forget both altimeter and compass, glowing companionably in front of him, a foot below his nose. Rashly, Peters chose rather to pin his faith on his physical senses, ignorant that these were becoming progressively less and less trustworthy with each passing minute. The doubts and confusions in these soon convinced Peters that he was flying upside down. Panic gripped him, and he joggled wildly at the stick. For a moment or two, the BE staggered unhappily; only the aircraft's inherent and often-abused stability overcame the effects of Peters's absurd and clumsy handling. Rigging and airframe whined or creaked in protest and the engine howled in alarm – brought to his senses, Peters mastered his panic and, to his relief, found that with his night-vision improving, the ground could just be seen, dimly but unmistakably, exactly where it should be – three thousand feet beneath his lower wing.

The discovery of this simple fact came as such an unexpected surprise to Peters that he laughed aloud. Belatedly, he remembered his compass and altimeter and set himself to climbing the rest of his long, slow haul to six thousand feet. His sense of humiliation and failure faded, leaving him feeling strong and brave, a man well worthy of those looks of admiration he sometimes saw written in the eyes of civilians when they spotted the wings on his chest. He forgot Gladys Biggs and the ignominious shame his manhood had endured at her hands. Peters sang. He was still singing when Whitstable passed unnoticed beneath his wings and the BE12 flew on out over the Estuary. His sudden realization of the sea's inimical blackness below him stopped Peters's song. Once more he panicked, and his subsequent turn south-east was so poorly controlled that even the patient BE jibbed at the roughness of her handling, precariously near to stalling and spinning.

As Peters regained the coastline, somewhere near Herne Bay, a battery of anti-aircraft gunners, mistaking Peters for an intruding enemy, let fly at him, startling the night with their spurting gun-muzzles and the flash of bursting shells. Although none of these came within a mile of Peters, the courage and confidence that had begun oozing through his veins fled incontinently. Once more, he felt lost and humiliated and horribly afraid. Why did it always have to be him who got hold of the dirty end of the stick, he whined aloud. Why? *Why?*

A few minutes behind Peters, young Browne had quickly recovered from his own wretched take-off. It had been, he told himself, like one of those awful shots an incoming batsman sometimes plays to the first ball he receives – an entirely thoughtless swish which, even though it might fail to be immediately disastrous, set an unhappy precedent for what was to follow. Well! Not tonight it wasn't – of that Browne was quite determined. His flying would be as blameless as the Archangel Gabriel's from now on. . . .

Browne grinned inwardly. What was it his old school reports had always said? 'Could do better. Careless. . . . Must try harder. . . . More concentration needed. . . .' Well, for once he'd take notice. He'd bloody-well better! Failure to take heed of such advice didn't just mean a wigging from old 'Sticky' Milton anymore, or six of the best from the Head Beak; – no, failure *now* meant a broken neck and fatigue-wallahs digging a six-by-four hole in the ground – always assuming, that is, enough of one was ever found to make a funeral worth while.

Browne's thoughts came back onto more cheerful paths as he realized that somewhere down there in the blackness beneath his wings lay Canterbury. Once again he allowed his mind to dwell on that glorious afternoon's batting with Perkins before they had succeeded together in diddling Kent. What a game that had been! And what a game this flying was, too, he thought, coming back to the present. Not for him the hideous unpleasantness of the trenches, or the endless boredom of swinging idly round a buoy up at Scapa. His was a different war altogether; exciting, glamorous even. . . . If he'd felt dismay on being sent to a rag-time outfit like 'D' Flight after completing his training instead of to a squadron in France, he knew he must control his patience. His time would come. And, in the meanwhile, it was really rather ripping being what he was now – a sort of aerial St George whose job it was to deal with any Jerry dragons trying to get their jaws into London.

With the cheerful optimism of extreme youth, Browne never doubted the final outcome of any encounter he might have with such a dragon. He'd bowl the blighter for a duck. . . .

Matching action to his belligerent line of thought, Browne reached up over his head to the twin Lewises angled upwards on their Forster mounting and fired a brief warming burst. No problems there. . . . Come on, Dragon! Browne pleaded cheerfully; have at you, sirrah!

Once, when loving Dolly Lyttleton – his mind leaping towards its long-imagined images of flight – Destrier had known himself drawn, Icarus-like, into the tawny eye of the sun. Now, there was only darkness – darkness and cold and the infinite emptiness of sorrow and despair. There was hate, too. Hate for those who had killed Dolly.

As the Bristol climbed, reaching easily for her patrol height, the sub-zero temperature began to permeate through Destrier's leathers to the scarred body beneath, complementing his mental *acedia* with an icy physical lassitude.

Heedless of what lay outside himself, his sorrow and hate draining to a numb indifference, this last, small remaining spark of what had once been Laurie Destrier continued to shrink inwards on itself, self-forgetting yet totally self-absorbed. The world below became as a formless, rumoured echo of something half-remembered; something vaguely familiar, yet never properly known. . . .

With the Falcon's throttle wide open, and with Destrier's claw-like hands clutching unconsciously at her control-column, the Bristol's climb steepened. Drawn on by her raging air-screw, she lifted upwards through the thinning, freezing air, past her patrol height – and then onwards towards her ceiling. . . .

In the Bristol's rear cockpit, Hopkins was slowly winning his battle with the surging waves of nausea that still threatened to drown him. In the ten days he had known Mackail, he and the sergeant had, of necessity, grown close to each other in their shared responsibility for licking into shape Brick-Kiln Farm's make-shift complement of men and material. But it was not this brief liking nor even Mackail's transparent decency that had so sickened Hopkins about his death. No, it had been the manner of his dying, the casual and callous way in which this had happened. Mackail's neck had been severed, his life put out, his body flung aside, as if his existence had been of no more importance than that of a beetle crushed beneath a man's foot. . . . And Destrier hadn't cared, because Destrier was now beyond such considerations, beyond kindness or humanity – dead. . . .

This thought made Hopkins sharply aware of his own situation. Christ! he thought, peering forwards, if Destrier was dead, then he was as good as in his own box himself. Paradoxically, this notion only served to steady him, and the fears that had been gnawing at him since he had made up his mind to join the patrol suddenly vanished. Once a man was beyond hope, Hopkins remembered reading somewhere, he became free. Bullshit, he'd thought at the time, but now he found the idea oddly truthful and comforting. His nausea disappeared and, despite the cold that was beginning to bite into his body, he felt surprisingly clear-headed.

The Bristol staggered uneasily and for the first time Hopkins became aware of the steepness of her climb. The strained bellow of the Falcon set his teeth on edge and he found himself on his feet, staring down past Destrier's head into the blackness of the for'ard cockpit. The slipstream nagged its way in under his goggles, blurring his vision, and for a few moments he was unable to read the dimly-lit altimeter. When he was at last able to, Hopkins thumped wildly on Destrier's shoulder with his gauntleted fist. 14,000 feet? What in God's name did Destrier think he was playing at?

The Bristol's climb eased; her engine-note softened. Hopkins slid back down onto the small, padded square that served him for a seat. Despite the roar of the engine and the blistering slipstream, he had no sense of place. For all he knew, the

Bristol was hung, solitary, in a limbo of her own, surrounded by shrieking, bellowing demons. Apart from the glow of the aircraft's own exhausts, there was no light; no light at all, so far as he could see in all the firmament – not a star, nor even a glimpse of that promised sliver of moon.

Suddenly, Hopkins became painfully aware of the Bristol's flying into a mass of something almost solid – a mass which broke round his head in a million stinging needles. Sleet! In a few seconds, his bowed head became plastered with the stuff which first caked and then froze upon his goggles and helmet. Again he felt the Bristol stagger unhappily in the air, and then her motion changed as she began plunging wildly downwards into the night, leaving the snow-squall far behind.

Between them, the squall and the subsequent dive fogged the clarity of thought Hopkins had so recently achieved. Apathetically, he crouched low in his seat. A small suspicion crept into his head that perhaps Destrier was now quite deliberately diving the Bristol downwards to destruction. Behind his ice-caked goggles, Hopkins closed his eyes. Well, if that was the case, there was bugger-all he could do about it. Besides, he told himself, almost anything would be better than another hour or two of this freezing misery.

After his return to R.45's cabin, von Trier sat himself at the navigation table and, toying with a pair of parallel rulers, rechecked the dog-leg course he had previously made up his mind would be the bomber's safest outward path over Kent. With a due-easterly turn to be made in a few minutes and the throttles kept at their present setting, Maidstone would be reached in just under another twenty minutes' flying. From Maidstone, a south-easterly turn and another half-hour would bring R.45 out over the sea near·Dover. Mentally, von Trier went over his calculations again and jotted the two courses down on a slip of paper before standing and moving forward to Horst. The pilot took this paper, read it and nodded in affirmation, his shoulders straightening at the sight of the word 'Dover'. Horst set his face into a martial scowl and banked R.45 ninety degrees to port.

Bloody fool, thought von Trier, by now too weary and cold to be amused by Horst's puerile chauvinism. But, as the Count returned to his seat at the rear of the cabin, he found himself questioning his right to the assumption of any marked superiority of mind over poor Horst. After all, when one considered the matter dispassionately, his own handiwork this evening had been childish enough in all conscience....

Once, as a schoolboy at that hated Military Academy, von Trier had led a group of similarly like-minded little urchins in a defiant raid on the house of an unpopular master. The intention had been to smash the man's front windows; to this end, von Trier and his gang had stationed themselves one evening in a shrubbery, fifty metres from the master's house. Before starting out on their expedition, each of the boys had filled his pockets with carefully chosen stones. After waiting for it to become quite dark, tremulous at their own temerity, the boys had moved out of cover and, at von Trier's signal, had taken aim at the lamplit and uncurtained windows of the house.

Their aim had been quite dreadful, von Trier remembered. The stones had thudded uselessly against the wall, and the windows had remained mockingly unbroken. Herr Klepp's front door had burst open – and the boys had fled in incontinent panic. There had been a great deal of noise, a lot of empty bravado, and little or no damage done....

Much as tonight, von Trier thought wryly. Sound and fury signifying nothing.... All in all, this evening's raid might have been specifically designed to illustrate the aptness of that old line about the child being father to the man.... He was *still* chucking stones at windows, and he was still running blindly away afterwards.... It was a salutary experience for a man to discover that in sixteen years he hadn't improved one whit....

On the ground at Brick-Kiln Farm, the mood was introverted and gloomily subdued. Mackail's body had been taken away and was now laid in one of the farm's tumbledown out-buildings, wrapped in Morton-Dunne's blood-drenched great-coat and a grey army blanket. But, out of sight though it was, the awareness of its existence lay like an uncomfortable shadow across everyone's mind. Many of the Farm's personnel had become used to violent death, but this totally unexpected and gratuitous blotting-out of Mackail – a personality so four-square and reliable – had brought home to every man who had seen the accident the unpalatable fact of his own mortality. One moment Mackail had been among them, ordering, direct-ing, encouraging, cajoling – a certain, if sometimes dryly caustic pillar of strength – and the next, he had been elimin-ated and reduced to so much butcher's meat by a single swipe of the Bristol's air-screw.

At least half of Brick-Kiln Farm's airmen had seen friends killed in action. Such deaths – if cruel and ugly – were never-theless an inescapable fact of war. And then, too, whether in action or not, pilots were always getting themselves killed in one way or another. But Mackail's death was somehow different – unnecessary and so inconsequential that tem-porarily it left Brick-Kiln Farm possessed by a demoralized rabble.

The officers were as much at fault as the men, who – less their two senior NCOs, the one flying, the other lying shrouded in that draughty shed – had no one left from their own ranks to look to. Only Morton-Dunne had remained un-touched by the confused and trance-like numbness into which everyone else seemed to have fallen. He had shed his air of remote and philosophical detachment and moved among the gape-mouthed and silent groups of mechanics and riggers, exhorting and encouraging, until slowly the men began mov-ing about their duties again. With the exception of one or two of the younger and tougher junior NCOs they worked like zombies, refilling the petrol-drums of the flare-path before returning to their sullen and unspeaking groups, waiting dully in the freezing cold, staring blankly upwards into the darkness. It was beginning to snow again now. Borne on sudden squalls of wind, the snow-flakes swirled and flurried about the waiting knots of airmen, buffeting their unheeding faces.

Then, three-quarters of an hour after the aircraft had taken off, there was a new source of worry. The distant drone of an aero-engine announced that one of the Flight's aircraft was near to completing the first lap of its patrol.

'Factory engine,' someone said, recognizing the chur of a returning BE12. The aircraft passed, some considerable distance to the south. Morton-Dunne fired a trio of Very lights – two green and a red – into the night. An answering green slanted palely down through the murk. The sound of the engine faded as the aircraft turned onto the second leg of its search. A minute or so later, the growl of a second approaching BE12 was heard. This time the roar grew louder until the plane was almost overhead, and its recognition flare dropped into a little coppice just beyond the airfield's perimeter. That was both the single-seaters accounted for. But where was the Bristol?

The minutes passed, relentlessly ticking themselves into oblivion. Now everyone knew that something must surely have gone wrong. Despite being the last of the three aircraft to take-off, the Bristol, with its advantages of greater speed and climb, should have been the first to return. But the Bristol hadn't returned. . . . And, the events of the evening having prepared 'D' Flight for wary pessimism, the near-certainty of probable disaster loomed ominously in everyone's mind. If a fool like Peters could manage to find his way home safely, then there was not much likelihood that the great Destrier had made a navigational mess of things. No, much more probable was the chance that the Bristol and her crew had been forced down somewhere out there in the icy vastness of the night, the victims of engine-failure. In which case, Destrier and Hopkins had by now almost certainly gone west and were lying dead somewhere in the smashed or burnt-out wreckage of their Brisfit. God help the poor sods. . . . There couldn't be much hope for anyone trying to force-land on a night like this . . . nor, if the crash had left them lying seriously injured, would either man be likely to survive till morning. Exposure would get them first.

Reluctantly, young Russell gave up any hope of ever seeing his sweaters and socks again. With the callous egotism of youth, he thanked his lucky stars that he wasn't inside them at this moment. Still, it was a pity about poor old Hoppy, though. For a Flight-Sergeant he had seemed a very reasonable sort of bloke. But that was the way things went, Russell told himself, remembering the sound of Peters's safely homing BE and the sight of Mackail's shattered body lying on the ground; it was always the decent blokes who bought it, and the bastards who survived.

Long miles to the north, the deep organ song of the Bristol's Falcon was booming out as strongly as ever and very far from failure. In the cramped, elbow-jarring rear cockpit of the big fighter, Hopkins's grieving and shock-confused mind was partially lulled by the engine's chorale. Seated now with his head well down below the cockpit coaming, a hand thrust up under his helmet and an elbow jammed against one of the fuselage members, Hopkins used the bones of his arms and wrist to bring the Falcon's multitudinous polyphony singing into his ear, knowing his work on the worn engine to have been good. But this work hadn't been solely his, Hopkins remembered; it had been Mackail's, too. Yet this splendidly singing artifice that he and Mackail had refurbished between them had been responsible for Mackail's death. . . .

Hopkins was puzzled. Things didn't make sense. The sounds in his ear added up to a testament of order and harmony. Let just one of these myriad voices sing a slightly different tune and the whole pattern would be lost, the music would become chaotic – and the engine fail.

Yet this same order had smashed Mackail with a casual and anarchic violence that of itself affronted and denied all the canons of discipline and control it supposedly represented. There was a paradox in this, if only he could see it; a paradox – and a sort of perversity, as if whatever fates there were sniggered up their sleeves to watch mortal man's blind and stumbling attempts to shape some sort of sanity for himself out of chaos.

A right sods'-opera.

The Falcon's roar deepened and Hopkins brought his mind back to the present with a jerk. He raised his head above the cockpit-coaming and out into the murderous slipstream. It seemed to him that his goggles – though now cleared of their ice – might just as well be a blindfold, for all that he could see through them. The night was as black and as solid and as impenetrable as ever. Even so, Hopkins was guiltily aware of his own abysmal failure as an observer since the Bristol's take-off. An observer's job was to observe, come what may – and never mind sickness, cold, grief, or his dear old gran's piles. . . . Since he'd been cowering in the bottom of his cockpit, the whole of the German bomber fleet might have gone thundering past, for all he knew. Besides . . . a new uneasiness began to steal over Hopkins: just how long was it since they'd taken off, for Gawd's sake? He ducked down below the cockpit-coaming again, scrabbling for the make-shift light-switch to get a glimpse at his watch. Hell's teeth! Thirty-five minutes they'd been up – and so far without making that scheduled south-easterly turn which should have come after ten or fifteen minutes' flying time. Now just what the devil did Destrier think he was up to? And where the blazes were they heading for?

Hopkins stood in the cockpit and leant forwards over Destrier, pummelling his shoulder and bellowing the words 'south-east!' close to his ear. But the syllables were broken and distorted by the slipstream, and blasted back into Hopkins's own throat, making him splutter and choke. The shoulder under his hand remained as unresponsive as that of a corpse.

Leaning even further into the wind, Hopkins looked past the lump of Destrier's head to the dimly-lit instrument panel. Again the slipstream got under his goggles, distorting his vision, and it was some moments before he was able to focus on the compass sufficiently well to be able to read the Bristol's course. North by east – nearly nor'nor'east. . . . What the hell did Destrier imagine he was up to, disobeying his own instructions like this?

With difficulty, Hopkins half-succeeded in smothering his disquiet. After all, who was he to question Destrier's chosen course of action? This sort of thing was Destrier's forte, not his. It was Destrier who was the predator, the hunter with an almost fabled reputation for seeking out and finding the enemy. For the hundredth time, Hopkins damned the conscience that had driven him to clambering into a cockpit again. He'd been a fool even to imagine he could bridge the gap between the sort of flying he remembered and this.... The war had changed and he was much too old a dog to learn new tricks. Yes – tomorrow night young Russell could have his cockpit back, and welcome.

In the meantime, Hopkins told himself, here he was – presumably somewhere over Essex – with the prospect of being flown even further and further north by someone whose sanity he could no longer take for granted, until they either turned back or continued onwards until the Bristol ran out of juice and they crashed somewhere in the icy loneliness of the North Sea.... Longingly, Hopkins thought of grabbing at those handholds on the rudder-cables running by his legs, and pulling the Bristol's nose round by mainforce until she was on a southerly course again. But the part of Hopkins that was a creature of military habit blanched at the very thought of such an action. Ashamed that his consciousness had even been able to shape such an idea, he slumped back again into the windy misery of his cockpit, huddling deep into his layers of woollens, trying to conserve the last of his rapidly vanishing body-heat. But supposing they *did* go down into the sea.... How long would a man last on a night like this? Three minutes? Four? Hopkins didn't know. An ironic fatalism stole over him; by an odd quirk of chance, his thoughts ran on identical lines to young Russell's back at Brick-Kiln Farm – thoughts concerned with his borrowed sweaters and socks.

That young man should be down on his knees and thanking the Almighty that it was some other fool who was wearing his blasted property at this moment....

EIGHT

Von Trier ticked off the remaining minutes of R.45's due easterly course. As he did so, his mind fell back onto an old and irritating riddle which – so far as he knew – had no solution. This, for want of a better name, he thought of as the riddle of Fate itself; in all its curious and unfathomably devious workings, and the way in which, rightly or wrongly, it appeared that an individual's life seemed to be governed by decisions, his own and other people's, so small as to be barely recognizable as decisions at all.... A man's fate could never entirely be a matter for himself alone: his whole pattern of existence was hedged about and subtly altered by the unconsidered whims and gestures of people he would never know, and who would never know him....

Come to think of it, whole generations owed their precarious foothold on existence to the fact that successions of unknown and shadowy ancestors had somehow contrived to go on missing death by inches. A man's gift for survival ensured his posterity. Besides, as if the hazards in this sort of thing were not enough, there was the further chancy miracle of each individual's conception.... Von Trier remembered reading somewhere of the exact number of sperm engaged at any one ejaculation in their blind race to the womb. The figure ran into millions, so far as he could recall. And, even when there *was* a winner to this race, only one single sperm out of all that vast number came safely home to harbour.... Yes, a man's singularity might seem very special and important to himself, but nature, or Fate, or call it what you would, simply didn't give a damn.

Von Trier picked up his dividers, pressing their points into the back of his hand until they hurt. He looked down at his chart and disliked what he saw. That change of course in a few minutes to fly out over Dover was an unnecessary piece of bravado in his estimation. Knowing there were enemy bombers about, the not inconsiderable port defences would be on their mettle at the first warning drone of R.45's engines. The night's secrecy would be laid bare by searchlights, and the air torn to shreds by every gun the defences could muster. Von Trier was well aware that the chances of these actually hitting anything were remote. But, nevertheless, those chances *did* exist; and, his night's work being complete, there was no point at all in courting danger.

Von Trier drew another line across his chart, one which was merely a continuation of R.45's present course, and one which would bring her safely out over the Channel somewhere just north of Sandwich. The Count wrote this change of intention on a fresh slip of paper and eyed it sardonically. That Horst would be affronted by its implied prudence he had little doubt. The Sausage would be in his element with the Dover defences and what would probably seem like half the Royal Navy giving R.45 an uncharitable send-off. For his own part, von Trier was quite sure he could do without so Wagnerian a conclusion to the night's fun. The shortest way home, and the one least likely to hold unpleasant possibilities, seemed the sanest course to him.

Tearing the slip of paper from his pad, von Trier stood up and made his way for'ard. Horst took the paper and digested its brief instructions, looking up at his Commander with much the same accusation in his doggy-brown eyes that a hound might have shown if deprived of a keenly anticipated after-noon in pursuit of wild boar. The abruptness with which Horst transferred the slip of paper to the clip-board on his knee was a remonstrance in itself, and once again von Trier felt a barely resistible urge to shake some sense into the man.

Bloody fool!

Annoyed by Horst's obtuse and stolid lack of imagination, von Trier returned to his seat. Just under another forty min-utes flying time, and the bomber would be safely out over the sea and able to say *Auf Wiedersehen* to England for one more night.

Von Trier looked down at his chart again with something

like complacency, quite unaware that by the drawing of one thin pencil line he had irrevocably triggered Fate.

For, quite unknown to the Count, there were other architects too, who – by intention or chance – were also taking their parts in shaping this night's ends. Far away to the north-east of R.45, Destrier was reaching towards the destination his subconscious mind had insistently but inexplicably ordained for him from the moment the Bristol had left the ground – Tolleswich. Perhaps, his wounded spirit argued, he would again see the silhouette of the monstrous cruciform that had so obsessed him since that night when death had come whistling down from it to destroy everything he loved. If so, he promised himself, then one way or another, he would make an end to its dark dominion. The same, preternatural skill that had been used without hatred – and, sometimes, with regret – to drive down forty of his king's enemies would this time be used with vindictive ire, and a complete carelessness as to the possibility of his own destruction.

'But what about Hopkins?' prompted a last, small, surviving spark of compassion within him. With callous deliberation, he snuffed the life out of this. Hopkins was as nothing beside this need of his for catharsis, for this destruction and blotting out of the evil that had so wantonly murdered his Dolly. To this end, Hopkins was but a tool – competent, reliable, and as expendable as himself. . . .

Destrier dropped the Bristol's long, purposeful nose for speed, seeing ahead of him the black, twisting estuary of the river on which Tolleswich lay. A sharp finger of light betrayed the exact locality of the town – a single searchlight, piercing the scud of drifting snow-squalls, before being joined by a second light, and then still others, as the harbour defences came alive to the sound of an approaching aircraft. Methodically, these began quartering the sky. Destrier dived the Bristol down, keeping just outside their perimeters, waiting for the monstrous shape which, he knew, must surely fly into their clutch. . . .

But no such shape materialized. Instead, after several minutes of search, the lights caught the Bristol and held her in their brilliant eye. Despite the fact that the aircraft above had only one engine, and that the silhouette was friendly, the Tolleswich gun-crews were obviously taking no chances. For no sooner had the searchlights caught the Bristol, than every gun beneath, on shore or in the destroyers moored at the mouth of the harbour, opened its mouth in hysterical wrath.

Instinctively, Hopkins now knew where they were. Awed, he leant over the side of his cockpit, staring down at the fury Destrier had stirred up. Tracer from small calibre guns yearned up at them and faded into the night. An ear-splitting crack above the starboard wing and the reek of cordite warned of heavier metal being used (three or four-inch, Hopkins guessed) and its unwelcome and dangerous accuracy. A second explosion, even nearer than the first, sent the Bristol skittering wildly across the sky. Shrapnel fragments tore through the fuselage. One piece struck the elevating-arm of the Scarff mounting, and then, its force nearly spent, struck Hopkins a numbing blow on the shoulder. He flinched and swore, and – for a moment or two – was tempted to duck back down again into the illusory safety of his cockpit. But, realizing the futility of this – the plywood and canvas floor of the cockpit was no defence against either machine-gun bullets or shrapnel – he unwillingly looked down again towards the ground, where the whole town and harbour of Tolleswich appeared to be a carpet of dancing, flickering gunfire.

Jesus Christ! They would have to get out of this – and fast! But strangely, Destrier made no attempt to evade or lose the searchlights' implacable and blinding glare. Instead, he turned towards the most brilliant and persistent of these and, dropping the Bristol's nose, dived nearly vertically down its long column of tormenting light. Dazzled, Hopkins fought to keep himself from closing his eyes. Now, without doubt, he knew Destrier to be insane. Mother of God! what did the man imagine he was going to do? Strafe the searchlight and its crew with the Bristol's Vickers? The dive continued down and down, the shriek of the wind through the aircraft's rigging rising in pitch as her speed increased. The guns, caught out by the Bristol's tactics, had momentarily lost their accuracy and were being directed above her. To Hopkins, it felt as though the fighter was falling down through the hollow centre of a cone of whining, shrieking, singing metal. The blinding, burning eye of the searchlight leapt into the whirling disc of the propeller, and now Hopkins knew without any further room for doubt, that strafing it *was* Destrier's intention....

Chri-i-ist! that would be the end....

Without much caring whether he fell out of the Bristol or not, Hopkins leaned far forward against the slipstream, grabbing Destrier's shoulders with both hands and shaking him, probing cruelly for the half-healed and knotted muscle at the base of the other's neck. He felt Destrier squirm with pain, and his hands lost their grip as Destrier's head was jerked backwards to butt him agonizingly in the mouth. Hopkins clenched his fists and pummelled Destrier's head and shoulders with a despairing savagery. Then, suddenly, the whine of the slipstream through the rigging altered in pitch as Destrier at last pulled back on the stick. With a shudder and a wing-tearing wrench they were out of the dive, out of the maddening, relentless glare of that searchlight, and streaking low across country a hundred or so feet up. A line of tracer from an outlying machine-gun leapt up at them – and was then left behind.

Hopkins fell back into his seat, shaking and momentarily spent, the searing glare of the searchlights still written on his retina, his mouth full of the iron-taste of blood from a badly cut lip. The Bristol swept round in a tight, banking turn, and Hopkins resigned himself to a second – this time probably fatal – run over Tolleswich. But no – passing to seaward of the town, Destrier this time outflanked its defences, apparently veering back the way they had come. Wearily, Hopkins got himself onto his feet again. Screwing up eyes that were still branded with the image of the searchlights' terrible candle-power, he squinted past Destrier's head towards the compass. It was some seconds before the after-echoes of light still stamped on his retina allowed him to focus his eyes with sufficient clarity to find that the Bristol was now flying south – south-east. That meant they would fetch up somewhere on the Kent coast again, which seemed to imply that Destrier had returned to at least some small semblance of sanity.

But God alone knew what was going to happen when – or, rather, if – they got down again at Brick-Kiln Farm. One way and another, there looked like being the very devil to pay....

The frenzied pounding of Hopkins's fists on his shoulders had indeed brought Destrier partially back from the remoteness into which he had allowed himself to be beguiled since taking-off from Brick-Kiln Farm. The imperative that had drawn him northwards, across the Thames Estuary and then across the flat desolation of Essex, had been irresistible – a whisper calling to him from a voice he had thought silenced for ever beneath its shroud of East Anglian clay. For months he had lain awake long nights trying to recapture the cadences and timbre of that voice, with its twin *liet-motifs* of kindness and laughter always lurking beneath its surface calm.

But the voice had remained lost and irrecoverable, its music no longer even an echo in his head. And then, this evening, as he had lifted the Bristol off over the dark waters of that dyke – waters that were as dark as those of Lethe – a murmur had begun, a voice shaping itself among the tremulous stresses of the aircraft, the elusive harmonics of the rigging, the undertones of the engine. And this voice was unmistakably Dolly's, even though it had spoken no words. Instead, it had communicated itself to him in an inchoate and constantly changing flow of rippling sounds whose pattern and meaning had become clearer and more insistent as the Bristol had eaten into the long miles north. This very wordlessness of the voice had made its message the more compelling, its nuances the more subtle, its truths the more direct. Beguiled, Destrier had allowed himself to be drawn northwards, convinced that now at last he was moving towards that one culminating moment of destiny he had always secretly known himself born for. And, in that moment, the voice promised him, the grief and anger of the last few months would be cancelled out, and he and Dolly miraculously restored to each other....

But the voice had cheated ... lied....

Over Tolleswich, no black shape had come swimming into the searchlights' glare for him to challenge and strike down. Instead, the searchlights had fixed on the Bristol, and the echo of Dolly's voice had faded, fragmenting and dissolving itself back into the separate aircraft noises from which his longing had formed it. Bereft, filled with a wild, despairing anger, he had dived down the cone of that one, too-persistent light intent on – intent on *what*? But the tattoo of Hopkins's fists pounding agonizingly at his neck and shoulders had brought him back to the present and its cold actualities – and he no longer remembered.

Destrier glanced down at the compass, and kicked hard at the rudder-bar. Allowing for drift, this new course should bring the Bristol back south again to somewhere near Deal on the second leg of her box search. Within the vortex of Destrier's brain, the last remaining shreds of his sanity told him to forget Deal, to fly straight home to Brick-Kiln Farm, to admit defeat, to follow Spring's advice and walk away from aircraft for good and learn to live with his grief like any normal person....

But then, something else within him whispered that it was already far too late for this, that by listening to that persuasive voice imagination had shaped for itself from the Bristol's murmuring prompting, his die had somehow been cast and that, willy-nilly, he was being drawn down a path which, however obliquely, led him towards fate....

Was this obsession? Madness? Destrier didn't know ... and neither did he care....

To Browne, now well into his second circuit, his patrol had resolved itself into a double-battle between boredom and cold. His habitual insouciance and youthful optimism had ebbed and shrunk within him like the mercury in some spiritual thermometer; physically and mentally he was moving towards his nadir. Poor Browne! His fit, slight, immature body was a fragile hostage to pit against this December night. Paradoxically, its very fitness told against it, having no cushioning layers of fat to insulate it against the blighting, inimical cold. As Browne's body chilled, so his senses slowed and his courage faded. Had he been a little older, he might have had deeper resources to call on, other than those of a somewhat gauche and schoolboyish youth who had yet to reach the full resilience and stamina of his masculine pride.

The laughter and foolery in Browne, his sense of the absurd, had all faded into misery long before he reached Brick-Kiln Farm at the end of his first circuit, and – too far to the south – had fired his Very pistol down into the night. The sight of Morton-Dunne's answering signal had filled him with something very like homesickness, a terrible sense of isolation and loneliness, and an almost irresistible urge to be down on the ground again, out of this damnable and icy blackness, safe and warm and surrounded by the cheerful bustle of his fellow men.

And, come to that, he had excuse enough, too. . . . Since somewhere near Deal, his engine had been dropping revs – not badly, but steadily and seriously enough for an older and wiser man than Browne to have called it a night, to have signalled Brick-Kiln Farm for the flare-path to be lit, and to have ghosted down only too happy for an honourable and legitimate excuse to feel his undercart touch solid ground. . . . But Browne did not come down; instead, with his engine beginning to sound increasingly uneven, he flew on, goaded not so much by courage or pride, but by sheer ignorance, his mind too full of the possibilities of what people might say should he land prematurely to understand that on this occasion, discretion was most certainly the better part of valour. In similar circumstances, neither Destrier nor Morton-Dunne would have hesitated to return and land. Indeed, before the patrol, it should have been Destrier's business to make it quite clear that in circumstances such as Browne's, continuance was neither praiseworthy nor heroic, but a stupidity liable to cost 'D' Flight one of its precious trio of serviceable aircraft. But Destrier, absorbed in his own private world of hate and grief was too preoccupied to have given the possibility of such an occurrence any mention at his scant and hasty briefing before the patrol, and Browne had not seen fit to ask, too awed by Destrier's reputation, his basilisk stare and the knowledge of that small slip of magenta ribbon hidden beneath the leather of his Flight Commander's coat.

But by now, with the stark blackness of the estuary-line opening below him again and Whitstable lost somewhere beneath his port wing, Browne was roused from his lethargy of cold and boredom by the alarming way in which the BE2's engine was beginning to lose power and by his consequent difficulty in maintaining speed and height. Again, a more experienced man might have decided to nurse his engine and turn, either directly back for home, or north-west across the narrow waters of the Swale to the RNAS station at Eastchurch. But young Browne chose to disregard both these alternatives. No, he would complete the second lap of his patrol, pray that his engine held out for long enough for him to get down safely at Brick-Kiln Farm – and then people could say what they liked. An awful and overpowering sense of his own loneliness began to permeate through him, much worse than anything he had experienced so far. The lightless dark and cold seemed directed against him personally, in a cruel and merciless conspiracy to crush and destroy him. For the first time in his young life it struck him that for all his hopeful promise and accomplishment he amounted to very, very little in the great scheme of things. . . .

Since the near-disaster of his take-off and the panic compounded by finding himself lost over the sea, Peters's confidence had gradually reasserted itself. This new morale had been boosted when his own hopeful flares had been answered by Morton-Dunne's bursting upwards from almost directly beneath him. Somehow – by luck or judgement (and Peters preferred to think of it as judgement) – he had managed to eliminate the navigational errors caused by that first overlong leg of his patrol and had found Brick-Kiln Farm with immaculate precision.

A new and unwonted optimism began to possess him, an intimation that it was at last within his power to lose, once and for all, his hateful reputation for incompetence. The confidence this aroused in Peters allowed him to bundle his old follies and indiscretions into the back of his memory. For what had these to do with his new and assured self who could fly a powerful, if second-rate, aircraft a mile high through the pitch-blackness of a winter's night with such splendid precision? Nothing! Despite the cold, Peters felt warm and full of vitality. It was borne in on him that this night was somehow marking a fateful watershed in his existence, and that in the last sixty or so minutes, he had become his own man – one very different from the whining, lack-lustre creature secretly despised even by himself. . . .

Even as Peters toyed with this exciting and intoxicating notion of his new and admirable self, he spotted the pale glow of an aircraft's exhaust, slightly to the south but on a heading parallel to his own. Peters felt his heart jump wildly with excitement, and he was filled with a strange and unfamiliar sense of exhaltation. Now, indeed, he knew his luck to have changed. A few more minutes, and no longer would he be Peters the absurd, Peters the incompetent, Peters the buffoon, Peters the butt of every squadron he had ever served with – no, rather would he soon be 'that chap who knocked a Gotha down over Kent, don't you know . . . that fellow who got his MC for finishing a bomber in a lumbering old crate of a BE12. . . .'

Kicking at the rudder-bar and opening his throttle to its widest, Peters brought the BE's nose round in pursuit of that dimly luminous exhaust. . . .

Peters had been seconded to 'D' Flight, a unit expressly created for one purpose – the interception and destruction of night-raiding enemy. So that now, after an hour's patrolling to this end, when at last – and against very long odds – he had spotted an aircraft, he wasted no time in questioning its probable identity, for that was a matter already settled in his mind. That the second aircraft could possibly be friendly, an ally bent on the same fool's errand as himself, simply never entered his head.

To a man long conscious of a string of bitter failures, suddenly presented with the apparent opportunity for redeeming himself at one swoop, the glow of that exhaust meant only one thing, that he had sighted his enemy, and that to live up to his new-found sense of strength and purpose, he must drive that enemy down. It never occurred to Peters to ask himself why he could only see the exhausts of a single engine, when the smallest spark of thought would have warned him that any intruding bomber would show him at least two, and possibly four, sets of manifolds set wide apart; no, Peters had already made up his mind, seeing no more and no less than what he wanted to see. In five minutes – ten at the most – the twin Lewises above his head would be brought into blistering action. Afterwards, no one would ever be able to dismiss him lightly or scornfully again; he would be someone to be reckoned with – in other men's eyes as well as his own.

Ninety-nine times out of a hundred, the original error that had taken Peters out over the Thames Estuary on the first leg of his patrol would have had neither importance nor significance once the mistake had been discovered and rectified; but this particular night, the errors, aberrations and honest judgements of individual men were to shape the separate parts from which a malicious fate was to shape a bloody and bitter whole....

What with Peters's error, and Destrier's decision to fly north, Browne's aircraft had become the leading one in the patrol. But now, with its engine fading, and palpably losing speed and height, it was Browne's aircraft that at this moment was falling back inexorably, yard by yard, to within range of Peters's guns.

Down the surprising length of R.45's cabin, von Trier looked at Horst's back, amusement replacing his recent irritation. If it came to a choice as to which was the more expressive – backs or faces – then, thought the Count, give him backs every time. Robbed of his promised exodus over Dover, Horst sat in the Staaken's left-hand seat, the rigid lines of his back a tautly eloquent expression of his suppressed disapproval of von Trier's change of course. With Maidstone and then Canterbury left behind, they were now flying over the loom of a landscape evidently flatter than that of the North Downs. In another ten or fifteen minutes, as von Trier knew, R.45 would be safely out over the Channel, and he would be able to kiss England goodbye for one more night. It would be a peaceful leave-taking, he hoped, one rather different to the sort of soldier's farewell to be expected from Dover. R.45 would become a fading echo on the night, an undiscovered presence slipping quietly away over the horizon, her night's work done.

The thought filled him with satisfaction. Von Trier reached into his flying-leathers and, after a little fumbling, managed to find his cigar-case. He took from it a small, black cheroot and despite the reek of petrol in the cabin, lit it and leant back in his chair. Wendel glanced forward at his Captain, his apparently unintelligent eyes deep with disapproval. And yet, at the same time, the sight of von Trier peacefully drawing on his cigar told the fuel-mechanic more eloquently than any words that the alarums and excursions to be expected from this night were as good as over. Wendel turned back to his pumps with a new heart. Pump no. 5 was by now the merest ghost of itself but, with the bomber relieved of the weight of her bombs, he knew he could keep it working well enough until they reached Gontrode. For a moment, Wendel was tempted towards feeling something very near to von Trier's obvious contentment ... but then the chimera of his doubts and misgivings returned to sober him. There still remained a long, long way between themselves and home; the long, dark sea-leagues in which anything might happen. Anything. Besides, there would be other raids after this one, raids that would go on till the war ended – if it ever did.

Down in the Staaken's belly, Rossi sat with both gauntleted hands pressed to his face. The bruising of his mouth and nose seemed to be making his whole head an agonized ball of pain. Buffeted by the relentless inpouring of the slipstream through the hatch beneath him, he no longer found it possible to think with any pretence at rationality. His whole world had become reduced to two things – wind and pain. There had never been anything else. . . .

Tomorrow – and at the risk of becoming even more of a laughing-stock among the Staaken's crew than he felt himself to be already – Rossi knew that he would have to go sick. Luckily, he also knew that the bomber herself would have to be out of service for a few days having her pumps replaced, so that no one would be able to accuse him of malingering. Not that Rossi found himself caring very much at this moment what people chose to think; he had a more frightening worry to occupy his mind. Normally, as he had long-since learned, his night-vision was better than anyone else's in R.45 – even von Trier's. But now, with his eyes closing up like a beaten boxer's, and further blasted and tormented by that icy gale raging up from beneath him, the terrifying possibility occurred to Rossi that he had hurt himself far more seriously than he had thought, and that he was going blind. The premonition that had come to him while he was lying on his bunk at Gontrode forced itself into the front of his mind with a new and sinister certainty, and he found himself moving his battered lips in prayer, repeating over and over again, 'Holy Mother of God, pray for us sinners now and at the hour of our death. . . . Holy Mother of God, pray for us sinners now and at the hour of our death. . . .'

With an effort he pulled his hands from his face and, with his head half turned against the searing, shrieking slipstream, squinted down into the night. A mist of dancing and inconsequential lights seemed to flicker across his eyes. Apart from that, he could see nothing.

Back in the cabin, Walter had silently approved von Trier's change of course. There was never any sense in stirring up hornets' nests or deliberately looking for trouble. For all his apparent flannel, the skipper had his head screwed on too firmly for that sort of game. The fattest, warmest wench in Bremen would have a lot to be thankful for. Studiously keeping his face expressionless, Walter stole a sideways glance at Horst. Poor old Sausage! His face was rigid with disappointment and disapproval. In Walter's opinion, if things had been left to Horst, then they'd have probably flown out over Dover, low down and with all guns blazing, like something out of a boys' adventure story.

Walter eased his cramped body in his seat and stretched his arms above his head in chilly but relieved contentment. Just ten more minutes and the possibility of any serious fun and games would be over for the night. He stretched again and met Horst's disapproving glare with an insolent wink, refusing to be intimidated by the officer's ridiculous hauteur.

'Officers ... I've shat 'em....' he said quietly, looking straight at Horst.

Horst's mouth opened in shocked disbelief.

'*Wha-at* did you say?' he bellowed above the roar of the Maybachs.

Walter creased his young-old face into a look of innocence.

'I said oil pressure slightly down on no. 3 engine, sir!'

The Sausage glared at him.

Out above that same no. 3 engine, Mendelssohn cradled the butt of his Lewis. His concerto continued to play itself in his head, and by now had reached the beginning of that unwritten third movement. But what was this? A new pattern of notes and sounds was tentatively shaping itself in his head. Mendelssohn did his best to ignore these and to pretend they had no interest for him. Composition – as he had long since discovered – was like fishing: strike too soon, and you lost your fish! Hurry was the enemy of Art. But even so, Mendelssohn was too much of a musician to be able to disregard this splendid extemporization handselling itself in his brain. For this music, it seemed, was growing out of some secret and as yet undiscovered part of himself, overflowing and flooding out into his whole being, so that, stiff and frozen as he was, he felt suddenly warmed and aglow as the long-elusive subject for his third movement came striding into his brain in a great unison of sound, the strings rising out of a ground of brass – pausing for the briefest moment – and then rolling relentlessly onwards like a river in spate. Against this, the voice of his solo violin eddied and spun like a leaf caught up and drawn ecstatically along by its tide. A great humility stole over Mendelssohn. Were these sounds really his? Was this splendid tumult roaring through his head something to be jotted down in black and white and claimed as his own? Such arrogance was absurd! From whatever source this miracle of creation came, it was too big to be born merely of his own poor brain. Like that solo fiddle, jigging and dancing in his head, he was but an instrument, a passive tool through which this glory might pour itself. . . .

Now, Mendelssohn knew, the labour and sweat were nearly done. He felt a serene contentment, like that of a seaman who has raised the lights of his home-port and knows the long fret and fever of voyaging on uncharted seas to be almost over. The moment R.45 landed, and he was at least marginally thawed out, enough to hold a pencil, Mendelssohn was determined to begin setting down the skeleton of these elusive sounds before they disappeared, silenced into the nothingness from which they had sprung.

Solitary and exposed as he was on R.45's shuddering wing-top, Mendelssohn, warmed by fulfilment, felt a glowing sense of oneness with all mankind.

The great music in his head opened out over newer and ever wider vistas of wonder and majesty. Awed, Mendelssohn listened to the harmony swelling and surging within him. For the moment at least, his earlier doubts about the sanity of his fellow men and the goodness of God were stilled. His faith was certain again – as certain and simple and whole as it had been when, as a child, he'd stood beside the comforting Sabbath massiveness of his grandfather in the Synagogue near his home, and listened to the words of the Psalmist:

'Great is the Lord, and greatly to be praised: and his greatness is unsearchable. . . .'

In sharp contrast to Mendelssohn, though marginally warmer, Hopkins had no such happy serenity of mind. As the Bristol racketed southwards, with the line of the Kent shore scrawled darkly beneath, he was in a mental turmoil.

Only one thing seemed clear: the bleak knowledge that had so dismayed him over Tolleswich – there would be the devil to pay for this night's work.

In his own mind, Hopkins was as certain as he could be of anything, that Destrier had been within a toucher of shooting-up and destroying that persistent and dangerous searchlight back at Tolleswich, and that but for his own equally un-military and indefensible behaviour (wilfully striking an officer, no less!), would have actually done so. Of one thing Hopkins was sure: that if Destrier chose to make anything of this little incident on landing, then he – Hopkins – was done for. What court martial would possibly take his word against Destrier's, or even consider listening to his reasons with anything other than amazed disbelief, any small intimations of doubt silenced by the sight of that slip of ribbon on his accuser's chest? Besides, even in his own defence – even through the neutral medium of a Prisoner's Friend – how could he even begin to consider saying that Destrier, the one really close friend he had ever made, was ga-ga, Doolali, bolo, completely off his chump? When you had known someone for twenty years, known him more thoroughly and intimately than most men appeared to know their own brothers, then decency, honour – love, even – put their own limits on what might, or might not, be said....

It was this prospect, and not that of his own court martial, that tormented Hopkins, crouched in the rear cockpit of the Bristol: the fact that, one way or another in the near future, it would be his *duty* to say what he suspected – or, rather, knew – about Destrier. Common sense told Hopkins that with Destrier in his present state of mind it was unlikely that he would be fallen in between an escort the moment they touched down at Brick-Kiln Farm. By Destrier, at least, the whole matter would probably be laid aside and forgotten as something trivial and insignificant, counting for nothing beside those greater obsessions by which he was now so obviously driven. Once down, Hopkins doubted the incident would even be mentioned.

But it *ought* to be. Destrier's madness over Tolleswich should not be forgotten, even if it meant bringing a great deal of unpleasantness down onto his own head in the process. Destrier's undoubted gift for destruction had been turned inwards on himself and was now as great a danger to his friends as to his enemies.

Yet, in the disordered and unmilitary make-shift base that was Brick-Kiln Farm, who was there for him to turn to? His course of action was unclear. Even in a proper squadron — one with its proper establishment and hierarchy of officers and warrant-officers through whom he could voice his fears — what he had to say would still be next-door to impossible. 'Please, sir, I respectfully beg to report that the Flight-Commander's gone off his head, and can something please be done about it?' — even in the most favourable of circumstances, the 'something that would be done' would most likely be himself. . . .

But Destrier could not be allowed to go on flying in his present state. It wasn't just a matter of the poor devil killing himself — though that might, perhaps, be the kindest solution; no, there was Destrier's observer to be considered — perhaps not himself next time, but young Russell — or one of the inexperienced subalterns back at Brick-Kiln Farm who, so far, seemed to have spent most of their time in keeping out of the way and avoiding Peters.

Peters! Hopkins's dismay deepened into despair as he considered the man. True, he was Brick-Kiln Farm's senior subaltern, but Hopkins knew that he could no more consider taking a matter of this sort to Peters than he would consider jumping out of the cockpit and doing handstands on the wings. Peters, in his own way, was every bit as big a headache as Destrier.

There was always Morton-Dunne, of course, Hopkins thought, clutching at straws. For all that he read philosophy or whatever in Ancient Greek, he seemed a pretty sound and sensible sort of chap – and decent. But, NO! Hopkins brought himself back to reality; decent or not, Morton-Dunne was too young, too junior, too greenly inexperienced in the ways of the Service to know what ought to be done, even if he could bring himself to believe what Hopkins had to say.

The more he chased the problem round in his own mind, the more insoluble it seemed. He could choose to do nothing, of course, and wait events. . . . Hopkins sucked at his torn and aching lip. Yes, he could do that – and then learn to live with himself afterwards when someone got killed. To take such a course would be a betrayal of himself, sheer cowardice. . . .

What a bloody awful mess the whole thing was.

In the freezing air, south-east of London, a dozen men spun out the thread of fate in the blackness over Kent. One, his engine abused until it seized, had already crash-landed on the southern flank of Shooter's Hill, and now, unconscious, was being revived by the anxious Special who had struck him down. A second would have no awakening: rigid and frozen, he bobbed and swayed in his harness above R.45's port wing. The others were reaching towards their destiny, too – ten airmen who, through choice or chance, had left their natural element for the air, and who, ill-met in this, the dark of their moon, would kill and be killed as the separate threads of their lives wove themselves briefly together in a single, apocalyptic strand.

Destiny was about to bring these ten men together – because Peters had fluffed his navigation; because Destrier had chosen to hunt northwards, pursuing the ghost of a remembered voice echoing in his head; because von Trier sought to take what seemed R.45's safest course back home to Gontrode; because of Browne's fading engine, his fear of being thought afraid, and his unexpected susceptibility to cold. . . .

These then, were the immediate causes of a brief and apparently indefinite – though bloody – encounter over Richborough and the Sandwich Flats. The immediate causes only – the real origins lay much further back, and had – if you like –

been brewing in the womb of time, since time itself had begun.

Somewhere to the east of Canterbury, it became clear to Browne that his faltering engine might just get him home. In the last five minutes or so since he had turned south-east, its note had got no better, but neither had it got any worse. Revs and temperature seemed to have settled on a constant and, albeit reluctantly, the BE12 appeared to be holding her own. Despite his frozen state, a small spark of optimism and sense revived within Browne. Honour was satisfied; no one would now be able to say he'd shown the white feather if, at the end of this second circuit, he chose to fire off the two greens that would see the flare-path lit for him. He would plonk the BE down gratefully, thankful to be done with the night's proceedings. Judging by the noises coming back to him from up front, it would be a day or two at least before the BE was serviceable again, and Browne admitted his relief to himself. It wasn't that he was windy exactly, or anything like that . . . it was – the return of his doubts about himself engendered a rising anger in Browne. What the devil did Hopkins and Mackail mean by sending him up in a rotten and unreliable old crate like this? Lord! But he'd jolly-well have a word or two to say to that pair when he got down! Between them, they might have got him killed. This small truculence growing in Browne helped to restore his confidence and waning *amour-propre*. He knew his resentment to be unfair – particularly aimed at the two NCOs. God alone knew how hard both had sweated in the last ten days. But still, the worst side of himself insisted, listening to any further deterioration of his engine note, it wouldn't do any harm to haze them along a bit. It would stop the blighters from slacking off and keep them up to the mark. Christ, the last, frozen particles of his normally decent self warned, he was beginning to sound just like that awful shite, Peters; yes, *exactly* like Peters. . . .

At this moment, the first shells from below began bursting round Browne's BE12. . . .

For five days the battery firing at Browne had been tucked away in a clearing barely large enough to contain it, at the edge of a wood, half a mile along a rutted and only just passable track. The Battery had sweated and cursed its way along this, hampered equally by unfamiliar equipment and its own lack of cohesion and proper training. Like 'D' Flight, it was very much a scratch eleven, and one which had been hastily brought into being for the same purpose – the detection and destruction of enemy raiders.

Of its officers, only two had been in action; and its NCOs, with the exception of the BSM, had been resentfully dug out from the selection of comfortable – and sometimes profitable – niches where they had esconced themselves in the hope of sitting-out the war. Now events had dragged them from the security of these and their displeasure expressed itself in a deliberate stupidity and slowness and in a sullen and perverse delight at each and every set-back the Battery suffered. And these had been many. Half-settled into its first gun-park, the Battery had been discovered (through some administrative error 'higher-up') to be sited on the wrong map-reference. The subsequent move had been dogged by one misfortune after another. The broken axle of a GS wagon had, for an hour, effectively blocked all progress through a narrow lane near Wickhambreux. A mile or two further on, a driver had had his knee pulped by a mule no whit less bloody-minded than his human masters. Tempers had frayed and then broken. A second driver had found himself under close arrest for striking a bombardier. Wearily, and long, long after dark, the Battery had found itself at last in its new home, a paddock engagingly named on the Ordnance Survey Map 'Bastards' Piece'.

Apart from the belligerent driver who was now awaiting court-martial for laying-out the bombardier, there was a fine crop of men who found themselves 'On Orders' as a result of their infractions during the move. These – charged with everything from wilful disobedience to dumb insolence – were dealt with in salutary fashion by their Battery Commander, in the corner of a tumbledown barn to one side of the clearing. Whether or not on home service he was strictly entitled to award no. 1 Field Punishment – whereby a man was spread-eagled against a wagon-wheel for several hours – Lockabee was unsure, and cared less. By and large, the men coming before him were not the new recruits, boys still in their teens, but the old sweats; the picture of wide-eyed innocence, they were marched up to his table in the makeshift Battery Office. And Major Lockabee wasted neither sympathy nor mercy on them.

He was a tall, spare man, this major, with an eye-patch hiding the still-weeping socket of a lost eye – the result of a one-sided duel between a battery of heavy German Artillery and his own eighteen-pounders, some months earlier. To his men it was no secret that 'the Major liked his drop'. Several times a day – even more frequently during the course of that dreadful move – Lockabee was seen to commune with the large spirit-flask he kept ready in his pocket.

And as the whisky in this was lowered, Lockabee's men learned to fear him. He was not a martinet by nature, but he *was* a man who mourned, and mourned deeply, for his lost eighteen pounders and for the slick and easy discipline of his annihilated battery. Deemed unfit for further duty overseas, his present command filled him with nothing but loathing and contempt. Still, it was his duty to do his best with the collection of rookies and King's-hard-bargains foisted on him; so Lockabee drove his Battery without care or mercy, until, in five days, it had at last achieved a pale facsimile of efficiency. Now, only Major Lockabee's telephone link was missing, preventing him from getting any information from the blind binaural operator listening for Gotha engines at the post near Canterbury. Despite an adjutant riding twice daily into the city about it, and the constant promises that something would be done 'tomorrow', Bastards' Piece remained as isolated and cut-off from the wide world as it had been five days previously.

But, whatever the faults in the organization higher-up, Lockabee was determined that when the enemy next came, his guns would be ready. . . .

Lockabee's determination had personal as well as Service

reasons. The Major hated aeroplanes – and with good reason. It had been a wandering Rumpler which had called down the murderous howitzer fire that had smashed his beloved battery – Lockabee felt he had a score to settle. In his heart of hearts, he knew such an emotion was absurd; searchlights, or fire from a battery such as his, were merely tell-tales designed to betray the line of a German bomber to patrolling night-fighters – much as that of a running fox is given away by crows or plovers rising from its path. But, even so – his face twitching horribly from a mixture of shattered nerves and whisky – Lockabee was determined that when the occasion arose, his unmilitary, and largely uncaring, collection of odds and sods would surprise everyone. . . .

Thus it was that, quite unable to distinguish the chur of a BE12's RAF engine from the deep quadruple roar of a Staaken's Maybachs, the Battery found itself expectantly standing-to as Browne's aircraft approached. Its engine-note grew louder and louder. Orders were shouted as to height and range. At a nod from Lockabee, the Battery Sergeant-Major opened his mouth and bellowed into the darkness:

'FIRE!'

Firing-lanyards were pulled, and the three-inch guns re-coiled as their uplifted muzzles bloomed and flung their fury into the sky.

Against all the odds, they made excellent practice. . . .

A mile ahead of him, and slightly below, Peters saw the cluster of shell-bursts amongst which an aircraft was briefly sil-houetted. For a few moments subsequent to this, the fine edge of his night-vision temporarily blunted, he lost sight of his quarry's exhausts, until a second salvo from the tell-tale guns beneath again showed him the black shape of his enemy now banking away to the south-east. Ever since he had first found himself in sight of another aircraft, Peters had been entirely sure in his own mind that this aircraft could only be German. Now, despite having had a fair glimpse of his 'enemy's' silhouette – a glimpse that should at least have caused him doubt – the attention with which the guns were greeting the aircraft ahead only confirmed Peters's certainty. His earlier optimism grew until it became an euphoric exultation, blotting out vigilance and caution. He was triumphantly aware that here, for once, he was the pursuer, and not – as he had so often found himself in France – the pursued. The pent-up terror and humiliation of that experience filled him with a vengeful lust to destroy and kill. Now, even more than just to shoot this enemy down, Peters wanted to see him burn, to know his remembered sense of ignominy wiped out, to watch as his absolution was scrawled in a terrible and fiery calligraphy down the starless December sky. The necessity for this last filled his loins like an overwhelming sexual desire. . . .

Peters had just enough remaining self-control to force himself to think logically and plan his next move. Keeping an eye on that tiny spark of exhaust ahead, Peters lifted the BE's nose in a gentle climb. He knew he must give himself the advantage of height, so that – when his moment was right – he would be able to dive down beneath his opponent's tail before zooming up to rake his vulnerable and defenceless belly.

Suddenly Peters found the wings of his aircraft rocking as he climbed through air still turbulent from the shells bursting below. A drift of acrid smoke was wafted back into his cockpit, hot and sharp with the reek of cordite. Though it made him choke, this smell only served to sharpen his mounting excitement still further. The feeling was new to him. He recognized in it the instinct for battle that up till now he had only seen in others and had never been able to share. He felt brave and strong and invulnerable: a nemesis about to fall on his country's enemy. . . .

He twisted his neck and, peering down over the side of his cockpit, stared at the enemy below him. Now – in shadowy outline, at least – the bomber was quite clearly defined. And – still failing to see in the 'enemy's' silhouette a replica of his own machine's – Peters was disappointed. In spite of the stories that he'd heard, the Gotha's size looked really quite ordinary – neither bigger nor smaller than that of any other aircraft. But in his feverish state of mind, Peters warned himself not to be fooled by this question of mere size. Other pilots had made this error and had allowed themselves to be deceived by it, failing to score because their subsequent attacks had not been pressed in closely enough. Well, he wasn't going to let himself be caught out in that way. No. Not him.

Judging his moment carefully, he pushed the stick forward and flung his aircraft down into the night. The tail of the bomber swept past him with disconcerting rapidity and, struggling desperately to keep control as his BE jibbed at the smack of the Gotha's slipstream, Peters stared frantically upwards, scared for an instant that he had lost his quarry.

But no, there it was, still flying serenely on, blissfully unaware of his presence. Peters pulled the control-column back into his stomach and reached up to struggle with the cocking-handles of the twin Lewises. As the BE zoomed upwards, Peters stared at the aircraft above. Christ! the storytellers hadn't lied after all. The bastard *was* big! So big and so close-seeming that he felt he could almost reach up and touch him. Even so, he would hold his fire for … a … moment … or so longer … until … until. …

NOW!

As he forced his attack close in, Peters' finger tautened on the trigger lever on his control column and was immediately deafened by the rapid yammer of his guns and blinded by their dancing muzzle-flash. A lambent trail of Pomeroy licked remorselessly upwards into the bomber's belly.

Peters's mouth opened in a wide gape of astonishment as he felt his bullets striking home – a gape that became a long-drawn yet soundless shriek of terror as, completely misjudging the size and distance of the aircraft above him, he took his BE12 slap into the underside of young Browne's. …

But Browne, luckily, was already dead. Peters's first shots, fired from the classic position of attack on a large aircraft and triggered from a range of yards, had carved up through the fragile flooring of the aircraft, up through the wicker bottom of Browne's seat, and had then ripped and smashed their way through his body from anus to neck. Browne was dead and done for before he even knew he was under attack, before his aircraft and Peters's locked themselves together in a deadly and final embrace, before the fuel from his shattered tank spilled out into the night and streamed over Peters's engine, where – vapourizing – it exploded with a sullen 'Whooo-OOMPH!'

Poor Browne ... and poor Peters, too. He had wanted to see his enemy burn all the way down, and would now do so.... Still alive and conscious, despite a body broken and crushed amongst the tangle of falling aircraft, and with the flames temporarily kept from him by some small freak of aero-dynamics, he felt little or no pain, and his mind resolved itself into a calm and self-indicting lucidity. Everything was all quite clear to him now. He was one of nature's fools, despised and unbeloved, even by God; a scapegoat. In his last few moments, Peters was able to view himself with neither self-pity nor contempt, but as a sad, pathetic creature at odds with a world which he had never begun to understand, and which had never understood him.

When the flames reached for him at last, as the falling debris cartwheeled down the sky, Peters made no sound. In that small last instant before he died, he saw his only enemy with luminous clarity – saw him with all his pretensions, his cowardice, his hopeless folly – himself....

With the one hand he could still move, Peters stretched forward towards the leaping flames, reached out for them almost imploringly – as he might to a lover. ... .

NINE

His ears lulled by the hypnotic sonorities of R.45's engines, it was some moments before von Trier's mind reluctantly allowed itself to become aware that something was troubling Horst and Walter at the front of the cabin. Even in the subdued blue light he could see that the normally phlegmatic and undemonstrative Horst was swivelling agitatedly in his seat, gesturing wildly at one of the cabin's side windows with a gauntleted hand. Beside him, Walter, too, was sitting open-mouthed, shaken out of the studied irony with which he armed himself for each operation.

Christ! Now what? Von Trier forced himself to stand and move forward calmly, covering the distance along the length of the cabin with the bent-kneed casualness of a man trying to find a seat in a tram-car.

'What's up?'

He leant over Horst, looking in the direction of the pilot's pointing finger. Yet, even as he asked his question, von Trier knew it to be redundant. As he had moved along the cabin, its side windows had shown him only too clearly the results of Peters's misjudgement falling like a comet from the sky.

'Ours or theirs, sir?' Horst asked.

Von Trier gazed at the blazing mass. Distance was difficult to gauge at any time in the air, let alone at night. Even so, he judged it couldn't be more than four or five miles away at most.

'It's one of ours – by the size of it. . . .' he said reluctantly.

'There was gunfire from the ground over that way a couple of minutes back. . . .'

'That settles it then.'

'Bastards!'

Von Trier had never heard Horst swear before; the Sausage's German was usually pedantic, middle-class, almost prissily respectable.

'*Dulce et decorum est pro patria mori....*'

Horst gawped back over his shoulder, shocked, and as if uncertain as to whether or not von Trier was trying to be funny.

'Like that?'

'What did you expect? A heavenly choir singing Wagner?'

'They died for the Fatherland!'

It was von Trier's turn to gape now. Great God in Heaven! Only a Horst could presume to start churning out the old platitudes at a time like this.

Von Trier gestured towards the throttles and snapped harshly, 'You'd better get those open and start climbing unless you've an overweening ambition to die for the Fatherland yourself.'

Horst's sheeplike mouth opened in protest – but von Trier was gone. He ducked down through the hatchway leading into the nose, feeling R.45 surge and lift as the thunder of her Maybachs became more urgent. Despite the frenzy of the slipstream, he felt a sense of relief at having left the cold yet claustrophobic fug of the cabin to be out again in the cleanness of the night. But it was now a tainted and poisoned cleanness.... Von Trier forced himself to turn and watch where that pillar of flame and smoke was still falling down the sky like some obscene firework.

Friend or foe, it wasn't good to have to see men dying like that. Was Horst really so devoid of imagination or sensibility that he couldn't imagine that happening to *himself*? If so, then perhaps Horst was lucky, locked in his safe and complacent carapace, content with platitudes and second-hand thought.

Fascinated despite himself, von Trier could not drag his eyes from that plunging aircraft drawing its long, horrific smear towards the ground. Vaguely he began to suspect that his decision not to change course might have been an unwise one after all.... Better to have faced the inevitable hate over Dover than to have seen this spectacle. God alone knew, but there were already horrors enough from this war stored in his subconscious; horrors that awoke him each night in the fretful and nightmare-haunted limbo that served him for sleep these days. . . .

Even as he watched, the flames ceased to fall. As the cascading wreckage at last hit the ground, the fire leapt upwards instead, springing like some exotic orchid opening its petals, transforming the small meadow in which the aircraft had crashed into a field of light. . . .

Von Trier turned away, sickened and numb. As if waiting their cue, the searchlights lanced up into the sky ahead of R.45, probing amongst the tenuous layers of squally overcast. Von Trier reached forward to grasp the icy comfort of the Lewis's angular butt, cocking the weapon as he did so. It would be ten minutes yet before the bomber reached the comparative safety of the sea, and – though none of the searchlights had as yet come near to finding them – his airman's instinct warned him that it would be as well to be prepared for trouble and that, empty as the dark sky seemed, the hunt was up. . . .

The mischance that makes a nonsense of sane and logical decisions was working against von Trier also that night. Had he kept to his original intention, he would still probably have seen the pyre that marked the deaths of Peters and Browne, though at something over twice the distance. Unchallenged and unpursued, R.45 would have thundered out over the lightless waters of the English Channel, and thence safely home.

It is absurd, of course, to see in this unfair throw of chance – as Morton-Dunne's Greeks might have done – the malignant and deliberate working of the Fates, Clotho, Lachesis and Atropos, working in unholy accord to spin and cut off the thread of seven more lives. Absurd – and, in the light of reason, unthinkable.

And yet. . . . And yet. . . ?

Destrier and Hopkins had only been back over Kent for a few minutes when they saw the meteor-fall of what, unknown to either, was the death-embrace of the two BE12s. Hopkins shuddered. Called out, as he had frequently been, to retrieve any salvagable scrap from such falls, he knew only too well how they ended: in the barely recognizable bits and pieces of what might once have been aircraft and in the totally unrecognizable and shrunken carcases of broiled meat that a fellow dared not let himself think of as having been men. Above all, Hopkins remembered the stench lingering around such crashes: the reek of scorched rubber and petrol-fumes; the obscene, Sunday-joint stink of roasted flesh....

As the pillar of flame at last hit the ground, erupting upward like a miniature volcano, Destrier banked the Bristol eastwards to where a line of searchlights was springing into life. From the distance of several miles, these looked like columns holding up a sullen canopy of snowcloud that was moving slowly inland from the sea. This cloud drove before itself small banks of outriders; almost immediately, as it seemed to Hopkins, the Bristol flew into the first of these. Its grey interior was a-swirl with a myriad tiny, icy particles which lashed at the exposed areas of his face and blanketed his goggles. The bellow of the Falcon was muffled to a dull roar. Hopkins cursed; bugger this for a game of soldiers! But the Bristol burst out of the squall as suddenly as she had entered it. Ahead, the searchlights still swept vainly backwards and forwards, quartering the sky – blind men's sticks searching for something that wasn't there.

And then Hopkins knew he was wrong – utterly and totally wrong. Something *was* there....

His first sight of R.45 was over so quickly, as the bomber was momentarily silhouetted against the cold radiance of one of the searchlights ahead, that, for a second or two, Hopkins doubted the truth of what he had seen. Then the bomber passed across the shaft of a second light and Hopkins stood upright in his cockpit, leaning over Destrier's shoulder and thumping wildly at him again, getting his head down close beside Destrier's ear and yelling with every ounce of his strength.

'Bomber! Fifteen degrees left!'

His shout was caught by the slipstream and flung back into his throat so that he coughed and half-choked again before regaining his breath. He leant forward to yell a second time, but there was no need – Destrier had either heard him the first time or had caught a fleeting glimpse of the bomber for himself. The Bristol's nose dropped slightly, and the increased pressure of the slipstream tugging at his right cheek told Hopkins that the fighter was turning.

He faced round to bring the Lewis into readiness. As his hands closed on butt and pistol-grip, he felt – despite his earlier compassion for the men dying in that falling plane – an atavistic surge of exhilaration. He took his right hand from the spade-grip and reached forward to the centre of the C-shaped elevating arm on which the gun was clamped, feeling for the Scarff-ring's locking-handle.

It was sometimes claimed by mechanics, disconcerted by Hopkins's apparently encyclopaedic knowledge of the training-manuals, that their Flight-Sergeant must either have written the bloody things himself or else be in the habit of taking them to bed with him. And it was true, as Hopkins sometimes admitted, that he got a strange kind of pleasure out of them, and found an odd sort of rightness in their gauntly matter-of-fact prose – so much so, that without conscious effort, he had learnt whole chunks of them off by heart, like holy writ. Now, as he released the locking-handle, he found himself reciting between clenched teeth the relevant passage from the book of words.

But with the locking-handle released, Hopkins found that the manual had remained treacherously silent on the subject of a hundred-knot slipstream on the combined fifty or so pounds of gun and mounting. For a mad, terrifying moment, Hopkins became uncertain as to which was in command – himself or the gun – as, struggling to bring the Lewis to the full elevation of its pivot arms, he was flung with bruising force against the side of the cockpit, and for a few heart-stopping seconds was quite sure that the slipstream was about to pluck him out of the Bristol like a cork out of a bottle. Breathlessly, he jammed his feet into the corners of the cockpit. Despite the windage of gun and mounting, he found that both moved freely on their revolving ring, the bearings of which had not become even partially seized by ice, as he had at first feared. He discovered that by locking his elbows as widely apart as possible and leaning his weight close into the gun, he was able to turn it slowly against the force of the wind, until at last it was pointing directly for'ard over the Bristol's top-plane. But the bomber, of course, had disappeared, and Hopkins peered along the barely perceptible line of the Lewis's barrel, knowing full-well that their chances of finding it again were slender, even allowing for the Bristol's superior speed. Still, he told himself, reaching a hand down into his cockpit for the reassurance of his six spare pans of ammunition wedged on their pegs, if they *did* catch up with the blighter, at least they'd be able to give him a damned good fright. . . .

As the Bristol flew eastwards, a part of Hopkins's mind found itself considering the war and the changes that had overtaken it since he'd first flown as an observer back in 1914. Then, despite its essential seriousness and danger, the war had possessed a sort of primal innocence, a glorious amateurishness, a schoolboy humour and the civilized chivalry of another age. But that war was long dead, and with it that innocence. In the three years that had since passed, the thing had become a business: cruel, calculating and lethally professional. The make-shift improvisation of everything had been replaced by a disciplined order and routine. Even the apparent inconsequentiality of units such as 'D' Flight were no longer 'make-do-and-mend' in the original and now old-fashioned sense, but expedients embarked on in the certainty that, thanks to three years of experience and practice, a basis had been laid down out of which would evolve new patterns, new routines, new methods.

And when, or rather if, they caught up with that bomber fleeing home through the murk, the battle which followed would not be remarkable either for its laughter or its chivalry; it would be a brief, vicious, bloody encounter whose victors would waste neither time nor tears in regretting the slain. In his early days as an observer, Hopkins remembered having been part-appalled, part-contemptuous, part-afraid of the cheerful insouciance with which the young officers who had been his pilots had fought their war. Now, too late, he found himself longing for the simple decencies that had lain behind such an attitude.

He found himself wondering just what sort of men were flying that bomber ahead – blokes whose guts it would be a joy to hate, or fellows he could like and sympathize with? Men who enjoyed their beer and tobacco, and who asked little more of life than merely to stay alive? But Hopkins bundled this last thought into the back of his mind. It was no good letting himself think of the enemy in that way. Once you did that you were lost. The trouble with flying – like the trouble with being tight – was that thought, for all its apparent lucidity, became simplistic and over-obvious. Things looked very different when a man sobered up – or came back down to earth.

And Destrier? That Destrier whose helmeted head was within touching distance in front of him in the darkness and who, for all the unlikely circumstances of his birth and breeding, had been one of those rare creatures who, by some chance, had been gifted from the cradle with the rare seed of originality and truth? Well, the war had taken Destrier, had made a hero of him and, at the same time, had snatched from him every last shred of anything he had ever found worth the possessing. It had taught him how to hate and, in so doing, had wantonly destroyed him.

Hopkins tore his thoughts away from Destrier. For Christ's sake! how much longer could he be expected to go on being his brother's keeper? And yet, in his heart of hearts, Hopkins knew there could be but one answer to that question: until the end.

Even as he realized this, a new brace of searchlights, well to the east of the first line – the one, as he guessed, somewhere to the north of Sandwich, the other to the south – groped upwards into the night, probed uncertainly amongst the layered overcast for a few moments and then, reaching inwards to each other, met in an inverted V with R.45 caught fair and square at its apex.

Hopkins stared at the sight, awed and daunted by the bomber's sheer size. His first instinct was one of pure terror. So this was one of the rumoured giants! Christ! the ruddy Alleymans had gone and put the tin lid on things this time! Even at something just over a mile in distance, the thing looked as big and as menacing as a bloody battle-cruiser. Hopkins fought down his rising edge of panic; just what had he gone and let himself in for? Taking on that monster with a Lewis would be about as pointless as taking on a bull-elephant with a pea-shooter.

At the risk of frost-bite he stripped off his heavy gauntlets. In action, they would be far too clumsy for him to be able to handle the Lewis effectively. He dropped them down onto the floor of the cockpit-well beneath his feet, making sure they were in no danger of fouling the control cables. He worked the cocking-handle of the Lewis and calmed by the gun's steely coldness, peered along the barrel in the direction of the fleeing enemy. There was this to be said, that when they caught up with the bomber, there'd be no excuse for missing it. . . .

As he'd half known it would, Hopkins's sense of apprehension slipped from him. Now he knew himself committed to action, he found himself able to examine his own feeling with a detached and clinical interest. He felt keyed up yet calm; excited yet cool – almost as if he'd moved onto a newer and quite different plane of consciousness.

As he stood peering ahead over Destrier's shoulder, the slipstream thrashed and snarled about his upright body. Even in the minute or so since he'd removed his gauntlets, he could feel his finger joints stiffening in the sub-zero temperatures; but, from the core of his being, a primitive and uncaring creature whose existence Hopkins would not have recognized nor admitted to under normal circumstances, began to sing its torrid song of bloodlust. . . .

When Destrier had climbed his Pup to face his attackers over Nine-Tree Wood, he had been afraid. Fear had given place to anger, and anger to courage. Now, he felt none of these things. In the stupendous image of that aircraft transfixed by the searchlights ahead, he recognized the cruciform silhouette whose lowering terror had haunted him since that evil night at Tolleswich. It did not occur to him to doubt that this was flown by the same man, the same murdering enemy. The certainty of this rang within him like a tocsin. And with this certainty came another – that here, at last, was that moment for which he'd always known himself to have been born. Those other times when he'd thought that moment to have arrived fell into their proper perspective as parts of the whole pattern – important clues, but clues only. Here, in the next few minutes, the final shape of that pattern would resolve itself, and its meaning be made plain – like the answer to some all-important yet baffling and apparently insoluble equation.

For the most fleeting of moments, Destrier saw himself again as a child – a small, unhappy boy sitting miserably in the corner of the orphanage playing-fields – while the swallows flickered shrilly about his head, self-absorbed and lost to all else but the taut perfection of flight.

Caught in the glare of the twin-searchlights, von Trier cursed. Knowing R.45 to be so near the sea, he had momentarily allowed himself to relax – and, in that moment, the lights had blazed upwards on either side of the bomber, hesitating only for the briefest of seconds before clutching her in their pincer grip. Not that von Trier was particularly worried even now, despite his curse. To be caught by searchlights at this late hour was not likely to be much more than a disconcerting nuisance. In two more minutes, R.45 would be safely out over the darkness of the sea and beyond the range of their Judas's kiss. Besides, having seen that funeral pyre falling out of the sky a few minutes ago, his gunners, Schmidt, Mendelssohn and Rossi, were hardly likely to be anything less than keyed up for the faintest sniff of a possible attacker. Even so, von

Trier wished that Horst would take some more positive action to shake off those damned lights instead of flying straight and level along their spillage reflected back from the base of a flat bank of overcast only a few hundred feet above. Why didn't Horst get up there? The cloud wasn't particularly thick, but, even so, it was probably just solid enough to cover the last few miles of their retreat. Away to the right, hopelessly inaccurate as it was, the splash of anti-aircraft fire made up von Trier's mind. He turned and hammered on the ice-edged windscreen behind him, gesturing upwards. The dimly outlined shape of Horst's head behind the armoured glass nodded, and von Trier felt R.45's tail sag as the bomber began to strain for precious height. He found himself groaning at the ponderous deliberation of her climb. It was at times like this that he most missed the nimble agility of his long-abandoned single-seaters with their cheerful ability to change sky in split seconds. In R.45, the slowness of her reactions gave a man the feeling that the bomber's every move was being telegraphed to the enemy. Although she had been lightened considerably by the dropping of her bomb-load, and seemed to be climbing easily, the searchlights found no difficulty in staying with her. Von Trier thundered at the windscreen again, his gauntleted fist eerily lit by the cold glow of light as he waved his hand to and fro in front of the glass: Weave!

In practice, the cumbrous antics of R.45 as she performed this simple manoeuvre amused him – like an elephant waltzing, as Schmidt described it. But now, tired, cold, and beginning to suffer from the nervous reaction that always began to grip him towards the end of each raid, von Trier found himself shaking with petulant anger at the bomber's sullen response to her controls. R.45's climb steepened and von Trier felt her sag away uncomfortably to port. He ducked back down into the narrow hatchway between nose and cabin. Just what in hell did that bloody fool Horst think he was up to now?

Alone in the small Antarctic of his open tunnel, Rossi had long since moved beyond coherent thought. The shrieking slipstream which, for an eternity – or so it seemed to him – had pounded every nerve in his bruised face had by now lulled him into an apathetic but not unpleasant limbo of semi-consciousness, so much more tolerable than the agonized misery of his waking state. When he had first found himself slipping into this, Rossi had thought to counter it by sucking at the mouthpiece of the oxygen-bottle clipped strategically close to his head, but he had pushed the temptation aside. Why bother? The oxygen-bottle could only promise him a return to the world of pain and cold and fear. It was better – better by far – to feel as he felt now, drifting away, with his senses dulled into an uncaring lethargy where even the terror of his apparent blindness didn't seem to matter any more.

Even when the searchlights blazing up at R.45 reached through his gun-hatch to illuminate her interior with a surrealistic clarity, Rossi remained unworried. He knew only that he was immersed and drowning in a cold and blinding light. Perhaps this was the death he had foreseen for himself back at Gontrode? If so, it didn't seem one half so frightening or terrible as he had feared. His lips moved feebly as he tried to pray again. But in his dulled state it occurred to him that perhaps prayer didn't matter very much now, either. . . .

The time for prayer was past; all that remained to him was acceptance. . . .

Out on R.45's port wing Otto Schmidt had some time since passed through the same shadowed valley that poor Rossi was now entering. His dead body, slumped in its harness, was jerked backwards and forwards in the slipstream like that of some uncouth and pathetic marionette. The light of his ebullient and unthinking spirit had proven too frail to endure against the night, and had been snuffed out.

But Schmidt had been right in one assumption, though: no bullet made by Vickers could ever reach him now.

In the Bristol, Destrier and Hopkins had seen R.45's barrelling climb for the cover of the thin bank of cloud above her. For a moment it looked as if the bomber might indeed succeed in breaking free from the cage of light in which she was enclosed. But, after a momentary falter, the faithful and unrelenting searchlights followed and caught the Staaken again, holding her as she began to weave.

Hopkins tried to gauge the distance now separating the two aircraft but found he had no yardstick by which to judge. The very size of the bomber confused the issue. Even now, he felt as though he could almost reach upwards and chuck bricks at the ruddy thing – and yet, she must still be – what? – a good half mile away, so far as he could tell.

Hopkins found himself praying. Oh, God! If only those lights could go on holding the bastard for just a few more minutes. If only. . . . If only. . . .

Seconds before the searchlights had sprung their ambush on R.45, the music surging through Mendelssohn's head had suffered a new and menacing change. So far it had suggested the closing of doors upon an old unhappiness, but then the serene mood had first been troubled and then smothered beneath a cacophony of noise that came dinning through his brain in mocking refutation of the order it destroyed. Mendelssohn shuddered as, against his will, this new music shaped itself into a demonaic and frenzied scherzo, made all the worse by its strident and brutish vulgarity. It was the music of a new, arrogant and apparently invincible barbarism, whose sole justification and argument would be the rule of boot and rifle-butt: the projection of some not far distant future, loud with the insensate, jeering laughter of a world that had given itself over to the sway of louts and corner-boys.

Somewhere beneath this clamour, the thread of his old music remained – but muted now, and in a minor key. The voice of his solo violin had become the cry of a people suffering under the lash of a new Babylon.

Even as Mendelssohn found himself bathed in the cold glow of the searchlight and began swinging his Lewis methodically through its arcs, the sounds of the scherzo refused to be stilled. Its oafish menace seemed directed at him personally, dinning its hatefulness in his ears.

It seemed to Hopkins that Destrier, rather than content himself with merely closing the range on the bomber, had, in an attempt to gain a height advantage first set himself the task of outclimbing his quarry as it reached towards that now thickening bank of overcast. Even so, the distance separating the two aircraft had closed considerably, and Hopkins was aware that should one of the searchlights be momentarily left behind, the Bristol's presence would, almost certainly, be given away completely, poised as she now was, a hundred or so feet above and a quarter of a mile astern of the bomber's tail. But neither searchlight lost its tenacious grip and the bomber flew on, taking no other evasive action than that slow weaving of its preposterous bulk.

The Giant showed up with startling clarity in the beam of the searchlights. As the Bristol climbed, Hopkins had time to take in the Staaken's details – the twin-finned bi-plane tail and ten-wheeled undercarriage; the neatly streamlined fairings of its under-pods and the familiar multi-coloured lozenges of its dazzle-painting. The insular Englishman in Hopkins was inclined to scoff at the apparent grandiosity and vainglory of what he saw. The mechanic in him was less sure and more objective. Here, Hopkins thought, was the possible – no! – the probable pattern of the future, when the world's capitals would be linked together by monsters such as this, just as they were by ocean liners now. The small dark voice of native pessimism within him insisted that it was far more likely that such aircraft would be used as was this one now – for nations to instil terror into each other, country outbidding country in frightfulness. . . .

He was called back to the present by the Bristol winning her race for the cloud and hiding herself in its wispy base. Destrier levelled off and made a slight adjustment of course –

obviously aiming to average out the mean of the bomber's weaving, so that when he dived out of the cloud again, the Bristol would still be squarely astern of her quarry.

The cloud was beginning to glow internally with the radiance of the searchlights now – a soft and strangely beautiful luminescence that seemed out of place with the violence that was about to happen. More likely the setting of a romantic play, Hopkins felt; perhaps that odd thing of Shakespeare's he had somehow found himself sitting through at the Old Vic a few months back. What was it? *The Tempest?*

Suddenly, in the dim glow, Hopkins became aware of Destrier's hand gesturing in front of him, describing a dipping motion: this was repeated two or three times. Hopkins leaned forward and slapped Destrier on the shoulder to show that he'd understood. They were to dive down beneath the bomber and then rake the length of her belly as they climbed.

Back in 1914, Hopkins had found that when the moment of battle was about to be joined, a small muscle in the left side of his face had begun to pulse with the regularity of a metronome. Before he had been grounded by Major Driscoll, the muscle had ceased its drumming, and Hopkins had known that this was a symptom of tiredness, a warning that the fine edge of his alertness had been dulled. Now, the best part of three years later, he was pleased to find that the muscle had become active again, ticking away in his face like a badly set tappet.

In front of him, he could see Destrier's right hand held vertically upwards. The hand remained lifted for perhaps five seconds before being brought down abruptly as Destrier pushed forwards on the stick. The Bristol dropped her nose obediently and plummeted downwards, bursting almost instantly out of the cloud no more than a couple of hundred yards behind the enemy. As they passed through the bomber's slipstream, the huge turbulence of the four Maybachs hit the Bristol like a hammer-blow, and Hopkins added a bitten tongue to his already damaged lip. But the bomber, it seemed, had still not seen them. No machine-gun fire leapt back to greet her as the Bristol swept upwards towards the great box-kite of the Staaken's tail. Then, at a range of no more than fifty yards, Destrier opened fire with the Vickers, sending a line of tracer and explosive Pomeroy needling along the length of the bomber. As his own gun bore – the right cross to the left jab of the Bristol's two-fisted attack – Hopkins also concentrated his fire on the Giant's fuselage.

And then, almost at the point of collision, so it felt to Hopkins, Destrier broke off the attack, the Bristol's port wing-tips barely scraping through the space between the wheels of the bomber's port and starboard under-carriages.

Je-sus! That was close! But Hopkins felt exhilarated rather than afraid. He swung the Lewis round and, giving way to his excitement, emptied the Lewis haphazardly in the general direction of the now-distant enemy.

Bloody fool! he accused himself as he changed pans. For Christ's sake, just what in hell had he thought he was doing, blasting off at a lot of empty sky like some green-arsed sprog?

Even so, thanks to the complete surprise of Destrier's attack, in those first few seconds they'd given Jerry a proper browning. But where was the big so-and-so now? Hopkins asked himself, when the fresh pan was on the Lewis. He saw at once that Destrier had taken the Bristol well beyond the tell-tale glare of the searchlights. Hopkins looked towards these. Calmly and inimically, these were still keeping pace with the retreating bomber which, apparently undamaged, for all the sudden savagery of the Bristol's attack, continued to reach upwards for that elusive cloudbank.

With the element of surprise now gone, Hopkins was grimly aware that subsequent attacks were going to see the sky full of metal coming in the opposite direction. Round one had definitely gone to the home side – on points. But this was now surely going to develop into a slugging match. David had hurled his piddling little stone at Goliath – and the Giant had shrugged it off. In whatever followed, David would now only survive just as long as he was slippy on his pins. If he once stumbled or failed to side-step, then it would be a case of –

Hopkins jerked his head angrily, as if throwing the thought aside; the muscle in his jaw pulsed angrily – they'd cross that particular bloody bridge if and when they ever came to it. . . .

When von Trier emerged from the hatchway back into R.45's cabin, its interior bright with the eerie and icy spill of the searchlights, he found that the heavy yawing during the bomber's climb had not been caused by Horst's clumsy-handedness but by the loss of power in the leading port-engine, due to petrol starvation. This owed itself to that recal-citrant and ever-doubtful no. 5 pump. Von Trier moved quickly aft, but by the time he reached Wendel, the fuel-mechanic had sorted the problem out, and the engine was picking up strongly again. Von Trier raised his thumb in approbation at Wendel before moving for'ard. He stood, legs braced wide apart, behind Horst's seat, listening to the surg-ing yet now even beat of the Maybachs. Tomorrow, with luck, he and the rest of R.45's aircrew would take a couple of days' well-deserved rest while the bloody pumps were being re-placed. The Count thought of the plumply pretty little Bel-gian girl whom he would go and see in Ghent, and grinned sardonically. It all depended what you meant by 'rest', he sup-posed. The thought occurred to him that it might be amusing and educative to take Horst along to meet one of the girl's putative 'sisters'. But perhaps not. . . . Poor Richard, laced in the strait-jacket of his provincial morality, would only be shocked and more than likely put a damper on some pleasantly diverting proceedings.

The crack and whine of machine-gun bullets slashing their way through R.45's cabin took von Trier completely by sur-prise. For a few seconds, the air was full of the sob and howl of incandescent metal, and the bomber's shell rattled as though stung by hailstones. It was as though a nest of hor-nets had been suddenly disturbed, and he stood paralysed as a storm of tracer ricocheted through the thin, plywood floor and sides of the cabin, adding to their own danger that of flying splinters.

Fascinated, he watched the floor, as, starting from the rear of the cabin, a line of jagged holes appeared, as regularly and neatly spaced as lettering on a typewriter. The windscreen in front of Horst shattered, and the mica windows along the starboard side of the cabin became opaque and pocked with holes.

Before he had time to move, the attack was over.

Miraculously, no one in the cabin appeared to have been hit. The trellis of flying metal had somehow – while reducing the neat order of the cabin to a shambles – done no major damage. The slipstream whined into the bomber through a hundred holes, dispersing the cabin's comparative stillness and warmth and setting up a swirling maelstrom of conflicting currents in which charts, papers and dust flew about madly.

Von Trier cursed himself. Even when caught by those bloody searchlights he had allowed himself to trade on the dangerous assumption that regarded R.45's sheer size as a guarantee of invulnerability in itself. And damn that little Belgian bitch, too! He had allowed his mind to wander down below his navel – and this had been the result. The Count looked at the chaos about him, at the splintered floor and colander sides of the cabin. Sergeant-Major Mann wasn't going to like this when he saw it. Only too easily von Trier could picture Mann's furrowed brow, his hurt, accusing look. . . .

But, in the meantime, the Count most wanted to know just why that useless article, Rossi, had failed to give the slightest warning of what was happening, and why he hadn't fired so much as a single shot in reply. Of course, their attacker had managed to get in under the blindest spot in R.45's defence. But even so, von Trier had long since planned for such an eventuality and had made the tactics to be followed perfectly clear. At his first glimpse of an enemy, Rossi – or either of the other gunners – was to fire a short burst, not so much in the hope of hitting anything but as a warning to the rest of the crew that they were under attack. Now Rossi had failed to carry out these simple and well-practised instructions, and by so doing, had nearly been the death of them all. Von Trier had long recognized in the Italian the one really potential weak link in R.45's crew. Now – much as he liked and felt rather sorry for the man – the last few minutes had made up he Count's mind. In the morning, Rossi would be gone.

But first things first. Instinct told him that instead of seek-
ng to pin down the blame for the surprise of that first attack,
is time would be better spent in preparing for the enemy's
ext move. And whatever his decision, it had better be right.
udging by the cunning of the attack and the shooting, the
ellow who was after them was good – damned good. Only the
ack of the devil had kept him from hitting anything vital in
is first attack. And even now, caught as R.45 was in the glare
f those blasted searchlights, he would certainly be prowling,
idden by the encircling darkness, waiting for a second chance
o pounce.

Von Trier pummelled Horst's shoulder.

'Corkscrew!'

Horst turned his big moonface upwards to stare blankly
ack, and for a moment, von Trier was tempted to hit it.

'Corkscrew, fool!'

The bomber's nose dropped as she sideslipped into a series
f sickening diving turns which, as the Count knew, took her
o the very limits of her construction and manoeuverability. It
vas an uncomfortably hair-raising tactic, even when practised
y daylight, but now – temporarily at least – it served its pur-
ose. The glare of the searchlights faded from within the
abin's interior, leaving only the subdued glow of its normal
ghting.

Von Trier turned to the second pilot.

'Get up front, Walter!'

Without even bothering to acknowledge the order, the little
nan eased himself stiffly out of his seat and ducked down into
he hatchway.

Von Trier turned to go aft. The violence of Horst's man-
euvring hurled him backwards and forwards against the
ides of the cabin. Once, where two or three bullets had
mashed their way in close together, weakening the structure,
is steadying hand went clean through the plywood and out
nto the night. For a heart-stopping second, he more than half
xpected the whole side of the cabin to give way, hurling him
ut into space, but nothing happened. As he dragged his hand

back in through the hole, those damnable lights caught up with the bomber again. Reaching the rear of the cabin, he noted with academic detachment that his seat and navigating table had both been reduced to matchwood and that the already useless radio looked as though it had been attacked with the flat of a spade. As he passed Wendel, von Trier felt a brief stab of envy for the fuel-mechanic's apparent calm; for all the lack of excitement showing on the Saxon's bovine face, they might as well have been engaged on a routine exercise. . . .

Once again it occurred to von Trier just how lucky they had been despite being caught with their breeches round their ankles. That R.45 was still to all intents and purposes relatively undamaged was the merest fluke. As he ducked down through the hatchway into the draughty tunnel of the bomber's after-fuselage, von Trier felt a mounting anger for Rossi's stupidity. The fool could have killed them all. By the time he'd finished with that useless bastard he'd be – von Trier's anger died as he was brought to his knees by something soft and yielding. In the light flooding up through the gun-hatch he saw that anger was now quite pointless. Whatever it was that had caused Rossi to miss seeing their attacker no longer much mattered. The enemy's first shots had caught the gunner fair and square in face and chest, leaving him half-lying, half-hanging in his harness.

It took von Trier some time to unclip Rossi's body from its webbing and push its horrid limpness out of the way against the side of the fuselage. The slipstream tugged and dragged at him as he did so and, once, caught off balance for a moment by Horst's manoeuvring, he all but fell through the black hole of the gun-hatch. For a second, he teetered precariously on the lip of this, before an even wilder side-slip flung him stunningly but safely against the tunnel bulkhead. He struggled into Rossi's harness, trying to ignore the ugly stickiness in which it was soaked and the stiffness of its securing clip which had been dented by a bullet. He knelt beside the gun-hatch and examined the twin Lewises. As far as he could see, neither guns nor mounting had been damaged, though there was a bloom of bright metal on the elevating-arm where

bullet had kissed it in passing. Von Trier released the
cocking-handle but kept the guns trained dead-aft, instinct
telling him that when their attacker made his second pass, it
would most probably be a near repetition of his opening gam-
bit.

Well, he told himself savagely: this time, that damned
Englishman wasn't going to get things all his own way.

Although the searchlights had brought Mendelssohn at least
partially onto the *qui-vive*, the suddenness of Destrier's attack
had caught him as wrong-footed as it had everyone else. He
had heard the chatter of machine-gun fire from beneath R.45's
tail, had felt the smack of bullets striking home underneath
him but had only glimpsed their assailant for the briefest of
moments as the enemy had broken off his attack.

Fear had gripped Mendelssohn for a moment as R.45 had
began her plunging, corkscrewing dive. God! They were out
of control! But no.... The panic that had momentarily threatened him died as he recognized in the gut-tearing motion the
evasive tactics that von Trier had devised and petrified them
all with in a series of scarifying and merciless rehearsals. During these, as he remembered, his friend Otto had disgraced
himself by returning to earth an unbecoming grey-green in
colour. The thought of Schmidt's probable discomfort at the
present moment steadied Mendelssohn; that would teach
friend Otto, for all his remarks about bare-bottoms in holly
bushes.

Reasoning along similar lines to von Trier, Mendelssohn
swung the barrel of his Lewis round, calculating the point
where his field of fire began under R.45's tail. The top part of
his mind was now crystal clear. But beneath this lucid surface ran those depths in which a terrible music would not
let him be. Now, against this, the voice of his solo violin spoke
out, clear and unafraid: the voice of infinite calm and hope.

s with Mendelssohn, R.45's belated but violent manoeuvring

had, for an instant, deceived Hopkins into thinking that the big bomber had been harder hit than first appearances suggested. He felt like shouting aloud with joy – not so much in triumph at the bomber's destruction, but in his relief that a second run at their ponderous adversary would not be necessary. But the relief had died as he realized that the Giant was still very far from being out of control and that, on the contrary, her diving, corkscrewing turns were all part of a careful stratagem to throw an attacker off. In that moment when the searchlights lost her, it seemed to Hopkins that she had been successful in this, and his emotions were conflicting ones: disappointment, certainly – but also a shameful sense of reprieve. But first one and then the other of the two searchlights had cast around like a pair of hunting dogs, picking up their quarry again and holding grimly on, despite every trick the bomber's pilot could try. Grudgingly, Hopkins mentally congratulated the searchlight operators for their ruthless persistence. Those fellows knew their stuff, whoever they were. But now, low-angled, and with the light at their apex palpably dimmed, it was clear that the searchlights had nearly been outrun by the bomber and were at the extreme usefulness of their range.

As the Bristol circled warily, hidden in the penumbra of shadow outside the circle of light, Hopkins had a second chance to examine the Staaken. Up till now, few in the Flying Corps had done more than glimpse one of these fabulous beasts. The stories these few had told, filtering from mouth to mouth through the service, had sounded pretty tall to him. But now, privileged as he was to be getting a grandstand view, Hopkins reckoned rumour to have erred on the side of understatement rather than otherwise. But it wasn't the sheer size of the bomber that was its most compelling feature. No, it was something that went deeper than this: the suggestion of sheer primitive destructiveness and uncompromising enmity written into every angular line. As a boy Hopkins remembered having come across a picture of a pterodactyl in a book he had found in the orphanage library. The drawing had been a good one, showing in great detail the creature's loathsome boniness

246

d leathery skin, its dreadful saw-edged beak and cold, cruel
es. Somehow the picture had suggested a total and wholly
il malevolence, and its image had stayed with Hopkins
ross the years, as if in some ways it epitomized for him an
stinctive and ultimate definition of diabolic force. Now, in
e reptilian lineaments of the bomber dodging and weaving
the searchlights' glare, it was as if this interior knowledge
d been made manifest. Here, it seemed to him, were the
rces of darkness and despair fleeing from that one power
whose sight they could not live – the light.

The bomber's pilot appeared to have sensed that the search-
hts could not now hold him for much longer, and his
anoeuvring had become less violent. Still weaving, but with
r nose held down to gain as much speed as possible, the
mber dived towards the sea. Destrier tightened his circling
fly from right to left across the bomber's tail. For the second
ne, Hopkins felt the slam of that giant hand as they passed
rough the bomber's slipstream. And then Destrier tightened
s banking curve still further and further, boring in beneath
e Staaken's exposed quarter. This time, at an impossible
nge, a short burst of fire came back at them from the
mber's belly. At an impossible range or not, the fellow be-
nd that gun was either very good or very lucky. A line of
acer yearned at the Bristol before flickering away between
e port wing-tips.

To Hopkins, it seemed that Destrier had decided to change
s point of aim. No longer was he attempting to strafe the
ng box of the bomber's fuselage but was this time going for
e port engine-pod, cantilevered on its bracing of struts be-
een the bomber's wings. The angle of their raking turn was
epening and, as the range inexorably closed, the gunner in
e Giant's belly became busy again. Hopkins watched in a
scination that was beyond fear as the tracer streamed to-
ards him for a second time. It was well-aimed, almost too
ll-aimed, perhaps. It slid between the inner bays of the
istol's wings in a line of liquid fire, hitting nothing. And
ll Destrier held his own fire, so that for one horrified mo-
ent, the terrifying notion came into Hopkins's head that

the madman in front of him intended ramming their oppor
ent. Then, with the Bristol's bank still tightening, and wit
the range now down to bare yards, the Vickers spat out i
fury in a blaze of light that splashed against the meta
panelling of the bomber's engine-pod. For a moment – th
most fleeting and transitory of moments, but one which woul
stay photographed on his memory as long as he lived – Hop
kins saw, half-below, half-above the line of the Staaken
wing, the jerking, black figure of a gunner crouched over h
weapon. To Hopkins, it seemed that the barrel of this wa
pointing straight down at his head, and almost within touch
ing distance. He shrank into himself as he waited for the gun
ner to open fire. But no shots came. . . .

And then the Bristol juddered and fought at her contro
as Destrier squeezed her upwards through the space betwee
the bomber's wings and tail and she was caught aback by th
mighty wind-lash of the Maybach's propellers.

But Hopkins had no time to notice this. If the gunner o
the port-wing had been too petrified or startled to open fir
his colleague on the starboard wing was not. As the Brist
shot upwards over the bomber, he engaged her at a distan
of no more than twenty yards. Adding to the bucking, jerkin
climb of the Bristol as she fought ailerons and rudder, Ho
kins felt the smack and jar of bullets lashing into fuselage ar
wings. Desperately he fought against wind and the forc
generated by the Bristol's antics to bring his own gun to be
– but for a few vital seconds found his target blanked off b
neath the trailing edge of the starboard wing. Then they we
above the bomber, the Bristol seemingly hanging on the silv
disc of her airscrew. In the split second before she final
stalled, Hopkins aimed down into the source of that machin
gun fire still searing up at him.

The Lewis spoke once – and then stopped. . . .

As the Bristol stalled and fell away, Destrier kicked ha
on the port-rudder-bar, flicking the aircraft over into t
graceful stall-turn he had first seen practised by that pair
swallows twenty years before. But hardly had the Brist

dropped into the dive following this, than the stick was pulled back and the rudder-bar kicked hard again, bringing her round onto a course parallel to, but slightly above the bomber. As if in protest at the violence of this manoeuvre, every part of the two-seater whined, creaked or groaned in anguish.

But Hopkins, struggling to clear the stoppage in the Lewis, noticed none of this. He was in the grip of a fever – a fury – such as he had never experienced before, one which, paradoxically seemed to leave his mind stripped to its bare essentials and working at several times its normal speed. To clear the stoppage he stripped his hands of their woollen gloves. Without caring overmuch, he felt the gun's icy metal flaying the skin from his hands. He worked methodically, checking off the drill-book sequence for clearing stoppages as he did so, until he knew the gun was ready again.

This time, it seemed, Destrier intended making his attack from above, diving down along the length of the Staaken and then lifting the Bristol's head to rake the bomber from tail to nose. For his own part, Hopkins struggled to bring his recalcitrant Lewis round to bear on the Giant's port engines again. The effort involved was greater now: keyed by anger or not, a terrible weariness, born of the cold, was beginning to seep treacherously through his body.

The Bristol continued her dive down on the bomber's tail. But this time no storm of defiant tracer leapt upwards to greet the two-seater, and for Mendelssohn, the battle had ceased to have either sound or significance. For Mendelssohn had escaped. A few minutes earlier, as he crouched over his Lewis, firing up into the Bristol after Destrier's second attack, that intolerable scherzo in his head had seemed reiterated and reinforced by the yammering fury of the Lewis jerking and snarling in his grasp and reaching towards a climax that was like the promise of a world which he knew he had no wish to survive to experience. Instead, he longed only for release and silence – and swiftly, both had come to him, reaching down from the aircraft above, in the form of an apparently innocent and innocuous blob of glowing light, dropping towards

249

him with a lazy yet unerring certainty. As a man might lift his face towards spring rain, or to receive a kiss of peace, so Mendelssohn acceptingly lifted his....

The one bullet that Hopkins had managed to fire before his gun jammed took Mendelssohn cleanly through the centre of his forehead.

The Bristol dived to within fifty yards of R.45, then her long, pugnacious nose lifted and she jibbed momentarily, like a startled mare, as the Vickers resumed its murderous commination. Hopkins noticed that this time both gunners were slumped in their harness, their bodies bobbing and swaying grotesquely. An unlucky pair of sods, he thought bleakly. Taking careful aim at the Staaken's port engines, he opened fire again.

And then, Hopkins felt the Bristol hit – and hit hard from almost directly beneath. In his early days as a sapper, Hopkins had done a bit of boxing. Once, when all over a clumsy but notoriously dirty opponent, he had felt himself hit hard and deliberately in that vulnerable six inches between groin and belt. The world had immediately exploded into a vermilion mist of pain and gathering unconsciousness. Unknown to him, the referee, having seen the foul, had been moving in to stop the fight. But all Hopkins could see was his opponent, his fists held low, confident and triumphantly cocky. Hopkins's reply had been unorthodox, and he had stopped the fight in his own, decisive way. Bunching both fists together, he had raised them like a club before bringing them down on the other boxer's head, hammering the blighter down onto the canvas like a man driving in a nail.

Now, with the Bristol being savagely mauled from below as Walter in the Giant's nose fired upwards at point-blank range, Hopkins instinctively settled for the same sort of impromptu riposte that had once saved him with that foul but effective two-handed blow. He swung the Lewis round till it was pointing directly at the Bristol's own tail, and then, taking aim at a spot halfway between himself and the fin, and knowing full-well — but not caring very much — that by so doing he could destroy both himself and Destrier, emptied the magazine down into the Staaken through the wood and canvas of the fighter's own fuselage....

However bad a nightmare may be, there is usually lurking at the core of its terror the illogical knowledge that the sleeper will somehow — and against all apparent likelihood — wake again to the familiar world of the safe and commonplace. But when the nightmare is repeated, night in, night out, doubt settles in, and the suspicion — amounting almost to a resigned certainty — that one day there will be no relief, no blessed re-awakening, and that the nightmare will have become the living moment's reality....

For Wendel, that time had now arrived.

As the Bristol swept a bare twenty feet above R.45, it seemed to the fuel-mechanic that his world was disintegrating into a chaos of flying, shrieking metal, amongst which he alone stood unhurt and invulnerable. Compared with this, the violence of their assailant's earlier assaults had been as nothing. The plywood structure of the cabin was split and riven as though by pickaxes and the air was full of the heavy reek of petrol spilling from holed tanks. Upright to the last, Horst's body jerked twice, and his head seemed to burst as though exploding from within, a hideous grey mush showing through his torn helmet. But even in death, Horst's body automatically remembered its duty. His heavy spatulate hands remained locked round the wheel at the top of the control-column, and R.45 flew steadily on.

As if detached from the chaos about him and set apart in some mysterious bubble of immunity, Wendel watched as the last remaining shreds of order in his world were shattered and destroyed around him. He had seen all this before, in his nightmares; not once, but many times, and was not surprised.

With a terrible certainty and quite powerless to prevent

what he knew must happen next, Wendel saw von Trier emerge from the hatchway beside him, accept the fact of Horst's death, and then move forward to take up piloting the bomber in his place. But in that rage of fire still tearing through R.45, he had barely gone two steps before he was struck down by its fury. Like a boxer refusing to take a count, von Trier staggered to his feet, only to be hit again. Even as he fell the second time he began inching his body forwards towards Horst. But Wendel knew he would never reach the lieutenant. Hit again and again, von Trier was finally still. He lay – as Wendel had known he would – with his face turned back, the ghost of his usual sardonic smile frozen on his face.

As if seeking relief in the familiar, Wendel turned his attention back to his pumps. His hands moved swiftly and automatically, valving off fuel from damaged tanks, and trimming others to redress the increasing mushiness in R.45's flight. He worked in near-darkness again. For now, when it was too late, those damnable searchlights had at last lost their grip on the bomber.

As the searchlights were left behind and the Bristol zoomed up above R.45 to disappear into the starless night, Sergeant Walter found himself wondering just what sort of madmen the enemy must be. He had heard stories of observers firing downwards through the tails of their own aircaft but till now had always dismissed and discounted them as the products of over-imaginative minds, or downright lies. Now, he had experienced such determination for himself – and the discovery had frightened him far more than the plain and simple fact of being shot at. To be on the receiving end of such unremitting and suicidal hostility gave a fellow the sense of being up against an enemy who was both more and less than human. Besides, the fighter's riposte to his own upward fire had been terrifyingly effective. He had felt the weight and savagery of the enemy's metal smashing into the bomber all round him, and the butt of the Lewis had been wrenched from his hands as something had smacked him abruptly in the chest, throwing him heavily against the cockpit coaming.

Now, with the action broken off, he knew himself to have been lucky. Fearfully, he had torn off both gauntlets and gloves for a tentative examination of his own chest. His flying-leathers had been torn, but, to his relief, he had found none of the ominous stickiness of blood. Presumably he must have been hit by a nearly-spent ricochet. The fattest, warmest wench in Bremen still had her chance. . . .

Even so, Walter felt shaken and weary. Lucky as he knew himself to have been, the bullet had still struck his chest with numbing force. The whole of his right side from shoulder to thorax felt badly bruised. Still, he thought, given luck, the Tommies might even have unwittingly done him a favour by cracking a rib or two. In which case, he could look forward to a couple of days in a nice warm bed attended by pretty nurses, perhaps, and with a few days sick leave to follow. The twin prospects of warmth and femininity pleased him. Both seemed infinitely preferable to flying and the ever-present menace of this damnable and crushing cold.

His legs felt shaky – he had to resist the urge to duck back down through the hatchway behind him into the comparative warmth of the cabin and the restful sanctuary of his seat beside Horst. But he fought down this temptation. The search-lights might have lost R.45 at last, but somewhere ahead of them lurked that blasted fighter and its bitterly determined crew. The likelihood was that these had been given the slip. But the chance remained – a slim chance, maybe – that the Bristol's pilot might just pick up R.45 silhouetted against the loom of the searchlights now left hopelessly behind. And supposing this was to happen, any new attack could only come from one possible direction – dead ahead. In which case, the battle would go to whoever kept his head coolest, held his fire longest – and then fired straightest. . . .

But with the cold and the leaden lassitude of fatigue making it more and more difficult for him to concentrate, Walter stared blindly into the darkness ahead. The chances of the enemy finding R.45 were remote, as he knew, and growing more so with every passing second. If that bloody Bristol didn't spot them in the next couple of minutes, they would all be quite safe. . . .

In the labyrinthine and no longer wholly logical recesses of Destrier's mind, it seemed to him that the voice which had earlier betrayed him into going north – that voice he had mistaken for Dolly's – had, after all, in the barely comprehensible way of such things, brought him face to face with his enemy. So far he had failed to destroy that enemy and had now even lost him. With the frantic certainty of madness, Destrier knew he was being tested. Now, as surely as he had ever known anything, he was certain his climacteric was almost upon him; that consummate moment which would explain and justify his conception and birth in that Fratton bedroom. Now his mind was made up: those other critical moments in his life had been but passing – though necessary – steps along the way. Now, in the next few minutes, he would find his last step of all, and, in its surmounting, he would pass beyond the world of men and their little dreams, and rise like some homing seraph into the infinite. . . .

He had loved Dolly Lyttleton; this last enemy that he must now overcome, would, in some way, be a test of that love. He had loved flight, and was – even at this moment – climbing towards an apogee from which there would be no descent; no mundane falling back to earth. . . . The gods gave a man breath, talent, love – and, in return, demanded the willing sacrifice of all three upon some cryptic yet compelling altar. . . .

Any second now, Destrier was certain he would find his enemy. And when that moment came, he knew he would – must – destroy him in the one sure and inescapable way left. . . . *This* was the purpose for which he had been born.

The Bristol, Hopkins, *himself*, were, all three, tools: tools with no other purpose or duty but to serve this end. . . .

It was Hopkins who spotted R.45 first – much as Walter had suspected the fighter's crew might – silhouetted against the last, pale glow of the searchlights. For a moment he glimpsed the faintest solidifying of the night between themselves and the land and, thumping on Destrier's shoulder, reached down to yell in his ear. As the Bristol banked round to cast back for her quarry, Hopkins saw with surprise that they were over the sea. Or *was* it the sea? Perhaps, he thought, with tiredness and cold tempting him into a rare lapse from logic, what lay beneath was *not* the sea at all but only an infinite extension of the darkness that stretched above them.... Perhaps the ordinary, everyday world of men was nothing but a dream, an illusion his mind had created for itself. In this world of darkness and burning cold, there were few realities left any more: himself, Destrier, the Bristol –, and that bomber towards which they were now turning.

With an effort, Hopkins pulled himself together, changed the pan on his Lewis, then screwed up his eyes to stare hopefully into the darkness ahead. And – Yes! – there it was still – a barely tangible solidification of that darkness, moving slowly and deliberately to meet them.

Grimly, Hopkins noted that Destrier was taking no risk of missing the bomber on what – surely – must be their last chance to destroy it. He was pointing the Bristol right into the centre of its sable shadow, aiming the fighter like a bayonet at the enemy's heart.

This time Hopkins felt no welling of the fighting-madness that had made him fire down through the Bristol's tail. As he trained the Lewis round for'ard over the upper-wing, he was conscious only of tiredness and cold, and a resigned apathy of spirit. He waited for Destrier to open fire – but the Vickers remained silent. And it was only as that great and terrible shadow of the bomber swept forward to engulf them that he at last understood Destrier's intention. Hopkins stared ahead into the darkness, open-mouthed, his eyes wide in horrified disbelief. A bayonet, he'd thought....

'Oh, Christ Jesus!' a voice within him screamed as the

Bristol leapt towards the bomber. 'Oh, Christ Jesus!'

Despite the bruised feeling in his chest and the increasing difficulty he was finding in getting his breath, Walter began to feel light-headed. Absurd snatches of children's rhymes and bawdy barrack-room songs floated through his mind, mixed with inconsequential scraps and fragments of long-forgotten conversations. Even so, one part of his mind – the same, small, icily-accusing part that will tell a drunken man just how drunk he is – remained alert, yet coolly detached.

It was unsurprised when Walter spotted the blue-green flame of the Bristol's exhaust crossing in front of R.45, and undismayed when that exhaust narrowed, and then became two, as the enemy nosed round to resume the attack.

Fixedly, Walter kept the muzzle of his Lewis aimed between those twin approaching points of light. He was resolved to hold his fire as long as possible, knowing that the instant he pressed the trigger, these would disappear, blotted out by the leaping muzzle-flash.

It was only when the Bristol seemed poised on the very tip of his gun-barrel that the cold little voice from within first guessed, then screamed the enemy's intention.

Oh, Christ! The mad bastard was going to ram.

Almost by reflex, Walter's finger tightened on the trigger. The night ahead of him was stabbed and seared by a jagged, dancing curtain of flame – and through the glare of this, he caught a glimpse of the Bristol's tail-plane hanging vertically in front of him for a small eternity, before plunging abruptly out of sight.

R.45 staggered as though she had run into a solid wall – staggered, recovered – and then flew heavily on.

Hopkins had been unconscious for no more than a few seconds. Snatched from his chilling hands, the butt of the Lewis had caught him a stunning yet glancing clout beneath his jaw. Now, as his senses returned to him, he became aware of a distant voice reciting a flat and matter-of-fact litany, a known and familiar progression of words that he knew ought to make sense for him but which somehow didn't.

'"The gunner's emergency control,"' the voice said, '"consists of a socket projecting through the floor on the right-hand side, which is intended to accommodate a detachable control-lever, the latter normally being carried in two clips on the floor. The socket is mounted on the fulcrum pin carried by two angle brackets bolted to the floor, and projects through the aperture cut in the latter. . . ."'

Once, during 'D' Flight's first week at Brick-Kiln Farm, Hopkins had found Russell seated in the Bristol's rear cockpit meditatively exploring its interior. Rushed off his feet, Hopkins had been briefly tempted to bawl out the young aircraftman for idleness. But the boy had disarmed him by turning, grinning broadly, and waving something triumphantly aloft for the Flight-Sergeant's inspection. Hopkins had recognized in the object the Bristol's emergency control-lever and had understood Russell's feeling. He himself had experienced the nightmare of being flown home by a badly wounded pilot, knowing that, without dual-control, he was entirely helpless in the event of his pilot's final collapse. Those forty-five minutes, he remembered, had stretched themselves out into an eternity, during which he had learned that 'to die a hundred deaths' was no mere figure of speech. In the event, his pilot had not collapsed – and Hopkins had survived. Others – God alone knew just how many – had been less fortunate. . . .

Remembering this, Hopkins's annoyance with Russell had faded, and he had moved close to the Bristol and asked, 'D'you reckon you could use that if you had to?'

The corners of Russell's mouth had quirked down comically.

'I could have a bloody good try, Flight.' His grin had broadened. 'At least this gives a chap something to occupy his mind while he's waiting to go west. . . . I think I might learn pretty fast in the circumstances.'

Hopkins had found himself liking the youngster's coolness

but hadn't been able to restrain himself from pointing out the difficulties of using the rudder-controls, activated by exiguous handgrips sleeved onto the rudder-control cables.

'You'd need to be built like a bloody octopus to use those and the stick at the same time, son.'

Russell had shaken his head.

'Look,' he'd said, tucking up his legs and placing a booted foot on each handgrip, 'I've got that one worked out, too. See?'

He pressed down alternately on each cable, and the rudder moved from left to right, then back again.

Hopkins saw but refrained from pointing out that what seemed so easily done on the ground and what might happen several thousand feet in the air – when cold, terrified, and maybe wounded – were two quite utterly different kettles of fish.

Yes, two *very* different kettles of fish, the coalescing strands of returning consciousness argued, while that strange litany continued its relentless nagging in his head.

' "The emergency control lever is connected up to the rocking shaft by a link member, and works in one direction only, namely, fore and aft; it therefore only operates the elevators. The tubular socket in the floor of the gunner's cockpit, which receives the detachable control column, is a piece of $1\frac{1}{4}$ inch 17 SWG mild steel tube, closed at the lower end with a spruce plug. The upper end of the jaw clip –" '

Hopkins was jerked back to full consciousness. The words 'jaw' and 'clip' rang warning bells in his brain, and he woke to find himself slumped in his harness against the for'ard coaming of his cockpit.

The Bristol was falling. Falling and spinning down wildly widdershins through the winter night. . . .

He remembered Destrier's obvious intention of ramming the bomber and the sudden leap of flame and scream of flying metal hurtling back from the Giant's nose. Vaguely he remembered the Bristol leaping like a gaffed salmon, the butt of the Lewis being wrenched out of his hands, and the agonizing smack of something hitting him under the jaw before succeeding waves of darkening mist had dragged him down into their depths and he had thought himself hit and dying. . . .

Now he stood again and beat down wildly on Destrier's slumped shoulders. But Destrier's body remained inert: dead, unconscious – or simply uncaring.

Hopkins heard his own voice begin sobbing and cursing. He groped wildly on the floor of the cockpit, and Russell's voice came mockingly back at him as he struggled to remove the emergency control lever from its retaining clips. The lever came free at last and he had a second battle to find the elusive socket on the rocking shaft. He struggled to raise his feet onto the rudder control cables in the way Russell had shown him, blaspheming hysterically as his bruised and aching limbs refused to obey him despite their mortal danger. Only by clenching his hand and arm round his recalcitrant left foot could he hook it up into position – a position from which it promptly and oafishly slipped down onto the cockpit floor again. For a second time he forced the near-senseless limb into place, gritting his teeth in agony as a piercing shaft of cramp bit viciously into his thigh.

It was this knife-like lancination that killed the panic rising in him and set his mind working lucidly. What was it he remembered Russell saying? Something about a chap learning pretty fast in the circumstances? Hopkins found himself laughing as he struggled to centre the controls, exerting all his strength to pull the stick back against the dead-weight of Destrier's slumped body. Well, now was his bloody chance to learn all right! It was a pity that in the way of things he was unlikely to survive and be able to tell young Russell just how truly he had spoken. . . .

Lifting his weight onto the bony point of his right buttock and thanking providence that the cramp was in his left leg and not his right, Hopkins thrust down with all his strength on the starboard rudder cable, struggling to put on full opposite rudder. He felt the cable give and sag under his foot and knew that he was succeeding. . . .

'Now, you old bitch, you – NOW!' he pleaded with the Bristol. But, relentlessly, remorselessly, irrevocably, the fighter's spin went on, and the black and uncaring sea leapt up to meet her.

Walter found he no longer cared whether the Bristol had been destroyed or not. The creeping lassitude that had been eating into him ever since he'd been hit by that ricochet, the cold and that other lassitude which always overtook him after battle, combined together within him to give a feeling of distance and remoteness. Detached and somehow separate from himself, he looked inwards at his own weakness with amused compassion.

'You, poor old sod, Ernst. . . .' he murmured, in a voice that though kind was devoid of self-pity.

It took him longer than he expected to get back through the hatchway to the cabin behind. Half in, half out of its narrow tunnel, he found it necessary to stop and rest for a while, gathering his strength. The splintered shambles represented by the cabin left him neither surprised nor dismayed. As he struggled to stand upright before moving to his seat, the subdued glow of the cabin's lighting seemed almost blinding after the absolute blackness of the night outside. Without emotion he took in the sight of von Trier's contorted body and Horst's shattered skull. A last small imp of Walter's somewhat graveyard sense of humour was mildly surprised and amused to discover that in life – despite rumours to the contrary – the poor old Sausage must have possessed roughly the same amount of grey matter as everyone else. . . .

As he looked down the length of R.45's cabin, Walter noted the look of relief on Wendel's face at his appearance, and would have made some small gesture of reassurance, or even spoken to the fuel-mechanic, had not the effort to do either seemed just too much. He slumped down into the co-pilot's seat and failed to see Wendel's relief turn to horrified dismay as he saw the blackly coagulating mess of blood covering the whole back of Walter's flying-leathers.

Tiredly, Walter thought he would rest for a moment before loosening the grip of Horst's dead hands from the control-column. In death the poor fool had been doing his duty every bit as faithfully as he had in life. Let him go on doing it a bit longer. . . .

Walter stared ahead of him into the windscreen. But it seemed to him that what he saw was no longer an ice-rimmed rectangle separating him from the night, but a threshold, beyond which he was free to walk into a landscape that was suddenly brilliant and warm with sunlight. But the power to rise and walk was beyond him. Dazzled by the brilliance before him, he saw that a path led away into that landscape beyond the windscreen – a pathway down which the figure of a girl was coming towards him: not that crude image he'd so often fashioned for himself of 'the fattest woman in Bremen', but a pleasing looking creature, with generous and shapely breasts and thighs which, moving loosely beneath her loose shift, promised a man an infinity of warmth and rest. . . .

When she reached him, the girl turned her face towards Walter as though understanding it was beyond his power to come to her, and as if trying to tell him she didn't mind this in the least, that she knew why, and that she would come to him. Unconcernedly she stepped in through the glowing place where R.45's windscreen should have been, and Walter sat transfixed by the rich, baroque splendours of her body showing through her gossamer dress. Without a word, the girl leant down over him, brushing his lips with her own and folding his tired body in the sanctuary of her warm brown arms.

'*Liebschen*. . . .' he heard himself murmur – then drowned in the blood that had been surging into his lungs ever since Destrier's bullet had hit him.

The nightmare was proving itself true, then.

For a few, brief, treacherous moments after Walter's return to R.45's cabin, Wendel had almost allowed himself to believe that its pattern had been broken, that the terrors and images his subconscious mind had shaped for itself were chimerae rather than the true sum of this night's reckoning. For a fleeting instant – despite R.45's shattered condition and the still, bullet-torn bodies of von Trier and Horst – a spark of optimism, a sense that everything – despite appearances – would now be all right, had briefly possessed him. But even as Walter had turned to slump wearily into his seat beside Horst, and Wendel had seen the evidence of his blood-encrusted back, the small spark of optimism had died and Wendel knew that his nightmare had not lied.

He was able to watch Walter's slight body relax into death with something like indifference. Now that the nightmare had proved itself to be the waking reality, he was beyond emotion. The long nights of his private and unsharable nightmares had left him spent. He turned back to the reassurance of his pumps, his clumsy ploughman's hands picking up their duties mechanically. By now, pump no. 5 had virtually ceased functioning altogether. Petrol-starved, the leading port engine began to lose power once more, and R.45 yawed heavily round, her nose dropping from its easterly heading and only steadying when the bomber was pointing into the landless wastes of the German Ocean, as Wendel once more coaxed the recalcitrant pump into life and the leading port engine's doubtful rumble deepened into its habitual roar. With her control column safely held in Horst's stiffening grasp and Wendel mindlessly feeding them with their precious fuel, R.45's Maybachs would go on tirelessly functioning for hours yet, turning their huge wooden propellers. Only when the bomber's tanks were at last dry would the engines stop, and R.45 falter, before tumbling down out of the sky to be swallowed up by the freezing waters beneath.

Until that moment, then, she flew on.

There were still several hours to go yet, before, in the bitter half-light that passed for a midwinter's dawn, Sergeant-Major Mann and a handful of·his groundcrew would stand, their faces rimmed with snow, their feet frozen, staring westwards, waiting for the familiar WhooooOOm-Whoooo-OOOOM of R.45's homing engines. They would wait – and continue to wait – long after sense and logic had told them

hey were fools, that the bomber's fuel must long since be
pent, that neither she nor her crew would ever now return
ome. . . .

Nor would anyone ever hear Mendelssohn's completed con-
erto. . . . The NCO detailed to clear away the little Jew's be-
ongings would shrug his shoulders scornfully and uncom-
prehendingly at the untidy and dog-eared sheets of his manuscript before tossing them into a waste-bin – the same waste-
bin from which he would most gratefully retrieve Rossi's dis-
arded and grossly libidinous photographs.

The von Trier estates would fall into the uncaring hands
of an oafish play-boy cousin – a cousin who would waste their
substance in promoting the interests of an hysterical, yet hyp-
otic ex-corporal. . . .

The remainder of R.45's crew would be mourned by their
amilies and friends: Wendel, by a widower father, outwardly as dull and phlegmatically insensitive as his son; Otto
Schmidt, by a mother who, till his death, had been as gaily
inconsequential as himself; Rossi, by parents and sisters – including his favourite, Bianca, who would take his memory
with her into her convent and, as Sister Maria-Conceptua,
pray daily for his soul.

The Mendelssohns would mourn, too – mourn, that is, until
– despite the fact that their only son had died for the Father-
and – they were taken away and herded in cattle-trucks across
the cruel vastnesses of Germany to be murdered in Ausch-
witz. . . .

Walter would be wept for – not by the fattest wench in
Bremen but by a wisp of a girl as small and slight as himself. . . .

For Horst, there was no girl to mourn – only the down-
trodden official who had fathered him and who had secretly
been so proud of his officer son. But Herr Horst's grief would
not last long. Overworked and half-starved – thanks to the
British blockade – he would die quietly at his desk six months
later. . . . Nor would Gruber – Horst's soldier-servant – ever be
called upon to account for his petty pilfering. 'Ah . . . Horst,'
he would be heard to say, recalling his old master in later

years, 'now he was the softest touch I've ever come across in my life....'

But, for this moment, and for a few hours at least, the casualty returns remained unwritten, and the next-of-kin telegrams unsent. And in the meantime, R.45 flew on with her dead crew, while Wendel juggled and sweated with pumps that would never now be torn out of her and replaced. Like some primordial reptile seeking a place to die, she flew on northwards into the black night, occasionally battered by snow-squalls, while the slipstream whistled and shrieked its requiem through her rigging, and the great organ note of her engines bellowed its ominous threat at the future.

Hopkins had long since given himself up for dead when the Bristol at last came out of her spin. The fighter's recovery seemed something quite separate from himself and his despairing manipulation of stick and rudder-cables. Indeed, past caring whether the aircraft came out of her fall or not, he had finally left these to their own devices. No, it was almost as though the aircraft herself did not choose to demean her kind by dying in such a graceless and unseemly way. The whickering howl of air over fabric and rigging softened into its normal sussuration. The Falcon ceased its uneven, lawn-mower clattering and roared out strongly on all cylinders again. The long nose of the plane lifted – albeit unsteadily – above the invisible line of the horizon, though, looking over the side of his cockpit, Hopkins saw that the Bristol was only just skimming above the ruckled surface of the sea. Then, quite without warning, the engine suddenly ceased altogether. The big biplane slowed and hung uncertainly on the air for a few seconds before sliding quietly into the sea with a surprising lack of fuss.

Immediately, the nose, weighted down by its heavy engine, dipped low into the water; spray hissed and spat on the hot exhaust manifolds. Hopkins frantically unstrapped himself, climbing laboriously over the side of his cockpit and out onto the wing-root. Even as he did so, a blinding shaft of light

retched out towards him across the water, found the ditched
ristol, swept on past her, found her again – and then held
enaciously on. Hopkins breathed a silent prayer of gratitude:
nank God for the Dover Patrol. . . .

Suddenly – guiltily – he remembered Destrier and edged
is way precariously forward to try and help the other out
f his cockpit. In the cold glare of the destroyer's searchlight,
Iopkins saw Destrier's face quite clearly – or, rather – saw
nat disturbing, inimical blankness of his leather mask. Des-
ier's head was turned towards him and, through the mask's
ye-slits, Hopkins saw Destrier's eyes full on him, their pupils
linting like agate in the harsh light.

Hopkins reached down to grab his friend's shoulder.

'Come on, Lol – time to go. . . .'

Destrier appeared not to have heard him.

'Are you hurt?'

Again Destrier failed to answer and Hopkins, feeling the
Bristol growing increasingly heavy and sluggish beneath his
eet, reached down into the for'ard cockpit, struggling to re-
ease Destrier from his harness and hearing himself begin to
eg and plead with the other to try and help himself. But Des-
rier remained, sitting quite still – though, so far as Hopkins
ould see, he had not been hit. But he could not be sure of
his, for below the level of its coaming, the cockpit was beyond
each of the searchlight's spillage: a black void.

The Bristol lurched, and Hopkins reached down to grab
Destrier beneath his armpits, exerting the last of his rapidly
ading strength in an attempt to hoist the other to safety. But
ecause of the water now swirling over the camber of the
Bristol's wing, he could not get a sufficient purchase with his
eet to be able to lift Destrier's weight.

The fighter lurched again, her nose burrowing deeply under
he water, as if she had had enough of things and was anxious
o be gone. Hopkins's feet slithered from under him and he
lung on desperately, his hands scrabbling at the cockpit
oaming as they were snatched from Destrier's shoulders.
The sea swirled about his knees, dragging him away from the
uselage. He snatched desperately for a handhold and felt

his gloveless hand slashed through to the bone as, grabbing a
a flying-wire, he struggled in the water among the struts and
rigging of the Bristol's wing.

Abruptly, the aircraft plunged her nose vertically downwards into the sea, lifting her tail high in the air before slipping beneath the surface with scarcely a sound or ripple.

Hopkins was left struggling in the sea. He heard himself
shrieking Destrier's name until, weighed down by fug-boots
and flying-leathers, he too was dragged inexorably beneath
the water's surface and knew himself to be drowning....

As consciousness slipped away from him, he was aware of
one last thought: that perhaps it was all for the best, really...
But whether he meant for Destrier, or himself, or for them
both, he was quite unable to say.

CODA

Midsummer, 19——.

After flying out over the Channel for some time, Juliet Echo
had turned landwards again, crossing the coastline over the
Martello Towers at Dengechurch, before backtracking –
though higher this time – across the velvet counterpane of the
Roman Marsh. It was trying, talking against the racket of the
engine; conversation in the Pup had dwindled, firstly to mono-
syllables and then to nothing. Inland, the day's blueness had
become transmuted, and the whole weald was enclosed in an
aureate web of heat-haze. Liz spoke briefly into her micro-
phone, was evidently answered, and then banked the Pup
away westwards. She brought the aircraft low down over the
end of the airstrip at Shenley Farm – a primitive boundary
that was no more than a post-and-wire fence marked with
red fertilizer bags. Apart from this, there was little to suggest that the meadow into which they were descending was
an airfield: only a limp, yellow wind-sock sentinelling a narrow, fenced-off strip of coarsely-mown grass, running between
two buttercup-gilded pastures full of ewes, placidly grazing
with their half-grown lambs. Only two other aircraft were to
be seen on the field itself – an old Tiger Moth and an ugly
little spraying monoplane, both looking disarmingly pastoral,
lost to their axle-trees in a tangle of grass and clover. A
cluster of farm buildings bordered the airfield on one side,
though separated by a narrow lane; the club-house looked
what it had once been – an implement shed; and, beyond one
corner of the meadow, along a trackway white with summer
dust, a long Dutch barn housed an oddly juxtaposed collection of aeroplanes and farm machinery.

Liz touched the Pup down, bumping over the blurring, uneven grass. She throttled the motor back and then taxied off

the mown runway, the Pup lurching unsteadily across it unt
it was parked companionably close to the Moth's wing-ti
Liz switched the engine off and opened the cabin door, dis
persing the cockpit's hot stuffiness and letting in the shar
and sappy Wealden scents: the mingling aromas of dog
rose, mown hay and sheep dung. For a few moments, the ol
man remained quite still in his seat. For him it was almost a
though the clock had been turned back fifty or sixty years. I
this context, neither the Moth nor the engagingly gawk
monoplane looked at all out of place, both being archa
enough in appearance not to clash in the slightest with h
memory.... The dying whir of the gyro, a solitary thrus
singing against the afternoon's heat, and the distant chereu
chereu of a light aeroplane lost somewhere above in the hea
haze only emphasized the midsummer silence. The old ma
found himself half-expecting to be brought face to face wit
his half-forgotten and much younger self, overalled or i
breeches and collarless greyback, spanner in hand and stra
in mouth, sauntering unhurriedly across the field, pleasantl
but not burdensomely busy. *He* would recognize that cheerf
young mechanic, maybe, but would that boy be able to loo
at him with anything more than a vague and uncomprehend
ing politeness? Once again, Hopkins found himself ponderin
that question he'd first asked over half-a-century back in th
freezing, candlelit bedroom at Brick-Kiln Farm: just whe
the hell did the days of a man's lifetime go to? Now, with h
eightieth birthday a month or so behind him, he found th
key to this riddle every bit as elusive as he'd found it then.

Liz broke into his reverie.

'A cup of tea, Gramps?'

The old man brought himself back to the present, reache
for his Panama hat, and opened the door on his own side
the aircraft.

'Now that doesn't sound a bad idea at all, young Liz....'

He stepped out onto the wing, closed the cabin door behin
him, and then dropped down onto the grass with only th
merest suggestion of elderly stiffness. Together, he and L
walked over to the tumbledown clubhouse, empty this afte

noon but for its part-time steward, who passed a quietly cheerful time of day with them and then brought their tea, setting it down on the grass beside them where they sat in a pair of sagging deckchairs out in the June sunshine.

For a few minutes, neither the girl nor the old man spoke. Liz watched her grandfather with affection as he lit a battered briar pipe, puffing contented clouds of blue smoke that drifted lazily away in the still air.

'So. . . .' she said at last, 'you weren't drowned.'

'No. . . .' he agreed gravely, 'I didn't drown.'

'How did you manage that?'

The old man laughed.

'I didn't. I'd gone under – right under – for good so I thought. The Navy got me out. A couple of bluejackets came in after me – and damned nearly went down themselves, I believe – though I don't remember anything about it.'

'Not a thing?'

'Not till I came to with someone shoving pusser's rum down my throat. I thought St Peter had slipped up, and that I'd got to heaven after all.'

'And your bomber?'

'Oh, at the time I was convinced we must have browned it pretty badly – but it seems I was wrong. Jerry *did* lose a Staaken that night – but that must have been through navigational error. One of their subs is supposed to have spotted some wreckage while patrolling near the Dogger – and that's a long way too far north for the bomber ever to have been ours.'

'And Destrier?'

'He . . . went down with the Brisfit. . . .'

'Perhaps it was for the best, really. . . .' Liz said gently.

Her grandfather didn't answer her. Yes, that's more or less what he'd been at pains to convince himself at the time . . . and for a goodish while after. But now, he wasn't so sure . . . For maybe Destrier, too, would have learnt to make his peace with the world eventually – just as everyone else had had to, returning from the war. Those who *had* returned. . . .

For his own part, quietude of mind had taken long enough

to achieve in all conscience. Years. But, he too, had conclude
his peace in the end. To do otherwise, he had gradually com
to see, was ungrateful – a breach of faith with all those lac
who had never had the chance to find out for themselves –
denial of life.

All Futura Books are available at your bookshop or newsagent, or can be ordered from the following address:

Futura Books, Cash Sales Department,
P.O. Box 11, Falmouth, Cornwall.

Please send cheque or postal order (no currency), and allow 30p for postage and packing for the first book plus 15p for the second book and 12p for each additional book ordered up to a maximum charge of £1.29 in U.K.

Customers in Eire and B.F.P.O. please allow 30p for the first book, 15p for the second book plus 12p per copy for the next 7 books, thereafter 6p per book.

Overseas customers please allow 50p for postage and packing for the first book and 10p per copy for each additional book.